JAIMIE ADMANS is a 35-year-old English-sounding Welsh girl with an awkward-to-spell name. She lives in South Wales and enjoys writing, gardening, watching horror movies and drinking tea, although she's seriously considering marrying her coffee machine. She loves autumn and winter, and singing songs from musicals despite the fact she's got the voice of a dying hyena. She hates spiders, hot weather, and cheese and onion crisps. She spends far too much time on Twitter and owns too many pairs of boots. She will never have time to read all the books she wants to read.

Jaimie loves to hear from readers. You can visit her website at jaimieadmans.com or connect on Twitter @be_the_spark.

Also by Jaimie Admans

The Little Christmas Shop on Nutcracker Lane

JAIMIE ADMANS

ONE PLACE. MANY STORIES

This novel is entirely a work of fiction. The names, characters
and incidents portrayed in it are the work of the author's
imagination. Any resemblance to actual persons, living or
dead, events or localities is entirely coincidental.

HQ
An imprint of HarperCollins*Publishers* Ltd
1 London Bridge Street
London SE1 9GF

1

First published in Great Britain by
HQ, an imprint of HarperCollins*Publishers* Ltd 2020

Copyright © Jaimie Admans 2020

Jaimie Admans asserts the moral right to be
identified as the author of this work.
A catalogue record for this book is
available from the British Library.

ISBN: 9780008400347

MIX
Paper from
responsible sources
FSC
www.fsc.org   FSC™ C007454

This book is produced from independently certified FSC™ paper
to ensure responsible forest management.

For more information visit: www.harpercollins.co.uk/green

Printed and bound in Great Britain by
CPI Group (UK) Ltd, Melksham, SN12 6TR

*For everyone who still believes
in the magic of Christmas ...*

Chapter 1

My phone beeps with a text message and I look up from the nutcracker bunting I'm painting. Hopefully the guy I'm seeing telling me he's missing me and he's sorry I've got to work late again. It's not serious yet, but maybe it could be one day. After so many disappointing relationships, it's nice to be dating such a reassuring man for a change. He's always texting to ask where I am and what I'm doing.

Can't wait to see you tonight. That's odd. I'm not seeing him tonight. *Wear that purple lingerie set I bought you. It looks sexy on you but it will look even better on the bedroom floor.* Again, odd. I don't own a purple lingerie set. *Nia's working late again. Thank God for this shop she's got. We'll have all night without her constant needy texts.*

It instantly makes sense. Oh, great. Not only am I dating another cheater, I'm dating a cheater who thinks "it'll look better on the bedroom floor" is original or even slightly seductive *and* thinks my texts are needy. I thought I was being romantic. I thought he liked me because he's always texting to find out what I'm up to. I should've realised it's because he's carefully scheduling his purple lingerie appointments.

A few seconds later, my phone beeps again.

Hah! Had you going, didn't I? Ha ha ha ha ha ha ha ha!

Does he think it becomes funnier with the more "ha"s he includes?

It beeps again. *Obviously I was joking. Nia? Nia?? Nia???*

I wait until he's added an abnormal number of question marks and then text back. *Oh, go schnitzel yourself, twatspangle. Enjoy your night with Ms Purple Lingerie. You won't be getting to see my lingerie ever again, purple or not.*

I delete the last bit before I send it. My lingerie is mostly a sort of off-greyish colour because I accidentally washed it with a black T-shirt. The mention of it is not going to make him fall at my feet and question his life choices.

I should probably feel sad, but we'd only been seeing each other for a couple of months. It wasn't serious. And there's become a sense of inevitability about it now. Every relationship is the same. Boy meets Girl, Boy is cute and funny, Girl does everything by the book and presents herself as most perfect specimen of normality she can muster – IE: Boy doesn't know Girl bleaches arm hair and plucks out occasional hag whisker. Things seem to be going well for Boy and Girl, and then … Boy cheats on Girl. Repeat *ad infinitum*.

My phone beeps again. *Sorry, Nia.*

At least he sent it to the right person this time. And had the decency to apologise, which is more than can be said for the last three cheating boyfriends.

I put my phone down on the desk and pick up one of the blank nutcracker silhouettes I'm painting and lift it away from the string it's attached to. 'What am I doing wrong?' I ask it.

It doesn't answer. Maybe it's the answer in itself – talking to wooden Christmas decorations.

Strings of tiny, flat nutcracker soldiers are laid out in front of me and I move along the desk as I put a coat of primer on each wooden figure so they've got plenty of time to dry overnight, and tomorrow I can start painting in the details like faces and brightly coloured clothing.

Maybe it's a good thing that it's ended. Now I won't have to worry about working late and not spending enough time with someone and can concentrate entirely on the shop and making it the biggest success it can be. Having my own shop on Nutcracker Lane is what I've wanted my entire life. It's good that I won't have any distractions. I keep repeating that to myself as I move from one hand-cut MDF figure to the next, trying not to let my mind wander to the text message. It's not like it was a serious relationship. Just a guy I met on a dating app a couple of months ago, chatted a bit with online, and have met up with a few times since. I didn't really think it was going anywhere, but I *did* think I was the only woman in his life. Another lie.

Tears blur the workbench in front of me and I try to blink them back as the tip of my brush dunks into the white primer. It's not even *him* – it's the fact that it's happened again. Yet another guy who can't be satisfied with just one person. Is it me? Am I not good enough for them? Other men get married and stay in committed happy relationships and their eyes don't wander. And yet, even when I meet someone who seems like one of the good ones, I repel them like water on oil paint. This makes it the fifth guy who's cheated on me in the last five relationships. That is not a promising ratio. And I'm the common denominator.

Maybe it's time to give up on love forever. I don't know why I keep trying when it's becoming clear that *every* relationship is going to end the same way.

I shake my head, sniff and wipe my eyes, and hum "Little Drummer Boy" as loudly as I can. Painting nutcrackers always makes me think of this song. No use dwelling on it. Another unfaithful man is not worth any more tears – not when it's December tomorrow and Nutcracker Lane will open to the public for the first time this year and my decorations will be for sale. This is something I've dreamed about my entire life and Stacey and I have spent the past few years trying to make it happen. Sharing a Christmas shop with my best friend. Yet another cheating boyfriend makes no difference to how amazing that is.

*

It's late by the time I've got the strings of nutcracker bunting finished and transferred to the little workshop in the back room behind the main shop. I should've been painting out the back, but this is my first year, and I wanted to watch from the window as the other shop owners finished their final preparations before tomorrow and left one by one. I wanted to watch the last of the Christmas lights be turned off as the sky gradually darkened above us.

The clear roof has always been my favourite thing about Nutcracker Lane – the way you can watch the skies and experience the weather. Even though it's warm and dry inside, the rain still patters down and the snow still blankets us, unlike the fake layers of felt snow that are piled up around the edges of the lane.

I pull on my red coat, tug my bag over my shoulder, and turn the lights off in the back room. One final walk through the shop floor reveals there's nothing else I can tweak or change. I've been here every day for the last month, transferring stock from my garden shed-slash-workshop, rearranging tables and display units, setting out everything *just right* and then setting it all out again in another formation until it really is *just right* and Stacey yells at me to stop fiddling.

I want it to be perfect. My own shop on Nutcracker Lane is what I've always wanted, and I'm desperate for nothing to go wrong. I could easily spend another hour carefully rearranging the wooden snowman family that is standing near the counter or displaying the array of hand-painted baubles and hanging decorations that are set out in wicker baskets on a table, but even I know that I'm tweaking for the sake of it, and the shop already looks like the cosy little Christmas haven I always imagined my shop on Nutcracker Lane would be.

4

I set a hand-painted "'Twas The Night Before Christmas" glittery plaque straight on the wall and then have to do it again because it was straight anyway and now it's wonky, and I adjust the gingerbread-house earrings on a mannequin in Stacey's side of the window. It's going to be amazing working here with my best friend. Going halves on the rent and sharing the shop space – her Christmas jewellery on one side, my Christmas decorations on the other, a window each, and one counter and till between us. We've done craft fairs at the weekends for years, but this is the first time either of us will have an actual shop for the season.

I give one of the retro Nineties-style foil garlands hung across the window a final fluff-up, hoping that my nostalgic display will encourage the feeling of walking into a homely cottage and not a shiny, flashy shop. My decorations are handmade and old-fashioned by modern standards, but I want them to invoke the feeling of Christmases gone by, before every decoration had to sing and dance and be controlled via a smartphone app.

I step out onto the honey-coloured crazy paving and bend down to turn off the multicoloured lights wrapped around the tree outside the door. There's an identical one outside every other shop doorway on the street, each one decorated in the owner's choice, usually displaying some of the goods. Ours is covered in hanging wooden stars and gingerbread men I've made, and acrylic holly leaves and candy canes that Stacey's made.

Every shop on Nutcracker Lane is identical – all large redwood log cabins with fake snow draped across their slanting roofs and a three-foot-tall Christmas tree in a red Santa's sack planter outside the door. The shopkeepers are allowed to decorate their own cabins in any way they choose, and each one has a wide double window and a sign nailed above the door displaying the name of their shop and a slogan. I wood-burned ours in my shed at home and it reads *Starlight Rainbows. Handmade decorations and jewellery.*

I lock up and slip the keys into my bag and turn around to

take in the 11 p.m. atmosphere before the place fills with shoppers tomorrow morning. Well, hopefully. It's been many years since Nutcracker Lane was as packed as it used to be when I was little and my grandma used to bring me here to visit Santa, see the lights, and buy a new decoration for the tree that year, and of course, make a wish on the magical nutcracker.

It's deserted at this time of night. Even the Victorian-style streetlamps that line the lane on either side and emit a warm orange glow in the evenings are off, but there's still the faint whiff of peppermint from the production of peppermint bark in the sweetshop next door today.

The only thing that's unusual is the empty shop directly across from me. I can never recall seeing an empty shop on Nutcracker Lane before. Getting a shop here is more difficult than scoring an invitation to afternoon tea at Buckingham Palace with the Queen. Not that I'm likely to manage that either, but since I started making decorations and selling them online, I've applied every year to rent a shop for the season, and this is the first year I've been a successful applicant.

It's odd to see the log cabin opposite completely dark inside, with nothing in the windows and no sign above the door, not even a Christmas tree outside. Were they really that short of applicants this year? I know things have been deteriorating, but an empty shop is unprecedented. A shiver runs down my spine, and not just from the chill in the air as a cold breeze blows through the lane. Is this a sign of things to come? Is Nutcracker Lane really going downhill so fast that they can no longer fill all the shops?

I turn away and start walking towards the exit. Even with the lights off and the log cabin shops shut, the lane still looks festive. Without any gingerbread baking in the Nutcracker Lane bakery, the balsam scent of the Christmas trees mingles with the faint peppermint from earlier, making me wish I could stay here all night and breathe it in.

'Goodnight, Mr Nutcracker.' I approach the supposedly magical giant nutcracker. When I was little, I thought he was the most magical thing in the world – even better than Santa. He was the talk of the town. *Everyone* knew about the magical wish-granting nutcracker on Nutcracker Lane. He's old. I don't know how old, but he's carved of solid wood, and his mouth and the lever at his back to operate it are his only moving parts, unlike modern-day nutcrackers that are all pins and dowels and glue. He's an older version of the nutcrackers we see everywhere today, with eyes and a moustache carved into dark brown polished wood, and inlaid cherry-stained wood to make his rosy red cheeks, instead of being painted on like they are these days. He has the same white furry beard, long and slightly threadbare now, and his once-bright soldier's outfit, painted in shades of yellow and red, is faded and chipped after so many years of cracking nuts. He holds a carved candy-cane wand and his black boots are encased in cement and buried in the floor to prevent him being stolen.

He's the main attraction of Nutcracker Lane, and he stands proud, over eight-foot tall, in the middle of the big court inside the entrance. He's surrounded by a wooden fence, Astroturf, and white-spotted red mushrooms with little wooden doors on their stems to make up an elf garden.

Next to him are a few large plastic cases of various nuts – walnuts, hazelnuts, and a fake nut alternative for allergy sufferers, and there's a sign up that reads – *Nutcrackers are brimming with magical powers. It's long been said that if a wish is made at the exact moment a nut is being cracked, when the stars shine bright and the wind rustles his beard, and you can almost hear the sparkling of Christmas magic in the air all around, the nutcracker will grant the wish. Try it!*

Surrounding the nutcracker's feet are a bed of broken nutshells where people can throw them, ready to be composted after Christmas, and there are steps up to the handle so even little ones can reach, although a far more popular position is on the shoulders of parents, the way my granddad used to lift me up to crack a nut and make a wish.

The poor old thing might need a fresh coat of paint and some wood filler, but he's stood here for as long as I can remember – if anything, he's the most reliable man in my life. He's here every year without fail. Every year as strong as stone, like an old friend you look forward to catching up with in the festive season, who brings a smile to your face when you remember them throughout the year.

This old nutcracker has seen so many years go by. Things aren't how they used to be, but he's still here, watching over his lane, even though wish-granting is a thing of the past now, and it's been a long time since Christmas magic sparkled around here.

'You're the kind of man I need, Mr Nutcracker,' I say to him as I go to walk away. 'Goodnight.'

And for the weirdest moment, a chill goes down my spine as the breeze through the lane suddenly picks up and ripples his beard. It's a crisp, clear night and I look up and see the stars twinkling through the glass roof and a crescent moon glowing to the east.

I glance back at the nutcracker, half-expecting him to have moved, what with the similarity to the sign about the stars twinkling and the wind rustling his beard.

I turn around and walk back towards him. 'I know when the universe is trying to tell me something. And I suppose a wish couldn't hurt …'

I go through the gap in the fence surrounding him and pick a walnut from one of the nut-vending machines. I reach around him to pull the lever up and open his mouth, put the nut in, and pull the lever gently back down.

I look up at his cheery, red-cheeked woodgrain face. A face I've looked into many times and always felt was smiling back at me. I was fifteen the last time I made a wish on him, and my last wish was that one day I'd get to work on Nutcracker Lane, and even though I am now working here, it's taken twenty years to come true, and determination not to give up even when every application for a shop has been rejected, so I don't think I can quite credit Christmas magic for that one.

'Ah, what the heck …' I pull the lever until the nutcracker's jaws touch the walnut shell. 'I wish to finally find Prince Charming. A prince like you, Mr Nutcracker. A strong, dependable, handsome man who will be loyal and charming and kind. Is that too much to ask?'

The breeze whispers through the lane again and the walnut splits. I take it out of the nutcracker's smiling mouth, throw the shell into the nutshell garden, and pop the kernel into my mouth. 'Goodnight.'

A cloud passes over the moon above and for just a moment, it looks like he winks at me.

I shake my head at myself as I walk away. Apparently break-ups cause hallucinations now too. It reminds me that I'm alone again, and I decide to take the long way round and pop into the 24-hour supermarket on the way home. Never mind magical nutcrackers and walnut wishes, there's only one thing that'll make me feel better in this situation – Ben & Jerry's. Several tubs. And one of those gigantic tubs of chocolates they bring out for Christmas.

In 65,903 calories' time, yet another cheating man will be nothing but a distant memory. It won't matter that I'm alone again because it's Christmas and Nutcracker Lane opens in the morning, and it's my first year here. It's going to be the best Christmas ever.

Chapter 2

The chill in the air is icy as I step out the door of my cottage and lock up behind me, still finding it weird not to say goodbye to my grandma as I leave, even though she's been gone for over four years now. The concrete of the driveway is sparkling with frost, and as I open the front gate and go through it onto the pavement, I see Stacey standing on the corner where my little side street meets the main street, bouncing on her feet to keep warm as she waits for me. She lives two streets down the hill, so we always meet at this intersection and walk up to Nutcracker Lane together.

'Another one bites the dust, huh?' She rubs gloved hands together as I approach.

At first I think she means Ben or Jerry, several tubs of which bit the dust last night and it takes me a moment to realise she's talking about the cheating ex and not ice cream or Cadbury's chocolate.

'Another one bites the purple lingerie, to be precise.' I shove my hands into my pockets as we start walking up the hill towards Nutcracker Lane. 'Probably tearing it off with his teeth as we speak.'

'Nah, far too early for that kind of naughtiness. She's probably too busy trying to get pillow creases out of her face while he's brushing his furry tongue to get rid of the morning breath. Remember him that way. It'll make it easier.'

I laugh out loud at the mental image. I love my best friend. She knows it wasn't a serious relationship, and even though she's happily married with a daughter, she gets that it still hurts when someone cheats on you, no matter what. Thinking about it makes the loneliness sidle in again, having been blocked out by rushing to get ready this morning. It's opening day and I thought we'd better get there early. 'Am I ever going to find a decent man? Is there even *one* out there? What is it with all these guys who go for sexy purple lingerie instead of comfort and commitment – both in lingerie *and* in a relationship? Aren't there any decent men on the planet?'

'Yeah, there are loads, there's just the slight problem of them all being married or otherwise taken. It's a shame single men don't grow on Christmas trees.' She snuggles further into her scarf.

'My relationship problems are solved anyway,' I say as we reach the top of the hill and turn left, walking through another residential street. 'I asked the nutcracker for a handsome prince last night, so one is bound to be along any minute. Can you hear the clip-clopping of horses' hooves?' I put my hand to my ear. 'Probably him on the way in his fairy-tale carriage right now.'

'Yep. There's bound to be a single, gorgeous, gentlemanly prince waiting in the entranceway as soon as we get in, magically summoned by an old wooden toy to find his princess,' she says with a laugh. 'And any prince is bound to be entranced by your collection of Christmas jumpers. Which one did you go with today?'

I open my coat to reveal my Christmas jumper, which is black with lots of green trees all over it, each one with tiny lights that flash from a battery pack hidden inside the hem.

'Flashing trees for opening day. Good choice.'

'Nothing like a Christmas jumper to get you in the mood.

11

And an added bonus of sending customers to Mrs Brissett in the Nutcracker Lane jumper shop when they ask where I got it.'

We come out the other end of the residential street, go up another slope, and shortcut across the frosty shrub border surrounding the Nutcracker Lane car park. Even though the nutcracker manufacturing plant that runs behind the lane hasn't started work yet, the hint of fresh-cut wood is in the air, mixing with the balsam and pine smell as the tree seller unloads netted Christmas trees from the back of a pick-up truck that's reversed up to the end of our little Christmas village where her tree lot stands.

We walk around the perimeter of the building on the pavements surrounding it until we get to the wide glass doors, a huge clear-sided foyer full of signs advertising Nutcracker Lane's attractions – signs that have lessened every year as more and more things disappear.

'No prince, then.' Stacey pushes open the second set of doors into the main entrance court. 'Just a giant nutcracker who, admittedly, is better company than some of the men you've dated.'

'Aww, I think the nutcracker's a prince in his own right.' I wave to him as we walk past his little elf-garden enclosure. 'Good morning, Mr Nutcracker.'

'You're only polite to it so when they rise up as an army on Christmas Eve and take over the world, they'll remember you fondly and spare you.'

I poke my tongue out at her. She doesn't get why nutcrackers have always been my favourite Christmas decoration or why I like that one quite so much.

'You know it was the staff here who granted your childhood Christmas wishes and he's not really magical ... Unless Prince Charming randomly turns up this morning. Then I'll take it all back.'

'I think we can safely say *that's* not going to happen ...'

Santa chooses that moment to stroll out of the gents' toilets pulling his trousers out of his bum.

12

Stacey and I hold each other's gaze for a long moment and then burst into giggles. 'Nah.'

'God, it's bleak, isn't it?' She says as we continue down the lane, the first signs of the log cabins coming to life around us. Lights on in the back rooms, a few of the Christmas trees with their lights twinkling already. 'They don't even decorate anymore.' She wraps her hand around a bare iron lamppost as we pass it. In years gone by, the posts were wrapped with sparkling green tinsel wound with white fairy lights, finished with an oversized red bow and a bunch of fresh mistletoe hanging from the top of each one. The ceilings were decked with fairy-light-wrapped garlands and you couldn't turn around without coming face-to-face with a poinsettia.

'I always imagined bringing my children here one day, and it's so sad that Lily has never got to see it as I remember it. She doesn't believe me when I tell her what it used to be like. It's such a shame to see it on its last legs.'

'Do you really think it is?' I try to stamp down the sadness that rears up. I haven't got as far as thinking about having children, but if I ever do, I can't imagine *not* being able to bring them to Nutcracker Lane where I spent so many happy childhood days back in the Eighties and Nineties.

'Look around, Nee. It's faded gradually every year, and this is the worst one yet. Opening day and … this is it. There are no staff except the shopkeepers themselves, no one keeping the actual lane running, no maintenance, no cleaners, and if you dare to turn around right now, you'll see Santa picking his nose. How much worse can it get than Santa pulling bogeys out of his nose hair and examining them … Oh, wait, now he's eating them as well. Lovely.'

'It just needs one good year to recover – one year with even a fraction of the visitors it used to get. Most people don't even realise it's still here. The only person who seems to have any interest in it these days is the horrible Scrooge-like accountant who keeps slashing the budget every year. That lovely couple who owned it haven't been seen for months. I was chatting to Rhonda in the hat shop the other day and she said she didn't see them once last year— What the hell is that?'

We turn the bend in the lane towards Starlight Rainbows and I stop in my tracks. The empty shop opposite is no longer empty. Its window is ablaze with white light, and instead of a Christmas tree outside the door, there's a six-foot-tall animatronic dancing Santa wearing a tropical shirt with a Hawaiian lei around his neck who's currently doing some depiction of the Macarena. The hand-painted sign above the window reads "Tinkles and Trinkets" and in smaller letters underneath "The BEST Christmas decorations for all your holiday needs."

'But that's ...' I splutter, unable to get my words out properly. 'That was empty last night. There was *nothing* in there. How did they get it set up so fast?'

'Elves?' Stacey pulls a face at the dancing Santa.

'But we sell decorations. I *make* decorations. And now we've got to compete with *that*? And look at it.' We both peer into the window. There are so many fairy lights glowing in the display that somewhere in the next county, there's a bloke wondering why the sun just came out and the National Grid has probably started groaning. The animatronic theme continues as the window display is full of dancing Santas of various sizes, musical nutcrackers, light-up feather wreaths, branches of lit-up twigs, twinkling garlands, a giant snowglobe with lights around the base that's playing some kind of conflicting tune with one of the singing festive teddy bears, and even a model Christmas village with plastic nutcrackers moving in a mechanical circle in and out of a tiny factory building.

Even the term "plastic nutcrackers" is offensive. Nutcrackers are always, always made of wood. It's traditional.

Something inside is playing a Christmas tune, but it sounds like its batteries are going flat, and there's so much twisting and jiggling and dancing in the window that I can't even tell which one it is.

'It's impressive,' Stacey says. '*Everyone* is going to stop to look at it.'

'Exactly.' I look over my shoulder at our darkened little shop opposite. 'It's a million times better than our rustic wooden decorations and Nineties-style foil garlands and sets of lights taped round the windows. You can see Tinkles and Trinkets from space. There are probably aliens on Jupiter right now scratching their heads and trying to work out who turned the lights on.'

'Well, it's not *better*, it's different. Personally, I like the nostalgic side of Christmas and think all this singing and dancing stuff is distasteful tat.'

'Does it look like familiar distasteful tat to you?' I cock my head to the side and try to hear the strains of a tune the nutcracker model factory is playing, but it's drowned out by the toy with the dying batteries and the creaking of the Macarena-ing Santa.

'I can't see anyone inside.' Stacey cups her hands around her eyes and peers through the glass, but the glare of the lights is too bright to see anything beyond the window display.

'I don't understand how it can have been empty last night. No one could've got this done so quickly, could they? It must've been a whole team of people.' I peer in the window too, but all I can make out is rows and rows of shelves. 'It's like it's sprung up from nowhere.'

'Like magic.' She slots her arm through mine and yanks me across the paving stones to Starlight Rainbows. 'It's not worth worrying about. We sell totally different types of decorations and there's room for all of us on Nutcracker Lane.'

I give the dazzling shop one last glance. Every other log cabin on our lane has been setting up for a month now. We all got our keys on the first day of November, and since then, everyone has been back and forth unloading stock and setting up their displays. Except this one. And in the space of the nine hours since I left last night, this owner has managed to create the most spectacular display of all.

15

I unlock our little wooden door and turn the wood-burned wreath sign on it over from "closed" to "open". Our shop smells of fresh-cut wood from my decorations and that inimitable scent of tinsel and foil Christmas decorations when they've been shut away for a while. I flip the light switch and pick up a letter that's been posted through the letterbox.

'You were here for hours tweaking last night then?' Stacey looks around like she can tell every earring I adjusted on her jewellery side of the shop.

'I was priming some nutcracker bunting so it had time to dry before today.' I switch the electric wax burner behind the counter on to fill the shop with the scent of vanilla and balsam and dump my bag on the counter as I split the letter open and unfold it.

'Factory space!' I stare at the letter in horror. 'How could they do this? Listen …' I start reading it aloud.

Dear esteemed Nutcracker Lane lease holder,

I am writing to inform you that commencing January 1st, Nutcracker Lane will be under new ownership. As the acting manager until the new owner joins us, it falls to me to ensure we will not be carrying deadweight into the new year. Next year will see things change for the better. Next year your leases will not automatically be renewed – instead, you will have to work for the privilege. Only the most profitable shops will be going forward to the next festive season – the rest will be sold off for factory space to the nutcracker factory next door. I will review your accounts in January and let you know in due course whether you will have a place on the improved and streamlined Nutcracker Lane next year.

Do your best this festive season!

Regards,
Mr E.B. Neaser
Head accountant and acting manager, Nutcracker Lane

'Wow.' Stacey runs a hand through her short hair.

'Do you think this was hand-delivered? It's early for the postman.' I turn over the envelope in my hands but there's not even an address on it. 'Everyone must've got one.'

'Not even a "kind regards" or a "best wishes" or anything. How rude. And he's still using that stupid name. It's like he knows we call him Scrooge and he's mocking us.'

'There's no way it's his real name,' I agree. 'We've dealt with this guy before. There's definitely nothing kind about him. We've already had three letters this year telling us of yet more budget cuts and restrictions and a rent increase for the privilege. He seems to take pleasure in it. 'This is like a cross between a motivational speech and a condescending headteacher telling off naughty schoolchildren who have run riot with the crayons.'

I open the door and look outside to see Hubert from the sweetshop looking around too, the letter clutched in his hand.

Before I have a chance to speak, Rhonda who runs the Christmas hat shop, opens her door and steps out. 'You got one too?'

Hubert and I both nod.

'This is terrible.' Mrs Thwaite opens the door of the Christmas candle shop two doors down, her letter balled up in her fist. 'How dare they!'

'This is the same Scrooge who's been cutting the budget every year, and now he's eschewed the budget and started on the shops themselves,' Hubert says.

'What are we going to do?' I step outside to join them. 'We've only just got our shop. I quit my job to work here. I was relying on it being renewed next year.'

That's one of the reasons it's so hard to get a spot on Nutcracker Lane. Once you're in, all existing shop owners get first right of renewal, and this used to be such a lovely place that if you had a shop here, you wouldn't give it up. Hardly any new leases come up each year and the competition to get them is fierce, and the owners have always been selective about which shops they choose to be part of Nutcracker Lane. They have to add something new and unique and not have any crossover with any of the items already available here.

I glance at the shining new decoration shop. Clearly that rule has gone down the pan this year.

My job was only stacking supermarket shelves, but it would've been impossible to do both that and Nutcracker Lane. For the past few years, I've been working dead-end part-time jobs, spending as many hours as I can in the evening making decorations, and Stacey and I have been driving to every craft fair that would have us at the weekends, and selling via our own websites, eBay, and Etsy shops. I'd hoped to make enough profit from this to have a bit of leeway in the coming months until next year here.

'We all were. I've been here for nine years,' Rhonda from the Christmas hat shop says.

'Fifteen.' Mrs Brissett from the jumper shop comes down the lane towards us, letter in hand. 'This is ridiculous.'

'Twenty-something.' Carmen, the amazing chocolatier who runs Nutcracker Lane's very own chocolate shop follows her.

'This is my biggest earner.' The tree seller joins the group too. 'And now what? They're going to chuck out those of us who don't make the grade?'

'They can't do that, can they?' Rhonda asks.

'This Scrooge-like accountant seems to be able to do whatever he wants,' Hubert says. 'He's been running this place into the ground for years with his continual budget cuts, and now this. He couldn't sound much more gleeful in his letter, could he? He may as well have thrown us into *The Hunger Games* arena and told us to have at it.'

'Aren't we all competition now?' Mrs Thwaite from the candle shop asks.

'Aww, no, you lot are like a second family. I don't want to be in competition with you,' Mrs Brissett says.

18

'But that's exactly what it's saying.' I scan over the letter again as Stacey appears in the open doorway of our shop. 'Whichever shops earn the most money will stay, the rest of the lane will be sold off to the nutcracker factory …'

'… who will waste no time in bulldozing it,' Stace adds. 'There will be nothing left. And where are our parameters? How many shops are staying? How much do they need to earn?'

'Scrooge can pick and choose whenever he fancies it,' Hubert says. 'If we don't know what the rules are, how can we possibly win the game?'

Another chill goes down my spine. It's cold and heartless, just like the rest of Scrooge's letter.

'And this part of the lane is closest to the factory,' Rhonda says. 'So what's he going to do, move whoever's left into the entrance court and get rid of this bit entirely?'

'That's awful,' I say. 'How can you have Nutcracker Lane without the lane?'

'And how can he say "earn the most money or get out" just like that? How can he pit friends against each other? And how is it possibly fair? Little shops like you …' Rhonda points to me and Stacey. 'You're selling things that cost two, three, four quid. How can you compete with the chap who sells custom-made snowglobes at twenty quid each? Or whoever this is.' She points to the dazzling new shop opposite. 'There's a £300 price tag on that dancing Santa.'

We all look at the animatronic Santa who is *still* moving his hands out in front of him, to his shoulders, and then his hips and back again. 'One of those gone and this new arrival will have beaten the lot of us. I'll have to sell sixty hats to outdo one item.'

'No one's actually going to buy that though,' Stacey says. '*Who* would want a Hawaiian Santa doing the Macarena in their house, never mind be able to transport the gigantic thing home?'

A few of us gradually migrate towards the glowing window, which seems even fuller now than it did ten minutes ago.

19

'Who's the newcomer?' Carmen asks.

'I don't know, do you?' Hubert scratches his head. 'Funny they weren't here before, whoever they are.'

'Funny they're allowed to sell things that cross over with what the rest of us are selling.' I nod towards the lit-up snowglobe in the window, which must be plugged in somewhere because the snow is swirling around in it like a lava lamp as it plays a tune that clashes with the one the model nutcracker factory is playing in the busy window.

That tune again. One that sounds so familiar …

After a few moments of silence, Hubert says, 'It seems that a lot of things that once made Nutcracker Lane special have gone out the window this year.'

The sadness is palpable as all the shopkeepers, people I've known for years, people who have been the heart of Nutcracker Lane for as long as I can remember, realise that things *have* changed, and they're changing more every day.

'Good luck for opening day, folks,' Mrs Brissett says as she starts to walk back towards the jumper shop.

'No, you can't say that now,' Carmen corrects her. 'We're not all working together for Nutcracker Lane anymore – we all have to be out for ourselves and looking after our own interests. This isn't a normal year – this is a fight for survival now. I'm sorry, but I don't want to lose my shop. I won't be sending any more business your way and I don't expect you lot to send any my way. We've got to put ourselves first or we'll all be jobless next year.'

'I agree,' Rhonda from the hat shop says sadly.

'I don't!' Hubert smacks his hand against the paper he's holding. 'I'm not sure I even want to stay and work for this new owner. Anyone who can agree to a scheme like this is never going to be a decent person, are they? Whoever he is, he obviously cares for Nutcracker Lane as little as Scrooge does. You'd have thought any new owner would've been keen to reinvigorate it, but it's

20

screamingly obvious that he's only interested in the money. The same as Scrooge. Money, money, money.'

He's got a point there. The atmosphere on Nutcracker Lane has already changed because of Scrooge. Even as we stand here, a few other shopkeepers have stepped out their doors and come to see what's going on, and I can see everyone side-eyeing each other, weighing up the competition. It doesn't bode well for any of us, and Hubert has certainly got a point. Will the new owner be so horrible to work for that no one wants to stay here anyway?

Everyone starts to file away with no wishes of good luck or "happy opening day". Instead there are mutterings of competition and everyone for themselves. The atmosphere is prickly and tense – something I've never felt on Nutcracker Lane before.

'Good luck,' Hubert says when there are only me and Stacey left. He raises his hand with the letter in it. 'I'm not going to stop supporting my friends. Scrooge wants to divide us, and he won't succeed, not with me.'

'Me neither,' I say, sounding more confident than I am. One glance at Tinkles and Trinkets across from us has siphoned my positivity away. Stacey and I can't compete with £300 dancing Santas and electric-powered snowglobes. And what about the others? We're not just in competition with another decoration shop – we're in competition with *everyone*. I don't want to lose our shop, but I don't want them to lose theirs either. Some of those shops have been here for longer than I've been alive.

I remember Hubert from when I was young, peering over the counter in his candy-striped apron and taking my grandma's money from my fist as I tried to buy everything in the shop and he patiently counted out seasonal penny sweets to the value of the two pound coins I had while Grandma and Granddad discussed what to choose for my parents and he slipped me a free Christmas tree lollipop while they weren't looking. Nutcracker Lane would never be the same without him.

And Carmen who makes the most intricate chocolate creations,

Rhonda with her short spiky hair in a bright pink Mohawk who sells every type of Christmas hat you can imagine, or Mrs Brissett who's got the best selection of Christmas jumpers in the northern hemisphere, or the dear old man who painstakingly crafts the most beautiful snowglobes from photographs of real places.

'There's nothing we can do about it,' Stacey says from the doorway.

When I make a noncommittal noise, she comes over and takes the letter out of my hand and puts her arm around my shoulders. 'Let's give Scrooge what he wants and "do our best this festive season". That's all we can do. At least if this is our only year, you'll have got your wish – to work on Nutcracker Lane before it changes for good.'

*

'Don't worry about the competition,' Stacey says as I peer out the window at the shop opposite for approximately the ninety-third time this morning and it's only 11 a.m. 'No one's going to buy those things. The pricing is ridiculous. It's Christmas, for God's sake. Very few people have got excess cash at this time of year, and *no one* is going to drop £300 on a dancing Santa or the £96 that's attached to that model nutcracker factory. Whoever's running it has got no idea about competitive pricing. Expecting that much for Christmas decorations is pointless because there's so much other stuff to buy at this time of year. Customers are going to come in here and spend a fiver on one of your hand-painted wall plaques or £2.50 on a pair of candy-cane earrings without worrying about it, but the stuff over there is a seriously *big* purchase. They won't be as much competition as you think they will.'

'Have you seen the number of people going in?'

'And leaving with nothing. At least we've made a few sales so far.'

'It doesn't even look like there's anyone in there.' The light

22

spilling out is so bright that it obscures everything else and I hold my hand up like I'm shading my eyes from the sun, but it doesn't help. 'Do those garlands around the window look familiar to you?'

She glances over but a woman takes a gingerbread-house necklace and a standing red bow ornament up to the counter and she stops to serve her.

It's quiet for an opening day. I remember the days when you could barely move through the lane and there were queues to get into each shop. Maybe Scrooge has got the right idea – put it out of its misery before it gets any worse. Things will probably pick up at the weekend when children are off school, but it's only Tuesday. Is this as good as it gets until then? There's a bit of noise coming from the upper end of the lane around the magical nutcracker and Santa's grotto, but down this end … footsteps of a middle-aged couple echo across the paving slabs as they walk straight past, not even lingering to admire the decorations like people used to when there were any to admire.

'I'm sure those are the garlands that used to be draped from the ceiling.'

'Nia, you're obsessed. You've barely been away from that window all morning.'

'Seriously, look. That new shop has got them around their window like a frame. They're the same ones. And that nutcracker village. I've seen it before …'

She's gone off to tidy a basket full of wooden baubles that a customer has rifled through and I'm talking to myself. A customer leaves empty-handed, giving me a wary look as he passes.

I *am* obsessing. I should be concentrating on *our* shop, not whoever's over there and whatever they're selling. It's nothing to do with me.

Although the door *is* wide open and it really doesn't look like there's anyone inside … I could go over and pop my head in, couldn't I? Have a peep and see if the inside is as spectacular as the window display. If the owner does happen to be there, I'll make an excuse of welcoming the new arrival to the lane. There's nothing wrong with being friendly, after all …

'Can you hold down the fort for a minute?' I'm out the door before Stacey's had a chance to reply.

I run across the lane and stop in the open doorway. 'Hello?' I whisper, telling myself I'm trying not to startle anyone rather than I'm hoping there's no one manning the place so I can have a nose around.

No answer. I take a tentative step inside, feeling as light on my feet as a ballet dancer as I tiptoe in.

Wow. If anything, the spectacularity of the shop itself is blocked by the spectacular window, because the inside is even better. Every wall is lined with a waterfall of twinkling white lights, a curtain of fairy lights that make it look like the walls themselves are sparkling. The shop is absolutely packed with decorations in all shapes, sizes, and colours, all lined up on chunky white shelves in perfectly size-ordered rows, like armies waiting to be called into action. There's a metallic-y scent of glitter in the air, and every so often, a flake of fake snow floats down from the ceiling, while the music "Dance of the Sugar Plum Fairy" from *The Nutcracker* ballet plays quietly from a speaker in the far corner.

I keep telling myself I'm not going to worry about the competition. Everything Stacey said is right, and all we can do is put all our effort in and hope for the best, but looking around this shop makes me realise we've already lost. It's like stepping into a winter wonderland, and the feeling I get is probably not dissimilar to the feeling Lucy Pevensie got when she stepped out of the wardrobe and into the snowy lands of Narnia for the first time. It would be easy to spend a couple of hours *and* a couple of hundred quid in here. Heck, even *I'm* suddenly prepared to pay £300 for a Macarena-dancing Santa and I definitely don't have any spare cash *or* appreciation for Hawaiian-style Santas.

It's weird that there's no one here though. The light's on out the back so maybe they're still unloading goods. There's plenty of space between shelves to fit more in, making it look minimalistic and still stuffed full of choice, unlike ours which just looks full because Stacey and I wanted to get as much stock out as possible and that means using every inch of wall space and getting as many display tables in as could reasonably fit while still meeting health and safety guidelines. I'd like to think our shop is relaxed, warm, homely and comforting, whereas this could be the set of a Christmas film.

But that strange familiarity is back again. Those curtains of lights covering the walls look like ones that used to be hung around the entrance foyer of Nutcracker Lane, and there's an LED mountain range – a huge stand displaying a range of snowy peaks from one foot to four foot tall at the edge of the window display with a £256 price tag. There *cannot* be two of those, and I'm almost positive this one used to form part of the backdrop behind Santa's grotto.

In one corner is a wooden crate full of soft toys that used to be given away to children who needed them. Now there's a price sticker on the front – £16 each. I tiptoe further in for a closer look and find myself stopping to bend over the window display and peer at the mechanical nutcracker factory model. It's playing a muffled repetition of the most recognisable bars of the first march from *The Nutcracker* ballet, and at the back, there's a drip mark in the navy paint, which proves it. This used to be in a display stand at the point where the lane ends and there's a short, covered walkway between the car parks for us and the nutcracker manufacturing plant next door. Why would it be on sale here? Why are any of these things on sale here?

The more I look around, the more I'm sure of it. Whoever owns this shop is selling off the decorations that have been taken from Nutcracker Lane. Decorations that were once used to decorate this place itself.

I back up and sidle along a shelf, looking at rows and rows of miniature snowglobes, metal reindeer ornaments, and wooden gingerbread men not unlike the ones I've been making with my CNC woodcutting machine in my garden shed workshop for months. Mine are four quid each and hand-painted, whereas these look like mass-printed Chinese imports with uneven eyes and wonky noses. I pick one up and read the price tag on the bottom.

'Twelve quid for *that*!' I put it down and step back quickly, except I don't realise there's anything behind me until something wooden hits me in the back. I yelp in surprise and turn around to see a six-foot-tall giant nutcracker staring back at me, wobbling precariously from the force of me backing into it.

'No, no, no, no, no, no, no!' I try to catch it but the momentum is too much and the smooth wood slips out of my hand and it goes crashing to the floor with such a loud bang that people in France probably heard it, and a shower of gemstones from his elegant green-trimmed coat clatter down and go skittering across the floor.

I squeeze my eyes tight shut and wish the ground could swallow me up. So much for a sneaky look around without anyone knowing. When I force myself to open them again to assess the damage, the giant nutcracker is lying on the floor surrounded by wood splinters. His left arm is broken jaggedly in two, and the broken bit has skidded across the aisle along with the sceptre he was holding.

Oh no. Oh *no*. I love nutcrackers and he was such a hand-some one. Longish furry hair that's such a dark brown it looks black from some angles, a matching beard, and painted black moustache and eyebrows above almond-shaped white eyes with big brown pupils, red cheeks and a hint of the same red on the tip of his nose. He's dressed in red with a green trim, navy cuffs around his wrists, black boots with gold accents, and a gold crown on his head.

'I'm so sorry, you lovely thing. I'll pay for the damage—' I catch sight of a price tag tied around his unbroken arm and lean across to read it, turning the tree-shaped cardboard over in my

26

fingers. '£926!' I say aloud. I've never had a heart attack before, but I suspect this is what one might feel like.

I've heard people use the phrase "eye-wateringly expensive" but this is the first time I've ever looked at a price tag and felt my eyes actually start to water.

Nearly a thousand pounds. Every part of my body has tensed up. I *cannot* pay that. I'd struggle to find a spare £26 at the moment, never mind the £900 as well.

I drop the price tag and look around in panic. There's still no one here. Wherever the shop owner has gone, even the noise of the nutcracker falling hasn't brought anyone running back.

No one has seen me. No one knows it was me. If I just left …

That £926 is pulsing in my head like a sign flashing in neon red. I've got *so* much stuff to buy to host Christmas for my family this year, never mind supplies to make stock, and food and presents, and in January, I won't have a job. Not a proper job anyway, only my online sales and whichever craft fairs Stacey and I can get a spot at, not including the petrol it takes to get there. And that's only assuming they'd let me pay it off in small amounts. The thought of being expected to find nearly a thousand quid right now makes a cold sweat prickle my forehead.

'I'm so sorry,' I whisper. And I run away.

I dash back across the lane and into Starlight Rainbows, kicking the weighted Santa hat doorstop I made out of the way and slamming the door behind me, even though we've decided to keep it open to make the shop more inviting.

'What's wrong with you?' Stacey looks up from replacing one of her necklaces that's been bought from the mannequin in the window.

'I knocked over a giant nutcracker and broke it and now I'm going to owe that shop nine hundred quid,' I say in such a rush that even a professional translator wouldn't be able to decipher it.

'Can you split that sentence into more than one word?'

I lean against the wall and knock a bauble skew-whiff and

27

don't even bother to straighten it as I take deep breaths and try to calm my heart rate while I repeat myself.

'You have to go back,' Stacey says when I've finished. 'Explain that it was an accident and ask if they'll let you start paying it off in January. They run a Christmas shop; they must understand how tight things can be at this time of year.'

'Or I could hide in the back room and never come out. I'll go home after dark and stay in my shed making decorations and you can sell them, and between us, I'll never have to show my face here again and no one will ever know it was me. How's that for a plan?'

We both know I'm not serious, but I start pacing the floor anyway. 'What am I going to say? And I've run away and made it all worse. Now I've made myself look like a criminal. I'm a fugitive. A life on the run beckons. Oh my God, I'm going to get involved in organised crime and be indoctrinated into a gang, and all sorts.'

'Your only crime is murdering a nutcracker. I don't *think* the punishment is twenty-five years behind bars, but maybe they've changed the charge of second-degree murder to include wooden dolls now.'

I narrow my eyes at her sarcasm and she laughs. 'I need a cup of tea, so go on, go back over there and confess so you can watch the shop while I go and get one, or there might end up being a real murder committed due to tea desperation.'

I try to delay the inevitable for a few moments longer, but I know she's right. I'm not a good enough liar to pretend it wasn't me, and my conscience is already getting the better of me. Stacey and I have done craft fairs where people pick things up and pull them around and break them and then hastily put them down and hurry guiltily away, or even better are the ones who draw your attention to it and say, 'This is broken, love. It was like that when I picked it up. I wonder how that happened …' I would much rather someone outright apologise and offer to pay for it, even though it doesn't matter as much with a £2.50 pair of earrings as it does with a £926 nutcracker. 'And what is with that weird pricing?' I say to Stacey.

'Nia!' she snaps. 'You're delaying. Get on with it.'

I've known Stace since the first day of secondary school, and sometimes I wish I hadn't because she can see right through me. I grumble as I set the door open again and force one foot in front of the other to traipse back across to the open door with the Santa *still* Macarena-ing outside, feeling like some sort of hefty cyclops rather than an elegant ballerina this time.

Inside, the shop is still empty. Where on earth is this person? The nutcracker made such a crash when it fell that I'm surprised someone from the UK's seismology team hasn't turned up to investigate the unexplained earthquake that just registered on their scales, and yet there's still no one in sight. This is getting weird now. I suppose I should pick the nutcracker up and wait with it until someone gets back …

I round the corner of the aisle where the nutcracker was, but the giant wooden soldier has gone, along with the broken bit of his arm, his sceptre and every splinter of wood, and lying on the floor in his place is a man. I scream.

The man is lying on his back and his head and right arm are under a shelf, looking like he's trying to reach for something. His left arm is in a plaster cast and held across his chest by a sling.

He yelps in surprise at my noise and jumps so much that he clonks his forehead on the shelf hard enough to make the whole thing shake, causing such a reverberation that the rows of fifteen-centimetre-tall nutcrackers wobble and fall off, pelting down at him as he tries to curl in on himself and makes a noise of pain.

'What are you doing there?' I snap, the shock of seeing him making all logical thought fly out the window.

'I work here. You?' he snaps back as he wriggles himself out from under the shelf, every movement slow and stilted and followed by a noise of pain that he's probably not aware he's making out loud. He crunches the nutcrackers under his legs as he moves, until eventually he's fully free of the shelf and is lying on the aisle floor, surrounded by a sea of little wooden nutcrackers, and squinting up at me in the brightness of the shop.

My heart is still pounding from the shock of his unexpected appearance and I'm sure he must be able to see it bouncing in and out of my chest like a cartoon character's.

He's got something clutched in the hand of his unbroken arm and he rubs his forehead with his free fingers. 'Is your jumper flashing or is this the festive equivalent of seeing stars?'

It makes me snort with laughter. 'It's flashing.'

'I thought you worked in the decoration shop opposite?'

'I do.' I can't hide my surprise that he knows that.

'Not the jumper shop?'

'No.'

'So you're wearing that *without* contractual obligation?'

'It's Christmas,' I say when I finally fall in to where his line of questioning was going.

'And that makes it socially acceptable to wear a set of traffic lights?'

'Ah, traffic lights only have three colours. This jumper has many more.'

'Believe me, I can *see* that.' He groans and clonks his head back onto the floor. 'So, my arm breaker. You came back.'

'I had to. I'm so sor— Wait, *your* arm breaker?' The music playing in the background of the shop is now "The Waltz of the Snowflakes" from *The Nutcracker* and the ballet pops into my head. The nutcracker soldier given as a gift on Christmas Eve, who gets broken and then turns into a prince at the stroke of midnight and takes the young ballerina on a magical journey through a land of sweets and snowflakes.

He mutters something about the nutcracker, but all I can think about is the ballet and the nineteenth-century story behind it. About the nutcracker who turns into a real-life prince after being broken …

30

He's just lying there, trying to catch his breath, pain obvious in every line that flashes across his face when he winces.

'Are you okay?'

'I did not think this through at all. Getting down here was hard enough, but I have absolutely no idea how to get up. I regret this decision.' His face is still pinched but there's a jokey tone in his voice that makes me smile.

'Do you need a hand?'

'No, I need a crane. Or a forklift truck.'

His tone makes me giggle again and when I look back at him, he's smiling for the first time and his smile is so much like Flynn Rider's that it stops me in my tracks. In that moment, he looks so much like the Disney prince that it's almost like the animated version has stepped out of the screen and into real life. Wait … A Disney prince. A nutcracker prince. A prince … I wished for last night?

No, it couldn't be. Like I've somehow developed the ability to see through walls, I look in the direction of the magical nutcracker. I wished for a prince. A prince like the nutcracker himself. And they say nutcrackers grant wishes if the wish is made at the moment a nut is being cracked, and the stars *were* twinkling just right and the wind *did* whisper in his beard. This man is even wearing a dark blue shirt with threads of green running through it, not unlike the nutcracker's navy cuffs and green-trimmed coat.

It couldn't be, could it? *He* couldn't be … he couldn't actually *be* the nutcracker I knocked over … could he?

No. Of course he couldn't. What am I thinking? Maybe *I'm* the one who's fallen over and hit my head. In the real world, outside of much-loved festive ballets, broken nutcracker soldiers don't magically turn into real men. I think. Hope. I mean, it would be nice, but …

'Can you take this?' He's holding his good hand up to me and sounding like it's not the first time he's said it. I put my hand out and his warm fingers touch my palm as he drops something into it.

I go to offer help again but the look he gives me makes me cut off the sentence, and I look down instead, trying to give him some privacy as he starts moving.

In my hand is an amber gemstone that I recognise from the front of the nutcracker's gold crown, one of the many that must've fallen off and skidded under the shelf when I knocked it over, which explains what he was doing down there. I'm trying to look away, but he's making so many grunts of pain that I can't help watching him worriedly, hovering like I might be able to help even though he's made it obvious that he doesn't want any assistance. His legs move against the smooth laminate wood flooring, the fallen nutcrackers scattering around him as he tries to get upright.

He seems to be hurting more than a broken arm would cause, but I've never broken anything, so I wouldn't know.

Eventually he gets onto his knees and has to stop. His good arm is laid along a low shelf and his forehead is resting against it, his chest heaving as he pants for breath.

I go to ask if he's okay, but it's obvious he isn't. 'What happened to your arm?' I ask instead.

'I got knocked over,' he says without looking up.

I freeze again. My fingers tighten on the amber stone I was fiddling with, hoping he's going to elaborate, but he doesn't. No. *No* … it *can't* be. Obviously he doesn't mean by *me*. Just now. When I knocked over the nutcracker and happened to break the exact same arm. That's ridiculous. Even though I wished for a prince last night and the more I look at him, the more strongly he resembles a Disney prince. He's like Aladdin, Prince Eric, and Flynn Rider got together and had all the best parts of themselves put into one person. He's got Eric's floppy dark hair, Aladdin's wide-set brown eyes, and Flynn's smile, and I feel every childhood crush coming back with a vengeance. It's some kind of sign – it's *got* to be. Obviously he can't actually be the nutcracker come to life, but what if the whole nutcracker thing is some kind of nod from the universe and this is a sign? What if this guy really *is* the Prince Charming I've been waiting for?

When he looks up, there's sweat beading on his forehead from the effort it's taken him, but he gives me a soft smile that makes every thought disappear from my mind and my body goes hot all over, and I realise I've spent the last few minutes staring at him.

'I'll clear these up.' I look away and start gathering up the mini bare-wood nutcrackers, anything to give myself something to do besides stare at him.

I take a couple of armfuls over to the counter, and he doesn't look up again until I go back for the third and final lot. 'At least it wasn't the snowglobes. That would've finished the job for the multiple things that have been trying to kill me this week.' He glances at the tiny globes lined up on the next shelf along. 'And been a lot messier to clean up.'

It makes me smile as I put the nutcrackers down and go back to hold my hand out. 'Now do you need a hand up?'

He smiles gently up at me and seems to consider it for a moment before reaching out and slotting his right hand into mine. My fingers close around his and I widen my feet and brace my knees and pull him up. Agony crosses his face as he stumbles to his feet and when he gets upright, he doesn't let go of my hand, even as he leans against the shelf for support, short of breath again. I can't imagine how badly that arm must be broken if it's causing him this much pain.

Eventually he opens big brown eyes with dark circles under them and moves from holding on to my hand to shaking it softly. 'Seeing as we're shaking hands anyway, I'm James.'

'Nia,' I murmur, feeling ridiculously entranced by his eyes. They're light brown, an unusual wood-like colour. You'd expect someone with such dark hair to have dark eyes, but his are so light they're almost out of place. 'Are you all right?'

'Well, let's just say it's a good thing the painkillers from last

33

night are still in my system or I wouldn't be functional at all.' He ducks his head and his hair flops forwards, and I can't help noticing he's around six foot tall – exactly the same height as the nutcracker.

Somehow, my hand is still in his, and we're still mindlessly shaking them even though the introduction phase *and* the awkward phase have passed and we're now just two strangers staring at each other and holding hands. A little tingle has sparked from the touch of his fingers and I can feel it gradually sparkling up my arm, across my shoulders, and down my spine, and it takes a long few minutes for me to realise I came here for a reason.

'I'm so sorry about your nutcracker,' I say in a rush.

'My what?' He blinks, looking dazed for a second, and then awareness seems to hit him hard enough to make him jump and he yanks his hand back and pushes it through his hair, which instantly falls across his forehead again anyway. 'Oh, that. Don't worry about it.'

'I'm so sorry. I broke it, I have to pay for the damage.' I don't add "assuming you *aren't* actually it come to life" to the end of the sentence. That would be one way to make an impression and not the good kind.

'Oh, please. I couldn't give a toss. You've done me a favour – I'll mend it and sell it at a reduced price. It needed to be reduced anyway – believe me, *no one* is going to pay £926 for that thing.'

'Yeah, but I damaged your stock. Everyone knows about the "you break it, you buy it" rule. I can't afford it outright, but if you'd let me start paying—'

'Nia, don't worry about it. It doesn't matter.'

'Yeah, but—' I start again, but he cuts me off.

'It's nice of you to offer, but forget it. It's just another Christmas decoration – *exactly* what everyone needs around here.'

'You work in a Christmas decoration shop ...' I say slowly, confused by his attitude. I thought he'd be calling the police to

34

have me done for criminal damage given half a chance, and now he's telling me I don't even have to pay it off?

'Exactly. I think there are enough nutcrackers to go round, don't you?' He waves his good hand towards the pile on the counter. 'You can smash up the rest of the shop too, if you want. I hate Christmas.'

I take a step back in surprise and quickly think better of it and check behind me, lest we have another nutcracker-related disaster. 'You *hate* Christmas?' I shake my head in disbelief. Surely he's winding me up? 'You own a Christmas decoration shop in the most Christmassy place in the country.'

'Exposure therapy?'

'Are you serious?'

He laughs a sarcastic laugh, which quickly turns into a wince of pain. 'I didn't think it through, okay? I usually do an office job but I needed a change this year. I took a wrong turn and pulled into your car park to turn around and saw a "Help Wanted" sign. And it seemed like a sign. You know, from the universe. And a literal sign. So I don't own it, I just work here.'

'I didn't know there had ever been a "Help Wanted" sign up …' I rack my brain, trying to think of a sign I might've missed. I go to push further but I realise how weird I must sound and stop myself quickly. 'Sorry, it's just that you're selling off Nutcracker Lane stock …'

'Am I?' He looks around, seeming surprised by this. 'I collected my keys this morning from Santa who was rolling his own earwax into balls and flicking it at passers-by. I have *never* been so grateful for antibacterial hand gel.'

It makes me giggle again, even though with that Santa, I doubt he's joking. 'All this stuff used to decorate Nutcracker Lane. Where did you get this from?'

He shrugs again but I can tell he's being careful this time because it's a muted shrug, and I want to ask him if he's okay again, but he doesn't seem like he's going to elaborate either way.

35

'I don't know, it's nothing to do with me. All I've been told is that the new owner's selling off stock and needed someone to man the shop.'

'It's not his to sell!'

'Well, if he's bought the place, technically it *is* his and he can do whatever he wants with it ...' He sounds cautious, like he's waiting for me to yell at him.

'Have you met him? Do you know who he is? He sounds like an absolute monster.'

'No.' He shrugs with a blank look on his face. 'Like I said, I've just got a job here until after Christmas. I needed to get out of the office for a while.'

'And you thought this was the ideal place for someone who hates Christmas?'

He pushes his floppy hair back again. 'Look, I may not have thought it through properly, okay? I needed to do something different while I still can, and this came up and I grabbed it. It was only afterwards that I realised what I'd be doing and how festive it'd be.' He pulls a face.

While he still can? It makes it sound like he's dying ... Or like he's a magical nutcracker come to life for a limited time ... No. I have to keep repeating it until I believe it myself – he is *not* a giant nutcracker come to life who's going to turn back into a wooden soldier on Christmas Eve. 'What does that mean?'

'Nothing. Forget I said anything. I think we shook hands for so long that I feel like I've known you for months, not minutes. Ignore me, I probably hit my head harder than I thought.' He rubs his forehead at the spot where he clonked it on the shelf.

I smile because, despite hating the thing I love most, there's something about him. Something that makes me wish we were still shaking hands. Something that makes it impossible to look away from his brown eyes and hesitant smile. He must be in his late thirties, probably a couple of years older than me, and he's definitely from around here because he's got a local Wiltshire accent that's warm and animated.

'It doesn't seem right that you're selling stuff that doesn't belong to you. Nutcracker Lane is all about handmade goods and shop owners who really care about their products, make bespoke orders for customers, and put their heart and soul into every festive season.'

'Well, I'll put my heart and soul into getting rid of this festive tat. Does that help?'

'It's not festive tat.'

'No? God help the person who sees that Macarena-ing Santa and thinks, "That's it! *That's* what's been missing from my life!" and rushes in to throw money at me and then Macarenas all the way home with it.'

His sarcasm makes me laugh and I let out a very unflattering snort that makes him smile his Flynn Rider smile again, and I *really* do have to stop staring. I force myself to turn away and my eyes fall on the miniature mechanical nutcracker factory in the window. 'That used to mark the spot between Nutcracker Lane and the factory next door, and now you're selling it for £96. And that snow.' I point upwards as another flake of fake snow floats down from an unseen machine in the ceiling. 'Nutcracker Lane used to have a snow machine but it broke down.'

'I know, I mended it.'

'You *mended* it? I thought you only picked up your keys an hour ago.'

Something flashes across his face but it's gone in the space of a blink. 'I'm a fast worker.'

I'm not sure I believe him. It took him ten minutes to inch his way up off the floor, but he has been missing from the shop for ages; it's not unfeasible that he could've been out the back mending a broken snow machine. One-handed.

I'm distracted from the line of thought as singing reaches my ears. 'The carollers are back!'

37

James groans, but I rush to the open door to see them. One of my favourite things about Nutcracker Lane was always the carollers. A group of women and men in full Victorian dress, carrying lanterns and singing traditional Christmas carols from sheets. When I was young, they were employees of Nutcracker Lane, paid to walk up and down during opening hours. They always carried spare lyric sheets and anyone who wanted could join in and walk with them or sing along when they passed, but the budget for carol singing was cut by Mr E.B. Neaser years ago, and now they're just a group of five volunteers who come by whenever they've got time.

I hum along to "Hark the Herald Angels Sing" as they come into view from the end of the lane and wave excitedly as they get nearer, glad to see that other shopkeepers are in their doorways doing the same. Now they don't get paid to do this anymore and their number has dwindled over the years, everyone is expecting the day when they don't come back, and it's heart-warming to see that customers have stopped to join in too. Maybe if enough people get behind them, we could convince the new owner that it's worth adding carol singers back to the budget.

I wave and shout "hello" as the group of carollers get nearer. The leader of the group is a wonderful woman called Angela who handmakes all their Victorian clothing and has been doing this for longer than I can remember, and she waves back, unable to stop to chat mid-song, but she points towards Starlight Rainbows and gives me a thumbs up, looking slightly confused that I'm in the wrong doorway.

I turn around at a noise and see James throwing and catching a resin reindeer in his one hand as if testing the weight of it. 'What are you doing?'

He holds it up to his head. 'Debating how much force it would take to knock myself out until it's over and if it would be worth the pain of getting up from the floor again.'

'I really hope you're joking.'

He grins, letting me know that he is.

'Don't you think that's lovely?' I force myself to look away from his smile because it's doing something to me. 'You don't have to like Christmas to appreciate nice music and talented singers.'

'Pardon? I can't hear you over that racket!'

He's deliberately winding me up now. 'You must like some Christmas music. You have *The Nutcracker* score playing in your shop.'

'I'm left with no options. The only tolerable Christmas music are songs without any words in them. I don't know how anyone can bear this lot waltzing around with their constant "Hosanna in Excelsis-ing". They need to fa-la-la off.'

I'm trying to be annoyed but I can't help the snort of laughter that escapes at his turn of phrase, and he smiles back at me, and I lose track of everything for a minute as we smile at each other across the shop, and by the time I come back to myself, the carollers are off in the distance and have moved on to "Away In A Manger".

'Well, your shop is amazing so you must be doing something right ...' I pause for a minute and then blurt it out anyway. 'Other than the name. And what's with the weird pricing?'

'When people try to haggle, I can knock a six or twenty-six off and customers think they've got a bargain. It works better when it's not a round number.'

'Shrewd.'

He bows his head like it's a compliment. 'And what's wrong with the name?'

'Tinkles sounds like something you need the bathroom for.'

'I hadn't even thought of that. I was thinking of Tinker Bell, you know, fairies on top of Christmas trees and stuff like that ...'

'Well, other than that, it looks like a real winter wonderland – just like Nutcracker Lane used to be.'

'I hear things are changing now ...'

'Yeah,' I say sadly. He obviously got a letter this morning too.

39

'Good. This place is old and tired. It's long past time it was put out of its misery.'

'No, it's not. It's long past time it was owned by someone who cares about it and thinks it's worth saving and putting money back into rather than selling off everything that's not nailed down and putting some miserly accountant in charge to squeeze every penny out of the budget. And this competition to be the most profitable shop is terrible. It pits us all against each other. It turns friends into enemies.' I pick up a little nutcracker that had ricocheted off a plastic snowman and tried to hide under a shelf and point it at him. 'You and me are officially rivals.'

'Ah, but I don't want anything to do with that. This is a one-off for me. I won't be back next year, and this shop'll only be here until the stock's gone. Sorry to disappoint you, but I'm not the rival type. We might have to be friends instead.'

I know my face has gone red because there's something so sweet about his innocent words. I'm trying not to smile, but there's something about him that's impossible not to smile at. 'I don't think I can get along with someone who hates Christmas as much as you do.'

He pushes his bottom lip out, pretending to pout, and I go back into the aisle where he's still standing and go to give him the nutcracker back but he shakes his head. 'Keep it. As a reminder of your Christmas-hating shop neighbour. You can put it on the counter and throw darts at it.'

They're unusual little nutcrackers – bare wood from the bottom of their circular stand to the peak of their top hat, their only facial feature is the traditional wedge-shaped nose and opening mouth, and there's no decoration whatsoever apart from a shock of furry white hair and a patch of white beard. 'I could never throw darts at a nutcracker ... but I'm absolutely fine with knocking them over and breaking their arms, obviously.' I regret the words before I've finished the sentence. Well done, Nia: first you cause clumsy destruction in his shop, then you keep mentioning it just to keep the embarrassment nice and fresh.

He goes to say something, but I hold up the little nutcracker. 'Thank you. I'll hang him on my Christmas tree when I put it up.'

'That reminds me – why are Christmas trees such bad knitters?'

'What?' I say in confusion because it sounds like the start of a bad Christmas joke.

'Because they keep losing their needles!'

Oh, what do you know, it *is* a bad Christmas joke. 'Did you seriously just pull a Christmas cracker joke on me?'

'Did *you* seriously just use "pull" and "cracker" in the same sentence?'

My traitorous face goes red at the terrible pun. 'That was unintentional.'

He raises an eyebrow and his mouth curves up into a smile at one side, and I literally can't get the smile off my face. Every time I try to stop smiling, I smile more. Who *is* this guy? He seems serious and pained, and then he comes out with *that*? I could stand here and talk to him all day, but Stacey is *still* waiting for her cup of tea. 'I'd better ...' I point at the door and back away towards it. 'See you around, Grinch.'

'See you around, Mrs Claus!' he calls after me.

It's probably the most perfect parting line ever, and he definitely thinks Mrs Claus is an insult, but even though he's a Grinch, I *probably* won't complain about seeing him around. Not with those eyes and that smile and the little hint of butterflies that are fluttering around inside me.

*

I must float back across the lane because I don't realise I've got there until Stacey says, 'There you are! I thought you'd taken a wrong turn and ended up in Narnia or something. I was about to send for a Search and Rescue team.'

It feels like I've been gone for hours, even though it's only been about twenty minutes.

'What happened? Did they let you have a payment plan?'

'No, he—'

'He!' she squeals, frightening the two customers who are browsing at the back. 'I *knew* I recognised that smile on your face! I haven't seen that smile since you met Brad.'

The reminder of my first boyfriend brings me back down to earth with a crash. 'That's a terrible comparison! I don't want to be reminded of the guy who cheated on me and apparently kicked off a trend for every subsequent guy to end a relationship in the same way.'

'Yeah, but he was the only guy you've ever been in love with. He was the only one who's ever made you smile like that.'

'I'm just happy because of the carol singers. Did you see them?'

She narrows her eyes at me, but maybe the reminder of Brad was a timely one. I spent most of my twenties living with him, the man I thought I'd end up marrying and having children with, only to walk past his parked car one night and discover him having sex with someone from his office in the back of it, and it set the trend for every subsequent relationship.

From then on, every time I've come close to letting someone in again, they do the same. Every relationship since then has ended with cheating or lying. There's no point thinking about James's eyes or warm smile. Men cannot be trusted. I learnt that much-repeated lesson yet *again* last night.

'What's this *he* like?'

'Oh my God, Stace, he's like a cross between every Disney prince you've ever had a crush on. He's got the most unbelievable smile, and eyes like I've never seen before, and—' I cut myself off when I realise I'm not following my own advice.

'But you're happy because of the carol singers, right?' She crosses her arms over her chest.

'It's not about that.' I give the customers a wary glance and step closer to the counter, beckoning her to lean over. 'I think he might be an actual prince. You know the story of *The Nutcracker*? Where the nutcracker gets broken on Christmas Eve and the girl mends him and he grows to life-size and defeats the evil mouse king, and it turns out he was a prince all along, cursed to take the form of a nutcracker?' I tell her about how I found James when I went into his shop.

'And you don't think it's far more likely that he heard the crash of the nutcracker falling, saw it, moved it, and got down to find the missing gemstones?'

'I was only back here for a couple of minutes. He wouldn't have had time.'

'You were back here for ages.'

'It wasn't that long ... was it?' I seem to have lost all track of time this morning. 'And I wished for a nutcracker prince last night. I made a wish on the magical nutcracker for a prince just like him. And *The Nutcracker* score was playing in the shop. And James said he got knocked over, Stace. *Knocked over*. I *knocked over* the nutcracker. He even said "*my* arm breaker" when I went in.'

'Poor guy was probably concussed from banging his head on the shelf.' She shrugs. 'I know you love Christmas, and nutcrackers, *and* the idea of Christmas magic, but I really don't think it's likely that he's a wooden doll turned into a real live man ...'

'Well, when you put it like *that* ...' I trail off, realising just how mad I sound as a customer approaches the counter with a basket full of decorations and jewellery and Stacey goes to serve her.

All right, it's a bit unlikely, and even I don't *really* think James is a giant nutcracker come to life, but it can't just be a coincidence, can it? Not with the wish last night as well, the green flecks in his blue shirt, saying he got knocked over and the same arm broken. It has to be a sign. It has to mean *something*.

'It's just ... I don't know ... weird,' I say to her when the customer has left after complimenting us both on the shop. I watch her go across the lane and into Tinkles and Trinkets,

43

hoping she didn't overhear any of our conversation to relay to the most gorgeous man I've ever seen. 'Did you ever see a "Help Wanted" sign?'

'No, but we've spent the last month hauling stock up that hill and using the back entrance by the tree lot …'

Hmm. Good point. I suppose it's feasible that there was a sign up somewhere that we could've missed by shortcutting around the back. 'But why would someone who hates Christmas voluntarily run a Christmas shop in a Christmas village? And since when are there vacancies here? You know how crazy the availability for these shops was. I had to register our interest at 12.01 a.m. on a January morning, submit an application by February along with our stock samples, and then we had to wait months while they assessed all applicants and chose the most suited ones. He makes it sound like he wandered past and they happened to have a spare shop. And if they *did* have a vacancy, why not go back to the original applications and offer it to the next best?'

'I think you might be overthinking this …'

Once again, I'm annoyed by how well she knows me. What am I doing – looking for flaws in his story that might somehow prove he's a wooden doll come to life? Trying to prove that you can't take anything a man says at face value?

'Do you know you haven't stopped smiling since you got back in here? And even mentioning Brad hasn't done it. Maybe this James guy *is* some kind of magical prince after all … It would definitely take magical powers to put a smile like that on your face.'

'Nooo,' I say quickly. 'He's exactly the type of person I hate, Stace. He *hates* Christmas and is keen to tell everyone how much he hates it at any opportunity. It's fine if people don't like this time of year, but they have no right to try to stop other people's enjoyment of it.'

'He's selling Christmas decorations. And judging by that nutcracker you're lovingly caressing, he's giving them away too.

44

It doesn't sound like he's trying to spoil anyone's enjoyment of it. Is he single?'

'I don't know, but there's no way. You haven't seen him. Men who look like that *aren't* single. And he was nice too – sweet, funny, engaging. No wedding ring, but his left arm is in a cast up to his thumb; he'd probably have taken it off.'

'Or he could be a magical nutcracker come to life solely meant for you to fulfil your wish on another magical nutcracker … There seems to be an influx of magical nutcrackers around this place.'

'Which, once upon a time, was what made it so popular.' Thinking about Nutcracker Lane and its rapid decline is one thing guaranteed to get the smile off my face. 'And I don't *actually* think he's a nutcracker, I just think there are a lot of coincidences.'

'Like the universe is winking at you—'

I cut Stacey off with the old British excuse for everything. 'Didn't you say something about a cup of tea?'

I hurry off to the back room to make it with our little kettle, because I can't think about things like that. James seemed lovely, and even though there was *something* about him, he's just going to have to be lovely from a distance. Single or not is irrelevant. I'm nowhere near ready to trust another man, and after so many relationships ending in lies and cheating, I'm not sure I ever will be again.

45

Chapter 3

'Well, that explains the spring in your step this morning,' Stacey says as we both huddle at the window of our shop the next day, watching James across the way. 'What is he doing?'

'Taking my advice.' He's standing on a stool outside his shop, repainting the sign to read "Twinkles" instead of "Tinkles". He's already been out there a few times to paint over the original T to blank it out, and now he's up there again with a much smaller brush, gliding a smooth outline to the new letters in gold paint. His left arm is still in a sling so he's got the paint pot balancing on the outer ledge of the shop window and he keeps having to lean down to reach it and wobbling around precariously on the stool, and I'd be lying if I said my heart wasn't in my throat. I don't want to watch in case he slips, but I can't tear my eyes away.

'He's going to break the other arm if he's not careful,' Stacey mutters.

'He's going to break his neck.' I groan as he bends to reach the paint again. 'Come on, James, get down from there,' I say even though he can't hear me. 'I wish I hadn't said anything about his shop name now.'

'You're *very* concerned about his wellbeing.'

'Oh, I didn't mean it in that way. I'm cheering him on. Y'know,

46

woohoo, go on, break the other arm. Close your shop because you won't have enough functional limbs to run it.' I wave an imaginary pompom.

She laughs and shakes her blonde hair back. 'I thought he wasn't getting involved in the competition.'

'Well, it's easy to say that, but not everything in his shop is Nutcracker Lane stuff. He's got rows and rows of cheap import decorations that the new owner wants shifted too. *Everyone* is competition now. That's what's so horrible. Even if *he's* not back next year, the shop will be if it makes more money than us.'

'Which it's practically guaranteed to do. Look at the number of customers he's got going in.' She nods towards him as he clambers down off the stool and rushes inside to serve a woman standing at the counter with an armful of decorations. 'So far this morning, we've only sold two necklaces and one of those make-your-own wooden gingerbread house kits you put together.'

'That's because you can see his shop from Scotland.'

'Did he say what other job he does? Because he's exceptionally good at retail. His shop looks magical, and ours looks like a glorified craft fair. We could use some tips.'

'It's not right that someone who's that much of a Grinch can run a Christmas decoration shop and be so frustratingly good at it,' I mutter.

The customer comes out the door carrying a bulging bag and James reappears behind her and gets back onto the stool, wobbling on the uneven paving stones. He's wearing navy jeans and a plain black T-shirt today, but it's way too cold for T-shirt weather, so it makes me wonder if he's having trouble with his arm. He was clearly hurting yesterday, maybe it's prohibitive to getting dressed easily too.

Thoughts of James getting dressed lead to thoughts of him *un*dressed and I suddenly feel a lot warmer than I did just now. I snuggle tighter into my Christmas jumper, this one dark blue with a big fluffy snowman on it and glittered-thread snowflakes

47

all around. 'And that's a good point too – what sort of office job lets him have the whole of December off to go and do a *different* job? That's a bit strange, isn't it?'

'Annual leave? He could've been stacking up holidays all year?'

'So he can spend them working? And in a Christmas village when he hates Christmas? It doesn't add up. I keep thinking about the other thing he said – the "while I still can" bit. Is this some sort of twisted bucket list thing?'

'Maybe he *is* going to turn back into wood on Christmas Eve.' She elbows me even though I can't take my eyes off him. 'Go and ask.'

I let out a burst of laughter. 'Firstly I'm not going over there to ask him if he's really a nutcracker soldier, and secondly, I don't want to know. I don't want to get involved, Stace.'

'Because you like him too much?'

'No, because … no more men. I can't take another relationship that's going to end with me crying into a tub of ice cream. And look at him. There's no way he *doesn't* have a real-life Rapunzel counterpart to his Flynn Rider looks. What's the point?' I say, because I'm about the furthest thing from Rapunzel you can get with my round face and fringe that was recommended to make my face look *less* round and I'm never quite sure if it works or not, which is why said fringe is currently at a length where I either have to commit to it and cut it again or tackle months of growing it out, at which point I will inevitably decide I miss my fringe and start the whole cycle again.

'Have you seen how many times he's looked over here this morning?'

'No, I've seen how many times he's wobbled on that flipping thing. He's not looking over here, he's trying to get his balance.'

She lets out a huff that says exactly how frustrated she's getting with me. 'And he's good with his hands. Well, *hand*. Look at that lettering.'

'You see? He said he works in an office and only picked up his shop keys yesterday morning, but look at how well that painting matches up. Are you seriously telling me he didn't hand-paint the rest of that sign too?'

'So what if he did? It's not impossible to work in an office and be good with a paintbrush in your spare time. You're looking for holes. Because you like him too much.'

Before I have a chance to deny it, James gets down off the stool again and looks over here, directly at us. He's still holding his paintbrush but he salutes us with his right hand and the widest grin.

'Oh my God, he is literally the personification of Flynn Rider.' Stacey fans a hand in front of her face. 'Look at that smile.'

Oh, believe me, I *am* looking at that smile. I've thought of very little else apart from that smile since yesterday morning. 'And on that note, I'm going to go and do some work so we might have a chance of beating him in this competition. The more stock we can get out, the more chance we've got of selling it.'

As if on cue, another customer calls James back inside, and Stacey makes a noise of disappointment. 'It's a shame he didn't fall on that Macarena-ing Santa. If anything deserves to be crushed from a great height, it's that.'

'Finally, one thing we can both agree on. That and our empty shop.' We both cast our eyes around until we're looking at each other again. We're the only two people who have been in here for hours. It's not a great start for our second day.

*

Stacey left at five so she, her husband Simon, and Lily could have a family evening together, and I'm still in the back room working. My tools are in the shed at home, so I do all my cutting and make the bases of everything there, but cutting MDF wood creates dust so it makes sense to bring them into work to paint when the shop's quiet rather than risk the dust settling into the paint. It's been quiet all day.

49

I look at the array of Christmas jumper hanging decorations set out in various stages of priming and drying on the workbench. One of my favourite things about crafting is how you can get a little production line going by painting all the same colours at once and let your mind go without having to think about anything. I love Christmas jumpers and hand-painting miniature wooden ones in any design I can come up with is one of my favourite things. Red with snowflakes and sparkles, a night sky with Santa's sleigh being pulled across it by reindeer, a tiny forest of snowy Christmas trees, and many more. They're a big hit with buyers too.

When I finally catch sight of the clock, it's gone 8 p.m., and I stand up and stretch my back out and wander onto the darkened shop floor. Everything's silent outside and darkness has long since fallen. The lights on the Christmas trees have been turned off as their owners have left. Nutcracker Lane's late opening hours to meet the demand of visitors who wanted to come after work or school or to see the Christmas lights in the dark are long gone now. It used to be open until 10 p.m. most nights, but the traditional nine-to-five opening hours were enforced on the shopkeepers a few years ago by E.B. Neaser as a budget-saving measure.

I open the shop door and stand in the doorway, wishing the café was open for a peppermint hot chocolate. I can't help noticing there's a light on in the back of James's shop, although his front window is dark and the giant Santa outside is mercifully quiet.

Everything is so quiet. Walking through Nutcracker Lane at night used to be a magical experience. My grandma and I would often take this way home, even after the shops were shut, because the trees would be sparkling, heavy with ornaments and tinsel, and the garlands would still be twinkling, hung in boughs from the roof.

I wonder if any of that stuff is left. There's a huge stockroom in the basement level of Nutcracker Lane, and it used to be packed to the brim with decorations, props, and lights, and shopkeepers were free to go down and help themselves to anything they wanted. I wonder if we could use some of it. I mean, there are no staff here anymore; there's no one monitoring what we do. What if we found some of that old stuff and put it up? What if we made Nutcracker Lane a bit brighter? It would probably be ages before anyone noticed the increase in electricity being used, and surely even E.B. Neaser couldn't complain about the shopkeepers trying to make things better for everyone?

I close the shop door behind me and start walking towards the end of the lane. There's a corridor between the Christmas craft shop and the snowglobe shop that leads to a staff-only door, and I tap in the code and let myself into a narrow corridor that runs underneath Nutcracker Lane. It sounds like some mystical underground vault full of Christmas magic, but it's actually quite scary and the first time I came down here last month, I went back to the shop to get Stacey and made her come with me because I thought I might get lost or find a serial killer lurking down here. In reality, it's a cold basement with squeaky lino flooring and multiple storage rooms, some of which haven't been opened for years. It's *not* where Santa stores his sleigh for the rest of the year like my granddad used to tell me when I was little.

I'm also not alone. As I get further along the hollow corridor, I realise one of the doors to a storage room is open and there's light spilling out. I gulp. 'Hello?' I call out, unable to hide the tremble in my voice.

'In here,' a voice calls back. Hopefully a good sign. I had visions of catching the bloke who plays Santa down here in a compromising position. What he does in public is bad enough – the thought of what he might get up to behind closed doors is enough to give anyone nightmares.

'Ah, my arm breaker,' the voice says as I get near the doorway and I'm already breathing a sigh of relief at it being James and not the Santa bloke doing something unthinkable with bodily excretions.

51

'Hi, Grinch.' I put my head round the door and spot him in a corner, examining a set of plastic light-up reindeer that used to be put on the roof every December.

He looks up and smiles as our eyes meet across the room. 'I know that's meant as an insult but it doesn't sound like one.'

'It is.' Why can't I stop smiling? No matter how much I tell myself not to, a great big smile spreads across my face every time I see him. And somehow he looks even more gorgeous tonight than he did earlier. He's got elegant cheekbones and a pointed kind of dainty nose, and the stubble covering his angled jawline is scruffier than it was yesterday.

He looks like he believes me about as much as I believe myself. 'Interesting jumper choice,' he says as he straightens up and moves away from the reindeer. 'Not quite as exciting as yesterday's flashing one.'

I look down at my snowman jumper. 'I buy a Christmas jumper every year. I love them. I usually keep the flashing ones for special occasions, like opening day and Christmas Eve.'

'Yeah. I think light-up jumpers should be saved for special occasions too. Like when hell freezes over – would that count as a special occasion?'

I go to snap something sarcastic back, but as he moves, a look of pain crosses his face and he seems to be shuffling rather than walking. 'Are you okay?'

'All the better for seeing that jumper.' He gives me a tight and completely mocking smile, but there's obviously something wrong. His face is pale and the dark circles under his eyes look much bigger than they did yesterday.

'Seriously, James. You don't look well.'

'I'm fine.' His left arm is still held across his chest by the sling, and he moves around the boxes, opening them with his right hand and peering inside. 'It's a shame spiders don't count as Christmas decorations.'

I shudder. 'I saw you renamed your shop?'

'Yeah, thanks for the advice. And about pricing. I reduced everything and made loads of sales today.'

'Good,' I say, even though what I'm thinking is "bollocks". Despite what he says, the last thing I'm supposed to be doing is *helping* the competition. I shouldn't have said anything. I should've let him get on with selling his hideously overpriced all-singing all-dancing decorations. Our shop has been empty today and his has been heaving. And his decorating is spot-on. He certainly doesn't need my advice on that front.

'What are you doing?'

'Replacing some of the things I sold today. Trying to, anyway. I don't see why anyone would buy this trash.' He pulls out a polar bear soft toy and squeezes its belly so it flashes and growls a "Merry Christmas". 'I mean, why? Why does a polar bear flash? Why does it wish you a merry Christmas?'

'Says the man whose shop is guarded by a plastic Santa inexplicably doing the Macarena!'

'Exactly – so it's *outside* where I don't have to put up with it.'

I roll my eyes as he uses his foot to tip the box on its side and one-handedly rifles through it, pulling out tinsel and lights and tossing them aside.

'So is this where you're getting your stock? Just stealing it from the storeroom?'

'Stealing it?' His head jerks up to look at me but it obviously hurts something because his right hand curls around the cardboard and his chin drops down to his chest as he breathes slowly through his nose. 'I'm doing what I've been told to do. Following orders, not stealing,' he says eventually, but his voice is quiet, and he sounds like he wants to be annoyed but he can't quite muster it.

'These are Nutcracker Lane's decorations!'

'Exactly. They belong to the new owner of Nutcracker Lane and whoever that is wants them sold.'

'He must be a monster, even worse than that horrible accountant!'

53

'I'm sorry,' James says eventually. 'I'm just doing my job. What are you doing down here at this time of night anyway?'

'It sounds stupid but I remembered some of this old stuff and wanted to see if any of it was still here. I thought we could put some of it up again.'

His eyes, which have been heavy-lidded until now, go wide. 'You don't have permission to do that.'

'Of course not, but someone has to do *something*. Nutcracker Lane is dying in front of us. No one cares about it anymore. And why am I talking about it to you? You hate Christmas. What do you care if our special little Christmas village closes down?'

He's quiet for so long that I think he's not going to answer. 'I liked it when I was little. It was different back then. *I* was different back then.'

'You've been here before?'

The corner of his mouth tips up. 'Didn't *every* child in Wiltshire and the surrounding counties come here when they were little? If you didn't come with your family, there were school trips every year ...'

'Yeah.' I can't take my eyes off him, and not just because of the soft, nostalgic smile on his face, but because his skin has gone from pale to a distinctly grey tone and he doesn't look like he'd stay upright in a light breeze. 'So you haven't always been a Grinch then?'

'For long enough that I can barely remember a time befor— Oh, he'll do.' He pulls a three-foot-tall wooden nutcracker soldier out of the box. 'Nutcrackers are always popular.'

I haven't realised I've drifted closer as we've been talking until I'm leaning on the other side of the box. 'You can't sell him!' I reach across and grab the nutcracker out of his hand. 'I know him!'

'Personally?' He raises an eyebrow, and I give him a scathing look.

'No. He and his family used to stand in the entrance foyer. There was one of each size, from tiny to life-size. They were lined up in size order like a family of Russian dolls.' I rub my fingers across the dusty wooden drum around the nutcracker's waist, a drumstick in each of his hands. 'One of them was a musical one and it played the tune of "Little Drummer Boy" and the sticks moved up and down. It was amazing.'

'Well, find me the others and I'll sell them as well.' He reaches across the box, gets his hand around the nutcracker's head and pulls it out of my grasp, but as he twists away, he lets out the harshest cry of pain I've ever heard and the nutcracker clatters to the floor as his hand shoots to his chest under the sling.

'James, what's wrong?'

'Nothing, I'm—'

I assume he was going to finish that sentence with "fine", which he is very clearly not. His face has gone from grey to so pale he'd camouflage against a white wall. His eyes are squeezed shut and his teeth clenched. A vein is throbbing in his forehead as he lets out a string of swearwords. He sways on his feet and I'm certain he's about to keel over.

'Come on, there's a box over there. You need to sit down before you fall down.' I slot my hands around his right arm and tug gently. I don't know where he's hurting but it's obviously more serious than a broken arm and I don't want to touch him anywhere that's going to make it worse.

There are tremors going through him. I can feel them through his black T-shirt, but he lets me tug him gently towards the far wall, his breathing fast and ragged.

'Sit.' I use his good arm to urge him downwards onto a long box against the back wall of the storage room.

Sweat is beading on his forehead as he positions his back against the wall and sinks down with a groan, and I sit on my knees in front of him and put my hands carefully on top of his knees. 'What's wrong? Where are you hurting? This is not just your arm, is it?'

'Broken left side.'

I eye his left side but it doesn't give anything away. 'Which part?'

'All of it.' His eyes open into slits. 'Feels like, anyway.'

His hair has fallen forward and stuck to his forehead and I reach up and brush it back. 'Shall I phone an ambulance?'

'No. God, no.' His good hand reaches up and closes softly around my wrist. 'No more hospitals. Just go, Nia. You don't have to worry about me.'

I almost laugh at the irony. 'You might be a Grinch, but you're clearly in agony and if you think I'm going to walk away and leave you here, you've got another think coming.' I keep brushing his hair back and his eyes drift closed again. His breathing is harsh, rapid and shallow, and I do what every adult does in a situation like this – look around for a better adult. An older adult. An adult who might know what to do. A more *adult* adult.

'Take four-second breaths,' I say, thinking of a meditation technique I once learnt. 'Four seconds in through your nose, hold for four seconds, then exhale through your mouth for four seconds. It's relaxing.' I do it too, encouraging him to join in, my little finger tapping his right knee in four-second bursts.

I don't stop reaching up to tuck his dark hair back, and his hand is still on my wrist and I'm not sure if his fingertips are rubbing minutely or if it's the tremors, but it doesn't seem like he wants me to stop, so I don't, and after a few long minutes, our breathing is in sync, and he's not panting quite so severely.

'James, seriously,' I say gently. 'What's broken?'

'Arm, two ribs, cartilage damage, and an impressive amount of bruising.'

'What happened?'

'I told you, I got knocked over. It was my own fault. On a business call, yelling at someone who didn't deserve yelling at, stepped out without looking where I was going, collided with an oncoming car.'

Things start slotting into place in my brain. 'So when you said you got knocked over … it was by a car?'

He nods almost imperceptibly.

'You were hit by a car! Oh my God, I'm so happy!' I push myself up onto my knees and pull his head down towards my chest, so overjoyed by the realisation that I can't stop myself hugging him right this instant, even though I'm being careful not to hurt him or jostle him in any way, and I end up half-smothering him somewhere between my boobs and my shoulder.

When I release him, his head drops back against the wall like it's too heavy for him to hold up, but he's blinking at me slowly, half a smile playing on his lips. 'And there was me thinking you didn't like me. I've never known anyone to be so pleased about a road traffic accident before.'

'I thought …' I think better of admitting I still had half a mind on the idea that he might be the wooden nutcracker come to life. 'Never mind. I could see you were in too much pain for just a broken arm. I'm glad I was right.'

'I'm glad my pain makes you so happy.'

I give him another scathing look but I still can't stop myself smiling. 'I didn't mean it like that. I meant I've been worried about you.'

'Hah.' He does a sarcastic laugh but abandons it halfway through because it obviously hurts. '*You've* been worried about *me*? We only met yesterday and you don't like people who don't like Christmas.'

'I don't dislike them *that* much.' In hugging him, I've re-smooshed his hair up, so when I sit back onto my knees, I reach up and tuck it back again, and his good hand drifts up to my wrist again, the backs of his fingers sort of rubbing against the skin of my inner wrist. He focuses on the point where we touch until his eyes start to close.

'When did this happen?' I ask because his fingers are doing such a good job of distracting me that I'd need a "phone a friend" lifeline if someone asked me my own name at the moment.

'Do you really care or are you just trying to keep my mind off it?'

'The first one,' I say with a grin. 'The second one's an added bonus.'

It seems to take him a moment to decide whether he trusts me or not. 'Last week. It's why I was so late starting here. I should've been setting up the shop but I wasn't functional for a couple of days after the accident.'

He doesn't look particularly functional at the moment. 'Did they get the driver?'

He rolls his head from side to side. 'They didn't stop.'

'It was a hit and run?' I feel my eyes getting wider with every word he says.

'It doesn't matter. It wasn't their fault – it genuinely was mine. I was frustrated and annoyed with work and I wasn't paying attention. I don't think they even realised they'd hit me. I bounced off the car, hit the pavement, and got straight back up and shook my fist at them and yelled a string of choice swearwords about their driving ability, picked up my phone and finished the conversation. I think it was the shock and adrenaline at first and it was only when I stopped for a minute and started processing it that I realised I was actually hurt and took myself to A&E.'

My hand on his knee must tighten because he says, 'Even without opening my eyes, you don't have to look so worried. I'm fine as long as I keep my upper body straight. I twisted it trying to grab that nutcracker off you. Serves me right for being such a Grinch, right?' He opens his eyes and looks at me. His fingers move on my wrist and my hand slips from brushing his hair back and slides down his face until my thumb brushes his jaw, and we hold each other's gaze for a moment, until I realise I'm stroking the jaw of a complete stranger.

I pull back so abruptly that it makes him jump and he winces again.

'I'm sorry,' I whisper. 'You sure you don't need an ambulance?'

He still hasn't lifted his head from where it's leaning against the wall, but he moves it slowly from side to side. 'I'll be fine. There's nothing they can do for broken ribs. I've just got to keep active, not lift anything heavy, and do a load of incredibly painful breathing exercises to keep my lungs clear so I don't get pneumonia.'

'Well, you've certainly been keeping active,' I say, picturing him climbing up and down on that stool today.

'That means you've been watching me ...'

Is he being deliberately obtuse or does he genuinely have no idea how difficult it is *not* to watch him? 'Actually, we were watching the Macarena-ing Santa. It's impossible to take your eyes off him.'

His face breaks into a smile and then he groans. 'Oh, please don't make me laugh, I beg of you.'

My concern must show on my face because he tells me again not to look so worried. 'I just twisted it, that's all. It's the end of a *long* day and I admit I overdid it this morning with the painting. I haven't been sleeping because the ribs are too painful to find a comfortable position, and I've already hit my pain threshold a few hours ago.'

'Why didn't you go home at closing time?'

He goes to shrug but thinks better of it. 'Nothing to go home for. How about you?'

'I like spending time here.' I hesitate because I'm sure he's going to make fun of me for it. 'It feels more and more like Nutcracker Lane as we know it is going to be gone soon, and I want to make the most of it while I still can.'

He pushes his bottom lip out and then pulls it back with his teeth, but I cut him off before he can say something sarcastic. 'You said something yesterday about painkillers?'

He laughs. 'Oh, I can't take them here.'

'Why not?'

'I've been taking them at night, at home, in private, because they make me fuzzy-headed. It's bad enough making a fool of

59

myself, I don't want to make a fool of myself in front of you too.' He uses his good hand to pat mine where it's still resting on his knee. 'So you have to go away and leave me alone because I'm not moving until I've taken them.'

'I'm not going anywhere.' I can't help smiling as I squeeze his knees. 'We're the only two people here and you're sorely mistaken if you think I'm going to leave you by yourself in this state.'

He laughs again, a shallow chuckle rather than a laugh. 'I'll be fine. I just need to take something and not move for a while. I've been alone for a long time – I can look after myself.'

'Good for you, but I'm not leaving.' I pat his knees again gently and use the box on either side of his legs to push myself up. 'Painkillers?'

He pats the front pocket of his jeans. I go to get him a cup of water from the staff water dispenser inside the door, and when I get back down the corridor, he's got the packet held between his teeth and is somehow managing to push two out with one hand, and I watch as he pops them into his mouth and takes the water with a nod of thanks, his hand shaking as he swallows it and puts it down on the box beside him.

'Right, tea. Sugar?' I ask, but stop him before he has a chance to respond. 'Actually, don't answer that – you need something hot and sweet so you're getting sugar whether you like it or not.' I pat his knee again. 'Back in a minute. Don't move.'

'I assure you I'm going to lose consciousness if I even *think* about moving.'

'Good.'

He cracks one eye open and raises an eyebrow. 'You really don't like me, do you?'

I grin. 'I meant because you're not going to think about it, and you know it.'

A smile spreads slowly across his face and I'm smiling back involuntarily even though he must think I'm a lunatic because so far tonight, I've been ecstatically happy that he was hit by a car and tried to smother him to death by boob. I'd better get that tea before he starts thinking I've got a vendetta.

When I get back up to the shop, I can't make the tea fast enough. I spoon at least three spoonfuls of sugar into each mug while I wait for the kettle to boil and I search the table and rifle through my handbag for something to eat, wishing Stacey and I hadn't polished off those mince pies I got from the Nutcracker Lane bakery this morning. I haven't got anything to offer him.

Generally, you don't need anything here. Nutcracker Lane has got its own bakery which sells all manner of Christmas-themed cakes and biscuits, and next door to that is the coffee shop which sells every festive flavour of hot drink you can imagine, but everything's closed at this time of night. Most of the shopkeepers have their own kettle in the back room, which will probably get more use now we're all in competition with each other and buying coffees from the coffee shop makes it more likely that they will be the winners. It makes me sad just thinking about it. I don't want to work somewhere that I can't even go and buy a gingerbread tiffin latte because of this awful competition between us.

I take the two mugs of tea in one hand and walk down the silent lane and back towards the staff-only entrance to the storage rooms.

'You still conscious, Grinch?' I call out as I enter the code one-handed and use my foot to manoeuvre round the door and close it behind me.

'Define conscious,' he replies from inside the storage room.

It makes me laugh. 'That counts,' I say as I go in the doorway and find him sitting in exactly the same place I left him. He doesn't look like he's moved a centimetre. 'How are you feeling?'

He opens his eyes and looks up at me. 'Extremely grateful to the doctor who prescribed these lovely painkillers.'

His cheeks are flushed and his skin tone looks a lot brighter than it did before. I put my own mug on the box and crouch down in front of him. Before he has a chance to move, I reach out and lift his good hand and push the hot mug into it, letting him curl shaking fingers around the handle and close them, and I keep mine curled over his for a moment too long. 'Here. Tea is clinically proven to help in all medical emergencies. Probably.'

He smiles his wide, open smile. 'I'm fine, Nia. This is not a medical emergency.'

'There are people in coffins who look better than you did just now.'

His mouth curves into one of those wide impossible-to-stop smiles as he lifts the mug of tea and takes a sip without taking his eyes off me. 'Flipping heck, do you take a bit of tea with your sugar?'

'Hot. Sweet. Drink up.' I give him my most menacing look and pick up my own mug, and have to hide the shudder as the sweetness assaults my taste buds. Maybe I overdid it a *little* on the sugar front.

'You should go, Nia,' he says as I sit down on the box next to him. 'My filter goes when I've taken these. Usually I take them behind closed doors so no one has to see me in this state.'

'So no one can look after you?'

'So no one can use it as blackmail material later.'

It sounds bitter and sad and makes me feel like an icy cold arrow has just hit my back. 'What kind of people do you have in your life?'

'Ones who aren't like you, obviously.' His wide brown eyes are blinking slower than usual. 'Usually I start asking my Alexa barely legible things that she can hardly decipher. I keep waking up in the mornings and finding the app on my phone has got a list of nonsensical questions I've been asking, like: "Why do I feel cold without my teeth?" and "How many photos of encyclopaedias do I need?" And I assure you I have all my own teeth and don't own any encyclopaedias, never mind take photos of them.'

I've made the mistake of taking another sip of tea and it comes out of my nose as I snort with laughter again.

He laughs too and then groans. 'And I can't believe I just told you that. That I ask my smart speaker nonsensical questions until I fall asleep *or* that it's the most exciting thing I've got to talk to.'

'Me too,' I say quietly. 'I mean, with the being alone thing, not with the nonsensical questions. I don't feel cold without my teeth or take many photos of encyclopaedias.'

He giggles even though it's obviously painful. 'Please ignore everything I say. I'm at the stage where I'd tell you my bank login details and my mother's maiden name and forget about it by morning, so feel free to take advantage.'

I'm sitting on his undamaged right side and I scooch a bit closer until my thigh presses against his and my arm grazes against his bare forearm.

I don't know what it is about this man, but there's something that makes me want to be closer than is normal with someone I only met yesterday. And I'm still not a *hundred* per cent sure he isn't a giant nutcracker come to life.

I'm so distracted by my thoughts that I jump when his head flops to the side to rest on my shoulder. 'Can I lean on you?' he mumbles, completely missing the fact that he already is. 'You can yell at me if I fall asleep then; it's only going to hurt more if I hit the floor.'

I instantly stiffen because it's been a heck of a long time since I had a man get quite this close, but he lets out a long, slow breath, and everything gets heavier as he relaxes, and after a few moments, I realise I don't actually mind. At all. I concentrate on the spot of heat where our arms are touching.

I love how open he seems tonight. Yesterday I thought he was so uptight that we'd never be friends, but he seems different now. I know I've caught him at a bad moment – hurting, vulnerable, and without his walls up, but there's something even more endearing about him tonight. Yesterday I thought he was so much of a Disney prince that he could've stepped out of an animated film. He seemed sarcastic and untouchable, and even though I could

63

see there was something more than a broken arm bothering him, he'd never admit it.

But now when his head's leaning heavily on my shoulder, his floppy hair is smooshed up in several different directions, and the dark circles under his eyes make it obvious that he hasn't been sleeping even without him telling me, he seems even better than a Disney prince – he seems like a real guy who isn't as infallible as he'd have people believe. And it's all down to a nutcracker yet again. Nutcrackers keep showing up in our lives.

He's still got his mug of tea in his right hand and he manages to sip it without moving his head from my shoulder. 'Thank you for the cup of … well, it couldn't really be called tea … but it's the best cup of liquefied sugar I've ever had.'

'I don't usually drink tea like this. You know why I made it sweet.'

'To give me such a sugar rush that I forget about the pain?'

I try to hold back the laugh because I don't want to shake him when he's leaning so heavily against me. 'Obviously.'

He rests the cup on his thigh, still holding on to the handle with his good hand, and I get one of my hands behind my head and pull my hair out from where it's trapped under his head. My grown-out bob cut is over my shoulders now and the longest layers have almost reached my armpits, and I can feel my head being pulled down by the weight of him against me.

'Sorry,' he mumbles, shifting just enough to let me free my hair. I was worried about moving in case he thought I didn't want him there, but I'm glad when he settles his head back on my shoulder. He can stay there all night, frankly. It's been a long time since I had a man this gorgeous sit this close. I've kept all men at arm's length since Brad. Even when I've been in relationships, I've never let my guard down, never truly been myself, never allowed anyone to get close enough to hurt me like Brad did. Never really relaxed with anyone.

But there's something so calming about him being so close,

still doing the four-second breathing technique, and I find my breathing falling into sync with his and feel myself relaxing too, surrounded by the heady scent of his cologne. He smells so delicious that I'm half-tempted to lick his neck just to make sure he doesn't taste as good as he smells. But that would be a bit too weird, even for me. He smells of nutmeg and cloves and something orangey – it's a surprisingly Christmassy cologne for someone who hates Christmas so much.

He takes another sip of tea and rests the cup on his knee again.

'What's your story then?' I murmur, afraid that speaking in my regular voice will break the calm quietness that's settled over us.

He groans. 'When I said you could take advantage of me, I meant my credit card's in my wallet, the PIN is 7829, and I won't remember this in the morning. Please don't make me talk as well.'

I'm not sure whether to laugh or snort and end up doing a disturbing mix of both. 'Did you seriously just give me your card number?'

'I don't know. Did I?'

'It's a good thing I'm not interested in robbing you blind then, isn't it?' I lean my head to the side so it rests against the top of his. 'Tell me, Grinch. How does someone who hates Christmas end up working in a Christmas decoration shop in a Christmas village in the most Christmassy part of Wiltshire?'

He lets out a long sigh and I can almost hear him resigning himself. 'My father runs a festive business and next Christmas, I have to take over. He's handing me the reins, so to speak.'

'You? Running a Christmas business?' I say in surprise, trying to ignore how much I want to laugh at the pun. 'It's not delivering toys, is it? In a sleigh? On Christmas Eve? He's not *literally* handing you the reins? Because there have been movies about Christmas-hating children having to take over from Santa Claus fathers ...'

He laughs too. 'No. It's ...' He goes quiet for a moment before he speaks again. 'It's Christmas crackers. You know, the pull, bang, party hat, joke things. It started with those and then branched out into seasonal decorations and accessories for other celebrations throughout the year. He and my mum built it up from scratch decades ago and it's been their baby for as long as I've known. My parents have put *every* waking hour into it for over forty years, and now it's my turn.'

'They're retiring?'

He hesitates again and lets out a long breath. 'Yeah. Well, my dad is, and my mum won't be able to do it on her own, so it's time for me to step up and take over.'

'That doesn't sound like your ideal job.'

'I've only known you for a day and you already know me too well.'

'It was the overflowing Christmas cheer in you that gave it away. You don't want to take over?'

'Of course I don't. I despise Christmas. It's bad enough that I already work there, but I'm in the office. Sales and distribution, figures, that sort of thing. I don't have to get involved in the Christmas stuff.'

I can't see his face but I can hear the scorn in his voice. 'So that's where the bad jokes come from.'

'Oi. My jokes are class. Why can't penguins fly?'

I grin because I know this one. 'Because they're a chocolate biscuit?'

'Because their feet can't reach the plane pedals.'

I try not to laugh. I really try because he seems so earnest, but it gets the better of me and I end up cackling so hard I'd make any witch jealous.

'You seriously work for a Christmas cracker company?' I say when I've recovered some dignity.

'They're just a thing I have to sell. I shut myself into my office and persuade distributors to take on a product. Actually running the whole company is so much responsibility. My mum and dad *love* Christmas, it really matters to them, and their whole company is based on their love of it and bringing people together, and all

66

that fun stuff you probably love too. And I just ... don't. I don't care about Christmas. And I'm not sure what to do about it. I'm not sure what to do *with* it. I can't let the company die because it means *so* much to my parents. They've put their whole lives into it and I don't want to let them down, but honestly, if I hear one more person *"donning now their gay apparel"* it's going to make me want to deck someone *with* a bough of holly.'

His bluntness makes me laugh again. 'So what are you doing here? Were you serious when you said exposure therapy yesterday?'

'No. Yes. I don't know.' He sighs. 'I've been getting really stressed at work. More than my usual amount of work stress. I've known this would be my father's last year for a while now and I've buried my head in the sand and convinced myself it wouldn't happen, and the closer it gets, the more stressed I get and the less I know what to do about it. The accident last week was just one in a long line of things that wouldn't have happened if everything wasn't getting on top of me.'

His head presses a bit harder against my shoulder like he's trying to get my attention. 'I could do without the excruciating pain of fireworks going off in my chest, but this feels like the first time I've breathed in months, so thank you.'

I can't help the little fizzle of warmth it sends through me. I don't even know him, but I can tell he's the kind of person who doesn't stop unless they're forced to. 'You make it sound like you're spending Christmas on the frontlines.'

'Exactly. I thought I'd spend this season on the ground, so to speak. I thought if I could spend Christmas in the heart of it, surrounded by people who love Christmas, somewhere that I can't hide in my office and ignore it, it might make me see what other people see. If I can understand why people love it, maybe it'll help me understand why the business is so important to my parents, because right now I don't. Christmas is a tough time of year for a lot of people. It's not all candy canes and snowflakes.'

'No one says it is,' I say gently, wondering if he's speaking from

67

personal experience. 'I know it's the worst time of year for many.' I sort of press my cheek against his hair in a weird attempt to let him know it's okay if he's talking about himself. 'But it can also be the most magical. There's something special about Christmas and those who love it should be allowed to enjoy it, and those who don't should be allowed to ignore it in peace.'

'And no one should be Grinched at by me, right?'

'That's the first time I've heard Grinch used as a verb,' I say, trying not to laugh out loud.

'Or maybe I'm just trying to grow my heart. That was the Grinch, right?' He moves his head until he can tilt it upwards and catch my eyes. 'His heart was two sizes too small?'

'You know something Christmassy!' I do a victory fist with the hand closest to him. 'You're not a complete lost cause after all!'

He laughs as he swallows the last of his tea and does an excellent job of disguising the shudder. 'Go on then.' He reaches across to put the empty mug down on his opposite side. 'Now you know more about me than most people who have been in my life for years, how about you? What's your story?'

'I don't have one … I've been coming to Nutcracker Lane every year since I was born. My grandma always used to tell me about pushing my pram up here when I was only a few months old and how much I liked looking up at the lights. I've wanted to work here forever, but this is the first year my application got accepted … and will probably be the last if Scrooge has his way.'

'From what I've seen so far, he seems to be the only sensible one around here.' His voice is jokey and I know he's only trying to wind me up, but I still hold my palm out like I'm going to smack his leg. 'If you weren't already hurt, I'd hit you for that. No one praises that awful man in my presence.'

He laughs and I can feel his face heating up through my jumper. 'What do you do the rest of the year?'

'As many part-time jobs as will have me. Until last month, I was doing the night shift stacking shelves in the supermarket, but

I handed in my notice when I got confirmation of having a shop here. For the past few weeks, Stacey and I have been working on our stock and setting the shop up.'

'Wait, so you've actually quit your job to work here?'

I nod gently so he'll feel it.

'What happens in January?'

'Blind panic. Followed by jobhunting. Me and Stace go to craft fairs up and down the country. We've got a van between us that we load up and go halves on petrol to get wherever we need to be, usually at weekends but sometimes we can get a spot for two or three days during the week as well. She's lucky because she's got a husband to support her, but I don't earn enough from making decorations so I have to do whatever I can to support myself in the meantime. A full-time job would be the end of my craft work, so I do whatever job I can for a few days a week to pay the bills and spend the rest of my time working on my business.'

'But … you'd …' He shakes his head against my shoulder. 'You'd actually give up a job, security in this unstable economy, solely to work *here*?'

Does he have to sound quite so incredulous? 'I love this place. I love making Christmas decorations in my shed at home and I want to do that as much as I can. I don't love stacking shelves, doing temp work, waitressing, or working at the drive thru of fast food restaurants, but I'll do anything that allows me the time to do what I really love. And *this* is special. Nutcracker Lane is where I've dreamed about working my whole life. I'd have given up anything to get here this year. The last time I made a wish on the magical nutcracker it was that I'd get to work here one day.'

'Hah!' He laughs so hard that it turns into a groan and his right hand shoots up to hold his ribs again. 'Why am I not surprised that you believe in wishes on the *non*-magical nutcracker?'

'Serves you right,' I mutter as he lets out a shaky breath. I leave out the fact that technically the last wish I made on the nutcracker was for Prince Charming. There's *no way* someone who laughs that hard at the suggestion of magic is really him. I was *so* mistaken on that line of thinking. Magical nutcrackers are more realistic than the idea that someone so grouchy and dismissive could be the answer to my wish.

'You do know it's not magical, right?'

'No, I had *no* idea. I also think flying reindeer are a good choice of transport and that Santa pops down the chimney of every house in the world on Christmas Eve and eats eight billion mince pies without putting on a single pound in weight.' I roll my eyes and lift my head from his to rest it back against the wall. What is it with people who hate Christmas being so keen to decry others for their love of it? 'Look, we're both adults. We both know that the nutcracker doesn't really grant wishes and that when wishes *were* granted on Nutcracker Lane, it was by a team of wish-granters who were paid to listen in and go above and beyond to make them come true, but don't you think it's nice for people to believe there's a little bit of magic in the world?'

'Not really, because there isn't.'

'Well, anyone who thinks that will never find it, will they?' I snap. 'How can you not believe in magic?'

'Because I'm a sane, adult human?'

'That's not being an adult – that's just sad. What's the harm in a Christmas wish? Where's the harm in allowing people to believe in the possibility of magic? In letting children grow up believing in Santa and the idea that Christmas wishes can come true?'

'The real world? Life? Disappointment? You can make wishes until you're blue in the face, and they *won't* come true. I learnt that *very* early on in my life.'

'But making a wish gives us something to dream about. Something to work towards. Something to look forward to – the possibility of it happening one day. It's not all about magical nutcrackers and witches stirring cauldrons and wizards waving wands. Magic is all around us. Don't you ever look up at the stars twinkling on a cold winter's night, or watch an autumn sun set across a blazing pink sky, or blow away the seeds of a dandelion clock, or make a wish when you see the time turn to 11.11, or salute a full moon, or stand outside when it snows, or get so completely lost in a good book that you emerge feeling like you've time-travelled and lived a different life for a few hours? That's *real* magic.' I sound like I'm about to burst into a rousing rendition of "Colours of the Wind" and stop myself quickly.

'I don't have time for that. And I've got into enough trouble lately for not looking where I'm going, so I won't be looking up at the stars anytime soon. The stars will still be there without me looking at them.'

I sigh, but it hits me right in the gut. 'No wonder you're such a Grinch.'

He laughs and does what is probably meant to be a shrug without moving his torso.

'One of the best things about Christmastime is believing that anything can happen. Magic always feels just a little bit closer to the surface at this time of year.' I wonder if I'm going a bit far. Usually when I meet a new person, I make an effort to hold back my weird side for a while, but here I am talking about Christmas magic to a guy who acts like he's due to have three ghosts turn up in his bedroom anytime now.

His hand flops down from holding his ribs and lands on his thigh right next to mine. My brain sputters to a halt and all I can think about is the weight of it resting against my leg. 'What would your wish be?'

He laughs again. 'I don't have one.'

'Seriously.' I prod his thigh gently. 'Everyone should have a Christmas wish. Imagine for just one moment that you were a person who believed in magic and you went to crack a nut in the magical nutcracker's mouth ... What would you wish for?'

'Someone to love me,' he says instantly and then hesitates. He's quiet for so long that I think he's going to leave it there and not elaborate. 'Last week I sat in the A&E department of the hospital

71

for five hours, in pain, a good deal of the way into shock, scared, and completely alone. I couldn't stop shaking, and all I wanted was someone to hold my hand and tell me it was going to be okay. Sorry if that makes me sound unmanly and unmacho, but that's the truth. How alone I was hit me harder than the car had. I wanted someone to care about me. I wanted someone to worry about me. To notice I hadn't come home. More than anything, I wanted someone to love me.'

'Your parents?'

'They've got their own problems.'

'Friends?'

'My friends are lads, y'know? Great to go out for a beer with, not so much for handholding through emotional trauma. And I've ... kind of pulled back this year. I've been busy with work and there's stuff I don't want to share with them and when they've invited me out, I've refused because I've been crap company for the past few months ... There's no one I could phone out of the blue and ask to come and sit with me.'

His voice has gone quiet and shaky, and it's clear that he's nowhere near as blasé about the accident as he seemed earlier. Something like that shakes a person up, no matter how determined he is to appear unaffected, and I'm surprised he's shared this with me because I get the feeling he isn't someone who admits vulnerability easily. His hand is open on his thigh, palm up, and I don't know what makes me do it, but I reach over and slip my fingers between his and squeeze tightly. 'Next time you can call me.'

'I'm going to endeavour not to get hit by any more cars, but I'll keep that in mind.' I expect him to recoil in horror at me holding his hand, but his fingers curl around mine and he squeezes back tighter than I expected. 'Thank you.' He turns inwards and sort of rubs his cheek against my shoulder. 'And just so you know, I'm going to blame this entire conversation on the painkillers tomorrow. If I was thinking clearly, I'm pretty sure I would never have admitted that out loud.'

'Your secret's safe with me,' I murmur against his hair.

I feel his face shift into a smile again, and he doesn't let go of my hand.

What the heck am I doing? Sitting in the storeroom holding hands with a guy I barely know. I don't *do* this sort of thing.

'What would yours be?'

This proximity and his cologne are making me feel fuzzy too. 'What?'

'Your Christmas wish. What would it be?'

I'm *not* telling him about the whole Prince Charming thing the other night. I might've let my guard down a bit, but not *that* much. 'For someone to care about Nutcracker Lane.'

'No one cares about it?' He sounds confused.

'No one who matters. No one in management. No one who can actually help. It feels like everyone's waiting for it to die forever. It used to be special, and now it's just a shell, consigned to the memories of the people who loved it. I wish there was someone who cared about it as much as the shopkeepers do, someone who'd realise it's worth saving and with a bit of time and investment, could be restored to its former glory. It doesn't matter to anyone anymore. No one will listen.'

'I'll listen.' His fingers tighten around mine. 'I mean, I don't think I can do anything to help, but you're clearly passionate about this place and passion is inspiring. Tell me about it.'

I didn't expect him to say that. I'm sure he's not even vaguely interested in our little outlet village dedicated to the thing he hates most, but it's sweet of him to offer.

'Our Santa used to be the jolliest for miles. Not the bum-scratching grumpy thin bloke we've got now, and there used to be such an emphasis on helping others. Nowadays, all the advertising is about sales and deals in the shops, but it used to be about donating toys for children who wouldn't have any on Christmas morning and the free Christmas dinner that Nutcracker Lane used to host for the homeless, and how they used to drive out and collect elderly people who would be alone for Christmas and bring them here and put on bingo games and raffles and then take them home where they'd all totter tipsily off the bus with new friends and hampers under their arms.

'The wish-granters would only ever grant the wishes that meant something to people. It was never about material things – the children who asked Santa for a long list of expensive toys were rarely given even one. The wishes granted were for those who wished for something that would help the people around them or make their lives better in some way …'

'An iPad could make many people's lives exponentially better …'

'This was the Nineties – thankfully we didn't have iPads then.'

'Exactly. Don't you think it's failing *because* it's old-fashioned in this day and age? Walking into this place is like stepping back in time.'

'Exactly,' I repeat. 'People need that now more than ever given the state of the world. Is there anyone who *doesn't* love a bit of nostalgia and would love to step back into the past for a little while?'

'Yes!' He sounds so incredulous that it makes me laugh. 'I can't think of anything worse.'

'This is exactly the kind of place everyone needs. Modern Christmases are all about stress and expensive presents that none of us can really afford, but what Christmas is really about is time with family and friends and appreciating what you have rather than making lists of stuff you want. Nutcracker Lane is a remnant of times gone by, with the paving slabs and the Victorian lampposts and the old-fashioned carollers singing traditional Christmas songs rather than, I don't know, that bloke from *The Royle Family* singing "Christmas, My Arse".'

'There's not seriously a Christmas song called that, is there?' I nod.

'If I could move enough to get my phone out of my pocket, I'd look that up right now. I think we both know what the soundtrack in *my* shop is going to be tomorrow. Forget Tchaikovsky, "Christmas, My Arse" is my new favourite song and I haven't even heard it yet.'

I know he's deliberately winding me up again, but there's something so good-natured about it that I don't mind.

'Did you know they used to do free-of-charge day trips here for people with terminal illnesses? People spent their last ever Christmas on Nutcracker Lane. That's something special – something that shouldn't be forgotten.'

He shakes his head. 'Yeah, but … I'm not so heartless that I can find an argument against that, but people stopped coming. If Nutcracker Lane was as important as you say it was, why isn't it still?'

'People stopped coming because the budget keeps being cut. The more stuff that's taken away, the fewer reasons there are for people to visit.'

'If it was earning enough money, the budget wouldn't have been cut in the first place.'

I hate that he's got a point there. Am I putting more value on it than there actually was? Just because it was special to me, was it really so special to other people too? Or did they just come here for whatever free stuff they could get out of the magical nutcracker's wish-granting abilities, and when the wish-granters left, so did the visitors?

'It was an escape for me. My dad died when I was young, and my granddad died not long after, and my grandma and I kind of connected through our grief. We used to come here almost every day during the Christmas season and it was a little haven. Inside these doors, you could forget about everything outside for a while and lose yourself in festive magic.'

'That sounds nice,' he murmurs.

'After my granddad died, my grandma let me have all his tools, and I've been making Christmas decorations since I was old enough to use them. She always said I'd have a shop here one day and I feel like it's my little way of honouring both of them now. I don't want to lose it.'

His elbow presses into the line where our thighs are touching as he lifts our joined hands and twists his wrist, turning them over and sort of examining them, his fingers tightening and then gently rubbing the back of my hand. He seems lost in thought for a curiously long time. 'We could help each other, you know …'

'We could?'

'I have to take over my father's business next year and I don't know what to do with it. I *need* to find some Christmas spirit. That's what I came here for, and I can't think of anyone more full of Christmas spirit than someone with your taste in jumpers. I don't "get" Christmas, Nia. I don't understand why so many people love it. And you do. I need someone like you in my life.'

No matter the context, I can't deny it's *nice* to hear that. Most of the men in my life have said the exact opposite.

'And I know a little bit about retail and I can't help but notice that your shop doesn't exactly stand out. Let me help you save it – and make sure you're one of the chosen few who come back next year, and in return, show me why Christmas means so much to you. Help me understand why it's important to people, why it matters so much, because I don't think I can do what's required of me next year without some help.'

'You want me to un-Grinch you?'

He starts singing, '*Un-Grinch my heart*,' to the tune of the Toni Braxton classic "Unbreak My Heart". '*Say you'll mistletoe me again.*'

I get so lost in the fit of giggles that I snort and it doesn't even matter because he's laughing so much too, even though it must be painful. How is it possible that one man can be so simultaneously adorable and as irritating as finding a paintbrush bristle in dried paint and having to sand the whole item down and start again?

It takes a few minutes for me to be able to breathe again, and I'm not sure if he's quiet because he's trying not to pressure me or if he's trying not to die because laughing seems like one of his most painful activities.

'Well, I've never been afraid of a challenge.' I glance down at his tousled dark hair still on my shoulder. 'A really challenging challenge.'

'Oh, thanks,' he says with another laugh.

'I've got my family coming for Christmas for the first time,' I say as I think about it, even though I can't imagine ever turning down a chance to turn a Christmas hater into a Christmas lover. 'Usually my mum hosts but she's got high blood pressure and her doctor's told her to avoid stress, so I said I'd do it, and then Mum said, "Oh, brilliant. Your brother's bringing his new girlfriend and those cousins we haven't seen for five years are coming," and long story short, I'm hosting Christmas for five extra people including distant relatives who weren't happy that Grandma left her cottage to me and are probably coming to inspect it and make sure I haven't wrecked the place yet, and my brother's new girlfriend who he met while travelling and who doesn't speak a word of English, *and* it has to live up to my mother's expectations. And she shops in Waitrose. I shop in Aldi. I need all the help I can get.'

'And you *enjoy* this?'

'Yeah. I mean, when I agreed I thought it'd just be me and Mum and maybe my brother if he was back from his travels, but unexpected guests are part of Christmas.'

'And you think I can help?'

'I have everything to do. I haven't even got a tree yet, never mind food shopping, baking, or present wrapping. The only thing I'm ahead on is gift shopping thanks to the traditional Black Friday "it's three weeks until Christmas and I've got *nothing* for anyone" panic and spending most of the day online shopping in the sales.'

'You've never heard of gift vouchers?'

'You can't give people gift vouchers for Christmas! You're supposed to think about what they'd like and put some thought and love into each gift.'

77

'What if the thing they'd like is gift vouchers? Or cash?'

I make a noise of horror. 'No! Cash is even worse. At least with a gift voucher, you've given some thought to a shop they might like.'

'I clearly have a lot to learn,' he says with a laugh. 'So, it's a deal then? I'll help with your shop and you help me find some joy in the festive season?'

I rest my head against his gently again and nod.

He's still holding our hands up and his fingers tighten around mine again. 'It's a deal. I'd say shake hands but we're already shaking hands.'

'We seem to do that a lot,' I mumble.

He rests our joined hands back on his thigh but makes no move to detach himself. Instead his middle finger rubs mindless circles on the back of my hand. 'So how does that work then, if your brother's girlfriend doesn't speak English?'

'That remains to be seen.'

'I'm not sure if he's an idiot or a genius. Maybe my relationships would've been better if we hadn't been able to communicate.'

'Maybe mine would've been better if we *had*.'

He laughs a gentle laugh of sympathy that makes me feel more connected to him than our joined hands and his head on my shoulder.

I lose track of how long we sit there. Everything's quieter than the normal after-closing hours of Nutcracker Lane because down here in the storage room, the noise of the weather outside is muted and the only sound is each other's breathing, and for the first time in months, I'm just concentrating on the weight of him beside me and the feel of his fingers between mine, and not on how many more reindeer I have to cut with my wood cutter, how many sheets of MDF I need to buy, or if I've got enough white paint to cover sixteen snowmen or the right shade of orange for a penguin's beak.

All the talk of the Grinch makes me start humming "Where

Are You, Christmas?" from the Jim Carrey film under my breath and I love the feel of his face shifting into another smile through my jumper.

'You've started my un-Grinching early.' He sounds half-asleep.

'I'd sing but you're already in enough pain without adding burst eardrums to the mix.'

'You can if you want. I'm pretty sure I won't remember this in the morning. Actually, I *hope* I won't remember it in the morning, given some of the things I've admitted out loud tonight.'

I squeeze his hand, which is inexplicably still in mine. In any other circumstance, I'm pretty sure this would be weird, but it feels completely natural with him, and I could quite comfortably sit here until we both fell asleep, even though the box of whatever decorations we're sitting on is getting increasingly uncomfortable and I'm fairly sure I've got a nutcracker's sceptre digging in my backside.

'Hey, do you have to drive home tonight?' It's ages later when the thought occurs to me.

'Yeah, but I've got a few hours of work ahead of me yet. I'll be fine by the time I'm done.'

'No.' I've completely lost track of time as we've been sitting here and I'm surprised it's past 10 p.m. when I check my watch. I pull my hand out of his and push gently at his arm so he knows he's got to move, then I stand up and stretch my legs out, fold my arms and give him my most authoritative look. 'Just no. Come on, I'm within walking distance – you can come home with me.'

He blinks up at me. 'I'm not good company. You barely know me and you want me at your house?'

'Nope.' I shrug. 'But you're not getting behind a wheel in that state – you've already been in enough accidents lately, and you're not staying here working for God knows how many more hours.'

'I'm not?'

I shake my head.

79

'Prevent other shopkeepers from working – one way to get rid of the competition, I suppose.'

'You can barely stay upright. How much work do you think you're going to get done in that condition?' I ask with a raised eyebrow.

He looks down at himself. 'Fair point, well made.'

'Good.' I give him a satisfied nod. 'I've got a veggie hotpot with cheesy dumplings in the slow cooker. When did you last have a proper meal?'

'Last night.'

'A proper homecooked meal? Which you cooked to perfection with your one arm?' I raise the other eyebrow. He does *not* look like he regularly eats well. He looks like he's struggling with the injuries more than he'll willingly let on.

'Well, no, a Big Mac. But it was a meal and it was cooked.'

I let out another snort. I really am going to have to stop snorting in front of him. He's going to think there's pig in my DNA at this rate. 'Well, Big Macs don't come with cheesy dumplings. If that doesn't sway you, nothing will. Can you move yet?'

'We'll find out …' He shifts minutely, edging himself upright.

I hold my hand out to pull him up like I did in the shop yesterday and he grins as he slips his hand into mine again and stumbles to his feet.

'I'm fine,' he says eventually, squeezing my hand once before letting it go and stepping back.

I miss the feel of his hand in mine as he moves carefully, stretching slightly and stamping his feet to get feeling back into them. He pulls his black T-shirt down and readjusts the sling while I pick up the nutcracker he dropped hours ago and go to put it back in the box.

'Keep it,' James says. 'I won't sell him. Or his family.'

I look at him questioningly, and he continues. 'Because you like him. We'll find the rest of them and put them out somewhere. Where they're meant to be.'

80

'Thanks. That's really nice of you.' I straighten the nutcracker's white beard and brush his hair down.

'Maybe I'm not a lost cause after all.'

I grin at him because underneath his sarcasm and quick wit, there's a softness there too, and I like his kindness and willingness to listen to me talking about Nutcracker Lane tonight, even though he hates Christmas and isn't going to think about this place again once the festive season is over.

As we walk out of the storeroom and along the corridor, he dodges past me and pulls the door open, and I look up at him with a smile and meet his pale brown eyes as he stands back to let me go through first.

A real Prince Charming.

Chapter 4

'It's freezing tonight.' James holds the entrance door open and lets me through before closing it behind him and pulling his oversized hoody tighter.

I shiver as we step out onto the walkway surrounding the car park. Our car park is on the opposite side of the building to the car park for the nutcracker factory, and now there's just one solitary car left in it, parked in the end space near the point where I shortcut across the border. It must be his. 'Can you still drive?'

'Yeah, without the sling on. Thankfully it's an automatic and I'm right-handed.'

It's parked under a lamppost so I can tell it's blue and looks like a sensible sort of car, and nothing like the flashy and impractical sports car I'd imagined him driving.

There's a little path through the stubby green bushes and the earth under our feet is crunchy and iced over as I take my usual route across the border and make sure he's following me.

He's got his hand shoved into his pocket and his black hoody zipped up to his chin, and his breath appears in front of his face every time he exhales. He's careful on the uneven icy ground of the border, and he puts his hand out for balance as we start down the hill, taking care with each step, and I'm not sure if he's just being careful in the dark, with the ice, or if he's still in more pain than he's letting on, or maybe all three.

I know I shouldn't touch him again, I've already got far too close to him tonight, but it seems wrong not to hold my hand out, and when I do, instead of taking it, he loops his right arm over my outstretched hand so my arm is hooked through his and he squeezes it against his good side.

Neither of us speaks, and I breathe into my scarf to avoid looking up at him because it should feel weird to walk arm in arm down the street with a man you barely know, but it doesn't.

I love walking home in the dark at this time of year and seeing all the Christmas lights twinkling from every house. All of my neighbours make an effort with their festive decorations, and each house has lights twinkling from porches and roofs; some have twinkly trees outside and others have left their curtains open to show their inside trees and star silhouettes in the windows.

We turn the corner where Stacey meets me every morning and start walking along the narrower street towards my cottage.

'Why can I already tell which one is yours?' James says, but he doesn't sound insulting about it.

I stop at the little wooden gate and unlatch it, letting my arm slip out of his as I pull away to dash up the garden path and unlock the door to let us in out of the cold, while frantically trying to remember if I've left bras hanging anywhere or knickers drying on the clothes airer. It's been a *long* time since I've invited a man home, and he's suffering enough tonight. He doesn't need to come face-to-face with my underwear too. When I turn around to invite him in, I'm surprised to see he's still standing at the gate, looking up at my house with an expression of awe.

'Your house looks like it should have gumdrops on the roof.'

'And now I know those painkillers really do make you loopy,' I say even though it's impossible not to grin at him. I don't have many Christmas lights outside, just one string stapled along each angle of the roof, and a string of candle-shaped bulbs wound through the picket fence separating me from my neighbours on either side of the narrow front garden, and I'm suddenly glad I've got them on a timer that's set to come on from five until midnight every night, even though my mother is keen to point out that I'm wasting electricity if I'm not home. I've been working late so often lately, and in the last couple of weeks – since it got close enough to Christmas to be socially acceptable to have lights up – it's made me happy to come home to the multicoloured twinkling bulbs, and I don't want to be the only house on the cul-de-sac not lit up after dark.

He's still dawdling so I duck inside to switch the heating on, kick my shoes off, and then go back to the doorway.

'It's like a picture-perfect little Christmas cottage. I'm not sure if it looks like it should belong in a snowglobe or like you live alone in the middle of the woods and leave trails of breadcrumbs out for unsuspecting children.'

I laugh out loud and quickly clamp my hand over my mouth for fear of waking any neighbours who have gone to bed early.

At least he looks suitably guilty for making me laugh as he wanders up the paving slab path, his fingers trailing over the holly bushes glistening with frost and leaving lines through the ice covering the wooden railing on the steps up to the door.

I stand back to let him inside while I go through to the living room, turning on the lights and the candle warmer, and wishing I already had my tree up because that always adds to the cosiness of any room. I throw a firelighter into the wood burner and add a couple of logs as it starts to burn, and then squeeze back past him as he's holding on to the wall inside the door and toeing his boots off. I go into the kitchen to check on the slow cooker and inhale the warm, homely scent of the veggie hotpot cooking.

'Wow,' he says from the living room. 'Do you have anything that *isn't* festive? Is there any one thing in your whole house that *doesn't* have some formation of reindeer and snowflakes on it?'

84

'Not at this time of year,' I call back cheerfully. I have a chest upstairs that my grandma left full of hand-knitted Christmas blankets she'd made or bought over the years, along with throws and cushion covers. Even the doormat has snowmen on it. 'It's only once a year, I like to make the most of it. It's nowhere near finished yet.'

'Not finished,' he mutters. You wouldn't expect to be able to hear someone rolling their eyes from another room, but surprisingly I can.

I take the lid off the slow cooker and give the hotpot a stir until I'm satisfied I haven't brought him back here to accidentally poison him. I fill the kettle, and when I go back to the living room, he's looking at my nutcracker collection on the window ledge.

'Have you got enough?' He's holding a medium-sized soldier with a furry hat and a sword and moving the lever in its back up and down to open and close its mouth.

'They were a thing. My grandma found one she thought looked like my granddad and bought it for him the first year they were married, and ever since they bought a new one every year. When he died, it became a tradition for me and her to walk up to Nutcracker Lane on opening day and choose a new one from the factory outlet shop to add to the collection every year.'

He puts the soldier back in the space it came from, being careful not to knock any of the others in case they fall over and we have a nutcracker domino effect on our hands. He picks up the little wood-coloured one he gave me yesterday and holds it out questioningly. 'No dart holes?'

I give him an offended look. 'I haven't had time to get one yet this year so he'll do for now. Opening day is different on Nutcracker Lane when you're working there. I didn't have a chance to go across to the factory outlet where they sell them.'

He puts it down and picks up another short, stumpy one with a glossy green sceptre and a glittered red jacket. 'I used to make these.' He sounds lost in thought.

'*You* used to make Christmas decorations?' I say, not intending for it to come out quite so disbelievingly.

'Only for crackers. The really tiny squat ones that are chiselled from one piece of wood and covered in glitter paint. A *long* time ago now.'

'Do you work with your hands much?' I think about how he said he was going to fix the nutcracker I broke yesterday and how he mentioned mending the snow machine, and his talents when it came to repainting the shop sign.

'I used to, but not anymore. Now I just sit in an office and stare at my computer, with numbers and figures blurring on the spreadsheet before my eyes.'

Before I have a chance to question him, he puts that nutcracker down and picks up a snowglobe, a clay Christmas tree inside with a tiny model of a young girl in a pink coat beside it.

'My granddad made that for me. He'd never made one before but he knew I liked snowglobes and he wanted to give me something special. I was surgically attached to my pink coat at the time.'

He shakes it and watches, mesmerised, as the snow and glitter float down around the miniature snow-covered branches of the tree, still as perfect today as the day my granddad gave it to me when I was seven years old.

'Okay, even I can admit that's kind of special.' He puts it down gently and his long fingers trail across the top of the glass dome. 'For a Christmas decoration.'

I narrow my eyes at him when he looks up and smiles.

'Your house is amazing.' He looks around with a soft kind of awestruck look on his face. 'It's so warm and inviting. This is what a house should be like. It's like coming home.'

'Where do you live?'

'I have a flat over in Melksham.' He points in the general direction of the area. 'About half an hour in the car, but near my parents and the office. It's *not* like this. This is a real home. I still have boxes I haven't unpacked from when I moved in four years ago.'

'I moved in with my grandma when I was a teenager and then looked after her when she got older, and she left the cottage to me when she died a few years ago, so I've lived here for a really long time. And accumulated enough Christmas decorations to show for it.' I indicate the army of nutcracker soldiers on the window ledge, and he looks at them again and his eyes shift to the warm yellow glow coming from the scented candle in the warmer.

'It even smells like Christmas.' He takes a deep breath and as he breathes out, his tummy lets out a loud rumble, and his face instantly glows adorably red.

I can't help giggling as I point to the coffee table in front of the sofa. 'Help yourself to biscuits and chocolate.'

His eyes go wide as he spots the tub of chocolates and the biscuit selection box on the low rectangular table. 'You have chocolate and biscuits just there for the taking?'

'It's Christmas. You have to have a tub of chocolates and a biscuit selection box.'

'It's December the 2nd.'

'Exactly. Only three weeks to work my way through as many as possible. And they're all on offer at this time of year – it'd be rude not to.'

His smile is so wide as he goes across and tears the lid off the tub of Roses and picks out a hazel-in-caramel. He makes a noise of pleasure as he rips the wrapper off and puts it in his mouth and I watch his shoulders droop in contentment as he sucks it. Then I realise that standing in the doorway and watching him enjoy a chocolate is probably weird, so I nod towards the sofa. 'Sit. Help yourself. Put your feet up on the table if it's comfier. That's what it's there for. Food won't be long now.'

He's barely swallowed before he takes a strawberry cream and tears into it, and I kind of like that he's gone for my favourites. We might not have a love of Christmas in common, but at least we can appreciate the same chocolate.

'Is there room for me with all the festive cushions?' he says with his mouth full.

'You can use them to get your ribs comfortable. Pack them around yourself or chuck them off if they don't help.'

He pulls a red-and-white knitted Fair Isle cushion aside and sinks down with a sigh of relief, sounding as tired as he looks. He plonks first one leg and then the other up onto the coffee table with a heavy clunk and settles back, letting his head rest against the back and closing his eyes. He goes to speak but all that comes out is a giant yawn.

Thankfully the kettle chooses that moment to click off and I back away to the kitchen rather than getting caught up in how nice it is not to come home alone or how *good* he looks sitting there. 'I'll make us a cuppa.'

'Can I just have two sugars this time?' He calls after me. 'Not sixty-two like last time?'

'You're hilarious,' I call back as I get two Christmas mugs out of the cupboard and throw a teabag into each. 'The remote's on the table in front of you. Choose something to watch. You've got a choice between Christmas music or Christmas movies. We may as well start your un-Grinching straightaway.'

'Don't I get tortured enough with Christmas music twenty-four hours a day at the lane?'

'Movies it is, then,' I call out. 'I recorded *Elf* last night. You'll like that one.'

'There has never been and never will be a Christmas movie that I'll enjoy.'

'You'll love *How the Grinch Stole Christmas*!'

Even he laughs at that, and I have to admit I'm impressed when the sound of the TV comes on and it sounds like he's following instructions. I make the two cups of tea and set out two china bowls with a pattern of holly heaves and red berries weaved across them.

'Are you actually going to watch all these?' he asks, muffled

88

around another chocolate. 'I'm going through your DVR box and I've lost count of how many Christmas movies you've got recorded. I'm not a mathematician but I'm pretty sure there aren't this many hours in the day between now and next August and that's not taking into account things like working and sleeping.'

'I don't like to miss any,' I say, half-annoyed because surely commenting on the contents of someone else's TV box isn't good etiquette and on the other hand, half-impressed that he's comfortable enough to do so. 'In January, I'll delete any that I don't get around to.'

'At least you're optimistic.'

I turn off the cooker and dole out two bowlfuls of the veggie hotpot and position chunky cheesy dumplings around the edge, and finish off the teas with a splash of milk. By the time I carry his into the living room, he's got *Elf* ready to play and he hands me the remote, and I put the snowy robin tray holding the bowl and mug onto his lap.

'Christmas mugs *and* Christmas bowls *and* a Christmas tray. I'm not even horrified anymore, I'm intrigued by what other Christmassy things you're going to bring out, like a never-ending *Generation Game* conveyor belt.'

I put the remote on the arm of one of the chairs and go to fetch my own food.

'Nia, thank you,' he says when I come back in. 'Seriously. Tonight is the nicest thing anyone's ever done for me. I couldn't have chosen a better person to nearly pass out on in the store-room.'

It makes me laugh again. 'You're welcome. Next time you need to keel over on a random stranger, you know where I am.'

He smiles and doesn't drop his gaze from mine as I sit down in the armchair opposite him and fold my legs up underneath me. His teeth pull his lower lip into his mouth and I get the feeling he wants to say something else, but he doesn't. 'This looks amazing.'

I blush, even though he has no idea how it tastes yet. Looks

89

can be deceiving, especially when it comes to my cooking. This could be the epitome of that glossy turkey in *National Lampoon's Christmas Vacation* when Chevy Chase cuts into it and it bursts apart with a puff of air and shrivels to gristle.

'I can't believe you're making me watch a Christmas movie,' he says as I press play and the credits fill the blue screen. 'I can't remember the last time I watched a movie. It's not going to make me laugh, is it?'

Oops. I hadn't thought of that. 'Er, no. *Elf* is absolutely the unfunniest Christmas movie ever. No laughter guaranteed.'

By the time we get to the scene of Will Ferrell trying to go up an escalator, James has realised I was being sarcastic. There are tears of laughter running down his cheeks – or possibly tears of pain – and he's got a cushion held against his side by his elbow to give his ribs some padding.

'I can't remember the last time I laughed like this,' he croaks out. 'If I hadn't taken enough painkillers to bring down a donkey, I'd hate you for this. If it was possible to hate someone who had just cooked me the best thing I've ever eaten.'

I go to brush the compliment off, but he stops me. 'Seriously, Nia. This is so good. When I remember it tomorrow, I'm going to think I hallucinated it.'

He seems to know exactly what to say. I don't cook for many people and it's *nice* to hear that, in the same way I don't have many people over to the house apart from Stacey, Lily when I babysit, and Mum occasionally, and there's something about seeing him so at home here. Since Brad, keeping relationships at arm's length has meant I've not invited anyone into my heart, let alone my house or let anyone try my cooking, and seeing him enjoy it has done a better job of warming me up than the log fire has.

I also love that he's clearly enjoying *Elf*. I've seen it enough times to be able to quote it word for word but I concentrate intently on it as a way of stopping myself watching him and the way crow's feet crinkle around his eyes as they dance with laughter when Buddy and Jovie sing "Baby, It's Cold Outside", and the way I can feel his eyes on me too, and every time I look over, he smiles and it makes something unclench in my stomach and warmth fill my chest.

He even looks disappointed when I pause the film to go and cut a slice of Yule Log each for afters, and he's so much of a gentleman that he offers to do the washing up afterwards, which I refuse because he still looks so tired that a stiff breeze would finish him off.

There's a point at the end of *Elf* that always makes me cry – when Jovie starts singing "Santa Claus Is Coming To Town" and the crowd in Central Park join in – and when I risk a glance across the room at him, trying to hide my tears so he won't laugh at my sappiness when it comes to Christmas movies, he's fallen asleep. I squeeze my reindeer cushion tighter and watch the last five minutes of the film, and then turn it off as quietly as possible.

I get up and take the plates out to the kitchen and slip them into the sink a millimetre at a time. The last thing I want to do is clatter around and wake him up. I tiptoe back into the living room and gently lift the biscuit selection tin from his lap. His broken arm is still across his chest and his good arm is propped up on a snowman cushion, while the pile of cushions stacked around him is keeping him upright. His head is leaning back against the sofa and his breathing is shallow and even, his hair has flopped over his forehead again, thick and straight, and I wish I could risk tucking it back into the rest of his mussed soft hair.

There's a red fleece throw with a pattern of white holly leaves and mistletoe berries over the back of the sofa and I tug it down and unfold it, and carefully pull it across until it's covering him. I inch it up gently to his neck so at least his broken arm and ribs will be warm. He looks like he's gone for the night, and maybe it's weird to have a stranger sleeping in your house, but he seemed so tired today that there is no part of me that would even consider waking him.

I creep up to bed, painstakingly avoiding every creaky stair, and wonder if I should be concerned that it doesn't feel weird at all. James falling asleep on my sofa seems like exactly the way this night was supposed to end.

Chapter 5

My alarm goes off as usual at seven-thirty and I hit the snooze button and roll over, stretching out with a groan and pulling the duvet tighter around myself, feeling the pleasant ache of having had a really good night's sleep. Even though it was late by the time the film finished, I'd usually have gone out to the bright lights of the garden shed and worked for a couple of hours, but I couldn't risk waking—

'James!' I say loudly as I sit bolt upright and the events of last night come flooding back.

I scramble out of bed, shove my arms into my blue penguin-patterned dressing gown and fight with the door handle, stiff after not being used for so long. There's no need to close a bedroom door when you live alone, but I didn't want to risk James waking up and looking for the bathroom only to accidentally come across me snoring and drooling into my pillow. He's traumatised enough from the accident.

I fly down the stairs. 'James, are you—'

Gone. The living room is empty. The blanket is folded neatly in the space where he was, and my keys are on the doormat where he's let himself out, locked up, and put them back through the letterbox. He's found my stack of Post-it Notes by the landline phone because there's a neon-yellow square stuck to the coffee table, with *"Thank you. ~ J"* written on it in scrawled handwriting. When I go in the kitchen, the washing up is done and stacked neatly on the draining board, and I can't help smiling as I pull my dressing gown tighter and huddle into it. Even Prince Charming never did the washing up.

I can't help the spike of disappointment that bursts through me too. I was looking forward to seeing him this morning. I imagined coming downstairs to find him still sleeping, going to the kitchen to make breakfast and putting the coffee machine on, waking him up with the smell of fresh-ground coffee and waffles from the ill-advised waffle maker my mum got me for Christmas last year, despite the fact I've never eaten a waffle in my life, and never managed to successfully make one in it since. In my fantasy of this morning, it produced soft and fluffy buttery waffles, and not the crumbled pieces of charcoal it actually produces.

Maybe it's a good thing. The sight of me first thing in the morning is enough to terrify anyone, and James has suffered enough lately. But having him here was nice. Not being alone was nice. Having someone to chat to, and eat with, and watch a film with was nice.

I can smell his cinnamony cologne on the throw when I put it back where it came from and it definitely *doesn't* make my knees go weak. I wonder when he woke up, when he left, if he went to the lane or back home. It must've been a few hours ago. I'm pretty sure the biscuit tin has moved from where I left it last night and I kind of love the idea of him helping himself to biscuits for breakfast.

I suddenly can't wait to get to work this morning to see him. I go back upstairs for a shower, and then return to shovel cereal down my throat and put away the plates from last night. I'm usually as slow as a turtle in the mornings, but today I'm dressed and ready faster than ever before, and I have to make myself

94

pace inside the door for ten minutes before I walk out to meet Stacey on the corner.

I'm bouncing on the balls of my feet by the time I spot her trudging up the frosty hill towards me.

'You're early.' She checks for cars and then crosses my street to the corner. 'You're *never* early. What's wrong?'

'Nothi—'

'And you're smiling! You *never* smile at eight-thirty in the morning.' She takes hold of my shoulders, turns me round to face her and peers at me, looking for clues. 'What's with the spring in your step?'

'You know that guy? James from the shop opposite?' I try to sound casual as I shrug myself out of her grip and we start walking up the hill.

She's not buying my casualness. 'Oh, just that gorgeous guy you happen to think might be a nutcracker come to life ...'

I pull my scarf further up my face so it covers my mouth, muffling my words. 'He kind of came home with me last night.'

She grabs my arm, pulls me to a stop and looks all around, straining to see past the corner of my street. 'Where is he?'

'He left early.'

Stace narrows her eyes. 'He didn't leave when you woke up, did he? Literally a *dream* guy in all senses of the word?'

'No, he left before I woke up. He was—'

'A one-night stand!' She shouts loud enough to attract the attention of a smart business-suited father and well-dressed mother packing their two impressionable young children into the back of the frightfully posh car in their driveway. They give us a suitably dirty look.

'Nia Maddison!' Stacey ignores them and carries on at a normal volume. 'That's not like you! Have you been at the festive spirit or what?'

'It wasn't like that. He was hurt and tired and I wouldn't let him drive ... He even did the washing up, Stace.'

'What's that? A euphemism? A kinky sex position?'

'No, the actual washing up. With one hand.'

'Are you sure you didn't sleep with him? Because Simon only does actual washing up in exchange for sexual favours.'

'No, he's just that much of a gent.'

'Like the kind you wished for?'

'No. Well, maybe. But it's ridiculous. He couldn't be.'

'He couldn't be a Christmas decoration come to life or he couldn't be an actual real-life man who just happens to have some prince-like qualities and isn't as much of a wanker as the other guys you've dated in recent years?'

'He hates my favourite time of year, Stace. He's no prince,' I mumble as she slots her arm through mine and makes me fill her in with as much info as possible in the five-minute walk to Nutcracker Lane.

'His car's gone,' I say the instant the car park comes into view.

'Did you expect it not to be?' She pushes herself up on tiptoes to follow my gaze to the empty space under the lamppost.

'No. I don't know. I guess he'd go home to shower and change. I was just hoping …' I can't finish the sentence. What was I hoping? That he'd be there so I didn't have to wait a moment longer to see him? 'I just want to know he's okay. He wasn't in good shape last night.'

'Hmm.' She sounds like she isn't sure which one of us I'm trying to convince either.

*

'Nia, you're blocking customers' view of the goods – will you come away from that flipping window?'

I jump when Stacey barks at me for *not* the first time this morning. 'It's half past ten and he isn't in yet. Where *is* he?'

'I don't know, but maybe if you stop watching his shop for three seconds, he'll turn up.'

96

I tidy the same display stand of Stacey's earrings that I've tidied approximately seventy times so far this morning. Turning each backing card of tiny resin holly-leaf earrings so each point of the holly faces the exact same way. I should be working – using every opportunity when the shop's not busy to be out the back, painting as much stock as possible to give us the most chance of outselling the other shops, but the fact James hasn't come into work yet is at the forefront of my mind and I can't concentrate on anything else.

'What does it matter if he doesn't open up anyway?' Stacey says after she's served a customer buying a glittery hand-painted set of standing snowmen ornaments. 'It's a good thing because we might get some of his customers. Why are you so worried?'

'Because he's …' I trail off as a customer comes through the door and says good morning to us both. It's another sentence I can't finish anyway.

'Can you man the till while I replace the two necklaces that have sold from the mannequin busts in the window?'

I give James's dark shop another look like something might've changed in the 0.02 seconds since I last looked. Whoever would've thought I'd miss a Macarena-ing Santa?

Stacey disappears into the back and the woman who just came in asks me about the custom 'Christmas with the …' wall plaques I make and how many letters can be fitted into the family name and says she'll talk it over with her husband and retreats, unlikely to ever be seen again.

'Do you prefer the—' Stacey comes back onto the shop floor with three necklaces in her hands and stops in her tracks, her eyes fixed on the door. 'What the …'

I follow her gaze to where a man who is clearly James is hovering in the doorway with his left arm still in the sling, a poinsettia in a pot under his good arm, a cardboard tray containing three takeaway coffees in the same hand, and a brown paper bag over his head. There are eye holes cut out, a hole for his mouth,

97

and two bright red circular cheeks drawn on in the brightest marker pen.

The surprise at his appearance couples with the relief of finally seeing him and I burst into such maniacal, unhinged laughter that a customer goes to come in but quickly reconsiders.

'What are you doing?' I say when I can breathe again. 'Other than trying to break the other arm by walking around with that on your head?'

'Trying to frighten people half to death?' Stacey asks. 'I thought we were about to be robbed!'

'Ah, sorry.' James apologises to her. 'I hadn't thought of that.'

He turns back to me. 'It's the Bag Of Shame. I'm so sorry about last night.' I can see him cringing through the bag. 'I'm too embarrassed to show my face this morning. I thought this'd help.'

'You have nothing to be embarrassed about,' I say. He's come near enough to the counter that I can reach him, so I lean across and pluck the bag off his head, pulling his hair up with it so it stands on end and then flops down again, revealing his gorgeous face and cheeks that are redder than the marker pen on the bag. 'Good morning, Grinch.'

He ducks his head, trying to hide his smile which is so wide that it almost touches each ear.

I'm so glad to see him that it takes all I have not to launch myself across the counter and pull him into a hug.

After I properly introduce him to Stacey, James turns back to me. 'I'm seriously so sorry. I can't believe I fell asleep on you. That was *not* meant to happen.'

'Don't worry about it.' Stacey jumps in before I can say anything. 'Nia's had far worse happen with some of the guys she dated.'

'It wasn't a date,' James and I say in unison, then meet each other's eyes and smile. He holds my gaze and puts first the coffees and then the plant down on the counter. 'Apology in plant and caffeine form. I'm so sorry about last night. I'm not usually that ...' He trails off, not managing to find the right word.

'It's fine, Nia's not usually *that* either.' Stacey helps herself to a coffee.

His cheeks are still as red as the leaves of the poinsettia plant and I reach out to run my fingers over them. The leaves, not his cheeks. That would just be weird.

'Flowers and hot drinks.' Stacey takes a sip of her coffee and looks between us. 'I'm still waiting for an explanation about *what* exactly happened between you two last night.'

'Nothing,' James and I say in perfect unison again. We look at each other and I have to bite my cheek to stop myself giggling, and he quickly drops my gaze and takes his own coffee out of the cardboard tray on the counter.

'Thank you for the flower.' I stroke the stunningly bright leaves, edged with glitter by the florist up the lane, and lift the pot across the till and settle it in the little gap on the other side by the wall.

'You're welcome. Thank you for ... everything.' He looks down and kicks one foot against the other and I'm kind of glad that he's struggling for words because I am too.

'She appreciated the washing up.'

'Stace!' I hiss.

His cheeks burn even redder and he sips his coffee to avoid eye contact. I want to say something funny and witty, but my mind's gone blank so I take the last cup out of the tray and try a sip too.

'This isn't festive!' My face contorts and it takes all my will-power not to spit it out. 'It's December and you bought a coffee that *isn't* a festive one?'

'I don't like festive coffees?' He asks like it's a question I might know the answer to.

'Have you tried one?'

'I don't need to. I don't like anything festive.'

'You liked the Yule Log last night.'

99

He sighs, trying and failing not to smile. 'Have I failed in my first assignment, oh Christmas master?'

'We're supposed to be un-Grinching you. You cannot drink a non-festive drink in December. It's the law. You can have normal coffees the other eleven months of the year. In December, they *have* to be cinnamon, or hazelnut caramel, or clementine, eggnog, toffee nut, or spiced shortbread.' I point a threatening finger at him, hoping he knows I'm only *half* joking. The variety of Christmas-themed hot drinks from the coffee shop on Nutcracker Lane is one of the best things about this place.

The look he gives me is both impressed and concerned that I know the coffee shop's menu off by heart. He salutes me with his coffee cup. 'Duly noted.'

I grin at him and he grins back at me and it's like everything else disappears. Stacey isn't there silently appraising him, that customer wiggling the antler of a reindeer to see how much force it'll take to break isn't there, the couple walking past arguing about the height of the Christmas tree they're going to get aren't there – it's just him, his ridiculously wide smile and light brown eyes, and the bubbles I feel in my chest from seeing him again. I want to ask him if he's okay, how his ribs are, if he got home all right, but Stacey is waiting for every morsel of info she can get from this conversation, and he's clearly embarrassed.

We realise we're just standing there staring at each other at the exact same moment because we both jump and avert our eyes, and I'm surprised to see that three people have come in and are browsing the decorations and jewellery.

'I should ...' He points to the door.

'Yeah. Er ...' I nod towards the customers. 'Busy.'

'I'll see you around ...' He starts walking away while I'm still desperately searching for something to say to make him stay a bit longer.

'Hey, last night ...' He abandons walking away and comes

back to the counter. 'Was there a movie about a giant elf or did I hallucinate that?'

I giggle with relief at him not leaving. 'It was real. I seem to remember you enjoying it.'

'I seem to remember you promising me it wasn't funny. How will we ever know if I fell asleep or just lost consciousness from the pain of laughing so much?'

I give him a self-satisfied grin because he was so proud of announcing there would never be a Christmas movie he'd enjoy. And I'm certain he only fell asleep. Probably.

'So you know how I kind of slept through the end ... What, er ... what happened?'

I do an overexaggerated gasp and stand up straighter. 'Are you telling me you actually enjoyed a Christmas movie so much that you're desperate to know the ending?'

'No. Absolutely not! I just have, um ...' He looks up at the ceiling as if searching for inspiration. 'I just have this thing where I hate starting something and not seeing it through to the end.'

'Of course you do.' I give him my best smile and I know he knows that I can see right through his flimsy excuse. 'All right, so Santa's sleigh crashes in Central Park because of the lack of Christmas spirit—'

'No!' Stacey shouts so suddenly that one of the customers drops a wooden snowflake she was looking at and it clatters to the floor. 'You can't *tell* him the ending of *Elf*. It has to be *seen*.' She turns to him. 'So you'll just have to go over and watch it some other time with her, won't you?'

His eyes don't leave mine and his teeth pull his lower lip into his mouth. 'It's not the *worst* idea I've ever heard ...'

'She does have a point,' I say, wondering what on earth has got into me. Am I actively inviting a man over to my house? Again? And not just any man, but the most gorgeous and charming man I've ever met? 'And seeing as you enjoyed *Elf* so much, there's a whole host of other Christmas movies you'll love too ...'

I'm still at the till behind the counter so I have to stop abruptly when a customer comes over with a handful of Stacey's jewellery and a load of my hand-painted wooden baubles for her grand-daughters and starts telling us about them as I ring up every item. I expect James to leave, but he wanders instead, still sipping his coffee and looking around as Stacey goes to replace the necklaces from the window display.

'You do remember our deal, don't you?' I ask him when the customer has left.

He looks up from the wooden gingerbread house he was studying, a display model of the build-your-own gingerbread house kits I've made, and he looks at me blankly. 'What deal?'

'James! You were going to … and I was going to …'

He bursts out laughing and then stops with an 'Ow.'

'Of course I remember,' he says when he comes back over to the counter. 'I wasn't *that* far gone. In fact, I'm pretty sure I remember every excruciatingly embarrassing detail of last night.'

The scent of his cologne has followed him across the shop. He smells of ruby red oranges and cinnamon and ginger. It's not right that someone who hates Christmas can smell like they've just stepped out of a Christmas tree.

'I studied retail back when I thought I'd be doing something different with my life. I know a bit about merchandising and marketing,' he's saying even though I've got lost in smelling him. Again.

'I can see that. Your shop is amazing.'

'Yours is as warm and homely as your house. It just needs to stand out a bit more.' He turns and points his coffee cup towards my side of the window. 'In trying to make the display cosy, you've made the windows too dark. And I think there's too much division between your products. You're in this together, and you'd probably get more customers if it *looked* like you were in it together. At the moment, it's not clear what you sell, and from the outside, you find yourself looking around for another door because it looks like two separate shops.'

I blink in surprise and look over at our cosy little window displays. He's got a point. And I'd never considered that it looks like two separate shops from the outside, but I *have* noticed customers hovering out there before hesitantly coming in, like they're not sure they're in the right place.

'And your windows should be a *feature*,' he continues. 'Right now, you just display products in them for customers to come and pick at, but they're not a showcase. You're using them as an extension of your shop space rather than a way to *make* people stop and look.'

Again, I know he's right. Me and Stacey haven't had a clue what to do with the windows, and we've opted for displaying as many products as possible in the hope they catch someone's eye. 'You're really good at this. Thank you.'

Stacey's watching us with both eyebrows looking like they're having a competition between themselves for the World High-Jump record.

'I should go anyway. Again.' He still makes no move to leave.

'Your Santa's not going to Macarena by himself.'

He goes to agree and then rethinks. 'Oh, I don't know, I wouldn't be surprised if he was possessed by some sort of evil spirit.'

'Well, nutcrackers are supposed to guard against evil spirits, aren't they?'

'Oh yeah, I'd forgotten that.' He smiles a nostalgic smile. 'I guess I'll just have to put more out then, won't I? Do you want to pop by later and smash a few up for me?'

I laugh and jokingly threaten to hit him but he steps out of my way too quickly. 'Not that I'd hit someone who'd just bought me plant life.'

'And coffee.' He holds his cardboard cup up in a toast and I knock mine against it and he smiles at me and I smile at him

103

and lose all sense of time again until Stacey plonks her empty cup loudly on the counter.

'I should …' He points towards the door again and takes a few steps towards it this time. 'I'll see you around, right?'

See me around? I'm going to find *every* excuse possible to go over there today. I'm already calculating how long I can reasonably leave it before taking him a cup of tea. 'Definitely.'

'Okay, see you—' He backs into a table with a clunk because his eyes are on mine and not on where he's going, and he goes red again and scurries out, and I can't take my eyes off him as he crosses the lane and has to put his coffee cup down on the window ledge of his shop to dig out his keys and let himself in one-handed.

'Linger much?' Stacey says.

'Do you think so?' I feel myself flittering at the prospect.

'I don't know, but I can't remember the last time you sounded that hopeful about anything.' She leans across me and runs her finger down one glittery edge of a poinsettia leaf. 'He seems really nice, Nee. And he's definitely gorgeous enough to be a magical prince. And he's clearly only got eyes for you, which is more than can be said for any of your last five relationships.'

'It's not like that. He's just a friend. I might even be pushing it to call him that. I've only known him since Monday and he hates Christmas. It's a fundamental part of my life. We're never going to get on.'

'If he'd have lingered any harder, he'd have started singing that song by The Cranberries.'

I burst out laughing at exactly the moment the Santa outside James's shop bursts into life and starts Macarena-ing, and Stacey lets out a loud groan. 'Couldn't you have knocked that over instead of a giant nutcracker? It needs putting out of its misery.'

Within five minutes, as I'm leaning over the till trying to fix a jammed receipt roll, Stacey elbows me sharply and I look up to see James standing there again, thankfully without the Bag

Of Shame this time. He slides another cardboard tray of three takeaway cups onto the counter in front of me and takes one out for himself.

'What are you doing?' I physically can *not* stop smiling at the cheeky glint in his eyes.

'Peppermint-cinnamon hot chocolates. I figured the coffee was enough caffeine for one five-minute period.'

'You didn't have to do that.'

'Trying to pull it back from my first failed assignment.' He grins. 'I've gotta go, I left my shop unattended.'

Instead of going, he puts his cup on the counter, reaches across the till and blindly moves a bit of plastic inside and the till roll I've been struggling with for ten minutes slots instantly into place.

'Brilliant. You're more capable with one hand than I am with two,' I mutter. 'Thanks, James. And for the hot chocolate.'

'You're welcome!' He salutes us both with his cup and hurries back across the lane.

'You passed with merit!' Stacey calls after him as she takes a hot chocolate out of the cardboard holder. She takes a sip and sighs with happiness, and then elbows me excitedly, ensuring I spill hot chocolate all over my hand as I pick up my cup. 'Wow. I love a guy who brings me coffee, but I *love* a guy who brings me hot chocolate. He is seriously a keeper, Nee. That's like the sweetest thing ever. *Who* does that?'

'Him, apparently.' I'm lost in a daydream as I look across the road to the open door of his shop. 'He does that.'

'And you are, like, a *hundred* per cent sure he's *not* a nutcracker come to life? I mean, a prince who was defeated by the mouse king and cursed to spend eternity as a wooden soldier … He's definitely handsome enough to be a prince. And this hot chocolate is delicious enough to suggest some sort of magic in its origin.' She elbows me again before I manage to get the cup up to my mouth and take a sip. 'Coffee, flowers, *and* chocolate. What the hell did you two get up to last night?'

'Nothing!'

'Well, I'm going to set my watch and time how long it takes him to find another excuse to come back. He can't keep away.'

'He came back *once*. With hot chocolates. If you're complaining, I'm sure he won't do it again.'

'It took him half an hour to leave in the first place. And he was losing trade all the time he was in here because his shop was shut.' She shakes her short hair back and sips from her cup again. '*And* he must've seen your nutcracker army last night and he doesn't think you're a weirdo. *Re-sult.*'

'Thanks, Stace,' I say, even though I'm pretty sure he liked them. Quite a lot.

*

'Excuse me?' An elderly woman with grey curly hair and a crocheted shawl around her shoulders appears in the doorway while Stacey's at the counter and I'm on my side of the window display, pulling out the dark green fabric that made up the background so we can start implementing some of James's suggestions. 'I've just bought this over there ...' She holds out a boxed snow-globe containing a mountain scene with miniature polar bears walking around it and gestures towards Twinkles and Trinkets. 'I wanted it gift-wrapped, but that poor chap with the broken arm couldn't manage it. He sent me over here and said he'd settle up with you later?'

'The nerve of—' Stacey splutters.

'Of course, no problem. Come on in,' I say instantly.

Stacey makes a noise of confusion, but I direct the woman to our gift-wrapping station at the back of the shop without hesitation. James is standing in his doorway looking a bit helpless, and I give him a thumbs up to let him know it's no problem. I would gift-wrap ten snowglobes on his behalf just to see the relieved smile he gives me. What am I thinking doing a thumbs up? No one does that beyond the age of five, do they? I should've popped over and given him a Chinese burn to really show my maturity.

I can feel Stacey's eyes burning into me as I follow the woman to the table at the back that contains three rolls of different wrapping paper, some spools of ribbon, and a selection of bows. I'm not the neatest at wrapping things, but you can't run a Christmas shop without offering some form of wrapping service, even if Stacey's having none of it. At least the snowglobe is boxed so it's relatively easy to wrap and she tells me about her grandson who collects them and how she comes to Nutcracker Lane to buy him one each year, reminding me of my own grandma and our nutcracker tradition.

She asks if I remember the inflatable snowglobes that used to be outside. I haven't thought about them in years, but I remember how much I loved them when I was little – they were like a bouncy castle, but covered by a transparent dome, and the bouncy bit was filled with fake snow and there was a wind machine that blew it around so you felt like you were inside a big, bouncy snowglobe. They're another thing on the long list of things that have been cut since the days of my childhood.

She tells me her grandson is expecting a baby of his own and always said he hoped he'd bring his own children here one day to play inside the bouncy snowglobes, and she looks forlorn as she comments about how different things are now.

'He's taking advantage because you owe him for the broken nutcracker,' Stacey says after I walk the lady to the door and wave her off.

'I don't think he is,' I say. 'He couldn't have cared less about it.'

'I know he bought us hot drinks this morning, but he can't send his customers over here for us to wrap *his* goods for him. If he can't do it, he should hire someone who can. He's our competition, Nia. We can't help each other out like this.'

The sadness hits me out of the blue, wiping out how good it felt as that woman picked out her favourite bow and ran her fingers through our ribbon selection to choose the perfect match. She's not wrong. We shouldn't be doing favours for other shops. That's the problem with Nutcracker Lane now. We *can't* care about our co-workers. It's every man for himself. 'I don't mind, Stace. I think it took a lot for him to ask that. He doesn't seem like the type who finds it easy to admit he can't do something.'

'If that woman couldn't have got it gift-wrapped, maybe she'd have reconsidered buying it. He would've lost a sale and you might've *given* him a sale by doing it for him. And now you've done it once, it'll be the first of many – you watch.'

'Is this what we've become?' I'm leaning on my folded arms on the counter opposite Stacey and I bang my head down and press my forehead into them. 'Splitting hairs about a single sale? He needed a favour and I was only too happy to help. Nutcracker Lane shouldn't be trying to stop that, and as it is, quite frankly I'm not even sure I want to work here next year.'

The realisation that *that's* the reality now is enough to make me blink back tears. 'It shouldn't be like this. Doing that reminded me of what Nutcracker Lane used to be like when everyone helped each other and it was about making Christmas the best it could be for everyone who visited here. That's what's missing from the place this year – goodwill and community spirit. This stupid competition and the Scroogey twit who organised it – pitting us all against each other rather than letting us be friends and help each other out … That's where we're going wrong. Do you remember when it was like one big happy family here?'

I stand up straight and push my fringe back. 'We should be happy to gift-wrap his items while he's injured. Do you remember how the jumper shop used to line the florist's poinsettias up along their window display, red and white ones alternating between the jumpers, and now they won't because someone might walk out without buying a jumper but go across to buy a poinsettia at the florist's instead, or how the florist used to dress up floral displays in children's Christmas jumpers and point customers across the lane if they asked about it? What about how Hubert in the sweetshop and Carmen in the chocolate shop used to have free samples of each other's products for customers to try, and the hat shop and jumper shop used to offer each other's customers a discount if they bought things from both of them?

'I saw Rhonda and Mrs Brissett walk past each other yesterday and neither of them even *looked* at each other, and they used to eat lunch together every day. This whole thing is so wrong. There's an atmosphere in the air and customers can sense it. That's going to kill off Nutcracker Lane faster than anything else.'

'Maybe that's what Scrooge is aiming for.'

'It goes against everything Nutcracker Lane has ever stood for. Christmas isn't meant to be about profiteering – it's meant to be about hope, and joy, and family, and saying goodbye to the year that's passed and appreciating the good things in life.'

'What are you going to do about it? Hubert said he'd been trying to get Scrooge on the phone but it just rings out. He's either gone for the year or he's screening us.'

'I don't know, but I'm not the only one who feels like this.' I point towards James's shop. 'Wrapping that snowglobe reminded me of the good parts of Nutcracker Lane that have been forgotten in the last few days. Maybe we just need to remind the others …'

She gives me a look of scepticism, but it's the most hopeful I've felt for a while. Surely we can fight this if we stand together and not divided?

*

Simon is working late so Stacey left at half past three to collect Lily from school, and it's nearly six o'clock before I've finished tidying and cashing up for the night. Since we made some changes to the window displays earlier, there's been an increase in people stopping to look, and it turned into quite a busy afternoon – so busy that I've even managed to stop obsessively watching James's shop and trying to think of reasonable excuses to go over there. I'm out the back putting tomorrow's cash float ready for the morning when there's a knock on the door, and I rush through from the back and across the shop floor to open it.

'I was hoping you'd still be here.'

'My favourite Grinch.' I feel myself light up at the sight of him. The name is supposed to be an insult, but it no longer sounds like one. It might help if I could stop smiling so wide that my face is already aching. He's only been here for half a second, but at least his smile matches mine.

He's leaning on the doorframe with his good shoulder, and as I'm up a step on the shop floor, I'm taller than him for once. A section of his hair has flopped over his forehead and my nails dig into my palms as I clench my fists to stop myself reaching out to tuck it back.

'What do I owe you?'

'What?' I look down at the wallet in his good hand.

'For the gift-wrapping. I said I'd settle up with you later.'

'Oh! God, don't be so daft – you don't owe me anything.'

'No, really, it's your paper, bows, ribbons, and most importantly, your time.' His fingers work to pull a note out of the brown leather wallet and my hand shoots out to stop him, my fingers tingling as they cover his hand.

'Don't you dare. You don't owe me anything, end of story. The world is a really sorry place if people can't help out their broken-armed friends once in a while.'

He raises an eyebrow but I hold his gaze and he eventually looks down at my hand on his. 'I got the impression your friend wasn't happy with me.'

'She's just thinking of the competition between the shop-keepers. She thought you were taking advantage because I owe you for the giant nutcracker.'

'You don't owe me anything. Don't worry about the nutcracker. You've given him a *whole* new lease of life …'

110

He doesn't mean … No, it's not possible. He means because it's being mended, not because it came to life. Probably. I shake my head as my mind wanders off to the story of the ballet and the magical nutcracker prince again.

'So how are you?' My hand is still on his. Why is my hand still on his? Why am I not removing it? 'You look better than you did last night.'

He grins and his cheeks take on a red tinge. 'I've made an effort not to twist my upper body or steal any nutcrackers today, so I'm functional. Marginally.'

The zip of his wallet is sticking into my palm, but his warm skin is under my fingertips and it feels nice to stand here with my hand on his, like a little throwback to yesterday.

'I wanted to see you anyway – I wanted to say thank you again for last night. I was too embarrassed to say much with an audience this morning, but I'm so sorry for the whole thing. Leaning on you, making you hold my hand, making you listen to my business woes … I think there was even singing at one point, wasn't there? And then topping it all off by falling asleep on your sofa … I'm so sorry, Nia. Now you know why I don't take those painkillers in public.'

My hand tightens on his. 'You were fine. You have nothing to be embarrassed about. I'm just glad you're looking better today.'

'Do you have any idea how comfortable your sofa is? I haven't slept properly since the accident, but using the cushions to prop myself upright meant I stayed in one place and didn't put the pressure on my ribs that lying down does. I was so surprised when I woke up and realised I'd had a good night's sleep.'

'Good. No offence, but you looked like you needed it.'

He smiles up at me and I smile down at him and his fingers wriggle out from under my hand so they can curl over the top of mine and hold them tighter. 'Nice jumper choice today, by the way.'

I glance down at my black jumper with a large rainbow-coloured

111

Christmas tree in the centre of it. It's so bright and cheerful that it makes me happy every time I look at it.

'Sorry, you're probably busy. I didn't mean to disturb you. I should go …' He looks vaguely back to the opposite side of the lane but makes no move to let go.

Why isn't this weird? It should be weird, right? Standing here smiling, half-holding hands with someone who's hardly more than a stranger. I didn't get any extra work done last night and I should be going home early and getting some new things cut in my shed so I can paint them when the shop's quiet tomorrow, but I can't make myself push him away.

'Thanks for your advice about the windows,' I say in a burst of inspiration for a way to make him stay a bit longer.

'It looks a lot better.' He moves his hand out from under mine, puts his wallet back in his pocket, and wanders across to my side of the window on the left of the door, and I step out and follow him.

'It's still under construction. Stace had to leave early but we were going to change the whole thing. I thought of making it look like a living room to showcase my decorations with a small tree in the corner and a little wooden fireplace with some painted flames coming out of it, and then putting in miniature manne-quins to look like a family wearing Stacey's jewellery. We're not sure what to do with the other side yet.'

'You need to take out all these awful foil things.'

'They're not—'

He doesn't let me finish the protest. 'They might be nostalgic, but your products are buried by them. Standing here, I can't tell what you make and what's just a decoration you got from the pound shop to make the window look nice. I get that you're trying to make it look festive, but what you're actually doing is hiding your own decorations.'

'Thank you.' I'm taken aback by his honesty, and impressed by his ability to hit the nail on the head. He's right. It's the best feedback we've had since starting this, even though my Nineties-style tinsel lamettas are *not* awful.

'I've got plenty of those little plain wooden nutcrackers if you want some to put in – they'd look quite fetching wearing necklaces and earrings.'

I can't help giggling at the mental image. 'As much as I love the idea of jewellery-wearing nutcrackers, you don't have to do that.'

'It's no problem. The old owner must've bought a whole shipping container of them and the new owner can't have any use for them because he wants the majority shifted before they go for firewood.'

'Firewood?' I say in such horror that it makes him laugh.

'Don't worry, no nutcrackers will die on your watch. I'll bring some over tomorrow. I don't want to keep you any longer tonight.'

'Yeah, I should …' It's my turn to gesture vaguely back towards the door of the shop.

'Yeah, me too.' He sounds as sad as I feel. 'Thanks again for last night. And for the gift-wrapping today.'

I take a step back and he does the same. 'So, I'll see you around then …'

I force myself to drag my eyes away from his and turn away and I hate the sound of his footsteps crossing the lane behind me. I don't want him to go.

'There's a chilli mac and cheese in the slow cooker,' I blurt out.

'About that ending of *Elf*,' he says at the exact same moment.

We both turn around and grin at each other across the lane. 'I made way too much. It'd be a shame for it to go to waste.'

He comes nearer again. 'And how am I ever going to be un-Grinched if I miss the end of *Elf*?'

'Exactly.' I nod sagely. 'So you pretty much *have* to come over again tonight, right?'

He closes his eyes and nods like it's a relief, and I can feel the tension drain from me too. I indicate the shop over my shoulder. 'I just need to finish cashing up. Give me five minutes.'

'I'll get my coat.'

Since I got the keys to the shop, I've not yet left Nutcracker Lane as early as six o'clock, but now I can't get out fast enough. I sort the cash float for the till in record timing, grab my coat and bag, and when I get back onto the shop floor, James has let himself in, dumped a pile of the fifteen-centimetre plain wood nutcrackers on the counter and is arranging some of them in the window display. He holds one up to show me with a pair of Stacey's tiny acrylic candy-cane earrings slid into the white hair on either side of its head and a gingerbread man necklace resting on top of its beard.

'Cross-dressing nutcrackers. What more could you want for Christmas?' I throw my hands out in a shrug.

James is wearing the same baggy black hoody he had on last night. It looks totally out of place with his uptight work outfit of charcoal slacks and a long-sleeved blue check shirt with the tight collar buttons undone, and I get the impression it's probably the easiest thing to shrug on with his arm in plaster.

'You could have a Christmas party in the other window.' He uses the nutcracker in his hand to point to Stacey's side. 'There are so many display stands of jewellery that they look like clutter. If you emptied it out and put up sparkly backing paper, another tree in the corner hung with your decorations, a flashing disco ball or something to attract attention, you could have all these nutcrackers standing around like they're at a party, all wearing a necklace and earrings each. Their plain bodies will make each piece stand out. They can all hold something, so how about miniature wine glasses?' He taps his thumb on the hole in the hand of the one he's holding, meant for a sceptre or sword or some other accessory to go through. 'Make it look like they're at a Christmas party enjoying themselves.'

'Cross-dressing drunken nutcrackers. It just gets better.' I can't help giggling at the thought.

'You want people to remember you.'

114

'I'll make a mini photocopier and have one photocopying his bum. No one will forget that.'

He grins, and when he sees I'm ready to leave, he positions the last nutcracker and darts across to open the door and holds it for me to go through first, only stepping aside to let me lock up behind us.

It's raining outside tonight and nowhere near as cold as it was last night when we start walking up the darkened lane towards the magical nutcracker at the entrance.

James suddenly stops. 'Do you hear that?'

'No, what?'

He doesn't say anything but puts his hand to his ear like he's listening to something. I listen too, but all I can hear is the pattering of rain on the roof above us.

'Nothing. The sound of silence.' He lets out a relieved sigh. 'We've been out here for a whole two minutes and no one's "fa-la-la-ed" at us yet. That's some kind of record.'

'How can you be talking about squiffy nutcracker parties one minute and then be so grumpy the next?' I screw up my nose at him, even though his way of putting things makes me smile. The carol singers have been walking up and down a lot today, cycling through the usual repertoire of songs like "We Wish You A Merry Christmas", "The First Noel", and "Silver Bells", and while I never get tired of it, the same can't be said for him. 'Your Grinching would be much more reasonable if we *weren't* on our way to watch Christmas films.'

He looks over and slowly raises an eyebrow. 'Films?'

'Well, I don't know how far into *Elf* you dropped off, but there can't be more than half an hour left, and it's barely six o'clock. That gives us plenty of time to expand your Christmas film horizon. Which ones have you seen?'

'Christmas films?' He makes a face. 'None of 'em.'

'Oh, come on. *National Lampoon's Christmas Vacation*? That's the best Christmas film ever.'

115

He shakes his head.

'*The Santa Clause*?'

'Nope.'

'*It's a Wonderful Life*?'

'I saw a bit of it years ago. Doesn't it go on forever? I think I died of boredom halfway through. I imagine "death by *It's a Wonderful Life*" is a common cause listed on death certificates.'

I glare at him for insulting one of the best Christmas films ever made. 'How about *The Muppet Christmas Carol*?'

'Muppets?' He screws his face up. 'I'm an adult.'

'The Muppets are not just for children. *The Muppet Christmas Carol* is one hundred per cent the definitive version of that story. The original Dickens pales in comparison to the Muppet version.'

His eyebrows knit together so hard that he might need a seam picker to untangle them.

'*Home Alone*? *Die Hard*?' I try again.

'I've seen *Die Hard*.'

'Good, because it's *not* a Christmas movie, no matter what anyone says,' I say as we walk up the darkened lane, past the silent windows of the bakery displaying gingerbread houses and cupcake wreaths, and the soap and bath bomb shop that sells Santa-shaped soaps, tiny holly-leaf bath pearls, and fizzing bath bombs modelled to look like snowmen and reindeer and Christmas puddings that smell as gorgeously festive as they look and leave you sparkling with glitter afterwards.

'I need to get out of the shop more often,' I say. 'I haven't bought a new jumper yet this year, or a new headband, or even any new socks. I buy a new pair of Christmas socks every year. My goal is to have twenty-five pairs – one a day from the 1st until the 25th.'

'Like some sort of weird sock advent calendar?'

'Exact— Flipping heck, I forgot to open my advent calendar this morning. What *is* wrong with me? Day three and I've already forgotten chocolate before breakfast.' I don't mention quite how distracted I was this morning, or that I was so eager to get in and see him that it even stopped me thinking about chocolate.

'*You* have an advent calendar?'

'Of course. Don't you?'

He laughs and clutches his ribs, his face slowly falling when I don't laugh with him. 'Do I look particularly young or something? I'm thirty-seven and I have to constantly remind you that I'm not a child. I've never had an advent calendar; I'm certainly not about to start now.'

'You've *never* had an advent calendar?'

He shakes his head, looking at me like *I'm* the weird one here. 'What's the point?'

'It's chocolate. Every morning before breakfast. Surely even *you* can see the upside of that?'

He shrugs. 'I barely function before breakfast. I don't have the coordination to get a little chocolate out of a fiddly cardboard door. At that time of day, all I want is coffee. If by some madness I wanted chocolate, I'd go to the kitchen cupboard and break a piece off one of the bars there.'

'You're missing the point. It's fun, it's a countdown to Christmas, and it's basically enforced chocolate.' I shake my head at his blank look. 'First thing tomorrow morning, I'm buying you an advent calendar. It'll only be the 4th – it's not too late. The Nutcracker Lane chocolate shop does some amazing ones.'

'I don't want—'

'Don't finish that sentence.' I point a threatening finger towards him. 'Even *you* are not so much of a Grinch that you can't appreciate chocolate for breakfast. And if you are then there's absolutely no hope for you.'

We round the bend in the lane and the giant wish-granting nutcracker comes into view.

'I don't mind nutcrackers, you know.'

I do a mock gasp and give him my best flabbergasted look. 'Did you just say there's something about Christmas you actually *like*?'

'I wouldn't go that far, but my dad used to read me the book when I was little, and apparently we had one that I used to carry around like a doll and I'd never let my mum put it away after Christmas.' He looks up at the eight-foot-tall carved nutcracker looming over us as we approach the fence and garden area surrounding him. 'I always thought it was hilarious how people used to make wishes on this thing though. They honestly believed it was magical. Thankfully I was never young enough to believe in that nonsense.'

'What?' I ask. How can anyone ever not be young enough to believe in magic? Unless he really is a nutcracker prince who magically appeared into life a couple of days ago.

'You know what I mean. My parents were always honest with me. I never believed in Santa, and when we visited here, they'd point out the wish-granters dressed as elves who were strategically positioned to listen in on wishes made at the giant nutcracker.'

'You never believed in Santa?'

He shakes his head. 'I don't believe in lying to children. Neither did my parents.'

'… lying to children,' I repeat in disbelief. 'It's not lying to help a child believe in Christmas magic. That's something people remember for the rest of their lives. Anyone, at *any* age, should look up to the sky on Christmas Eve night and hope they'll see something magical.'

'Again.' He points to himself. 'Adult.'

I roll my eyes. 'That makes you need to believe in Christmas magic even more. With all the stresses and worries and strains of adulthood, we need it *more* than kids do. We need to believe that our dreams can still come true and that anything can happen at this time of year.'

'And your wishes all came true, did they?'

'Sometimes. Our family got my childhood dog because I wished for one here. Obviously I now know that one of the elves took my dad aside and talked about the benefits of having a dog

118

and about how many dogs there are in rescue centres who need homes, gave him a free adoption voucher, and a few days later, we went to choose our dog. A little Jack Russell called Dasher who was with us for fifteen years. At the time, I thought she was a Christmas miracle, but I'd never have persuaded my mum and dad on my own. My mum's too uptight and doesn't like anything that makes a mess and my dad was always working, but that wish-granting elf tugged at his heartstrings and convinced him I was old enough to take on the responsibility.

'There was other stuff too. I wished for a special day for my gran and granddad before he died and they took them on the most magical sleigh ride. One of those big walk-and-talk dolls that were sold out worldwide. It was never about stuff though, I think they gave my parents that to put under the tree as a way of teaching me that Christmas wasn't about material things because it broke down on Boxing Day and I preferred the crafting kit my grandma and granddad had put together for me anyway.'

I wait for him to say something belittling but he doesn't. We've both stopped at the towering nutcracker and are looking up at it, my left hand next to his right hand on the fence, so close it would be easy to reach my little finger out and touch the side of his hand. I look up at the nutcracker to distract myself. 'I wish I knew what the story behind him is. I was intending to ask the old owners when I saw them this year, but they haven't been around.'

James is grinning as he pushes himself off the fence, goes inside the open gateway, and somehow manages to negotiate the walnut vending machine with just one hand. He comes back and holds a walnut out to me between thumb and forefinger. 'Here. You can't say you wish something in front of him without cracking a nut.'

I take it from him even though I'm not sure if he's humouring me or making fun of me, but I can feel his eyes on me as I go inside the fence and stand on the lowest step to reach up to the nutcracker's mouth, place the walnut in it, and lean around to pull the lever down. 'I wish I knew the story behind you,' I say aloud as the shell starts to splinter, but no wind whispers in his beard tonight and the rainclouds above us block out any prospect of stars twinkling.

'He was carved in the 1930s by a local artist, and you know how nutcrackers are said to be lucky and are supposed to protect the homes they're in? He was moved around a lot and eventually mounted on a church near here in 1940, and when the area was bombed during the war, that church was the only building that survived, and people thought he'd somehow protected it and started visiting him for good luck.'

I'm still standing on the step and I turn around in surprise. 'You know it?'

'See? Wishes can come true.' He holds his one hand out like he's shrugging. 'After that, he disappeared. Some say he was stolen, some say the artist took him back and hid him where he could never be found, some say that so many people thought he was lucky that they came to touch him and simply wore him down to nothing.' He nods towards it. 'That one's obviously not true.'

I collect my walnut from the nutcracker's mouth and step down onto the floor. James continues as I go back out the gate. 'Years and years later, somewhere around the 1970s, an antique dealer came across him in a collection he'd gone to appraise up in the Scottish borders, recognised him and came back here with the story, and there was a big local campaign to raise enough money to buy him back and transport him home, and the whole county got involved in fundraising, and just as they'd nearly reached their goal, he went missing again.'

I hold out the cracked walnut shell to offer him half of the nut, and I can't tear my eyes away from him as he takes it and pops it into his mouth. 'You are full of surprises.'

'I'm full of something.' He holds the walnut between his teeth and grins around it.

I take my half and throw the empty shell onto the garden, glad to see how many shells have piled up there since my last wish.

People are still coming. They're still cracking nuts and believing he can grant wishes. Not *all* people have given up hope that something magical can happen.

'Two years later, he was left right here leaning against the door of the nutcracker factory. It was founded in the 1930s and it's said his creator used to work here.' James points towards the entranceway. 'No one ever found out where he came from or who put him there. The factory was the only thing that was unchanged in the forty years since he was made, so the popular theory was that he walked by himself and found his way home.'

I feel myself inexplicably welling up and have to blink furiously to stop tears forming. While I doubt the giant wooden nutcracker uprooted himself and walked his way home, it's such a nice thought, and just the kind of magical feeling I was hoping would be in the story behind him. 'How on earth do you know all that?'

'It was the interest in the story of his return that prompted the factory to expand into the commercial side of things and Nutcracker Lane was opened in the early Eighties. My grandparents were around in the Forties when it all happened, so my parents grew up hearing it, and then they were around in the Seventies when he returned, so it was passed down to me as well. They've still got newspaper clippings from the time. I'll see if I can find them next time I go there.'

Something in his voice changes whenever he mentions his parents, and I'm as desperate to ask about them as I am certain that he wouldn't answer. 'My dad knew,' I say instead. 'He used to tell me about it but I was too young to remember, and my mum doesn't go in for "fairy stories" so she didn't know. He died when I was young and I've always wished I could remember his stories. Thank you for that.'

'You're welcome.' His little finger reaches towards mine like he's going to touch my hand but he pulls back and pushes himself upright instead, his hand trailing along the fence tops as he puts a bit of space between us.

121

'So community spirit saved the nutcracker once,' I say as cogs start turning in my mind. 'That's magic in itself. It's a shame we can't get people to care that much again.'

'Well, it *is* Christmas. A certain someone keeps telling me anything can happen at this time of year.'

His maple-coloured eyes are twinkling, showing up flecks of green in them that I'd never noticed before, and I know he's only humouring me, but he's got a point. Anything can happen at Christmas, even the impossible.

Chapter 6

'You cannot seriously be getting me an advent calendar,' James says when I meet him in the middle of the lane between our shops the next morning.

'Yep. No arguments. And I peeked into the chocolate shop this morning. They're all half price now we're four days into December. Come on.'

'Nee ...' he starts as he follows me up the lane. It's not even half past nine yet and it's still quiet. There's a bit of chatter filtering down from around the nutcracker but not a single customer has wandered down this far yet. 'I enjoyed last night. I can't believe you made me sit through the whole of *It's a Wonderful Life* without falling asleep ... or that I didn't *completely* hate it.'

'I've got a pie ready to go in the oven when I get home tonight,' I say before I have a chance to second-guess it.

'You seriously want me there again?'

'We've got a ton of Christmas movies to get through. We've come this far, we can't give up now. It's non-negotiable that you still have to watch at least *The Muppet Christmas Carol*, *Christmas Vacation*, *The Santa Clause*, and the Jim Carrey version of *The Grinch*. And that pie is *massive* – I can't eat it all myself. And I promise tonight we'll watch something with an ending that won't make you cry.'

When I look at him, his mouth is twitching as he tries not to smile. 'I wasn't crying. There was something in my eye.'

I giggle because I teased him mercilessly last night too. He deserved it after his disparaging comments about one of the best-loved Christmas films of all time.

Mrs Thwaite in the candle shop is rearranging her window and she looks up and gives us a dirty look. I slip my hand around his wrist and tug him onwards, wondering why it feels so natural to touch him. His fingers start to curl around mine and I let go quickly, because it would be so easy to intertwine our fingers and walk up to the chocolate shop hand-in-hand, but it's not right. I barely know him.

I woke up early this morning because I couldn't stop thinking about him, and I occupied the hours between getting up and leaving for work with making a butternut squash and baked camembert pie that I was hoping he'd like because I want nothing more than for him to come over again tonight. Five days ago, I'd sworn off men forever, and now he's appeared and smashed through my defences with one smile, I can't hold his hand as well. The other night in the storage room was different. He needed it then. Now I just want to hold it because his hands are elegant and long-fingered and he's surprisingly adept with just one functioning.

The window of the chocolate shop log cabin is almost always surrounded by children pressing their noses against it and cupping their hands around their eyes to stare in without reflections. It's empty today, and James is the one who stops to stare in longingly. 'Do I walk around with my eyes shut or something?' he murmurs. 'Why have I never looked in here before? Have you seen that sleigh? How can *anyone* do that with chocolate? This woman is insanely talented.'

'This woman is going to lose her shop like the rest of us,' I mutter. Carmen the chocolate maker has been a staple of Nutcracker Lane for more years than I can remember. My granddad used to buy us all a selection box of her chocolates when I was young, and it was one of my grandma's favourite shops on the lane. Carmen changes her display every week and it gets more magical each time, from families of chocolate snowmen, to a North Pole workshop manned by chocolate elves with moving piles of presents, to today's creation of white chocolate reindeers pulling a ruby chocolate sleigh on an actual track that judderingly transports them from one side of the window to the other.

I'm standing in the doorway waiting and I touch James's left shoulder with the gentlest touch I've ever used because I have no idea how far his bruising extends. He looks up, blinking like he was lost in his own little world.

'Magical, right?'

He swallows hard and gives me a tight nod, and his Flynn Rider hair falls forward to frame his face.

'Come to survey the competition?' Carmen sounds angry and unwelcoming when we step inside the shop.

'Of course not.' I'm taken aback by the venom in her voice. 'Come to buy my chocolateless friend here an advent calendar.'

'Back wall. Half price. Don't *touch* anything. If you ruin it, you pay for it.' Carmen is barely tall enough to see over her own counter, but she folds her arms across her chest, her strawberry-blonde hair pulled up into a high ponytail that makes her look more severe than usual.

James and I share a look. Never have I felt unwelcome in a shop on Nutcracker Lane before. I try to ignore it but the tone in her voice prickles at me as James follows me up to the back wall, and I'm all too aware of her eyes burning into us.

There aren't many advent calendars left and they're all down to £4 now instead of £8, and James picks out one with an idealistic-looking cottage on it, and we start wandering back towards the counter. I want to look around and see if there's something else I can treat us to, but Carmen hasn't taken her eyes off us and I get the feeling that a boiling hot oven on legs would be a more welcome guest.

'Just this, please.' I give her my brightest smile as James puts the advent calendar on the counter and I get my purse out to pay.

'No.'

'No?'

'You're not meant to be buying from me. We're in direct competition with each other. I can't take your money.'

'That's ridiculous.'

'It wouldn't be right, Nia. We're competitors now.'

'Yeah, but I'm not.' James gets his wallet out and deposits four pound coins onto the counter. 'She was just trying to do something nice for me, but I'm not involved in this competition, so I can give you mine instead.'

'That wouldn't be fair on her.' She nods towards me.

James rolls his eyes. 'I'll buy something of equal value in her shop to even it out, okay?'

Carmen looks dubious.

'A whole four pounds is not going to swing this thing far, is it?' he says. 'For God's sake, I'm throwing money at you. Take it. I promise I'll go and buy something from Nia's now.'

She reluctantly covers the coins with her hand and pulls them across the counter, stabs some numbers into the till and puts them in. She rips off the receipt it prints out and hands it to him without a word.

'Can I have a bag, please?' He digs out an extra 5p coin and hands it to her. 'Because I'm an adult and I don't want to be seen carrying around an advent calendar.'

'Only people who are insecure in their adulthood worry about things like that,' I say.

Carmen laughs and quickly straightens her face as she puts it in a Nutcracker Lane branded paper bag. 'This is a one-off. Don't come back here again, either of you. If you weren't my first customers today, I'd have refused you both.'

I bite my lip. The anger and hurt on her face are plain to see, and it confirms my fears that the whole lane *is* as quiet as it looks.

126

'You're worse than Hubert. He's always coming in here, pretending to be friendly, "accidentally" knocking over my display unit and damaging my stock. Underhanded tactics, I tell you.'

'Hubert did that?' I say in surprise. Hubert is the most lovable bumbling buffoon you could ever meet, like a cross between Santa and Mr Bean. He's unnaturally clumsy and spends most of his days chasing dropped humbugs across his sweetshop floor.

'He *said* it was an accident but things are never an accident when you're in direct competition. It's me or him, Nia.'

'I thought you liked him. You always used to have samples of each other's treats to inspire shared custom. You're always together. You *like* each other.'

'I'm going to lose my shop if he earns more money than me! There is no room for liking people on Nutcracker Lane now!'

To my horror, her voice breaks and tears form in her eyes. 'It's oka—' I try to comfort her, but she turns away.

'Get out!' she yells at the wall behind her. 'Both of you, get out now!'

James's hand slots around mine, the bag containing his advent calendar dangling between us as he pulls me out of the shop.

'Well, that was horrible,' I say, feeling close to tears myself. 'I've never seen Carmen without a smile on her face before. I didn't mean to make her cry.'

James looks shaken too as I extract my hand from his.

'This is so wrong. How could that rotten accountant do this to us? Pitting friends against friends and turning everyone against each other? And I know poor old Hubert – there's no way he did that on purpose. There's always been rumours of a secret couple on Nutcracker Lane and I would've put money on it being those two. And now look at them. She's obviously hurting and he's probably devastated at making her think he'd do that.'

He twists his fingers around the handle of the paper bag, looking like he'd be wringing his hands together if he had both available. 'I suspect it was something that sounded better on paper, but if your Scrooge saw the actual impact of his actions, he'd probably reconsider.'

'I don't think the heartless wanker would give a monkey's.' I practically spit the words out. 'Has the merciless skunk ever even set foot in the place? Or does he just sit behind his fancy desk juggling his money? Even on paper, *no one* could think this was a good idea.'

'On the plus side, at least Carmen wasn't unscrupulous enough to take your money. That was honourable, wanting to be fair and all that.'

'Yeah, but she used to be a friend. She was watching us like we were a pair of shoplifters. The shopkeepers here have always supported each other, and now I can't even buy something from one of the others. The best part about getting a shop here this year was finally getting to work with people I've called friends for years. I send Carmen a Christmas card every year and she could barely look at me.'

I'm stomping down the honey-coloured paving stones like they've come loose and I'm trying to stamp them back into place, and he reaches out and catches hold of my hand and pulls me back, wrapping his good arm around me and pulling me into his side.

'I'm sorry, Nee,' he murmurs, his lips so close to my forehead that I can feel every word.

His arm around me, and knowing he's probably hurting and holding an angry woman at this proximity to broken ribs and God knows how much bruising, is enough to make the fight drain out of me.

The advent calendar in the bag bangs against my arm as his fingers curl around my shoulder and he pulls me just a little bit tighter. I rest my head against the good side of his chest and reach up to give his left shoulder another gentle pat as I let out a long breath, trying not to think about how much I love that he trusts me not to hurt him.

When I've lingered in his embrace for longer than strictly reasonable, I reluctantly pull away and mouth a 'thank you' at him.

'We have to do something,' I say. 'We have to fight this. Nutcracker Lane can't end this way. And it can't be impossible. Even the real Scrooge changed his ways by the end of *A Christmas Carol.*'

'Do you know a few ghosts?' James gives me a wink.

It makes me smile, but it also makes me start thinking. The ghosts *showed* Scrooge that things hadn't always been the way they were and there was still time to change. If we could show our version that Nutcracker Lane is worth saving, maybe it would help. Maybe if he saw the place and met the people here, he'd realise that his "on paper" idea is terrible in practice. I just need to find him. His letters give no clue about an address for the office, and the contact number is still ringing out unanswered according to Hubert who's been trying it daily.

James follows me into Starlight Rainbows, waving a fiver at Stacey who's behind the counter having just served a woman buying one of my red-and-white striped North Pole signposts who ducks out as we enter. 'Four quid of your finest Christmas gear, please.'

'Take your pick.' I gesture to the shop, unable to take my eyes off him as he starts wandering around.

'I like what you did with the windows.' He nods towards the living-room scene in one and the nutcracker Christmas party in the other that Stacey and I finished this morning.

'Thanks for the advice. They're much better.'

Instead of looking at our products, he points upwards. 'What wattage are your lightbulbs?'

'They're not for sale.' Stacey's clearly confused by the question.

He laughs. 'I was trying to say they're not bright enough.'

'Are you buying something or appraising us?' I ask.

'I'm not being horrible.' He comes over to stand next to me. 'I said I'd help with your shop and I am. It's too dark in here.'

'We have Christmas lights.'

'Exactly. It looks pretty but you can't actually see anything.' He points out a customer who has picked up a sparkly wrapped present necklace and stepped back to tilt it under one of the main lights.

I meet Stacey's eyes and we both make the same face. He's got a point. Maybe we have gone a bit far in the "cosy Christmas evening" direction.

'We'll bear that in mind,' I say, unwilling to admit I'm going to dash down to the storeroom when he leaves and find brighter bulbs. 'Anything catch your eye yet?'

'Will you choose something for me? I'd prefer it if it came from you. Your choice of whatever Christmassy thing I desperately need in my life.'

I grin as I start wandering around the shop, trailing my hand over the festive fabric tablecloths covering our display tables. My eyes fall on the *perfect* thing. Stacey sells gorgeous, dainty, pretty festive jewellery, but we also have a few novelty bits, because Christmas is a time for garish, light-flashing, chunky plastic pieces that you can see coming halfway down the street. I hold it up so Stacey can see what I've bought and she rings it up on the till and gives James his change.

I tear the packet open and pull the tab out of the battery box and unwind it in my hands as I approach him.

'What is that? Why do you look so … gleeful? That look can only mean one thing – that you're about to do something horrible to me.'

'You've got a six-foot-tall Santa doing the Macarena all day, every day. You deserve everything you get,' Stacey tells him.

I hold up the necklace at full width ready to slip over his head. It's a string of plastic candle-shaped bulbs in red, green, blue, and yellow, that flash in different patterns. *Exactly* the thing someone who hates Christmas would be overjoyed to wear.

'That's not a necklace, those are the lights that are wound round your garden fence.'

130

'In wearable form.' I gesture for him to lower his head, and am quite surprised when he does. I push myself up on tiptoes and slip it over his head, my fingers accidentally catching his strokable dark hair before I step back to admire my work.

'I hate you.'

'I know you do.' I give him my most self-satisfied grin.

'Until now, I've thought you were the loveliest person I've ever met, but my opinion has done a total one-eighty-degree turn – you know that, don't you?' He's trying his absolute hardest not to smile as he says it, but his mouth keeps tipping up.

'I know,' I repeat.

'Good.'

'Good.' I reach up over his shoulder to get to the battery pack at the back of his neck, my fingers brushing the dusting of fine hairs there, which stand on end at my touch and I can feel the goose bumps rising in their wake, until my thumbnail finally finds the on-off switch and I flick it and step back as the necklace flashes each colour of bulb alternately.

James groans as he looks down at himself, and I reach out and straighten it over the sling. 'And, as a bonus, it can help with road safety. I bet that car would've noticed you if you'd been wearing this.'

'It probably would've veered off to the side and crashed due to being blinded by the flashing lights.'

'You can say what you want, but you're not getting out of wearing it, Grinch.' I grin at him and he grins at me and I know he's trying to be annoyed but it's just not working.

'Just so you know, I have *never* worn something that flashes before. You must have magical powers to talk me into this.'

'It'll be a Christmas jumper next.' I pull my own jumper down, this one navy with snowflakes and a large polar bear wearing a blue fluffy scarf on it.

He goes to protest but Stacey clears her throat and points to one of my plywood cut and hand-painted bunches of mistletoe,

131

something I'd thought the stems would be too flimsy to cut but seems to have worked so far and has had lots of comments from customers. 'That could be termed "standing under the mistletoe".'

I give her a look because it's on the wall behind his head and there's no way it counts. He turns around and looks too and then laughs because he's a good few feet from it, and instead of stepping further away like I thought he would, he sidesteps until he's standing next to it and beckons me closer.

I'm blushing furiously as I go over. Thank God I didn't choose a red jumper today because I'd be completely camouflaged.

The advent calendar bag is still hooked over his little finger as he holds his hand out, inviting me to slot mine into it.

His eyes don't leave mine as his fingers fold around my fingers and he lifts my hand to his mouth, like a prince would greet a princess, and his lips press gently against the back of it. Heat flares from my hand outwards, his stubble sending sparks zinging across my skin, followed by a trail of goose bumps, and the most delicious shiver goes down my spine.

How can he have that much of an effect on me with one innocent touch? Well, maybe not *quite* so innocent, judging by the twinkle in his eyes when he pulls back.

He's smirking like he knows exactly what he's done to me. 'I figured that was the most I could get away with considering the position of the mistletoe. Solely to say thank you for the advent calendar, obviously.'

After lingering for an absurd amount of time, my fingers finally slip from his, his thumb closing over them to hang on for every moment longer, and everything feels faraway and hazy, even the carol singers on one of their trips up the lane, singing "This Christmas" by Brian Alex, a beautiful, haunting melody about Christmas wishes.

'And on that note, I should probably open up.' At least his cheeks have gone as red as mine must be, judging by the pulsing heat I can feel pumping from them. He backs out of the shop without dropping my gaze until he nearly falls down the step and quickly grabs the doorframe to stay upright.

'You bought your own advent calendar!' I call after him when I come to my senses. He stops in the middle of the lane and turns around to wink at me.

When he's disappeared inside his shop, I sort of collapse against the counter and look up at Stacey who's fanning a hand in front of her face.

'Never mind a nutcracker prince, you *are* sure he's not actually Flynn Rider in real life, right?' She looks across the lane as the Santa starts up his Macarena dancing. 'Because he seems more and more like he belongs in a Disney movie every time I see him.'

'Maybe that's the problem.' I push myself upright. 'Either he *is* a magical answer to a wish I made on the nutcracker, or there's something wrong with him that hasn't come to light yet, because men like *that* don't exist in my life. He's single, he's gorgeous, he's sweet, charming, and chivalrous, and so far his only flaw is that he hates Christmas. And he's here because he *wants* to find some Christmas spirit … So what's wrong with him, Stace?'

'Do broken bones count as a character flaw?'

I laugh. 'No. And that means there's got to be a catch somewhere else.'

'Or maybe it means that you've dated your fair share of complete prats and now the universe has finally thrown you into the path of Prince Charming.'

I give her such a sceptical look that she giggles. 'Or maybe he is a wooden doll come to life. Maybe he *is* going to turn back into a nutcracker on Christmas Day and you'll wake up and this will all have been a dream.'

'Maybe,' I say, but from what I know of men and dating, it's a far more likely scenario than James actually being as perfect as he seems.

133

Chapter 7

It's a couple of days later as I lug my granddad's old hand truck trolley up the hill to work. Lily's got a parents' assembly in school this morning so Stacey won't be in until later, and it feels odd and lonely to be walking to work on my own. I hadn't realised how much I'd got used to not being alone. James was visiting his parents last night and I missed him a truly *ridiculous* amount for my seventh day of knowing him.

I hadn't realised how lonely I was until now. Even though I've dated, it never felt any less lonely. None of those men have ever come to my house. Never eaten my food. Never watched movies with me. I've realised how much I tend to put off going home, and how much I work in my shed with Christmas music playing from my phone to drown out the silence, and how nice it's been to go home with James, and how warm and cosy and Christmassy it's felt to sit in the living room with him, get the log fire going, and a bowl of something hearty and warming and a Christmas film on the TV, even without the tree up. I can't believe it's already the 7th and I haven't got one yet.

The folding trolley to transport the tree home tonight clonk-bonks along the pavement behind me, and as I reach the top of the hill and go to cross the shrub border surrounding the car park, James's car pulls into his usual space under the lamppost. I can't help the smile that breaks across my face. It's a foggy grey morning but seeing his matching smile through the windscreen makes it feel like the sun has burst through the clouds.

He turns the engine off and opens the door. 'I was hoping to catch you,' he says before I've reached him.

I put my hand on the open car door and peek around the edge at him. 'I missed you last ni—You're wearing a Christmas jumper!'

He grins. 'Thought you'd like it.'

'Where did you find that? It's *perfect* for you.' I can't tear my eyes away from the giant green face of the Grinch on the front of the black jumper.

I don't miss how difficult it is for him to get out of the car. Every movement is slow and considered as he turns in the driver's seat and inches each leg out before using the door to haul himself upright without twisting his upper body.

'Mrs Brissett at the jumper shop.' He's speaking through gritted teeth and holding on to the car roof to steady himself.

It makes me realise how much pain he must be in and how much he usually covers it. Since the night in the storage room, apart from the odd wince or intake of breath, you'd never know there was anything wrong, and my nails make crescent-shaped indents in my palms as I hold back from how much I want to put my hand on his back and just sort of rub. His arm is out of its sling for driving and the white plaster of his cast stands starkly against the black sleeve of the jumper that's pulled up to his elbow.

'And now I wish I'd been five minutes earlier so you didn't have to see how long it takes me to negotiate something as simple as getting out of a car. I'm not usually like this, I swear.'

'You're hurt, James,' I start, but all the moving has pulled his jumper skew-whiff and as he reaches one arm back and tries to pull it straight, I catch sight of the bare skin underneath. 'Holy hell, you're black and blue.'

The trolley clatters onto the pavement as I drop it and leap

135

forwards to stop him pulling the jumper down. I cover his hand with mine and roll the knitted material and the plain T-shirt underneath it back up again, sucking in air through my teeth as I uncover more and more skin of his left side, from hip to as far as I can go without risking pulling near his ribs.

'Nia, don't, please. It's just bruising – it happens when you're hit by a car.'

'Have you had this checked out?' His whole left side is an angry mottle of black, blue, and purple in more shades than you'd see on a standard colour chart, with yellowy-green edges that extend under the waistband of his jeans and further around his chest than I can see.

'Of course. They said I'd be bruised and it'd take a few days to come out and a couple of months to properly heal. It looks worse than it is, Nee. They're just bruises; it only hurts when I press them. Don't look, please. At some point in the future, I wouldn't mind if you found me attractive, and seeing my battered body is not going to help matters.'

So many things spring to mind – that he's the most gorgeous man I've ever met and a few bruises don't make any difference to that, how bruises that severe are not the kind that only hurt when you press them – bruises like that spread through your entire body and hurt with every step – and mainly, how much I wish I could reach my fingers out and trail them across his bare hip, but that would be asking for too much trust from someone I barely know, not to mention crossing God knows how many lines.

I also realise that even though it's warmer today with the low-lying fog and threatening rain clouds, it's still a December morning and he's standing in the car park with half his torso exposed and the cold air is undoubtedly not doing the bruising any good. I quickly tug the T-shirt and jumper back into place and step away, but all my good intentions fly away as he straightens up and turns around, pain visible in every taut line of his face.

Without thinking, I throw my arms around his neck. Well,

with enough thinking to be careful of not hurting him. I reach up and pull his head down to my shoulder, my hand sliding around the back of his neck and my fingers carding through the thick hair there. My other arm wraps around his good shoulder and tightens as much as it can without being painful. I half-expect him to shove me away, but his right arm curls around my back, his hand tangling in the hair hanging over my shoulders and sort of gathering it up and pulling it aside, and even his broken arm slides behind me, the elbow above the cast pressing into my back.

'What are you doing?'

'I don't know.' All I know is that I'm nearly in tears at the sight of his bruised body and the thought of seeing that and *not* hugging him was unthinkable.

'I don't either, but feel free to keep doing it.'

My arm gets impossibly tighter around his shoulders and my fingers curl into the thick strands of hair at the back of his neck, so dark it's almost the same colour as the black lamppost beside us, and uneven enough to feel like it's growing out of the neat cut it was once in. All I can think about is what he said in the storage room the other night about being alone and in shock, and I want to hug him hard enough to retroactively erase those memories.

'Call them knots in my woodgrain,' he murmurs into my ear.

He's still talking about the bruises, I *know* that, but it's another reminder of the nutcracker and I stiffen in his embrace, even though thinking of bruises as temporary knots in woodgrain is a nice sentiment. 'Is this hurting you?'

'Absolute agony but worth every second.' I can hear the smile in his voice and the way his arms tighten makes me smile too.

I could happily stay here and hug him for a good few hours yet, but I force myself to let go and take a step back, wondering if the half-dazed half-confused look on his face matches the one on mine.

'Just so you know, I've never started my workday with a cuddle in the car park before.'

'That's the power of Christmas jumpers.' I reach out and touch the furry green face of the giant Grinch head on the front of his jumper, being careful to stick to the right side of his chest.

Why can't I take my hands off him? What is it about him that makes me want to be close? I've just inappropriately hugged him and now I'm rubbing his chest, and I *still* can't make myself step away.

The jumper is knitted in black and has a huge face of the Grinch in the centre, made from green fur and wearing a Santa hat with a 3D bobble. 'See? There's a Christmas jumper out there for everyone – even you, Grinch.'

He grins at the nickname. What started off as an insult has become a term of endearment.

'What's with the trolley?' He nods towards the blue metal contraption forgotten on the pavement.

'I'm getting my tree tonight. My grandparents always used to get their tree from here. The seller collects them from a little Christmas tree farm in Scotland and drives down twice a week with a new batch straight from the farm. They have a small selection but they're always personally chosen from the absolute top-quality stock.' I nod towards the tiny tree lot at the end of Nutcracker Lane where a truck is backed in and the tree seller and driver are unloading netted trees.

'Can I borrow that? I've got some stuff for you and that will really help with carrying it in.'

'What stuff?'

He beckons me to follow him to the boot of his car and opens it. 'Shelving for the shop.'

His boot is completely stacked with narrow wooden boards, and I can see a toolkit on the back seat.

'I haven't fulfilled my end of the bargain yet to help you improve your shop. I was thinking about it last night. Can I be brutally honest?' He continues when I nod. 'In the nicest way possible, it looks like a jumble sale. All the tables and rifling

138

through baskets makes it feel like a craft fair, not the professional retail shop that customers are expecting. You don't have enough shelf space. I was at my parents' last night and I remembered that their garage was full of all this old pallet shelving I made when I was younger. I thought you might want it in the shop to get rid of some of those tables and display things properly ... if you'll help me put it together. My mum had to help me dismantle it to get it in the car. Furniture doesn't exactly mix with one functioning arm.'

I reach out and run my fingers over one of the smooth wooden boards. 'This is beautiful. These are all old delivery pallets?'

He nods.

'And you made these into shelving?'

'Many years ago,' he says before I can look too impressed. 'Three units here, more in my mum and dad's garage. I couldn't carry any more last night.'

I raise an eyebrow. 'You're not supposed to be lifting anything heavy.'

His eyebrows furrow in confusion.

'I googled broken ribs,' I explain. 'You're supposed to be taking it easy. I wanted to make sure you're looking after yourself.'

'I can't believe you googled broken ribs for me.' He ducks his head and his cheeks redden, and then he looks up and mouths 'thank you' so quietly that no words come out. He reaches out and takes my hand and just holds it for a long minute, his thumb brushing back and forth softly across my fingers, so gentle that my breath catches in my throat and my knees start shaking. I can't help wondering what it would be like if we didn't let go. If we crossed this car park and walked into Nutcracker Lane hand-in-hand.

'I'm sorry.' James jumps and drops my hand abruptly. 'I'm losing track of time here. What do you think?'

It takes me an embarrassingly long time to realise he's talking about the shelving. 'Oh! Yeah, these are amazing. I'd love them.

139

Thanks. And you're right, I know you are.' I once again appreciate his honesty. Stacey and I know the shop isn't brilliant, but neither of us have known how to fix it.

He turns around and ducks into the car to retrieve his sling from the seat and slams the door shut behind him, and I go over to pick up the folded transporter trolley. 'I'm glad I caught you actually. I have a favour to ask. You know those nutcrackers you said the owner had a shipping container to get rid of? Could I have some more of them?'

'Sure. As many as you want.'

'How many does a shipping container contain?'

'I don't know. I'd have to check the stock records for an exact amount, but I'd guess around ten thousand.'

'That's brilliant!'

He laughs and quickly stops himself when he sees I'm serious. 'You want ten *thousand* nutcrackers?'

'Well, no, we should probably pace ourselves with a thousand or so to start with. Here, look.' I stop walking and prop the trolley against my hip and start digging in my shoulder bag until I find the examples of flags and banners I made last night. I pull them out and hand them to him.

'Save Nutcracker Lane,' he reads aloud. 'This Christmas, I wish … One for all and all for one … Christmas magic is in the air …' He shuffles through the flags and banners in his hand and looks between them and me, confusion on his face. 'Are you going to enlighten me?'

'We're going to fight Scrooge with an army – a nutcracker army.'

'We are?' I don't need to look at him to see the raised eyebrow as we start walking across the car park again.

'You inspired me the other day, talking about the community banding together to save the nutcracker. If they've done it once, they could do it again.'

He does a half-snort half-laugh. 'I've never inspired anyone in my life, so thank you.'

I want to say I'm sure that's not true, but we step down from the pavement onto the tarmac and the trolley clatters down the step behind me, making me jump because I'd forgotten I was pulling it. I seem to forget a lot when James is in the vicinity, including my own name and how to breathe.

I give myself a shake. 'The point is that no one knows how much trouble Nutcracker Lane is in because no one comes here anymore. If people in the local community knew, people like me who loved this place in years gone by, people like that woman with the snowglobe-collecting grandson who wanted to bring his own children here one day, people who had wishes granted by the wish-granters or still have photographs up on their mantelpieces of their children with Santa here, or fond memories of the sleigh rides, or who were helped out by the gift donations Nutcracker Lane used to collect for local charities … If people *know* that this time next year, whatever part of this place that survives is going to be very different … maybe they wouldn't let it go. So we're going to take your little nutcrackers, attach these flags to their hands and send them out into the community.'

'Under their own power? Do you have a magic spell to make nutcrackers sentient?'

Maybe. 'We're going to *put* them out there. Everywhere. We're going to hide those little nutcrackers in every conceivable place. We're going to line them up along the lane, create a chain carrying the banners running through every shop window, and outside too. I'll get in touch with the local paper and ask them to run a story on the nutcrackers that are appearing everywhere. I was thinking on the way up this morning – garden walls, garden gates, trees, bushes, and hedges. On lampposts and flower pots and gathering around the recycling bins and waiting at bus stops and sitting on park benches.

'I'll print out a thousand more flags, and we'll give each shop-keeper a box of the nutcrackers to distribute. Everyone comes from different areas, so we'll cover more ground if the others get involved too. If people find these nutcrackers and start talking about them, they might come back to visit this place. At least people will know that Nutcracker Lane won't always be here. Magically appearing nutcrackers will get people talking. Parents will tell children about the good old days here and maybe children will want to come and see for themselves. You can't ignore a fifteen-centimetre nutcracker if it appears at your garden gate.'

He shakes his head, a huge smile on his face. 'You're incredible. You're the brightest spark I've ever met.'

'What?'

'I don't know, but nothing seems impossible with you around. Even a nutcracker army.'

I blush. 'I'm going to call a staff meeting at five tonight. Will you come?'

'You don't honestly think I'd miss it, do you? I'll bring a box of the nutcrackers I've got here and collect the rest from the warehouse tomorrow.'

'Thank you. Seriously, James, thank you so much. I couldn't do this without—' I let out a shout of joy as we approach the entrance and grab his arm excitedly. 'The nutcrackers are back!'

He smiles as I lift up my trolley and rush over to the floor-to-ceiling glass windows surrounding the entranceway. Inside, in *exactly* the same position as they used to be, is the family of nutcrackers in size order, lined up from the biggest at five-foot to the smallest at a few centimetres, including the one James and I fought over in the storage room the other night.

When I look up, James has let himself in the door and wound the key in the one that plays "Little Drummer Boy" and the tune filters out to me as the nutcracker's drumsticks start moving mechanically up and down to his drum. It's a sight I haven't seen for years and never thought I'd see again. The tune was my father's favourite Christmas song, and there used to be something comforting about hearing it played as you walked in or out of Nutcracker Lane.

And there's only one person who could've done this.

'You found them,' I say as he stands in the doorway, holding it open so we can hear the music.

'You don't know that I had anything to do with this,' he says, but his smile says otherwise. 'I'm a Grinch, remember?'

'I know.' It's all I can do not to throw my arms around his neck again, but how many times can you inappropriately hug someone in one morning? I reach out and stroke the green fur of the Grinch's face on his jumper again, trying to make him realise I'm rubbing his chest, not the jumper. 'But you're the best Grinch I've ever met. I thought you were going to sell them.'

'I couldn't. Not with knowing how much you liked them. I figured they deserved to be back in their rightful position for their ...'

He trails off but I can finish the sentence for him: '... final year.'

He nods, and I stop rubbing his chest to press one finger against it like I'm poking him in the gentlest way possible. 'Not if we and our ten thousand nutcrackers have anything to do with it.'

He reaches up and wraps his hand around mine, our fingers entwine and he tugs me through the door, and this time, we don't drop hands as we walk down the lane.

Chapter 8

'We can fight this,' I say, hoping I sound more confident than I feel. 'But we have to work together, not against each other. We shouldn't be trying to save our individual shops; we should be trying to save Nutcracker Lane – the whole of it!' I'm standing in the gap of the fence surrounding the wish-granting nutcracker. It's quarter past five, and I've somehow managed to gather every shopkeeper and member of staff, all the carol singers, and even the Santa and his elf are sitting at the back on the floor against the log cabin wall of a shop while Santa picks his nose, peers at what he exhumes like he's choosing his next delicacy, and promptly eats it. Everyone is looking very deliberately away from Santa, which means I have at least thirty pairs of eyes on me and I've never been good at public speaking. James is somewhere behind me on a bench, and the strains of "Little Drummer Boy" are still filtering through from the drum-playing musical nutcracker inside the entrance.

'We have to show Scrooge that he can't do this to us,' I try again. 'E.B. Neaser, who doesn't even have the decency to use his real name, is trying to divide us, and so far he's succeeding. We're all old friends. That's more important than anything else.'

'He damaged my stock!' Carmen points an accusatory finger at Hubert.

144

'She's been stealing my customers!' Mrs Brissett from the jumper shop shouts at Rhonda from the hat shop.

'She's been telling everyone that my hats are rubbish and fall apart in minutes!' Rhonda fires back.

'My poinsettias died because I asked him to close up for me and he left a window open so it got too cold for them,' the florist accuses the bloke from the coffee shop.

'That was an accident!' the guy from the coffee shop yells back.

The bickering continues and I ask myself why I ever thought this was a good idea. How can former friends turn into enemies so quickly? A week ago, these people were making lunch plans together; now they can't even be under the same spacious roof without a fight breaking out.

'This is just the first year,' I try again. 'What happens next year? Scrooge is culling so many of us now, but do you really think that'll be the end of it? Whoever "wins" this time around and comes back to their shops next year – won't he just do the same thing again? None of us are going to be winners in the end. The only chance we've got is if we all stick together and fight back as a whole.'

'Nee, how can we fight it?' Stacey says quietly from her spot next to me, her arms around Lily's shoulders, looking like she regrets bringing her seven-year-old daughter to what has turned out to be a festive re-enactment of *Fight Club*. 'No matter what we do, at the end of the year, Scrooge is going to calculate our earnings and keep the shops with the most profit. No amount of nutcrackers is going to change that.'

'We could combine our earnings and report equal amounts!' I shout as the idea suddenly hits me. 'What if we all make a pact to pool our earnings and when we send our accounting books in after Christmas, we split the total and each report an exactly equal amount? He wouldn't be able to argue with that. Following his *own* rules, we'd beat him at his own game. What do you think?'

Silence. I think they must be so stunned by my moment of

145

genius that they can't quite find the words to capture what a fantastic idea it is.

'I'm pretty sure that's tax dodging and comes with a prison sentence,' the snowglobe seller eventually pipes up.

Murmurs of "account fiddling" and "fraud" go through the crowd and I gulp. 'We'd show the taxman our actual sales, obviously. I only mean the ones we send to Scrooge. We have to show him that he can't just pick and choose and sell the rest off to the factory.'

'How could we trust anyone though?' Carmen asks. 'How do we know everyone else would stick to the plan and not add a few thousand onto their totals to ensure their own safety and shaft the rest of us?'

'We'd have to trust each other. Like we used to.' To be honest, I'm half-thinking I've imagined how much everyone on Nutcracker Lane liked each other. How can so many friendships be so quickly decimated over this?

'Pfft.'

'Pah!'

'As if!'

And that's just a selection of the responses to how well that suggestion goes down.

'And you.' The man from the craft shop points a finger directly at me. 'Young whippersnapper who's only been here for seven days. I've been here for twenty years, and you come barging in, thinking you can tell us all to break the law. You can't tell me what to do. What do you know about Nutcracker Lane that makes you able to change things?'

'But ... but I've known you all for years,' I say to the man who my grandma used to buy festive embellishments to make her own cards from every year. 'I've been a visitor for decades ...'

'Do you think this is the first year we've noticed things are going downhill?' he barks. 'Do you think we don't do our best every year to attract more customers? You swan in like some sort

146

of saviour come to pull us back from the brink of despair. If Nutcracker Lane was saveable, don't you think we'd have done it years ago? And we certainly wouldn't have resorted to tax evasion!'

'I wasn't suggesting that …' My voice shakes. I've lost the crowd. They're all muttering among themselves about various injustices they've faced over the years that I don't know anything about.

James drapes his good arm around my shoulder, making me jump because I hadn't heard him get up. He was the last person I expected to stand up for me in this. I'm pretty sure he'd like to never hear the words "Nutcracker Lane" again.

'What my law-abiding friend here is trying to say is simple – do you *want* to come back to Nutcracker Lane next year? Do you *all* want it to still be here?' His voice is calm and measured, and there's something about him when he speaks that makes everyone fall silent and listen.

'Yes,' comes a collective response.

'Great, because that's what we all want.' He takes his arm from around my shoulders and walks over to the wish-granting nutcracker and points up at it. 'Do you all remember how the community rallied to bring this guy home once before?'

There's inconclusive murmuring and James gives a quick recap of the story he told me the other night, and then continues. 'Nutcracker Lane works on the idea that wishes comes true … Well, they don't.'

Typical James. He hasn't changed that much then.

'We're all adults here. We know that cracking a nut in this thing's mouth won't make it a reality, but we also know that half the power of wishes is the idea of manifesting what you want and working towards it, effectively making your own wish come true. So if we want to save Nutcracker Lane, we can't just make a wish and stand back to hope for the best. We have to *make* it come true.'

God, he's good. Everyone's gone quiet to listen to him and he doesn't seem even vaguely perturbed by so many eyes on him.

147

He's still wearing his Grinch jumper and his arm is back in the sling now, and his hair has fallen to the opposite side than usual like he's pushed it back a few times. I never expected him to get involved in this. I thought his involvement would end at handing over the nutcrackers, but the fact he's got up too, and is trying to calm this crowd of people he barely knows, buoys my confidence.

'We all know that people used to love it, and we all know that in a few years' time, if it goes, people will reminisce fondly and wish it was still there,' I say. 'That interim time is where the magic happens, and we're currently standing in it. We have a chance to save Nutcracker Lane *before* people can start reminiscing about the good times when it used to be there.'

'Exactly,' James agrees. 'What if we don't report equal earnings, but we *all* earn enough that Scrooge can't possibly shut us down? What if we all have our best year ever?' He's got a sort of authority about him that makes anything sound possible when he says it.

'I'm in.' Hubert, bless him, is the first to agree even though he hasn't got a clue what we're suggesting yet.

'If it was that easy, we'd have done it years ago,' the bloke from the craft shop mutters.

His cutting remarks shook me just now, but James gives him a bright smile. 'But we're not talking about years ago. We're talking about right now. If we have one Christmas left before Scrooge does irreparable damage then we need to make the most of it. If we fail, at least we'll have tried.'

Craft Shop Man reluctantly mutters something about being "in".

While I explain a bit about my plan to spread the nutcrackers far and wide, James goes over to the box he left on the bench and gets a handful of nutcrackers out. He gives one to Lily and winks at her as he comes back. I attach a "Save Nutcracker Lane" flag around one's neck and give another two a string of bunting to hold, joining them together, and explain that we could line our shop windows with these, as well as hiding them in every

148

conceivable place around our county and getting people talking about Nutcracker Lane.

'A whole new generation of children will be captivated,' Hubert says excitedly.

'We could get the newspapers involved!' Carmen shouts, and I'm glad that we're on the same page. 'And the TV cameras!'

'People will talk about hundreds of nutcrackers popping up around town!' one of the carol singers shouts.

When I look up at him, James is grinning at me.

'People will love finding them. Like free Christmas decorations. Kids love that sort of thing. Have you seen how some places hide books for other people to find? It'll be like that but with nutcrackers!'

'And we can all take some and distribute them around where we live. We'll have covered all of Wiltshire in no time!'

James and I share another look. I don't mention that we've already thought of all this stuff because it's amazing to see everyone getting involved.

'But we have to work together,' I say loudly to be heard over the racket as everyone starts chattering between themselves about good places for putting nutcrackers. 'We have to go back to supporting each other, showcasing each other's products, talking each other up, helping each other out. We have to show Scrooge that we're in this together and each and every one of us deserves our place. Even if this fails and we lose Nutcracker Lane, at least we won't lose the friendships we've made here.'

Everyone mumbles an agreement and the group is suddenly filled with hugs and apologies and people saying things like, 'It's been so lonely without anyone to have lunch with,' and 'I'll be in first thing tomorrow for a batch of my annual peppermint crèmes. I haven't known what to do with myself without them this year.' It warms my heart to the core, and when I look up at James, he's looking proud and sentimental, and I step a bit closer to him and he does the same until our arms are touching.

'Thank you,' I whisper to him.

'Thank *you*.' He tilts his neck back until he can look up at the giant nutcracker behind us. 'Making wishes isn't what's magic here. It's having something to wish for that makes all the difference. Hope. This has given them all hope. *That's* something that's been in short supply lately. For all of us.'

I know he means himself by that, but someone asks a question about the nutcrackers before I have time to analyse it too deeply.

James promises to go and collect a carful tonight and I promise to make up a thousand more flags. The atmosphere feels instantly brighter. Even Santa has left his bodily functions to their own devices and is now flicking a nail uninterestedly against a paving stone.

As everyone starts filtering away from the meeting area, they all stop to crack a nut in the giant nutcracker's mouth, and this time, all our wishes echo each other's – to save not just our own shops, but Nutcracker Lane as a whole.

Stacey goes to get their coats and Lily tugs at the bottom of my Christmas jumper and I crouch down so she can reach Rudolph's nose and press it, making the big red bobble light up. 'Auntie Nia, are you going to have to grow your hair?'

'I don't think so …' I say carefully, waiting to see where her childhood logic is going.

'Only every time you start growing it, you get it cut again, so I don't think it's going to go very well.'

Great. Even a seven-year-old has noticed my inability to commit to a fringe. Although I must be doing something right if she thinks I "get" it cut because what I actually do is hack away at it with scissors in the bathroom mirror and then regret it. And try to fix it, which inevitably ends up going horribly wrong until there are porcupines with better haircuts.

'Mummy says you might have to because you've got your very own Flynn Rider now …' She blushes as she says it, and I remember feeling exactly the same about Aladdin when I was her age. Crushes on cartoon characters are definitely a thing that carries across the generations.

'Oh, honey, there's no part of him that's mine, but he does look like him, doesn't he?' I glance up at James and grin at him when he meets my eyes. 'Hey, Disney Prince, come over here. This is Stacey's daughter, Lily. She wanted to say hello because she thinks you look like Flynn Rider.'

I introduce them, but she still calls him Mr Rider when she thanks him for the nutcracker, and I'd be lying if I said my heart didn't melt at how sweet and gracious he is with her, and how at least he waits until she and Stacey are out of earshot before looking at me in confusion. 'Who's Flynn Rider?'

'Rapunzel's prince. *Tangled*.' I shake my head in despair. 'So after the Christmas movies, we're going to have to work on getting you acquainted with Disney movies then, are we?'

He grins and waggles his eyebrows. 'I'm remarkably okay with that idea.'

I am too, but I still shake my head fondly. Honestly, never mind under a rock, anyone would think he'd been living as a wooden soldier for years.

Chapter 9

'Where is he?' I say for approximately the sixty-third time this morning judging by the look on Stacey's face. 'His car's in but his shop's shut.'

'Honestly, Nia,' she mutters from behind the counter where she's crouched down folding up gift boxes. 'If you spent as much time making Christmas decorations as you do looking for that man ... At least if his shop's shut, that flipping Santa isn't dancing.'

'I think I might buy you that for Christmas.' I turn and wink at her and she pokes her tongue out at me. 'Can you hold the fort if I go looking?'

She laughs and nods, and I'm hit with a wave of how grateful I am to be working with my best friend. I think she's so surprised by the prospect of me actually wanting to spend time with a man that she never complains about the number of times I dash out to see him, or how at some point today, we've got to go and distribute nutcrackers to the other shopkeepers and there's no time to waste given that it's already the 8th of December.

I step out of Starlight Rainbows and look both ways, trying to decide where James might be.

Hubert and Carmen, sworn enemies yesterday, are now huddled in his sweetshop doorway sharing a plate of her chocolates with a cup of tea each. Before I have a chance to decide which way to go, they beckon me over.

'He's a good one you've got there,' Hubert says.

'I thought he was going to be a problem when I first met him,' Carmen says. 'He looked so uptight and like he belonged in an office. Not Nutcracker Lane's usual type at all.'

Hubert nods. 'He doesn't let the arm stop him, does he?'

'What do you mean?' I ask in confusion.

'The garlands.' They nod in unison towards the top of the lane.

I thank them and head in the direction of the wish-granting nutcracker, and the question of what they mean is quickly answered as I come out into the entrance court and spot James, balancing precariously on a stepladder near the nutcracker, hanging a thick green garland intertwined with twinkling white lights from a low ceiling beam to the top of a lamppost where they always used to hang.

I fold my arms and look up at him. 'What part of this counts as "taking it easy"?'

He obviously saw me coming because he isn't even slightly surprised. 'You don't have to worry about me so much, you know.'

I probably don't, but I'm pretty sure I'm the only person who knows quite how far his injuries extend and I can't stop myself. 'Can I help?'

'You can come and steady the ladder, if you want. It's a bit wobbly up here.'

'Yeah,' I mutter as I go across and put one foot on the bottom rung and lean my weight against it. 'I've always thought the best place for someone with their arm in a cast and two broken ribs is right at the top of a rickety ladder.'

He lets out a guffaw. 'And good morning to you too.'

I can't ignore the little flutter at the sight of his smile. 'Good morning, Grinch. And congratulations on another impressive Christmas jumper.'

He grins down at me and I find it impossible to tear my eyes away from his. I love that he's somehow managed to find *another* Grinch-themed Christmas jumper, this one black with smaller Grinch faces all over it. He's wearing butter-soft well-worn jeans and his broken arm isn't in the sling, the sleeve of the jumper once again hooked around his elbow above the white cast.

We're only a few feet away from the fence that surrounds the magical nutcracker, at one of the lampposts on the edge of the entrance court, and I'm distracted as a little blond boy holding his older sister's hand goes up to it. His sister helps him get a walnut from the vending machine and tries to take him up to the nutcracker, but he shouts at her to leave him alone. He's maybe five or six years old, and his sister looks in her pre-teen years, and she huffs and tells him he won't be able to reach it by himself, but he shouts and pushes her away so she goes to stand outside the fence.

The scene intrigues me, from the scowl on the girl's face as she pulls her phone out and starts prodding it instead, to the little boy making his way up the steps to the nutcracker, which he really is going to struggle to reach.

I glance up at James. The fingers of his good hand are still trying to attach the garland to the top of the lamppost, but I can tell he's not concentrating on what he's doing.

The steps were designed so that little ones of almost any height can reach, but the little boy still has to stand on tiptoes to put his nut into the open mouth, and then step back down and go around the back of the nutcracker to reach the lever and pull it down with both hands. The nut cracks and the little boy goes back up the steps to collect it, and I realise there are tears streaming down his face. The sister is still absorbed in her phone, and I bite my lip as I watch him reach up to collect his nut, and stand on the steps with it clutched in one hand. He leans up and touches the nutcracker's furry beard.

'I wish I had a friend,' he whispers to it.

I can't help the intake of breath and I have to chew my inside

154

cheek to stop my eyes filling up. I look at James again and he's not even pretending not to be listening now. He looks down at me and his mouth tips up in a sad half-smile.

No one else has heard. The sister is standing far enough away and still hasn't looked up from her phone. There's no one nearby, and the little boy hasn't noticed us at the ladder. The boy eats his nut without taking his eyes off the nutcracker's friendly face, and doesn't look like he wants to move, until his sister shoves her phone back in her pocket and shouts over to him. 'Hurry up. Mum and Dad are waiting by the trees.'

The little boy wipes his eyes and squares his shoulders, rallying himself as his sister hurries him away. He keeps looking back at the nutcracker, but still hasn't noticed me and James listening in.

I'm so focused on them that it makes me jump when James steps down the ladder.

'Oh God, right in the heart.' He puts his hand on his chest when he's back on solid ground and standing opposite me. 'I've got an idea. Will you stay with them and don't lose track of them? I'll be back in a minute.'

I nod and he starts jogging towards his shop but within one step, he gasps in pain and slows to a fast walk. He hurries past the little boy and his sister, and I loiter, keeping an eye on them as she drags him down the lane towards the tree lot. I follow slowly, not wanting them to see me or wonder why this strange woman is following them, hiding behind pillars and lampposts. I pass Hubert and Carmen who are now chatting to the snowglobe seller, and wave to Stacey as I pass Starlight Rainbows.

I'm hiding behind a pillar when the two of them meet their parents at the corner of the lane before the covered part ends and it opens into the tree seller's display at the edge of the car park. James reappears beside me, out of breath, probably from the pain of moving faster than broken ribs generally allow. He's got a big nutcracker in his hand – a fifty-centimetre tall one with a silver sword in its hand, and a blue jacket with white accents and a silver trim. He nudges my arm, grins at me, and rushes across to the family.

'Hi, excuse me?' I watch him catch up with them. 'I'm James. I work at Twinkles and Trinkets.' He uses the nutcracker to point towards his shop and I attempt to hold my stomach in so they don't see me lurking behind the nearest pillar when they look in this direction. 'I was wondering if you could do me a favour?'

I love how, although he nods to the parents and sister, he talks only to the little boy. He sits down cross-legged on the floor directly in front of him. 'See, I've got this very lonely nutcracker who's desperately in need of a family to take him home ...'

He holds the nutcracker out and the boy takes it cautiously, clasping both hands around its painted body.

'Do you know the story of *The Nutcracker*?' he continues. 'He's really a prince who was cursed to take the form of a wooden soldier after being defeated by an evil mouse king, and it's said that if he finds the right person to take care of him, he can become a real boy again. A real friend.'

The boy strokes the nutcracker's furry white hair as James talks. 'I had one of these when I was your age, and I used to drive my parents barmy because I'd never let them put it away after Christmas. I used to talk to it and tell it all my problems. Nutcrackers are renowned for being very good listeners. What do you think? Will you take him home with you?'

The boy nods enthusiastically and unexpectedly throws his arms around James's neck. I see him wince but he does an amazing job of not showing it as he returns the hug, carefully patting the boy's back with his right arm while holding his broken one out of harm's way.

The father must catch James's wince because he carefully extracts his son and both parents thank him. He even goes to get his wallet out but James stops him. 'Merry Christmas from Nutcracker Lane.'

156

The family all wish him a happy Christmas and I wait for them to go out of sight before I sidle out from behind my pillar. James is still sitting on the floor and I go over and hold out my hand to pull him up, and I can't ignore the little buzz as his fingers close around mine and I haul him to his feet, even though I'm sure he was perfectly capable of getting up by himself.

I go to speak and only realise how close to tears I am when it comes out as a choked-off sob. That was so touching, and I can't find the right words to convey it.

He doesn't let go of my hand as we start making our way back up the lane. 'If there's one thing that surprises me about this place, it's the number of unexpected hugs you get.'

I gurgle a half-sob and tighten my fingers around his. 'Thought you didn't believe in lying to children, Grinch.'

He goes to speak but nothing comes out. 'Well, it's … it's not … it'll help him …' He gets increasingly frustrated at not being able to find the right words. 'He already believes a magical nutcracker is going to grant his wish, how much worse can it get?' He snaps eventually, but there's no heat behind the words. 'What's a parent's favourite Christmas carol?'

'You can admit your heart has grown a size rather than trying to distract me with terrible jokes, you know.'

'"Silent Night".' He grins, deliberately ignoring me. 'See? It wasn't *terrible*.'

I can't help laughing, but mainly because he thinks his distraction techniques will work.

Hubert has obviously made his way down into the storage room because there's a big box of decorations outside his shop, and he's now directing Carmen and Mrs Brissett to string tinsel around a lamppost each and drape it between them, one on a set of steps and one on a stool. They greet us cheerily as we pass.

'Thanks for the idea, you two,' Hubert calls out. 'We didn't know these decorations were still here. Scrooge is going to kill us. Isn't it wonderful?'

157

He sounds abnormally excited about the prospect of impending murder.

'I was followed this morning when I went to find the garlands in the storage room,' James explains. 'I mentioned what you said the other night about putting them up without Scrooge's permission and before I knew it, he was calling in reinforcements and collecting boxes.'

I'm torn as I want to stay to help, but Carmen's eyes have homed in on our joined hands and I can feel them like two pinpricks in the back of my hand. We *have* left a stepladder unattended that we should get back to, and they look like they've got it under control.

There aren't enough people around to have bothered with the stepladder by the time we get back, and James goes back up it to pick up the garland he left hanging from the central ceiling beam and attach it to the top of the lamppost with ease, leaving it draped in perfect crescent shapes high above our heads. If we do this with the rest of them, they will come out like a wreath formed above the magical nutcracker.

For someone who only seems to have come here a few times as a kid, he certainly remembers exactly how this place used to be decorated.

The sound of the carollers coming up the lane reaches us as they harmonise through "Silver Bells".

'What's with all the bells in Christmas music?' he says, as if trying to prove he's still a Grinch in case anyone saw his look of joy when that little boy accepted the nutcracker. '"Silver Bells", sleigh bells, "Jingle Bells" …'

'"Carol of the Bells"?' I offer.

'Is that the really fast one from *Home Alone* that absolutely no one knows the lyrics to?'

I sing him the first verse.

'Of *course* you know it word for word.' He shakes his head, but he can't get the smile off his face.

'You don't have to prove your Grinchiness to me just because you granted a Christmas wish. I can teach you the words if you want. Come on, it's much less complicated than it sounds …' I sing the first four lines slowly and make him repeat them, looking like he's torn between humouring me and actually enjoying it.

We stop when the carollers come into view and Angela, the lead singer, waves when she spots us.

'Any requests?' she asks as they come to the end of "Silver Bells".

James rolls his eyes. 'Oh, go on then. "Carol of the Bells", please.'

They surround the fence around the nutcracker and launch into the fast, lilting tune, and I *love* that James hums along, his eyes shining and his smile brighter than any twinkling Christmas lights.

He's laughing as the carollers gather again and start walking back towards the other end of the lane, the tune fading as they disappear from view.

Among all the carollers, I haven't noticed Carmen appear, but when I look round, she's up two rungs on the ladder behind us and leaning over to hang a fresh bunch of mistletoe from the lamppost we're standing under.

'From the florist.' She winks at us. 'One on every lamppost, like there used to be.'

I follow the line of lampposts on either side of the lane and realise I've been so distracted by James that I've missed the fact we're not the only people working on the decorating. Mrs Brissett has just come into view and is wrapping tinsel around the post on the corner, and the florist is dragging a step between each one and hanging up a bunch of mistletoe, the stems wrapped with twine, although it's obvious Carmen has come to this particular lamppost for a reason.

She nods down at James and I. 'Go on, it would be rude not to.'

He catches my eyes and smiles his Flynn Rider smile as he steps closer and ducks towards me, aiming for my cheek.

My eyes close automatically as his lips touch my skin, and the green earthy scent of the fresh mistletoe above us is overpowered by his aftershave. He smells like the spices you'd use to make mulled wine, orange and star anise and fresh cinnamon curls with a hint of fiery ginger, his usual stubble freshly shaven this morning and his jaw smooth against my skin.

It's nothing more than a press of his lips, but it's slow and intense and somehow feels even more intimate than if he'd kissed me on the mouth. I can feel every tiny movement of his lips, leaving me in no doubt about what it would be like to kiss him properly. My fingernails make crescent shapes in my palms as I try to stop myself touching him because I've never wanted anything more than to curl my hands into the back of his head and pull his mouth to mine.

My knees feel shaky and I don't realise I'm holding my breath until my lungs start to burn, and even though it lasts for a matter of seconds, it feels like time has slowed down and seconds have stretched out to eternity.

The tip of his nose rubs against my skin as he pulls back, drawing the closeness out for even longer, and I don't open my eyes as I try to hang on to the moment, even though I'm pretty sure I'll still be able to feel the imprint of his lips on my skin next March.

'Mistletoe is something we've been sorely missing around here,' Carmen announces.

I've completely lost myself and have to blink for a few moments to remember where I am. I swallow before I can get any words out. 'I hope you and Hubert will be testing it out for yourselves soon.' My voice is so breathy and stuttery that she must be able to tell. How can a peck on the cheek have that much of an effect on me?

She waggles her eyebrows. 'Oh, we already have, Nia.'

James shakes himself out of the daze and offers his hand to help her down from the ladder. 'Oh, you are a gent. And I saw what you did for that boy.' She lets go of his hand and reaches out to pat his arm. 'You're a good lad, James. I wasn't sure at first, but you're really one of us.'

He looks touched by that and a soft look crosses his face, but he quickly squares his shoulders and clears his throat. 'I'm really not. I hate Christmas. *Nothing* will change my mind.'

She ignores him. 'I best get back. Those decorations won't put themselves up. You two have fun, and remember, *every* lamppost.' She points to the mistletoe again and gives us a wink, and waves over her shoulder as she goes back to help Mrs Brissett.

But his harsh words are a sharp reminder to me. He's leaving as soon as his shop shuts, and he'll never give Nutcracker Lane another thought again. I try to force it out of my mind, but it stays like flames licking in the background. He's never going to care about this place the way I do. 'We should do that more often.'

'Stand under mistletoe?' He raises an eyebrow. 'I *completely* agree.'

'No ... Well, that too, but I meant grant wishes. That was really special, James. With a tiny bit of effort and no cost other than one of many nutcrackers from your stock, you made that little boy feel important. You cheered him up and made his day. We could do that more often.'

'I can spare a nutcracker or two, but I don't know about a family trip to Disneyland or the latest thirty-gear mountain bike under someone's tree ...'

He's certainly got a point there. People will wish for expensive things. On the minuscule budget Scrooge has allocated us this year, we couldn't even manage a miniature bike under a doll's house tree. 'It doesn't have to be about money. In fact, it *shouldn't* be about it. Everything's been about money lately on Nutcracker Lane. Scrooge and his budget, can't afford this, can't afford that, cuts cuts cuts everywhere. The wish-granting when I was younger was about giving people something relatively valueless that made them feel like they mattered. Like someone was listening to them. It made people feel seen, like you did for that little boy.'

'Yeah, but how? Not everyone is going to want a Christmas decoration.'

'I don't know, but it's not about money. It's about feeling. Making people *feel* something. Giving them that heart-warming feeling that Christmas is all about. Letting them know that someone cares. We could start listening in to wishes, just like the wish-granters used to, and if it's something small or something that we can interpret in a different way, like you did this morning, then why can't we do it? We could ask all the shop owners to get involved ...'

'Most people are having their worst year ever ...'

'It doesn't have to be a financial contribution. Believe me, *none* of us can afford that. But if we can't grant a wish, we could do something else, like put together little gift baskets with a festive plant from the florist and a box of chocolates from the chocolate shop and a decoration from you and a fun necklace or pair of reindeer antlers from me and Stacey. Something that no one has to make any extra effort for and the only outlay is something from stock ... Why are you looking at me like that?'

'Because you're incredible.'

It's such a simple compliment, but it makes butterfly wings start beating in my chest and my knees feel wobbly again. I swear, wobbly knees were never this much of an issue in my life before I met James. 'It's you. What you did today was lovely. *That's* the true meaning of Christmas. You're inspirational.'

'I can honestly say no one's ever thought that about me before.' He looks down as he says it, kicking one boot against the paved floor, and his voice is so quiet that it makes me wonder about all the things he *isn't* saying. He hasn't said much about his life so far, nothing more than what he said in the storage room on that first night, about having to take over a Christmas cracker business when his father retires, and it makes me want to prod and wheedle and ask questions, but it doesn't seem like the time or place.

'What do you think?' I ask as a way of distracting myself.

'I don't know, but you could suggest a trek to the North Pole to find the real Rudolph and then a swift naked roll in some pine needles and I'd agree. You're very persuasive.'

I steadfastly ignore any ideas of James naked, with *or* without pine needles. 'Good, because I was about to try persuading you into reindeer antlers or a Santa hat. We've got you into the Christmas jumpers; now we need to start accessorising too.'

He laughs and it slowly trails off when he realises I'm not joking. 'I've already got a flashing bulb necklace. Isn't that punishment enough?'

'Oh, believe me, the flashing bulb necklace is just the beginning,' I say, and he still can't get the smile off his face.

Maybe, just maybe, he might not be such a Grinch after all.

Chapter 10

'Come on, sing along.' I nudge my elbow against his right arm as Christmas music plays from my phone on the counter.

'Do you know how many people I've sung in front of in my life? You could count them on one hand. If you add "while sober" to the mix, you could count them on these two fingers.' He holds up his thumb and forefinger to make a 0 shape. 'I'm not singing along – I like you far too much to subject you to that.'

The idea that he likes me in *any* way makes heat rise up my body and pool in my chest.

Nutcracker Lane closed hours ago, but we're in Starlight Rainbows, reassembling the handmade pallet shelving James brought the other day. It's been leaning against a wall in the back room since then because we've been too busy with the nutcrackers to attempt putting it together yet.

'Besides, I refuse to sing along to a song I'd never heard of a week ago, but I've now heard so many times that I unintentionally know every lyric off by heart. The music that plays over the main speakers in the lane is like torture. I've started having nightmares about Cliff Richard.'

'It's lovely.' I try not to laugh. I doubt many people have got a phobia of "Mistletoe and Wine". 'And you don't have to keep trying to prove you still hate Christmas. It's like you have a threshold of how many nice things you can do before you suddenly remember your Grinch status and feel you have to prove it.'

It's been another day of decorating Nutcracker Lane, and handing out boxes of the miniature nutcrackers holding flags and banners to shop owners, and getting their opinions on the wish-granting idea, which so far has been positive.

'Don't tell me you're not enjoying it.' I point a screw at him.

His brown eyes go distant as he thinks back to earlier. 'You didn't see that girl with the skateboard today.' He starts telling me again about the teenager who told the magical nutcracker she wanted a skateboard because all her friends had them, and how the bloke from the coffee shop happened to have one in his car that had been sitting there for weeks, waiting to be taken to a charity shop, and as the girl and her family walked across the car park, he and James hid behind cars and rolled it between them so it went right across her path. 'You should have seen her look of wonder when she picked it up. The way she glanced back through the doors towards the nutcracker.'

'I know, you've told me three times already.' I nudge my arm against his again. 'Thought you didn't believe in magic, Grinch.'

'I believe in a heck of a lot of things since I met you, Nia.'

We stare into each other's eyes and for a moment, I think he's going to kiss me. I find myself drifting closer, pushing myself up on tiptoes, close enough that if I reached out I could touch his hand, until "One More Sleep" by Leona Lewis ends and the silence of the gap between songs fills the room.

'I don't.' He steps away sharply. 'But it was something so simple, literally something the guy's son didn't want anymore and it brought someone so much joy. It felt good to be part of that. The guy from the coffee shop even invited me out for a drink sometime. In my usual job, I have a quiet office and I keep to myself as much as I can, so it's nice to feel like part of a bigger picture.'

Mariah's "All I Want For Christmas Is You" starts and James

gives himself a shake. 'I mean, it's good from a commercial point of view for the lane, that's all. I'll never understand all this trash.' He waves a dismissive hand towards the pile of fairy lights on the counter that we've taken down to make room for the shelving, and whether he likes it or not, are going back up once it's all in place. 'All you're "putting up" is your electricity bill.'

'Oh, you're so practical.' I roll my eyes. 'Don't you have a tree? Not even a little one?'

'No. Don't tell me that surprises you? What part of "I hate Christmas" is unclear? Do you want me to repeat it louder or on a different frequency? How about in a different language? *Dwi'n casau Nadolig* – there you go, Welsh. French too? *Je déteste Noël*.'

'You hate Christmas so much, you've taken the trouble to learn it in different languages?'

He laughs, but he's not getting out of this one as easily as he thinks he is. 'You say all that, but you've never told me *why* you hate it. You grouch and Grinch and bluster, but you've voluntarily worn *two* Christmas jumpers this week, and you've been up at the nutcracker listening to wishes at every opportunity. That is very un-Grinch-like behaviour.'

'The jumpers are comfortable. Getting dressed isn't exactly easy at the moment and finding anything comfy is next to impossible.' He holds up the broken arm. 'Besides, I don't want to disappoint you. You're trying so hard to un-Grinch me, I don't want you to realise I'm too much hard work and give up on me.'

It makes warmth pool in my belly and I suddenly want nothing more than to throw my arms around him, but I force myself not to. The words seem significant somehow, not like he just plucked them out of thin air, and I want to push him for an explanation, but I have to keep reminding myself that I still barely know this man. Even though it feels like I've known him for months, the reality is that I met him ten days ago and I *don't* know him well enough to read what each line on his face means or hear hidden meanings behind his words.

He's holding a screw between his teeth and he makes a noise that I've translated to mean "Can you hold this?" now we're on our second set of the surprisingly sturdy shelving units.

Each plank of wood has been sanded until it's silky and smooth with age, and each knot in the woodgrain is preserved with resin. The back and sides of each unit are made from long lengths of pallet planks, and the shelves are made of shorter chunks screwed onto a wooden base.

I go over and hold two wooden boards at a ninety-degree angle while he leans down to line up the hole.

He takes the screw out of his mouth and pushes it in, holding it carefully between the fingers of his left hand as the electric screwdriver in his right hand whirrs into life and he drives the screw into place. 'It's so much fuss for one day that always ends up being a complete let-down. I don't like all the expectation that hinges on this one "Big Day" being perfect. You're expected to be full of joy and cheer, and *certain* people' – he side-eyes me pointedly – 'act like there's something wrong with you if you're not.'

'Oi, *you* asked *me* to help you find some Christmas spirit.' I pick up the next set of planks, ready for another screw. 'I was quite happy to leave you in your non-Christmas-jumper-wearing misery. And just for the record, I have *never* thought there was anything wrong with you.'

He looks up and meets my eyes and his mouth tips slowly into a smile, and I get so lost in his Disney prince eyes that I don't realise I've reached out to touch him until the boards I was holding clatter to the floor and make us both jump.

'It's not about the "Big Day" itself – everyone knows that.' My cheeks flare red as I pick the boards up and try to get them back into the same position. 'It's about the build-up. This is the fun part of Christmas. It's nothing to do with the day itself. That's always full of stress and a total let-down. It's about this – *this* exact time of year when everything's bright and twinkly and people are just a little bit kinder than usual.'

167

'Kinder? People are rattier and more stressed and tired than usual.'

I ignore him. 'Don't you love getting boxes of decorations out and experiencing the nostalgia of going through all these gorgeous things you haven't seen for a year? I decorated my tree last night. I have miniature wreaths that my *great*-grandmother made. It feels special to still have decorations from a family member I never even got to meet. Doesn't your family have decorations passed down through the generations?'

He looks at me with one eyebrow up and one eyebrow down, like he can't work out what I'm talking about. 'No. I've never decorated a Christmas tree.'

'*Never*?' I can't hide the shock in my voice. 'What kind of tree did you have when you were a kid?'

'One of those pre-lit, pre-decorated fibre-optic ones that come out of a nice neat box from the attic on Christmas Eve and goes straight back into it on Boxing Day.'

I shake my head. 'That's just wrong. Don't your parents run a Christmas business?'

His eyes widen for just a second and then he looks down. 'Exactly. It's the busiest time of year.'

'Didn't you have any build-up at all?'

'Yeah – work.'

'I mean when you were young.'

'Schoolwork.'

I narrow my eyes at him because he's being deliberately obtuse now. 'How about writing cards?'

'You mean killing the environment and destroying trees for the privilege of wasting money on postage stamps for someone you check in with once a year because neither of you can think of a polite way to stop?'

I roll my eyes. 'Buying presents?'

'Spending money you don't have on things people don't want that will be returned in January, regifted, or stuffed into the loft until they think they're safe from you asking about them and can get away with chucking them out.'

'Wrapping presents?'

'Sticking yourself up with approximately seventeen thousand metres of Sellotape on *non*-recyclable wrapping paper that no one even *looks* at, which is just as well, because everything I've ever wrapped ends up looking like I've drunk three bottles of gin and broken *both* arms.'

It makes me howl with laughter and he's grinning at me when I've recovered enough to look at him without giggling. *That* I can believe. 'What about food you can only get at this time of year?'

'Yeah, except the supermarkets put it out in September so you can get it for at least four months. Your three hundredth mince pie of the year kind of loses its sparkle.'

'Festive baking?'

'Firstly, you can buy boxes of mince pies for £1.50 in the supermarket so there's no point, and secondly, you don't want to know what happened the last time I tried to cook something. They're still replastering the kitchen wall.'

I laugh again because he's got a way of saying things that's impossible not to laugh at even though I'm not *quite* sure if he's joking or not.

'And what's the deal with Christmas fruitcake?' he continues before I can counteract him. 'Who would ruin a perfectly good cake with fruit? The only exception to the fruit in cake rule is the jam in a Victoria sponge.'

'Oh, come on. It's not Christmas in Britain until you've had a leaden brick of fruitcake that you don't like and wouldn't touch with a bargepole at any other time of year, covered with an inch-thick layer of marzipan and an even thicker layer of dried-up white icing. It's all part of the fun.'

He makes a face and it sets me off giggling again. 'The music?'

He points at the phone on the counter, currently playing Ellie Goulding's cover of "River". 'Same old nonsense every year.

You're onto a winner here because I've never heard this before, but honestly, it's the 10th of December and I've heard "Driving Home For Christmas" at *least* 78,472 times, and no one even *is* driving home for Christmas yet; it's far too early.'

I can't help giggling at his literal interpretation. 'Films? I know you like Christmas movies now.'

'There are these weird shiny round disc things called DVDs, and there's no law against watching Christmas films at any time of year.'

'Yes there is because if I watch them in July, I'll get too excited about it and then be too disappointed that it's still months away. Besides, you *cannot* watch festive movies when it's thirty degrees and sunny outside. You *have* to watch them on a dark winter's night with a mug of hot chocolate and a cosy blanket ... Just like with festive books.'

'Also, oddly, available all year round.'

'What about seeing family?'

'Family you happily won't see again for another year?' He bites his lip as if trying to let me know he's only half-joking. 'And there's this really weird thing where if you want to see people, you can actually go at any time of year. Isn't that an amazing invention?'

I give him a sarcastic grin. 'Memories? Christmas is such a nostalgic time that makes you think of years gone by ...'

'Yeah, I just *love* thinking about that time Dad got drunk over the paperwork, Mum fell down the stairs, and for a real change of pace for the special dinner, we put the microwave meal in the oven, and when it came out, it was so charcoaled that if you chiselled it hard enough, there'd have been diamonds inside.'

'Scented candles?' I'm really clutching at straws now.

'Fire hazards.'

'What about the novelty clothing? Christmas jumpers, hats, and jewellery?'

'They're ridiculous.'

'No, they're not – they're fun. I love people who aren't afraid

170

of looking daft and really throw themselves into it and embrace the silliness of the season. Christmas is all about walking around with poinsettia flower headbands, jingling reindeer antlers, and Santa hats on your head.'

'All at the same time?' He pulls a face.

'Why not? There's no such thing as overkill at Christmas.' The grin I give him is tight and wary. There's something about his humorous way of talking that makes me unsure if he's only saying it to wind me up or if he's serious. And if he *is* serious, it gives me a sobering pause for thought. He hates everything I like. If he really thinks this way, he's never going to change. 'You are the most cheerful miserable person I've ever met.'

'Thank you.' He lets out an unexpected laugh and puts his hand on his chest and ducks his head in what probably would've been a proper bow if he didn't have broken ribs.

The song chooses that minute to change and "Deck the Halls" comes on. 'One of my favourites!' I grab his hand and tug him into the middle of the empty shop floor, the tables pushed aside to give us space to construct the shelves. I grab a nutcracker from one of the tables and hold it out to him like a microphone. 'Come on, sing along!' I try again, even though he's refused every time I've tried to make him so far. 'Go on, what are you afraid of?'

'Nutcracker Lane's double-glazing repair bill after I've shattered every piece of glass in the building.'

'It's stood here for forty years, I'm sure it can cope with a bit of "*troll the ancient yuletide carol*-ing" too.' I sigh. 'You said you were stressed out with work the other night, but I haven't seen you relax once since then. Your shoulders are so tense, they must be holding every muscle taut and making your injuries hurt more. You need to relax and let go of yourself.'

'Fa-la-la-ing's not going to help, is it?'

'How will you know if you don't give it a try?'

He looks between my face and the nutcracker I'm still holding out as a microphone. 'Fine. Fa la la la la,' he says in a totally deadpan voice. 'Happy now?'

'Go on ...'

He rolls his eyes but his mouth quirks up into a smile this time, and his face softens at the exact moment he gives in.

I push the nutcracker-microphone into his hand and grab another one for myself and I can't get the grin off my face when he joins in the sing-along because it's amazing to see him let go and relax, and judging by the impossibly wide smile and the way his eyes are shining, even enjoy himself. He's always uptight and self-aware, and even though he wears casual clothes to work now, he still seems as taut as if he was wearing a smart suit. For a while, I put it down to the injuries, but it seems to be more than that, almost like he's constantly looking over his shoulder for something.

'I love that I can be silly with you and you don't judge me for it,' he says when the song ends and his eyes are glinting like a tiger's eye gemstone when you move it under the light so it reflects different colours.

I know the feeling. It's been a long time since I let myself go in front of someone, and the only person I've *ever* sung in front of before is Stacey, but it doesn't seem to matter with him. 'Everyone needs a dose of silliness sometimes. I think we all get caught up in the stresses of life and forget that far too often.'

The opening bars of "A Winter's Tale" by David Essex start playing, and James takes the nutcracker out of my hand and puts them both down on the completed empty shelf behind him.

'C'mere,' he murmurs.

When I step towards him, his right arm slides around my waist and he pulls me against him, and his left arm rests around my shoulder, touching at the elbow above his cast. We start doing some sort of slow dance, mainly just stepping around the room to the sweet, melodic tune, occasionally stepping on each other's toes and murmuring an apology.

My head fits perfectly into the crook of his neck and his chin rests on my head, the first hint of his dark stubble catching on my hair. I let out a breath against his collarbone and sort of snuggle into his chest. I'm unsure of where to touch him that isn't going to hurt and one hand goes around his hip to rub gently at the right side of his spine and the other drifts up to his left shoulder, letting my fingers trail over the back of his neck.

He makes a noise and I still instantly. 'Am I hurting you?' I whisper, because everything feels so quiet and peaceful that talking at a normal volume would break the spell.

'The opposite.' His arms tighten around me, pulling me closer, and it *must* be hurting, I *must* be pressing against some of his bruises, but he whispers, 'This is the most comfortable I've ever been.'

I don't need to look up at his face to hear the blissed-out tone in his voice or tell that his eyes are closed or feel the way his shoulders droop as he exhales against my hair.

It would be so easy to tilt my head and kiss his jaw. He seems so quiet and relaxed and I wish there was a bit of mistletoe nearby to give me an excuse. I can't kiss him for no reason. I don't even *want* to kiss him. I just want to see if what I felt yesterday when he kissed my cheek was a one-off brought on by hysteria at granting wishes again, or proximity to too many nutcrackers or something. That's all. It was some weird sort of nervous system malfunction. Nothing more.

'This is such a lovely song. So romantic.' He says it so quietly that I'm not sure if I've heard the words so much as felt the vibration of them through his chest. 'Why have I never heard this before?'

'Because you close your heart to Christmas and decide you don't like things without giving them a chance.'

He doesn't say anything, just squeezes me tighter and I let the fingers around his shoulder trail up to play with the hair at the back of his neck, carding through it and drifting up and down to the collar of his jumper and back, and I feel the shiver that goes down his spine, and I have no doubt that it's the *good* kind of shiver. Maybe I'm not the only one who felt something under that mistletoe the other day.

We slow-dance aimlessly around the room, listening to David Essex sing his 1980s tale of failed love.

'Sorry, I dance like I'm made of wood.'

I stiffen in his embrace. I'm a hundred per cent sure he isn't a nutcracker come to life, and then every so often, he'll say something that makes me think … *is* he? 'You dance like you've got broken bones and severe bruising and should be sitting down with your feet up.' It's the end of a long day, and although he's clearly trying not to show it, there's a tautness around his eyes and a wince at certain movements that suggest he's already overdone things.

'Nia, I need to tell you …' He lifts his head and looks me in the eyes, his pupils wide. The look is so intense that it makes my knees turn to jelly, which must be something to do with the earth's magnetic field and not just from *looking* at him. Maybe we're due an earthquake. They're not exactly common in Wiltshire, but it's possible.

His fingers curl into my hip, five points of burning pressure where they touch my body. Bits of his straight hair have sprung forward around his ears and it's like a magnet is pulling my fingers up to tuck them back, trailing down his jaw, feeling every speck of stubble with every line of my fingertips. His eyes drift closed and he lowers his head, and my heart is pounding so loud I'm sure people on a passing cruise liner in the North Sea can hear it.

I can already sense the delicious friction of his jaw against my skin, his soft lips that I felt on my cheek the other day against mine. My hand grips his shoulder as I stand on tiptoes, and I realise that I'm going to kiss him … And I jump back with such abruptness that it startles him and makes him wince in pain at my sudden movement.

'Sorry,' I mumble. I can't kiss him. I barely know him. Another

174

relationship is the last thing I want. I can't bear the thought of being cheated on *again*, and with him … it feels like it would matter. It didn't matter with the previous couple of boyfriends because I held them at arm's length so it wouldn't hurt when they inevitably slept with someone else. James is already closer than I've let most of my previous relationships put together. The thought of him cheating on me is enough to make my throat close up and my nose start to burn, and we're nowhere *near* dating yet. I can't let it get that far because of how much it will hurt to lose him.

Every part of me feels wobbly, and my fingers curl into his good arm to keep myself upright because it's like hugging him has cut off the blood flow to my brain and it takes a few seconds for awareness to come back.

'The shelves!' I yelp with such fervour that you'd think the future of the human race depended on us getting these shelves together.

He scratches his head awkwardly, looking like he can't work out what just happened, and goes back over to position the next part of the frame for building up from the shelf we've just screwed together.

I thought it might be awkward after that … whatever that was between us, but within a couple of purrs of the electric screwdriver, it's like nothing ever happened.

'Why did you stop making things?' My fingers run over the sanded wood, smooth compared to the roughness of the chalky white paint on one of the sets, an experiment in distressed-look shabby chic. These are so beautiful, and they fit in so perfectly with our rustic style. If someone had told me to go out and buy shelving, I'd have chosen these.

'I don't have time. I made these when I was younger, when I had nothing *but* time. Now I just work. Trying to make my parents' unprofitable company profitable again. It takes more … energy than it sounds like it does.'

I get the impression he's talking about emotional energy instead of physical energy. 'You can't work *all* the time.'

The laugh he answers with is bitter and sarcastic, and leaves me in no doubt that he doesn't want to talk about it. 'I'm not creative like you. It's impressive to be able to earn a living from something you make with your own hands.'

I've never thought of it like that before. 'Most days, I'm just struggling to get by. It's hard to find the motivation sometimes, especially when you're working a part-time job as well. But it's also my escape. I feel tense and weird inside if I haven't made anything for a while, and that tension releases when I get out to my shed, put some music on, and disappear into my own little world for a while.'

'But you don't just make Christmas stuff, right?' He pushes screws around a handmade wooden box as he searches for the right ones to secure the side supports.

'No, of course not. That would be a terrible business model. Stace and I both do themed crafts for every time of year; you just happen to have come along in December. We do Valentine's Day, spring, Easter, summer, autumn, Halloween, and everything in between, and we both have non-seasonal year-round products. But Christmas is the most popular and we make a huge effort for it.'

'And you've never thought about a physical shop together until Nutcracker Lane?'

'That would be a dream come true, but it's way too big a commitment. You hear so many horror stories of high streets failing and shops closing down. Neither of us earn enough to stay afloat without a second job. Buying our van together was a huge investment. Buying or renting actual property seems doomed to fail and neither of us have got the money anyway. Somewhere with a guaranteed customer base like Nutcracker Lane that was open all year through would be perfect, but for now, our budgets are better spent on making more products and doing more online advertising.'

'Apart from Nutcracker Lane?'

'That's different. It's a labour of love. I've wanted to work here my whole life.' I'm kneeling on the floor with planks of wood laid out in front of me, trying to figure out which ones we'll need next.

'I've never thought it could mean that much to people before. It's just another retail park designed to part people from their money.'

'But that's the one thing it never used to be – about money. Not until Scrooge came along, anyway. Things used to be sold cheaply, or given away to people who needed them. The shop-keepers felt valued. The whole place used to feel special, like magic was fizzing in every corner and if you caught it at just the right time, you'd see a sparkle and catch the faint jingling of bells as elves zipped out of sight.'

'And Scrooge ruined that?'

'Nothing can run on empty. It's been a never-ending snowball for the past few years since he came onboard. I don't even know his real name. He just hides behind this Ebenezer façade.'

'You've got to admit it's a clever play on words.'

I sit back on my knees and point a warning finger at him. 'Don't you dare compliment that horrible man in front of me. One more word of praise for him and you're not coming back to mine for Christmas-tree-shaped crumpets for supper.'

'I was joking, Nee.' He takes hold of my pointing finger and folds it down. 'Is there seriously even festive-shaped food now? Do they taste better because they're in the shape of a tree?'

'Of course they do.' I pretend to be outraged. 'It's a known fact. Like Easter eggs. All chocolate tastes better when it's egg-shaped.'

He goes to protest but I interrupt him. 'Don't say it's the same chocolate in a different mould. There's science to it. All seasonally shaped food is better.'

I can't hold back the giggles any longer and it starts him off too.

'All I can say,' he says between gasps for breath, 'is that you have to prove it because it's been years since I had crumpets and now you've mentioned them, there is nothing I want more in the universe.'

I don't know if it's the promise of hot buttered festively shaped crumpets or James's desire to get away from the Christmas music, but time seems to fly after that. We make a good three-handed tag team of me lining up boards and keeping them in position while James drives screws in with his electric screwdriver, holding each screw gingerly with the fingers of his broken arm, and when we're done, it looks like a different shop.

It's already much brighter in here since I changed the lightbulbs the other day, and the distressed-look shelving fits perfectly with our handmade aesthetic. It lines the right wall opposite the till, and the shop floor in between looks much better without tables cluttering it up. James has already started redistributing our stock into prominent positions on the shelves and is lining up my wooden gingerbread houses like a miniature village when I start untangling fairy lights to wind around the edges.

I nudge my elbow carefully against his right arm as I walk around him. 'Thank you.'

He cocks his head to the side like he can't work out what I'm thanking him for.

'For all your help,' I clarify. 'For all the tips and pointers and your ex-retail professional eye or something.' I don't know much about his job and why he studied for a career in retail but works in an office, and he clearly isn't going to elaborate. 'We're already getting more customers coming in after looking at the windows, and a few people have commented about how much brighter it looks in here, which is a nice way of saying it was dull before.'

'It wasn't *dull*, but you were trying to sell Christmas itself rather than your own products. You can't rely on people to come in just because you're a Christmas shop, you have to give them something to come in for. Looking festive isn't a sales pitch. Nutcracker Lane no longer has the kind of excess customers who come for days out and spend hours wandering through every nook and cranny and meandering around every shop just for the experience of it. People come in for what they want, buy it, and get out. Not having all those tables to bang into will help too. It's much easier to navigate the shop now.'

He points to the centre of the floor. 'If you put one table there with a big display on it, it'll give the shop a focus point, and customers will have space to browse. My legs are covered in bruises from walking into your tables.'

'That's because you don't look where you're going.'

'Or because I'm distracted.' He waggles his eyebrows with a grin, and then looks down at the plaster cast on his arm. 'Admittedly, I think we both know I'm not the best at looking where I'm going.'

'You're amazing at retail though,' I say, glad he didn't continue the first part of that sentence. 'Seriously, James. Stace and I are used to stalls at craft fairs, and we went into this thinking it would be the same, but customers expect something more here. We needed more help than we realised.'

'You're welcome. I want your shop to be a success as much as you do. Nutcracker Lane wouldn't be the same without you, Nia.'

I go hot all over even though he must mean Starlight Rainbows, not me personally. 'It wouldn't be the same without your shop either.'

'Yeah, the Macarena-ing Santa adds *so* much to the lane.'

'I'll miss it when it's gone.' I don't add that I mean its owner, not the Santa itself. Believe me, no one's missing *that*.

'I won't. I can't wait to get out of here.' There's just enough of a waver in his voice to make me wonder which one of us needs the most convincing.

Chapter 11

'I don't think I've ever been this relaxed in my life. What are you doing to me?'

'Trying to prove that cosy nights in, tree lights, and festive food have some merits after all …'

He lets out a long sigh and sinks further into my couch cushions. 'Do you have any idea how long it's been since someone made me crumpets and butter for supper?'

'But Christmas-tree-shaped crumpets taste better than regular crumpets, right?'

He narrows his eyes at me. 'All right, I'll give you that one.'

'Yes!' I do a victory punch, being careful not to jog the sofa too much.

He came home with me after we finished in the shop, and now the living-room lights are off, and we're both sitting on the sofa to admire the tree I finally got around to putting up last night. He's got cushions packed around him to support the ribs, his broken arm is resting on his chest and his good arm is propped up on a line of cushions between us and holding on to a mug of tea.

I settle back and sip my own tea as we look across the room at the tree, watching the white lights glowing steadily while the rainbow lights chase each other across the branches, reflecting off the glittery decorations and making everything sparkle. It's raining outside, pattering down on the roof, but the room is lit only by the Christmas lights and the orange glow coming from the fireplace. It feels warm and homely and it's special not to be alone for once. It's been a long time since I shared evenings with anyone.

'Doesn't that make you happy?' I nod towards the tree when he looks over at me.

He looks me directly in the eyes, and even in the low light, the look in his is breathtakingly intense. 'Something does. And it's been an impossible task lately.'

My hand drifts towards his bare arm on the cushions between us but I pull it back before I touch him. It's bad enough to feel this comfortable with him, I can't keep touching him too. 'Why?'

His head flops back and he blinks at the tree for a few moments and then closes his eyes. 'My father's dying.'

'What?' I look across at him sharply.

'I lied to you when I said he was retiring. I mean, he *is* retiring but he's retiring because he's dying of cancer. That's why I have to take over the business. He won't be here this time next year.'

'Oh God, James, I had no idea.' I sit up straighter and put my mug on the coffee table, pull my legs up underneath me and turn to face him. And you can forget about not touching him because my hand is already on his forearm, my fingers running through the fine dark hair covering it. 'I'm so sorry.'

'He and my mum run it together. They've been married for nearly sixty years, and she is *terrified* of how she's going to cope with losing him.' He hasn't opened his eyes yet. 'She can't deal with the business as well, so it's up to me to take over. That's why I came here this year. That's why I need your help. Because that business is the only thing that's ever mattered to my parents and it's up to me to keep it going. And I've failed at everything I've ever done.'

'I'm sure that's not true.'

181

'No, it really is. That's not being self-deprecating, that's being realistic. Jobs, relationships, you name it. I can't even cross a road safely.' He lifts the broken arm and clonks it back down onto his chest.

'And you *have* to take over the Christmas cracker business?'

'What?' He blinks his eyes open and focuses on me. 'Oh, yeah, that.'

My finger is drawing circle patterns on his forearm and I can't help the little fizzle of joy when he smiles at the movement. 'Are you the only one who can do it? No siblings or anything?'

'No, it's just me. No one else. Not even any extended family. I can't let my parents down, Nia. It means so much to them. They've put their whole hearts and souls into it, built it up into something really special for years, but things have been going downhill for a while, and now it's going to be handed over to me. Next Christmas, I have to not only keep it afloat but also make it the success it once was.'

'And you still can't find any Christmas spirit?'

'No.'

That one simple word makes a jolt go through me, because that's it, isn't it? He's never going to like Christmas. It's something I look forward to all year. Stace and I are already talking about our Christmas stock for next year. From late summer onwards, every surface of my house is covered with drying painted snowmen and sparkly red bits from glittering the chests of robin redbreasts. Realistically, what kind of relationship could I ever have with someone who's going to ridicule that?

'I get why it's special to you. I get why people like this time of year, but I can't wait for it to be over. I can't wait to get away from Nutcracker Lane. I thought coming here might unlock some sort of inspiration in me and I'd magically know what to do. But I still don't. And now it's even worse because I can see how much this time of year matters to people, and I don't want to let anyone down. My whole life has to go into saving this business.'

'This is what you meant when you were talking about doing things "while you still can"?' I think back to the things he said that didn't make sense at first. 'And what you said you hadn't shared with your friends?'

'Yeah. Like I said, I've kind of pulled back this year. Dad was fighting it. Operations, chemo, scans … everything that comes with a cancer diagnosis. We thought he was going to make it, and then early this year, we found out the cancer had spread and wasn't responding to treatment. I don't feel like going out drinking with the lads. I don't feel like listening to their talk of conquests and football matches and cars and marriage and kids. I've just needed to be alone. I don't know why I told you. I didn't mean to. You make me feel so comfortable that it just fell out.'

I can't help the proud smile that spreads across my face. 'Isn't that what friends are for?'

'Friends. Yeah.' He meets my eyes and then looks away, lifting his mug and downing his now-cold tea like it's something much stronger.

"Friends" doesn't feel right. I've *never* felt quite so strongly towards a friend before, but what else can we be? I'm not looking for another relationship, and he's obviously got a lot more going on in his life than I thought. 'What are you going to do?'

'I don't know. Blunder in blindly, mess everything up, and hope my mum can survive the heartbreak of watching her only son destroy the business she's dedicated nearly forty years of her life to?'

I want to put my hand over his heart, but the fingers of his broken arm are resting on his chest and I reach out and cover them gently with mine, letting my fingertips touch the soft cotton of his T-shirt. It's the closest I've come to one of his injuries and I wonder if I'm pushing him too far, but he doesn't pull away.

'Your hand is freezing,' I say in surprise.

'Having your fingers constantly stuck out of a cast will do that.'

I hold my hand out. 'Lift your arm, let me warm you up.'

Surprisingly, he does. He positions his elbow so it's supported by a cushion and lets his broken arm sink towards me. I bite my lip, my hands shaking as I hold my palm under his icy fingers and cover them gently with my other hand.

He lets out a shuddery breath and closes his eyes, letting his head drop back against the sofa again. It feels like he's putting an insane amount of trust in me, to let me hold his broken limb like this and trust me not to hurt him, *and* to open up like that.

'Even your hand is bruised,' I murmur, my eyes focused on the blueish purple skin emerging from the stark white cast that ends at the base of his thumb.

'Moving cars tend to do that when people walk into them.'

I want to pull his hand up to my mouth and blow on his freezing fingers to warm them, but I daren't move a millimetre. And it's probably a good thing because I want to lean across and press my lips to his smooth cheek and tell him it'll all be okay, but it won't, will it? He's about to lose his father and gain a business he doesn't want. 'Do you want some brutally honest advice from someone who barely knows you and has no right to comment on your life decisions, or do you want me to shut up and keep my beak out?'

He doesn't open his eyes, but a smile spreads across his relaxed face where his head is still leaning back. 'Advice, please. All the advice. You're the only person I've talked to about this. I can't tell my parents how apprehensive I am because they're dealing with enough as it is.'

'What do you *want* to do?'

'I don't know. I've never known. I grew up doing business studies and accounting and retail in the knowledge I'd be taking over one day. I rebelled and tried different careers and failed at all of them. I had no money so Dad gave me a job at their company, probably thinking that working there would inspire their love of Christmas in me, but I've failed at that too. Working on Nutcracker Lane, meeting you, and being dragged headfirst into Christmas has made me feel like a child again. I get all giggly when I'm with you, and I *cannot* remember the last time I giggled.

'Fixing things in the shop and seeing your crafts have reminded me of how much I used to like working with my hands, not sitting at a computer staring at numbers all day. Putting the decorations up at the lane, doing window displays, even putting those shelves up tonight has made me remember I had a creative side once. And none of that helps with … selling Christmas crackers.' He sounds so dejected in those last few words that I have to grit my teeth to avoid dropping his arm and wrapping him in a bear hug tight enough to break a few more ribs.

'James, if you don't want to take over this business, maybe the best thing you can do is refuse. I don't know your family, and I don't know you very well—'

He opens his eyes and meets mine. 'On the contrary, I've told you stuff I've never told anyone before. You know me better than all my friends and my immediate family now.'

I vehemently ignore how special that makes me feel. 'They wouldn't want to see you making yourself miserable. If you *can't* do this, maybe the best thing you can do for your parents, yourself, *and* the business is to admit it and find someone else. Someone who'd love it like they did. Someone who'd want to put in the time and effort it needs. You're trying to force yourself into loving something you hate so you can do something you don't want to do.'

The index finger of his good arm comes up to draw patterns on my forearm and goose bumps rise in their wake, but I carry on. 'You have no enthusiasm for it. You don't *want* to take over your family business – you're resigning yourself to it. No one wants a job like that, and believe me, *no* parent would want to see their son doing that.'

'I'm just scared of letting them down. I've realised lately that my approach so far has been all wrong, and I don't know how to fix it.'

185

'Then the kindest thing you can do is admit that.'

'I know. Believe *me*, I know.' He sighs. 'But how would I ever trust anyone? How would I ever know it would matter as much to someone else as it did to Mum and Dad? No one else is going to have that personal connection to it. When the going gets tough, no one is going to put in the effort they'd have put in because it's never going to be as important to anyone else.'

'But do you realise how important it is that you think that?'

He slowly screws one eye up and tilts his head to the side. 'No?'

'You're willing to do something you hate for the rest of your life because you care about their business *that* much. You're willing to come here and try to love Christmas – to actually change yourself so you can be a better fit to take over. You're trying to do the best thing you can for it – no one can ask for more than that. But you have to do what's best for you too.'

'I don't know what's best for me, but I do know I'll never forgive myself if I walk away.'

I'm still holding the fingers of his broken arm and his right hand is wrapped around my forearm from underneath now, his index finger trailing up and down from my inner wrist to inner elbow, and I'm trying not to think about it because every touch makes me shiver in a good way.

'Which is your favourite nutcracker?' Without lifting his head from the back of the sofa, he nods towards the nutcracker army on the living-room window ledge.

'You could just ask if we can change the subject, you know.'

He smiles at me sleepily. 'Sorry. It's all I've thought about for the past year and being with you distracts me. And I'm enjoying being distracted.'

'You can always talk to me. Even if you think I won't get it because I love Christmas, I'd still listen.' I look between him and the window ledge. 'You know, I've got a soft spot for that little unpainted wooden one *someone* gave me this year. Although I've always wanted a life-size one like you see in Hallmark movie sets. I think that'd really complete my collection.'

'That'd make you less lonely on winter nights.'

I don't mention that I haven't been lonely at all this December and I'm currently snuggling up with the reason. 'Didn't you ever have a proper Christmas?' I blurt out.

'Define proper?'

'Tubs of Quality Street, arguments over the last strawberry cream, family squabbles, the annual Trivial Pursuit and Scrabble games while Grandpa's snoring in the armchair and Grandma's telling everyone to pipe down so she can hear the Queen at 3 p.m., all sitting around wearing silly paper hats and getting abnormally excited about cheeseboards.'

He lets out such a loud laugh that it's a welcome sound after all the seriousness. 'Well, I understand the getting abnormally excited about cheeseboards bit, but nothing else. I don't have a big family, and Christmas has always been about work for my parents. When I was little, they'd hand me an Argos catalogue in November and tell me to circle everything I wanted, and it would all be under the tree on Christmas morning, but it was the people who worked for my dad who put it there. Christmas was delegated to his paid staff.

'Yeah, it was great having all the toys I could've dreamed of, but what my parents didn't understand was that I wanted *them* to play *with* me. I didn't want the *stuff* – I wanted the happy family Christmases I saw on TV. And that's never going to happen when you work until late on Christmas Eve, Christmas Day is a chance to catch up on admin and paperwork, and then it all starts up again on Boxing Day with trying to shift the excess stock that hasn't sold this season. My parents sold the illusion of a perfect Christmas, but our own Christmases were just a box-ticking exercise. Another chore to tick off the list. An inconvenience.

'I spent Christmases alone, waiting for my parents to be done with their paperwork so we could do something together. Other

187

days were easier because I could go round to friends' houses and stuff, but you can't do that on Christmas Day when everyone's with their families. To me it was a normal day where you couldn't *be* normal. The world forces you to acknowledge it and criticises you if you don't.'

His words conjure up an image of a little boy sitting in front of a Christmas tree, surrounded by toys, but sad and alone in the middle of what should be a happy scene. It's a good thing I'm still holding the fingers of his broken arm and I'm too afraid of hurting him to move a millimetre because it's enough to make me want to leap on him, snog him senseless, and promise he'll never be lonely at Christmas again.

One of his fingers twitches where they're sandwiched between mine and I squeeze them minutely tighter. 'You don't have to look so upset. As soon as I was old enough, I worked through Christmas and appreciated the uninterrupted day to catch up on admin.'

'That's a *terrible* way to see Christmas.'

'So yours were all about the family stuff then?'

'Yeah. Mum's house is a fifteen-minute walk away, so when I was little, me and my mum and dad used to come here to my grandma and grandpa's cottage, and she'd invite loads of cousins and aunts and uncles who we never saw at any other time of the year, and then after my little brother was born, Mum didn't want to drag a baby and all his stuff up the hill, so Grandma and Grandpa started coming to us and less and less extended family were invited.

'Mum was always crazed with the cooking, so my favourite thing on Christmas morning was walking up here to meet Grandma and help her carry the plates of food she'd made back to the house, and after my dad and then my grandpa died, our family Christmases gradually got smaller and smaller, but they were always *ours*. Everyone's Christmases are individual, and—'

'And no one's doing anything wrong if they choose to spend it working?'

'I think you spend enough time working, Grinch.' The name comes out as a murmur and my voice shakes with a rush of affection for him. I'm suddenly unable to stop myself touching him. I lift my hand carefully from his fingers and reach up to stroke his cheek where his face is still turned towards me, letting my nails trail lightly down his stubbled jaw. 'I wouldn't mind betting you've got three broken bones that were a direct result of working too hard.'

He untangles his hand from my forearm and slides it across mine on his cheek, his fingers slotting through mine and closing as he lifts it and pulls it to his mouth, pressing his lips against my knuckles.

It has *never* been such a good thing that I'm already sitting down.

He settles our joined hands to rest between his collarbone and shoulder, tucked under his chin, his hint of stubble grazing the back of my hand, and I close the fingers of my left hand gently around the fingers emerging from his cast, rubbing my thumb over them carefully, still astounded that he trusts me so much.

His injuries are the only thing stopping me from kissing him. Every part of my body is alive and tingling with the desire to do just that, and at the same time, I'm warm and relaxed and comfortable. I settle my head down against the back of the sofa and curl in a bit tighter, wishing the wall of cushions wasn't between us, smiling at him when he mirrors my position. It's been a long time since I felt this peaceful and at ease with someone.

189

Chapter 12

I'm alone when I wake up on the sofa, but I'm covered with the red-and-white fleece throw that I definitely don't remember putting there, and my hand twitches instinctively like I can still feel the weight of his hand in mine and the warmth of his fingers where they were intertwined. I groan as I stretch and put my legs down to try to get feeling back into them. It's been a long time since I spent a night curled over on the settee, and even longer since I spent the night with a man, even if it wasn't in *that* way.

I lean around the corner so I can see into the hallway and spot my keys on the doormat where he's posted them back through, and another Post-it Note reading *"Thank you ~ J"* is on the coffee table. The light filtering through the glass in the front door shows it's nearly daylight and I can't help wondering how long he's been gone. How did I not wake up as he moved around? How did I fall asleep with him in the first place? The last bloke I actually slept with was Brad and that was only after we'd been dating for months. I barely know James and yet somehow I can be comfortable enough to fall asleep with him.

I stretch out like a starfish and slide halfway off the sofa, groaning again as I heave myself up and go over to unplug the Christmas tree lights that got left on. Hanging on a branch at the front is a tiny, blocky, glittery nutcracker that I don't recognise. It's carved from a single block of wood, with painted green legs, a red torso, and a black hat. It doesn't have a lever, or a face, or the traditional furry hair and beard. It looks like the sort of thing you'd find inside a Christmas cracker and I remember James saying he used to make them. It must be from him.

It's later than I thought when I check the clock and I quickly shower and scarf down a couple of Christmas-tree-shaped crumpets before I dash out the door to meet Stacey on the way to work.

James's car is already in the car park, and there's a light on in the back of his shop when we get in. There are quite a few shopkeepers in early judging by the number of lights on, and there's not yet a gap in the line of nutcrackers that run down either side of the lane, all the way from the entrance door to the tree lot at the opposite end. And even though James and I got involved in setting them up so they're standing side-by-side like an army hand-in-hand, a line through every shop window and along the ground, I have to admit it's an impressive sight when you walk in.

I'm even more impressed when we open the shop door at nine and there are already a couple of shoppers wandering around. Could the nutcracker army being sent out into the streets be working already? In the past couple of days, James and I have divided a thousand of his nutcrackers into boxes for every shop and asked every owner to hide them around their local area. It's Friday today, and everyone has said they'll hide them on dog walks and days out over the weekend, so hopefully it'll gain a bit of attention by Monday.

Stacey and Lily hid some last night on the way home from school, and James and I took the scenic route back to my house and poked some into hedges and trees and stood them at my neighbours' garden gates and leaning against their garden walls.

Within five minutes of being open, I'm behind the counter serving a lady buying a hand-painted "Joy to the World" sign

191

that shows the words entwined in a reindeer's curled antlers and has got 3D paper poinsettias glued on and leaves a trail of glitter everywhere it goes, when James pops his head in the door and grins at me. 'Hey, can I—'

'You're wearing an elf hat!' I feel like a Christmas tree when someone's just plugged the lights in at the sight of him. And it's not *just* the elf hat. Although it is adorable. And something I *never* thought I'd see him wear.

He does the Flynn Rider smile that's so wide, it's almost like he has to speak from the side of his mouth to accommodate it. 'You said you like people who throw themselves into the season and aren't afraid to wear silly things. I think this qualifies.'

I quickly finish the transaction and the lady nods at him as she leaves. 'It suits you, dear.' She turns back to me. 'You know you've got a handsome man when he can even make an elf hat look good.'

I dissolve into a fit of giggles as James's cheeks go the same colour as the red stripes in the knitted hat on his head.

'Hat shop, fourth on the left,' he calls after her as she heads up the lane.

'Encouraging shared custom – that's good.' Stacey comes out of the back room with an armful of new jewellery to restock what was sold yesterday. '*Nice* hat.'

The bell in the tip of the green-and-red-striped cable knit hat jingles when he moves as he steps inside. 'Do you mind if I borrow Nia for a minute?' he asks her. 'I keep stealing her for this, that, or the other.'

'Oh, I assure you, it's not *the other* I'm worried about.' Stacey shoos us both away. 'Go on. Make sure you get up to a bit of this, that, *and* the other.'

'Are you sure you don't mind?' I turn back to Stace as I go to follow James out. I keep leaving her to cover the shop while we've been busy setting the nutcrackers out, and although she always says she doesn't mind, it's becoming a daily thing.

'Of course not. Nee, one of the main reasons we decided to go into this together was so I can go to school assemblies and parent–teacher meetings and pick Lily up when Simon's working late, and so you can go off with hot men who look like Disney princes whenever you need to and neither of us have to worry about the shop being covered. It said those specific words in our contract.'

I grin. Our contract would've been a lot more fun if there *had* been a mention of Disney princes in it.

'Besides, you two are trying to *save* Nutcracker Lane – that benefits all of us in the long run,' she continues. 'And if Simon looked like *that*, I wouldn't want to leave his side for a moment either.'

'It's nothing to do with th—'

'Your whole demeanour changed when he popped his head in. We met when we were eleven, Nia, and I've *never* seen you react like that to a man. He's someone special, even if you don't realise it yet.'

I can tell from the grin on her face that she knows I've already realised it but I don't give her the satisfaction of admitting it. 'Back in a minute.'

'Take your time,' she calls after me. 'Take *all* your time. As much *time* as you need.'

I pull my gingerbread woman jumper down as I follow James and go up the step into his shop, giving the Macarena-ing Santa a wide berth.

'What are you up to?' I look around at the chaos. Almost everything from the window is strewn around the aisles and he's got the nutcracker village onto a shelf and is trying to lift it one-handed. I rush over and take the other side. 'You're not meant to be lifting heavy things.'

'It's not heavy, it's just so bulky that I don't have enough functioning arms to manage it.' He makes us turn around with the plastic village between us, even though I protest that if we

193

fall over, it's going to hurt him a lot more than it will me, but he's ever the perfect gent and insists on being the one to walk backwards.

'What are you doing with all this stuff?' I ask as we pull into the side to avoid the group of carollers walking up the lane and singing "We Wish You A Merry Christmas". Angela waves cheerily.

'Are there more?' I say to James, my eyes following the singers over my shoulder as they swish up the lane in their floor-length Victorian dresses. It's impossible to count them.

'Maybe. I don't know. I'm used to counting sales figures, I never thought I'd end up counting carol singers.'

It makes me laugh as we carry on moving.

'Giving it back,' he says quietly.

It takes me a moment to realise he's not still talking about the carol singers.

'You were right. It's not mine to sell. Why should I earn money for stuff that can be used to improve the lane?'

'What about what the new owner wanted? I thought you were "following orders"? Aren't you going to be in trouble?'

'Frosted reindeer bollocks to the owner. By the time anyone even realises, I'll be long gone. I won't be here after Christmas; I won't have to deal with the consequences. What's the worst anyone's going to do? I've still got shelves of the excess products he wants sold, but this big stuff that used to be part of the lane itself … Let's put it back.'

He winks at me and I feel so fluttery that I nearly trip over my own feet. Stacey's right – I can't remember the last time a man had this effect on me. I've *never* looked forward to seeing someone before. Never missed someone when they weren't there or searched for excuses to spend time with them. And yet, every time James smiles, I forget about everything else in the universe. Apart from the enthusiastic way he talks about not being here after Christmas and how it makes my stomach drop.

We turn the corner at the end of the lane by the Christmas

bookshop and go down the narrow offshoot from the main lane that leads to the point where the nutcracker factory behind joins. There are large security doors separating the two, but before you get to those, there's the outlet shop where my grandma used to bring me every year to buy a new nutcracker to add to our collection.

It's manned by factory staff rather than rented by independent shopkeepers like the rest of Nutcracker Lane, and although it used to be open all the time, the factory have obviously decided it's not worth it anymore because it now only seems to open whenever they've got an excess of staff and can spare someone to sit in there for a couple of hours.

'Have you bought this year's nutcracker yet?' James asks like he can tell what I'm thinking.

'I've yet to see it open this year. I check it every time I walk past. They've restocked the nutcrackers but seem to have given up on actually allowing people to buy them.'

'The lane's been too quiet. You can see why they wouldn't want to spare the staff. At least the ones being made in the factory are guaranteed to be shipped overseas or sold wholesale. Why waste time on a dead end – literally?' He uses his eyes to gesture to the corridor around us. It's narrower than the main part of Nutcracker Lane. The ceiling is low and claustrophobic, covered in unlike the rest of the lane, and all that's down here is the nutcracker outlet shop, the public toilets, and the security doors that lead to the covered walkway between the Christmas village and the factory. The factory that's soon to be expanded if Scrooge gets his way.

It really is a dead end. The doors are foreboding steel with plenty of "Danger: Keep Out" signs covering them and both a key and a security code required to enter them from this side, neither of which anyone on Nutcracker Lane has. When school trips came here to go on a tour of the nutcracker factory, this was always the meeting point where children and teachers would be greeted by a surly-looking bloke in a hard hat and yellow safety jacket with a clipboard and list of rules to follow.

The budget for school field trips is one of the many things that was cut years ago, back when Scrooge first decided they didn't pull in enough cash and cost too much in staff training and health and safety measures, regardless of how much enjoyment they gave children or how popular they were with people who could book tours during certain times in December.

'But the nutcrackers they sell are special.' I nod to the outlet shop. 'Not just standard mass-produced ones, but special ones from the factory – ones with mistakes and flaws, ones that were tested but never put into production, practice pieces, and ones that are wonky or otherwise unsellable, all with characteristics that you don't find in typical high-street stores. That's why my grandma always came here for the yearly nutcracker. She liked unusual things and things that didn't quite make the grade. She was the kind of person who felt sorry for the last little spindly tree in the lot and brought it home to nurture it back to health and would always buy the limp 10p plants on the sale shelves in the garden centre and lovingly plant them up and tell them how special they were and be oh so proud when they flowered beautifully the following year.'

'So doing well with broken things runs in the family then?' He looks down at himself, and it takes all my willpower not to drop the nutcracker village and throw my arms around him.

'You're not … I mean …' I swallow hard and shake my head at myself. 'If I plant you in the garden and tell you you're special every day, are you going to sprout daffodils from your head next spring?' I turn it into a joke because it's not normal to want to hug someone this often.

'If you make me feel that special, I'll turn into Santa and fly through the Northern Lights on a reindeer for you.'

I grin and take it for the joke it is, because I *can't* tell him I think he might be the most special person I've ever met.

There's a podium next to the security doors with an empty display case on it, and James balances his side of the nutcracker model village against his hip while he digs a set of keys out of his pocket to unlock it, and between us, we slide the model back onto the stand and switch it on. A tinny tune of the most recognisable bars of *The Nutcracker* ballet opening march plays and the miniature conveyor belt starts moving tiny plastic nutcrackers into the model factory and out the other side.

'It looks better here.'

I look up at him and smile. 'I approve of the hat.'

He reaches out towards my chest and lifts the glittery green resin Christmas tree necklace I pulled over my head this morning. 'One of Stace's test pieces. I get all of her trial runs before she decides whether to make a full batch of them, and she gets all of mine. Lily's got a whole box full of half-legged or one-antlered wooden reindeer to paint because she won't let me throw them away.'

He smiles as he settles the necklace back against my chest and his hand drifts down my arm until his fingers close around mine and he tugs gently. 'C'mere.'

Instead of pulling me to him, he pulls me back up the small corridor until we're huddled under a lamppost. 'What are you doing?'

'I wanted to say thank you for last night.' He casts his eyes upwards and before I realise what he's doing, he leans down to press his lips against my cheek. It's just a quick peck with no lingering this time, but it catches me off-guard and he pulls back before I have a chance to register that I wanted to grab him and pull him closer.

'And you just *had* to do that under the mistletoe?'

'No, but I thought it'd be more fun this way.' He's smiling in a way that says he couldn't stop if he tried to.

I can feel the smile on my face mirroring his and there isn't a single part of me that *doesn't* want to reach up and pull him down so we can do it again.

'You must think I suffer from narcolepsy,' he says, thankfully

197

before I have a chance to act on my desires. 'Every time you turn your back on me for two minutes, I fall asleep on your sofa.'

An unexpected laugh bursts loudly out of my mouth and takes the moment for kissing him away with it. 'I think you're stressed out with everything that's going on in your life and you're schlepping around three broken bones and a *hell* of a lot of bruising, and not giving yourself anywhere near enough credit for how draining that is. Pain is exhausting, and so is the way you've got to think about every little movement and change the way you do things to accommodate the injuries. I think you keep going and going and push through it, no matter how much you're hurting, and when you do finally take the weight off your feet, you realise you're so exhausted, you can barely hold your head up.'

I'm not sure I should have said all that, especially when he starts shaking his head, but his mouth tips up into a smile. 'I've known you for eleven days and you already know me better than my own family do.'

His eyes are sparkling, dancing under the warm orange glow of the lamp above our heads, and I think it's best to change the subject quickly. 'Thank you for the nutcracker on the tree.'

'It's been years since I made one. I can't even remember how to. Feel free to laugh.'

'You said you like working with your hands. If you ever want to play around in my shed when your arm's better ...'

'Is that like The Wizard inviting Dorothy behind the curtain?'

'Well, you *would* look rather fetching in sparkly red heels.'

He laughs so hard that he ends up pressing his upper arm against his ribcage in an attempt to cushion the broken ribs.

'We should get back,' I say, kind of hoping he can hear how reluctant I sound. Standing under the mistletoe with James for the rest of the day would be fine by me, but judging by the state of his shop when I went in, there's a lot more decorations to get out, and the fact I've left Stacey by herself again in our shop.

'Yeah, I know.' His voice is low and husky and despite his

words, he makes no attempt to move. Instead, he reaches out so his fingers drag down the sleeve of my gingerbread woman jumper and he lifts my hand. 'Nia, I need to—'

'There you are!'

I hadn't realised how quiet it was in this part of the building until Carmen's shriek makes us both jump and James drops my hand like we've been caught doing something unthinkable.

'Hubert said he'd seen you come this way. She wants a polar bear!'

'Who?' James looks as confused as I feel. 'Hubert?'

'Noooo, a darling young girl making a wish. I think she meant a real one but there's only so far we can go. You've got cuddly polar bears, haven't you? Come on, quickly. Mrs Brissett's keeping an eye so we don't lose her!' She takes hold of his arm and physically hauls him away. 'And you look just the ticket in that hat, a perfect Nutcracker Lane elf! Come on, Nia, you too!'

James rushes to keep up with her and I realise she doesn't even know his ribs are broken because I'm pretty sure I'm still the only person he's told.

When we get back onto the main part of the lane, Carmen invites herself inside James's shop and we watch from the doorway as she starts rooting through the basket of soft toys, digging through them and discarding them like a cartoon mole burrowing through a lawn. I go to check on Stacey and then stand next to James, watching Mrs Brissett surreptitiously stalking a young girl walking down the lane hand-in-hand with each parent.

'Where are you going?' I ask as Hubert races past.

'A scooter! He wants a scooter! They've got one in the window of that toy shop three streets away. He's gone to see Santa! I'll make it before he leaves if I rush.'

I look pointedly at the wallet in his hand. There's no way Nutcracker Lane has a budget for scooters. 'You're not supposed to be spending your own money on this.'

He stops, even though he's obviously in a hurry and already

199

out of breath. 'It's just a little expense, Nia, but it's worth it. I'm not made of money, but I can afford a little extra here and there. We have a chance to save Nutcracker Lane. You two have *given* us a chance. If it's not worth a little investment by the people who love it most, then what hope have we got?'

He doesn't give me a chance to protest any further as he rushes off. When I look up at James, I see the same feeling reflected in his eyes. I'm not sure if I feel uncomfortable or touched by shop-keepers spending their own money. That was never the intention, but it's heart-warming they want to.

'This one!' Carmen emerges from the shop victoriously, a fluffy white polar bear clutched in her fist, and charges off up the lane, leaving James and I to hurry after her.

Mrs Brissett meets us and we all huddle behind one of the pillars. Carmen thrusts the polar bear at James. 'You go.'

'Why me?' He says, half-laughing.

She shrugs. 'Your shop. Your polar bear. You've got an elf hat on. Go on, quick!'

Surveillance mission complete, Mrs Brissett departs for the magical nutcracker, and I watch with Carmen as James intercepts the family and explains who he is.

Carmen nods to where he's kneeling on the floor so he's the same height as the little girl. 'Nothing's going to show him the true meaning of Christmas faster than seeing children believe in magic. 'Tis the season of giving, after all. That's what Christmas is all about.'

The little girl clutches her polar bear happily and waves to James until she and her parents are out of sight.

'I'm never wearing an elf hat again,' he says with a groan as I hold my hand out to pull him up and his fingers slot around mine.

'Oh, I assure you, you are.' I haul him back onto his feet even though I don't think he needed any assistance. 'If it's not an elf hat, I have an *endless* supply of Christmas headbands and hats to force on you, including a big tinselly Christmas tree that sits on your head with flashing lights, and a hat depicting Santa's upside down legs going down the chimney. All very fetching, I'm sure you'll agree.'

He grins despite being threatened with festive headgear. 'And if I show up looking any less festive than *this* between now and December 25th, you're going to torture me with increasingly more awful Christmas hats daily until I beg for mercy?'

'Exactly,' I say cheerfully, my grin matching his.

He hasn't let go of my hand yet, and I think the closeness is scrambling my brain because I'm not even sure what we're talking about.

'Does it look busier to you?' He finally realises our hands are still entwined and extracts his fingers from mine.

'Kind of,' I say because I'd thought it but hadn't dared to hope it might be true, but I can't be imagining things if he's noticed it too. We're halfway up the lane between the florist and the coffee shop, and it *does* look busier than it has in recent days.

A woman walks past clutching one of the nutcrackers we've hidden and James nudges his shoulder into my arm excitedly, offering me a gleeful grin when I look up at him. We start wandering up towards the magical nutcracker and he nudges me every time we see people stopping to admire the line of nutcrackers. It really does seem busier, with people stepping out of shops and sitting on the benches eating cakes from the Nutcracker Lane bakery and carrying coffee cups from the coffee shop. Not a huge number, but it's been so quiet lately that even the smallest increase in visitors is noticeable.

Mrs Brissett's daughter is covering her shop, so Mrs Brissett is in full wish reconnaissance mode, lurking behind the giant nutcracker with a mop and bucket, pretending to be a cleaner to blend in.

Behind us, there's a commotion as Hubert whizzes back up the lane on the scooter he'd gone to buy, crashes, and tumbles head-first into the boy and family he'd bought it for. It's impossible not to laugh at the scene and I can't help looking up at James, at the crow's feet crinkling around his eyes and his bright, resplendent smile, a tell-tale dent in his cheek as he bites the inside of it to stop himself laughing out loud as we watch Hubert pick himself up, dust himself down, and hand the scooter safely over to its intended owner, along with a bag of peppermint sweets that are now crushed to smithereens.

'You look like you're having fun.'

'I am.' James looks surprised as the words pop out. I'm surprised too, because I'd expected him to mutter something Grinchy and walk away, but his eyes are shining when he looks back at me. 'I really am, Nee. This place … These people … I feel like part of something here. I've never felt like that before.'

'It feels like you were meant to be here this year.' I don't say *quite* how much he's added to my experience of Nutcracker Lane, and how different things would've been if his shop hadn't opened opposite ours. When I'm with him, I feel like anything's possible, even saving Nutcracker Lane, and a few weeks ago, that felt like a truly impossible dream. 'Things would be different if you hadn't come along.'

'Nia, I—' James is cut off by having to jump aside as Hubert's ward zooms past us on the scooter, and from the pained expression on his face, the jolt obviously hurt. The boy does a turn and zooms back and we decide it's safer to head up to the magical nutcracker and see how Mrs Brissett's doing with her wish-granting.

'A unicorn, and a snowstorm big enough to close the school for a whole year,' she reports as we approach, shaking her head of grey curls fondly. There's something so adorable about childhood innocence. Deep down inside, wouldn't we *all* like a unicorn and a snowstorm?

A boy goes towards the giant nutcracker, and James crouches down and pretends to be doing something to the lamppost control box and I turn around and examine the point where the end of the tinsel is attached to the metal post like it's so enthralling that it could be a miniature Colin Firth performing a striptease.

He inclines his head until he can look up and wink at me, and we listen as the boy takes his nut from the vending machine and goes up to the nutcracker. He's not the usual type of person you expect to make wishes on magical nutcrackers, and I can't help sidling around so I can see him, pretending to examine the lamppost so thoroughly that a tiny Hugh Grant could now have joined the miniature Colin Firth in this festive striptease.

The lad is about fifteen or sixteen with messy blond hair and an oversized hoody, and he keeps looking around like he's hoping his mates won't spot him. I expect him to wish for the latest iPhone or other hugely expensive technological thing, but he breaks his nut and says quietly, 'I wish for something to bring my family together.'

'What does that mean?' I whisper to James.

'People are so divided these days. You can live with a whole family you know nothing about. One of my best friends knows more about his own sister from following her on social media than he does from actual conversations. People spend every moment on their phones. Even when they have "family time", their phones are still on the table so they're distracted by the possibility of a notification or what they might be missing on Twitter.'

'Times were better when we were young. I'm eternally grateful for growing up in the Nineties.'

'A board game!' James gets to his feet, looking like the injuries force him to take longer than he wants to. He leans around the lamppost so he can whisper to me. 'My favourite ever Christmas gift was an original Waddington's Monopoly. It had a big red box with a white stripe down the middle, little metal pieces, red hotels and green houses that would somehow always escape the box and you'd only find out when you accidentally trod on one later. It was the only thing my parents ever played with me. The Christmas I got it, the electricity went off, so Mum made hot chocolate with marshmallows on a little camping stove and we all sat around with candles and played three games of Monopoly one after the other. I always feel like *that's* what Christmases should've been like and that was the closest we ever got to it.'

'Where are you going to find a board game?'

'I'll tell you what, at this rate, the place that's going to profit most from Nutcracker Lane is that toy shop Hubert mentioned. I'm going to … well, I was going to say run over there, but I tried to run the other day and it didn't end well. I'm going to *walk* in the fastest and least impactful way possible. Don't lose that kid. I'll be back as soon as I can.'

He's taken off before I even have a chance to tell him to be careful, and I don't want to shout after him because of drawing attention to myself when I'm supposed to be following the teenager like some sort of super spy.

Like luck is on our side, the lad goes into the coffee shop and sits down with his drink, so engrossed in his phone that he doesn't notice me lurking outside. When he comes out, he goes into the bakery and then the candle shop to pick a gift, and Mrs Thwaite notices me loitering, realises what's going on, and makes him smell every candle in the shop to see which one his mum might like, and by the time she lets him leave, James is hurrying up the lane with a paper bag in his hand, his face red and his forehead glistening under the band of the elf hat, looking like he's seriously overdone things.

'Here. Your turn.' He hands me the bag and sits down on a bench, short of breath. I don't have a chance to protest that it was his idea in the first place because the lad is almost out of sight and I'm certainly not about to drag James up and let him overexert himself anymore.

'Excuse me?' I rush after the boy and introduce myself when he turns around. I have no idea what to say. My mouth has gone dry. I've never granted a wish before. James seems to be a natural at it; he has an innate patter and charm, but I do not. I stutter and stumble my way through an explanation about how we're giving away things to improve people's Christmases and how board games are good for families spending time together, aware of James's eyes on me from further up the lane.

All the while in the back of my mind, I'm thinking we could have misinterpreted the wish and his parents could be divorced and fighting all the time and how many things "something to bring my family together" could mean, and I half-expect the teenage lad to laugh at being given a board game and shove it back in my face like I'm a random Christmas-jumper-wearing weirdo.

'Vintage. Cool!' A smile spreads across his face as he peers into the bag. 'You're not trying to scam me, are you, Mrs Gingerbread?' He nods to the image on my jumper.

I don't want to openly tell him that we overheard his wish on the nutcracker, because the most magical thing about it is the possibility that it *might* be magic – that people are going to get these things and wonder if they really are somehow an answer to a wish. 'Nope, just a promotion we're running today to try and bring families together.'

If he notices I've reused his own words, he doesn't show it. 'S'all right, this place. Only came coz I found a nutcracker hanging out by some traffic lights, but you got good coffee and free stuff. Cheers!'

'Merry Christmas,' I call after him as he walks away, swinging the bag on one finger. I'm nowhere near cool enough to communicate with teenagers.

I'm well aware that James hasn't taken his eyes off me as I walk back up the lane, muttering all the way about how Monopoly being described as "vintage" makes me feel old.

I fold my arms and give him a purposely stern look when I get back to the bench where he's sitting. 'I think you forget how much of a toll injuries take on your body.' I hold out my hand to pull him up, but he shakes his head so I sit down beside him instead.

I'm on his left side this time, next to his broken arm, and his head instantly drops onto my shoulder. I automatically reach up to play with the fluffy white pompom on the tip of his elf hat where it's dangling down and resting against his neck.

'Did that feel good?'

His head on my shoulder? Oh, his head on my shoulder feels *very* good indeed. It takes me an embarrassing amount of time to realise he's not talking about that. 'It really did. I don't know if he even recognised the significance between that and what he'd said to the nutcracker, but yeah. I wish we could do more. There are so many wishes we're not going to be able to touch.'

'We're just a few people doing what we can,' he says. 'No one can expect more than that. The shopkeepers are already spending their own money on this. I never expected that.'

'Who bought that board game?' I say even though it's a rhetorical question because we both know he isn't going to claim it back on expenses.

'We should move.' He lifts his head, deliberately avoiding the question.

I stand up and hold my hand out again, and this time he lets me haul him to his feet. The bench happens to be situated under a lamppost with a sprig of mistletoe hanging from it, and he leans forward and presses his lips to my cheek again. Another peck that isn't nearly long enough.

'Really, Miss Maddison, we're going to have to stop meeting like this.' He mouths the words against my skin before kissing my cheek again and pulling away.

'Decorating these lampposts was your idea. You should've known there'd be mistletoe involved.'

'Oh, I was counting on it.' He gives me such a cheeky wink that it makes my knees feel so weak that I'm glad we're standing in front of a bench in case they give out. I've never noticed any problems with my knees before but James is having a shockingly negative impact on them.

'In fact, I think we should put some mo ... That's a weird camera.'

I follow his gaze when his sentence trails off and I see a man photographing the line of nutcrackers with what can only be described as a professional camera.

'What are you up to?' James asks nonchalantly as we approach him.

'*The Wiltshire Walkabout*. Following up some comments we've been receiving online. Quite a few people talking about these little chaps on our social media accounts. Something to do with this old place closing down?'

Even the words make a cold shiver run down my spine, but it's instantly replaced by James's hand as he gently but determinedly encourages me forward. 'This is Nia Maddison, the organiser.'

'We're co-organisers,' I say quickly.

'Oh, excellent.' The man pulls his phone out, presses a couple of buttons, and holds it up to show me the microphone symbol to indicate it's recording audio. 'Can you say a few lines about what's going on here? I'm going to run this on the website because people are curious, but if it gets a good response, it'll get a spot in the local newspaper on Monday too.'

At first I think I'll be nervous, but it's so quick and informal, and James's hand doesn't move from the centre of my spine between my shoulder blades, his fingertips rubbing minutely against my jumper, and by the time I've finished talking about how wonderful Nutcracker Lane used to be and how much things have changed, the man looks like he regrets asking.

He thanks me and hurries away, but we watch him dart into a few shops with his phone still in hand, surely to get comments from some of the other shopkeepers too.

'You said you wanted someone to listen,' James says as we head back to Starlight Rainbows. 'Maybe wishes do come true.'

I look up at him and he grins back at me, his brown eyes dancing with all the shades of wood.

It's definitely not beyond the realm of possibility.

Chapter 13

'Don't eat that, that's the door!'

'Sorry,' James says with his mouth full. 'Can't it be an open house this year? Y'know, warm and welcoming? Inviting people in via the *open* door?'

'It's a good job there's still plenty of dough left.'

'I'm sorry, but you put fresh-baked warm gingerbread in front of me and I can't control myself. I'm just testing it to make sure it's up to standard. Call me Quality Control.'

By December 15th, to say I'm having a slight panic about all the baking I haven't done yet would be an understatement. James has come over after work to help, officially part of his un-Grinching, although judging by the number of wishes he's been granting lately, I'm not sure how much help he needs on that front.

I should be telling him off for eating everything I can make as soon as it comes out of the oven, but the truth is that I *love* seeing him enjoy it, even if it was a vital part in the construction of the gingerbread house that was supposed to be made weeks ago.

He eats the cut-out bit of the window. 'This is just going to stand there for decoration. Don't we deserve to enjoy it too? What's the point of making something edible look so nice when you can't actually consume it until it needs hoovering and dusting first?'

'They're made for visual enjoyment.' I try not to laugh even though he has a point. 'I'll make a batch of gingerbread men for edible enjoyment before Christmas.'

'Can I come and help?'

'Like you're helping with that?' I raise an eyebrow as I carry on spooning the royal icing into a piping bag, ready to stick the pieces together.

'I'm supervising!' He nods towards the sides and roof of the gingerbread house laid out on oven trays covering the kitchen unit. 'I'm supervising these getting cold enough to construct.'

'A vital job. The whole process would fall apart without you.'

He pops another window into his mouth and grins at me, and even though I'm trying to be annoyed, I *cannot* stop myself grinning back at him. He knows I'm teasing, and I'd be so embarrassed if he had even half a clue about how happy I was when he still wanted to follow through on his promise to help with the gingerbread house.

I've used my grandma's recipe for the walls and roof parts – one with less baking soda to stop it rising and less butter for a stronger, firmer gingerbread – and between us we've got the dough made, eaten dinner while it was chilling, and James has stood back while I've rolled and cut each panel to within a millimetre of its life and used every oven tray I own to get them baked. It's the first time since we lost my grandma that I've used this recipe, and the first time I've ever attempted a gingerbread house on my own. Well, not on my own – *with* James. I glance over at him. He's now eating the garden path.

'You know you're going to have to come over again sometime and help me replace all the bits you've eaten, don't you?'

His whole face brightens as a smile creeps slowly from one side of his mouth to the other. 'Why do you think I'm doing it?'

The oven has heated up the kitchen, but his words make me

feel even more overheated. I'm *sure* he's only joking, but the idea that he might not be makes butterflies start zipping around inside, and they don't dissipate when the construction begins.

My hair is up in a ponytail and my fringe is held back by a Mrs Claus red sequinned bow with fluffy white trim, and it's so warm in the kitchen that this is probably the first time James has ever seen me without a Christmas jumper on. He's wearing a grey T-shirt too, and I made him put an apron on – one that's patterned with rows of dancing mince pies and Christmas puddings, mainly because he seems to understand the benefit of novelty Christmas clothing now, and even he had to smile as I reached up and slipped it over his head. It's almost as adorable as the reindeer antlers I made him put on to keep his hair back while he muttered and grumbled something about dying of embarrassment if anyone saw him like this.

The apron also means there's not much fabric between us as I squeeze in between him and the unit and start setting all the pieces aside, wash and dry the worktop and lay down greaseproof paper to protect it from icing spills.

He goes over to the sink to wash his hands while I start lining up pieces of gingerbread house in some sort of formation and working out where they'll be glued together. It's been so many years since I've done this and I feel rusty and out of practice, but it doesn't matter. Gingerbread houses are never perfect – and they'd be boring if they were. Each one is individual – that's the point.

James comes back and instead of standing next to me like I expected, he stands halfway behind me, barely touching but close enough to feel the heat from his body. His chin is close enough that I can feel every breath against my hair, and the press of the elbow above his cast as he holds his broken arm out of the way and his right arm comes around from underneath my arm and he turns his hand over so it waves up at me. 'Use me in any way you want.'

All thoughts of gingerbread houses go out of my head because all I can think about doing is turning around in his kind-of embrace, wrapping my arms around his neck and snogging him senseless, and it takes a *lot* of willpower to concentrate on the freshly baked walls in front of me. I pick one up and pipe a line of royal icing along the bottom and stand it up on the silver cake board base. I position his hand to hold the wall until the icing sets hard enough to keep it upright, while I pipe another line of icing along two sides of the next wall and stick it alongside the first one. He holds it in place while I turn the base around and pipe another line of icing along the adjacent side, and then pick up the next wall and splodge it in, wiping up the icing that splurges out and using it to plug the gaps.

James supports the structure while I pipe wobbly lines of icing, which probably wouldn't be *quite* so wobbly if he wasn't filling each one of my senses. His cologne is in my nose, some warming spice that would go on top of a steamy cinnamon drink, with an earthy hint of something natural like the wood of a newly sawn tree trunk.

Every breath is in my ear or stirring the hairs on the back of my neck. His body is warm and solid behind me, and his good arm is resting on my hip where it's underneath my arm. I'm sure it's not the most sensible position for gingerbread house construction, but I wouldn't want it to be any other way, and it's definitely a good thing that both my hands are occupied because I want to reach blindly behind me and pull him closer. He's the perfect height to stand next to because my head tucks in under his chin and his stubble brushes against my hair every time he speaks, and I'm not sure if it's being this close to him or inhaling so much icing sugar that's scrambling my brain.

Somehow we get enough of a routine going that it doesn't take long for the gingerbread house to be complete, and I stand back, my hands braced around it but not touching, ready to catch it the moment it falls apart.

'Wow,' James murmurs. 'I had no idea how these were made.'

'Well, now it's your turn. You're going to decorate it.'

He bursts out laughing so hard that it makes him wince. 'It's not fair of you to make me laugh that much when laughing's still so painful. You *are* joking, right?'

'Of course not. Decorating a gingerbread house is a rite of Christmas passage.'

'Yeah, but *with* you. You do the bits that are supposed to look nice and I'll stick some gumdrops on or something. You don't have time to redo it when I destroy it.'

'You won't. And I *don't* have time, that's exactly why I'm delegating. You get on with that and I'm going to make a start on the Christmas cake. You know the one that's supposed to have been fed with brandy every week since November?'

He looks down at the biscuit structure like it might morph into a flying reindeer and take a lap round the room at any moment, chewing his lip so hard that I want to reach up and free it from his teeth before he bites through it. 'And you trust me not to ruin it?'

'Of course.'

He smiles like the words render him physically incapable of *not* smiling. 'No one in my life trusts me not to wreck anything. I am the most untrustworthy person when it comes to wrecking things.'

'You're also creative and artistic with a good eye for detail. And I think it's been a long while since you let that side out. Christmas is the best time of year for letting your imagination run wild, so let yourself go and imagine you're a child again and it doesn't matter what it looks like as long as you enjoy it.'

'I've only got one working hand!'

'Yeah, but it's your dominant hand. Squeeze the top of the bag with your right hand; all you need to do with your left is guide it. Say if it's too much and I'll take over.' I twist the top of the icing bag, pick up his hand and place the filled bag into it, and he lets me curl his fingers around it in roughly the positions they should be in. 'Use this thicker mix for the outlines and then we'll make it thinner for filling in or just go to town on the sweets over

212

there.' I nod towards the tray of various sweets and chocolates I bought last week for this sole purpose.

I decide not to overthink it or let him talk himself out of it and I go across and start filling the sink with the empty bowls we've used so far and wash up the ones I'll need for the Christmas cake, trying not to watch James as he stands in silence pondering the gingerbread house, turning the base occasionally, looking like an artist contemplating his next art exhibition.

I set out the mixing bowls I need on the other side of the kitchen unit with the sink in between us. 'Before you start covering things, can I scribble down an inventory of what we still need to make?' I grab my notebook and pencil and go over to him. 'Another door, that bit of the chimney that broke, and the outside stuff. Another path, a couple of bushes, and some Christmas trees.' I write them down as I say them. 'Oh, and we need a gingerbread man and woman to stand outside, inviting guests into their *open* door.' I give him a pointed look but I can't stop myself smiling. I don't think I've ever smiled as much as I have in the past few weeks.

'Oh, yeah, because *that's* realistic. A happy couple, even made of gingerbread, is laughable.'

'It's Christmas. We're supposed to believe in the impossible.'

He looks up and meets my eyes, and for just a moment, I see something in them. Understanding. Hurt. A pain that for once isn't caused by his physical injuries.

His gaze flickers and he looks away. 'Can we have her bit-on-the-side hiding round the back and the husband holding gingerbread divorce papers in his hand?'

I'm not sure whether to laugh or not, but he speaks again before I have a chance to figure it out. 'Sorry, that was cynical even for me.'

'I'm kind of ... adapting ... to your cynicism.'

He smiles but it doesn't reach his eyes, and I want to question him, but I force myself to go back to my side of the sink. I start getting Christmas cake ingredients out of the cupboards, filling the unit with packets of dried fruit and nuts and spice bottles, but by the time I've measured out the wrong amount of brown sugar and used the wrong kind of flour, I realise it's because he's all I can think about. I risk a glance at him and he's concentrating intensely on piping lines of royal icing onto the gingerbread roof. 'What happened?'

'What?' He doesn't look up although I'm certain he knows what I mean because his lines on the roof are so neat that I couldn't possibly be talking about the icing.

'Even you couldn't reach that level of cynicism without being hurt somewhere in the past. Whoever did a number on you before … what happened?' I wonder if I'm being too pushy. It's easy to forget that I've only know him for two weeks. We're friends, yeah, but are we *close* friends? Close enough that I have any right to pry into his past when he doesn't look like he wants to talk about it?

'I was cheated on,' he says eventually.

I carry on weighing out the dry ingredients one after another, moving from the dried fruit and mixed peel to the almonds, deliberately not saying anything because he looks like he's struggling to find the right words.

'I was in a long-term relationship, seven years, not married but living together. She wanted to have her cake and eat it too. She didn't want to disrupt the apparently happy life we had and thought she was doing me a favour by sleeping with someone else rather than ending things with me. She genuinely didn't grasp that she was doing anything wrong. She honestly said, "I thought you'd be happy because I was getting what I needed without bothering you."'

'Wow.' My nails make dents in my palms as I try to stop myself going over to hug him. 'Are there really people who think like that?'

'Apparently so.'

'And since then?'

He shakes his head. 'What's the point? I mean, what *is* the point in relationships if even when you think you're happy, your other half's off having an affair with her married colleague, who was also apparently doing it for some sort of payback on his own wife because he suspected *she* was cheating on *him* in some never-ending cycle of revenge shagging.'

As usual, his way of putting things makes me snort and I have to cover it quickly.

'She blamed me entirely,' he carries on. 'And don't get me wrong, I know I settled into the relationship and got a bit too comfortable and worked too much, but to be told it's your own fault for making the person you loved sleep with someone else once a fortnight when they regularly as clockwork "travelled for work", and then to be bought books on how to be a better partner and told I was too much hard work and the ruined relationship was *my* fault for finding the text messages ... It just took the biscuit.'

'Oh, James, I'm sorry.' Do not go and hug him. I repeat the words in my head. Do *not* go and hug him. He seems uncomfortable talking about it, but I'm not ready for him to stop yet. 'You found messages?'

'He phoned the house by mistake. I answered, he covered it well and I didn't think anything of it, quite normal for a colleague to phone another colleague especially when they worked so closely and "travelled for work" so often. She was *always* on her mobile and was ridiculously protective of it, and in the scramble to get the house phone off me, she'd left it unlocked on the sofa. I wasn't going to look or anything, I was working on my laptop, and as I was sitting there, a text message from him flashed up on the screen with a string of swearwords and "I didn't mean James to answer. That was close!" I couldn't ignore that.

'By the time she came back in, I'd read hundreds of text messages going back years between them. The kind of messages and photos you *don't* send a colleague. For me, that relationship was *it*. We were going to get married, have children, and go on cruises in our retirement. For her, I was just an acceptable substitute until the guy she really wanted left his wife.'

The reindeer antlers jingle with every movement, the happy sound the complete opposite of how flat and quiet his voice is, and I can't hold back anymore. I've practically pureed the dried fruit I was meant to be stirring gently, and I shove it onto the unit and march across to him.

'What are you—'

I cut him off by leaning up to get my arms around his neck and pulling him down carefully until I can kiss his cheek. 'I'm so sorry, James.' I hold his cheek against my face for far too long a moment. 'You deserved better than that.'

It's a bit awkward and a bit uncomfortable because I'm at his side rather than front-facing, and there's no physical way he can hug me back, but I feel him exhale and relax and when I open my eyes, his are closed.

'Is this hurting?' I murmur.

'No, but my icing's dribbling.'

I burst out a laugh mixed with a dash of mild hysteria and let go of him, not missing the groan as he stands back upright.

I force myself to step away because no gingerbread is going to get iced and no Christmas cake is going to be made if I hug him for as long as I want to.

I watch him as he shakes his head like he's trying to clear it. 'How long ago?'

'Four years ... well, closer to five now. I moved out and got a little flat because it was all I could afford until we sold the house, but that took a couple of years and I'm still in that "temporary" flat.'

'With your boxes still not unpacked?'

'Exactly. No wonder I keep coming over here.'

'Ah, so it's nothing to do with the biscuit selection tins and tubs of chocolate then?'

'Add in the homecooked food and freshly baked gingerbread ...'

He laughs but it trails off. 'No. Honestly, Nee, it's nothing to do with *anything* edible.'

This man should come with a health warning. I'm having so many hot flushes with him around that I've started to wonder if the menopause has come on fifteen years early.

I have no idea how to respond to that so I concentrate intently on spooning glacé cherries into a bowl and only realise when the bowl is overfull that weighing them out is actually a key part of the process. This will be the cherriest Christmas cake ever.

'Okay, my turn.' James goes back to icing scalloped roof tiles onto the gingerbread house. 'Now you've got to tell me about you. You're the most caring, sweet, funny, and beautiful person I've ever met, and I can't believe you're not seeing anyone. I'm *still* expecting a husband to pop out of the woodwork any second. How on earth are you still single? What's going on?'

'Waiting for Prince Charming?' I try to make a joke of it but he raises both eyebrows and I know I've got to carry on, even though his words make me feel like I'm going to choke on my own teeth. 'Cheating. There's been a lot of it in my life too.'

'Really?' I can feel his eyes on me, burning into my back until I force myself to turn around and look at him and he gives me a sympathetic smile.

'Yeah. I was with someone for nearly six years and I thought that was *it* too, until I caught him with someone else. It was so unexpected. I trusted him wholeheartedly. Cheating was something that had never even crossed my mind. After that, I could never really trust anyone. Eventually Stacey set me up with someone else. It lasted a few months, but he cheated too, and since then I've kind of kept men at arm's length and never let anyone get close enough to hurt me. I've dated here and there when Stacey's nagging has driven me mad, but nothing that's ever been more than a couple of dates, and every single one of them has ended with cheating too. One started messaging his other girlfriend while we were having coffee, one ghosted me for a bit and then posted an engagement announcement on Facebook, and one texted me a message meant for his other woman on the day before Nutcracker Lane opened.'

'Oh, wow. God, that's so bad.'

'It's okay. Since the first guy, it hasn't mattered. I push people away. I don't let anyone in or let myself get serious with anyone. It's inevitable that every relationship is going to end the same way, so what's the point? I don't want to do it again, not even casually. I'd rather be alone forever than feel as worthless as I did after that first time.' I've never said that out loud before, not even to Stacey, but everything James said about his own relationship puts me at ease because he understands what it's like. 'Unless Prince Charming steps out of the pages of a storybook, I'm done with relationships.'

'I hear you there … well, maybe not on the Prince Charming front, but on the relationships bit. How do you ever trust anyone again? Not even just relationships. It totally changed the way I saw everything. It made me feel like everyone's out for themselves and their own gain. I don't trust anyone now.'

I think about the guy half-asleep on my sofa the other night, letting me hold the fingers of his broken arm. The guy who lets me hug him despite being bruised from head to toe. How open and uninhibited he can be sometimes. 'I think you do. I think you just put up a massive front to stop yourself getting hurt. Like your Grinch side. Disengaging from all things festive is a way of shutting yourself off. Another wall up between you and the world …' I trail off as I realise I've just completely psychoanalysed him, firstly without permission, and secondly when I don't even know him well enough to know what his favourite colour is. 'Sorry, James, I had no right to—'

'I see behind your mask too, you know.' He sounds gentle and caring, and when I finally look up, he gives me a soft smile. 'I think you're lonely but you put on a happy, breezy front and pretend you're okay. You still hold out hope for a relationship but tell yourself you don't so you won't be disappointed. You have all those romantic Christmas movies on your TV box because you still believe in love and you want that happily-ever-after to happen to you but you're too scared to put yourself out there in case it actually does.'

'No, I'm scared in case it actually does and *then* it goes wrong.' I try to ignore the quiver at the thought of how well he can see through me. 'Besides, those movies are an escape. They don't actually happen, they're just fantasy, like Santa Claus or wishes on magical nutcrackers.'

He snorts. 'Throwing myself into Nutcracker Lane this year has been good for me. The people there are good. Kind and genuine. They've welcomed me like an old friend. Invested their time and money and energy into making Nutcracker Lane special. And it is special. A real community. I've never had anything like that to believe in before, but seeing how much *you* love it, how much it means to everyone there … it's enough to make me believe in magic again.'

I swallow so hard that he must've been able to hear it. 'And in love?'

'Oh, Nia, I don't get it.' He pipes bricks onto the chimney. 'I want to fall in love with someone – *one* person – and take on the rest of our lives together as a team. If there are problems, I want to be in it together with someone. I want to believe there's someone out there somewhere who was made for me forever. I want to wake up with someone every morning for the rest of my life and not worry that she's going to get fed up of me and find someone better. I want someone who'll be there for the good times and the bad. I want to know without a second thought that there's *always* someone who's got my back and for someone to feel that about me too. I want to be someone's favourite person, the first person they call if something happens – good or bad. I want to share every moment of my life with *one* person. Someone who'll do a celebratory dance with me or … hold my hand in a hospital waiting room.'

He still doesn't look up from his icing. 'The magic of love is in the security of it. Anyone can go on dating apps and hook up, but aren't we all searching for that one special person? An other half? A half you didn't realise was missing until the first time you saw them?'

Maybe he really is a nutcracker come to life because I'm pretty sure he's too perfect to be real. The answer to a magical Christmas wish is a more likely explanation than him actually being this perfect. He says everything I've always thought about love but never allowed myself to believe might be possible.

'What are you doing over Christmas?' I ask to distract myself and cover this weird tension between us because I don't think the cherries were supposed to be chopped with *quite* this much fervour.

'Working?' he says like it's a trick question. 'After the shop shuts, I'm straight back to my regular job.'

'Without even having a break?'

'Even less of a break this year. I'll have been away for a month by that time. I'll have even more catching up to do.'

That familiar feeling of my stomach dropping hits me again. It's so cut and dried. He's gone as soon as Nutcracker Lane closes for Christmas. That's it, over. 'Christmas is the only time of year that I *do* have a few days off. No working, no crafting, no online orders or customising bespoke stuff or packing products up to post. Just watching TV and eating too much. That's one of your tasks for this year, Grinch. You *have* to have a break. No work. Don't even get out of your pyjamas. Just curl up in front of the TV and eat cheese and chocolate. *Not* together. Well, unless you're into that sort of thing, but I can't see it working.'

I've gone off on a chocolate-and-cheese-related tangent because what's scary is how much I want to invite him over. I can't think of anything better than cuddling up with him and stuffing our faces while watching old movies on the television. I'm searching for a way to keep him in my life for longer. To make sure we have something outside of work, because for all his help, it's blatantly obvious that he's not sticking around.

'What about the day itself?' I tip the cherries into the bowl, give it a quick stir, and start sifting the flour over them.

'Taking enough painkillers and drinking enough mulled wine to wake up on December 27th?'

My hands still and the flour comes out in a whoosh, and I point my wooden spoon threateningly in his direction. 'You had better be joking.'

He turns the gingerbread house and starts icing window frames and doesn't say anything.

'Do you still go to your parents' on the "Big Day"?'

'Of course. I visit as often as I can, but I'm always getting in the way. My dad's still working – still trying to get the business in the best possible shape for me to take over.'

'Come to me for Christmas Day,' I blurt out.

'I have to spend it with my family. It's going to be my dad's last—' He can't finish the sentence.

'Is your dad still up to travelling? They can come too.'

'You can't …' His voice catches and he stops himself and takes a few breaths before he speaks again. 'It's family time for you too. You don't even know my family. You can't seriously be inviting—'

'It's not right that you're helping me with all this prep and then I won't even see you on Christmas Day. Seriously, James, I'm cooking anyway; it'd be no trouble to add a bit of extra veg and put a couple more chairs out. It'd take pressure off your mum having to do anything, and I always cook enough to feed half the country.'

'Nia, I …'

'I'd love to have you here. And my family won't mind at all. I could invite the local dog shelter and they wouldn't care as long as Mum didn't have to do the cooking.'

'I would *love* that. Spending Christmas with you *or* the dog shelter, but mainly you.' He puts the bag of icing down again and crosses the kitchen with a couple of long steps, and reaches out to take my hand, his fingers folding around mine.

My cheeks heat up. 'Will you ask your parents if they want to?'

'They don't care about Christmas. They won't mind what we do.'

'So it's settled then.' He's holding my left hand and I put down the wooden spoon that's still in my right and let my fingers travel up to his shoulder and squeeze gently, feeling ridiculously happy about the prospect of spending Christmas with him. For the first time in a long while, the world feels like it's spinning in the right direction again.

'And after Christmas ...' I take a deep breath before I can chicken out. 'There'll be a ton of leftover cheese that I'll need help eating, and there are always eleventy billion boxes of chocolates, and in that space between Christmas and new year, all the festive films are gone from the TV and they just play old musicals from the Fifties ...'

Another deep breath. In for a penny and all that. 'Come and have a break with me. I feel like you need a proper Christmas. The past couple of weeks have been all about trying to show you what Christmas should be like and it doesn't just stop on the 25th.' My fingers trail up and fiddle with the thick hair at the back of his head, the longer front bits pushed back by the headband, and I reach up and play with a felt-covered antler.

His eyes drift shut and he drops his head until his forehead is resting against mine, the reindeer antlers on his head tangling with the bow on mine. 'Nia, you should know that if you don't step back right this second, I'm not going to be able to stop myself kissing you.'

My arms tighten around his neck in response and he makes a noise from deep within his chest. Before I know it, his lips are ... not on mine. Instead he kisses me right at the side of the mouth, softly and oh-so-slowly touching his lips to my skin, both infuriatingly slow and gorgeously gentle, and nowhere near *enough*, and I think it might be the sexiest way anyone's ever kissed me.

I can feel his stubble with the skin of my lips, hear every shiver of his breath, my nails have started digging into his hand where he's still holding mine and the fingertips still in his hair can feel every strand as my fingers tighten. It's really nothing more than a peck, but it leaves no doubt about how incredible it would be to kiss him properly.

When he pulls back, I'm torn between holding on tighter so he stays, and feeling so overheated and flushy that I might swoon in his arms, which would do his injuries no good whatsoever. I reluctantly unfurl my hands from his body and try to furtively cling on to the edge of the counter to keep myself upright, and the half-dazed, half-seductive and ridiculously flirty look on his face lets me know that he *knows* exactly how much of an effect he's having on me.

'That was a yes, by the way.' He goes back to his side of the unit and picks up the icing bag. 'In case there was any doubt.'

I can't help giggling. For once, there was *no* doubt. 'I've never realised I could speak "kiss" before, but believe me, even I managed to translate that.'

'You can literally lip-read.' It's an adorably terrible pun and his cheeks are fittingly red, but mainly I'm relieved to see his hand is shaking when he picks up the icing bag. I'm not the only one feeling *something*. And I'm suddenly *really* looking forward to Christmas. I'm not usually a fan of the haziness of that time between Christmas and new year when no one knows what day it is and you feel generally bloated from overeating the whole time but all you do is keep eating … and it's always a bit sad because Christmas is over and you've got a whole year to go until the next one, but with him here … It's going to be my favourite part of Christmas.

'If you think I can concentrate on icing a gingerbread house now …' he says with a laugh.

I giggle too because my brain has simultaneously turned to mush and melted out of my ears. I'm glad I've made this Christmas cake many times before and have a well-used recipe to follow because all I can think about is that burning hot spot next to my lips and the tingling where his stubble grazed over the edge of my jaw.

We carry on in almost silence, but whenever I have to weave around him to get my fruitcake in the oven or check on it, the touches are lingering, and everything about him makes me want *more*.

'You know that's amazing, don't you?' I say when he finally steps out of the way and lets me see the gingerbread house.

He's used white and milk chocolate buttons as roof tiles between scalloped lines of icing. Each window and doorframe is lined with perfectly even dots and there are Jelly Tots along the middle of the roof and down each slanted side. He's used candy canes on either side of the door and stuck red and green M&M's on like Christmas lights. The traditional peppermint swirl is above the door, surrounded by tiny stuck-on snowflakes and colourful dots. He's even managed to do some lattice work at the back, and there are lines of icicles drying on the greaseproof paper, ready to be peeled off and stuck to the roof edges.

'You've seriously never done this before?' I carry on when he shakes his head. 'You've got such a steady hand and an incredible eye for detail. You've done better one-handed than I could do if I was the human equivalent of an eight-handed octopus. You're *wasted* in your day job. Do you seriously just sit in front of a computer all day?'

'Yep.' He shrugs and aborts the movement when it clearly pulls on his ribs. 'Analysing figures. Sometimes for a change of pace, I spin around in my spinny chair and stare at the wall.' He lifts his arm and drops it around my shoulders. 'That was so much fun, and surprisingly relaxing.'

Relaxing. Not a word I would ever usually associate with

224

baking.

I must look dubious because he squeezes my shoulders tighter. 'Honestly, Nia. I never do stuff like this. It was fun.'

I've thought he had a creative side since that morning Stacey and I watched him repaint his shop sign, and it gives me a weird thrill to see this gorgeous man, who I thought was so uptight at first, wearing reindeer antlers and an apron that's now covered with splotches of multicoloured icing and so much powdered sugar that it looks like he's just come in out of a snowstorm.

'There is *no* part of tonight that hasn't been fun.' My hand involuntarily drifts towards the imagined imprint of his lips covering the edge of mine. Everything seems to have been fun since I met him and I can't remember what my life was like before he came into it. He's easily the best thing about Christmas this year.

Chapter 14

'We've got a budget increase!' Hubert bounces out of his sweetshop door as Stacey and I walk past on the way to work a couple of mornings later. His red cheeks match the red stripes in his red-and-white candy-esque striped shirt and his smile looks like it's trying to expand past the width of his face while he waves around a letter.

'Who – Scrooge?' I ask and he nods excitedly.

'Maybe the ghosts of Past, Present, and Future finally got to him,' Stacey says.

'The sales reports finally got to his desk, more like.' I fold my arms as she unlocks our door and retrieves our letter from the doormat. 'Or the mention we got in the local paper last weekend, or the amount of foot traffic through the door, or the comments and pictures of the hidden nutcrackers on social media. People are talking about our little wooden army.'

'One of my neighbours stopped me as I was going out my gate this morning and asked me if the magic was really back on Nutcracker Lane,' Stacey says. 'Even Scrooge isn't immune.'

'You don't think he did it out of the goodness of his kind 'ickle heart, do you?' I ask as she tears the letter open. 'And it's December 17th. Couldn't he have done it earlier? We needed a budget increase in November. A week before Christmas is not good enough.'

'From now until Christmas, he's increased our budget.' Stacey summarises the letter. 'It doesn't say how much by.'

'Of course not. Scrooge would never let us have goalposts we could actually see – that would be too easy.'

'It says to build and expand on wish-granting because it's getting people talking,' she continues. 'Nothing about the competition between shops or keeping the lane. Just a cheery "keep doing what you're doing" tacked onto the end.'

'Keep earning what you're earning so I can screw you all over in January,' I translate the letter as she hands it to me. 'Scrooge doesn't do anything to benefit the lane, only him—'

I'm cut off when the door to James's shop opens from inside and he appears in the doorway. All thoughts of Scrooge disappear instantaneously at the sight of him. He's wearing jeans and another Christmas jumper, this time depicting Max, the Grinch's dog, sitting in the snow with a Santa hat on, and his arm is in the sling across his chest again. On his head is a brown and white Christmas pudding beanie with crocheted green holly leaves and three red berries on top.

'You're early.' I want to go over and kiss him good morning or something, but with Hubert looking fit to burst and Mrs Brissett heading down the lane towards us with her letter in hand, I think better of it, especially when there's no mistletoe nearby to use as an excuse.

'Couldn't sleep.' His mouth tips up at one side. 'For *some* reason.'

My cheeks redden as I catch Hubert looking between the two of us with interest. I've not been getting much sleep lately either. I've barely stopped thinking about him for nearly three weeks.

'Budget's being increased.' I hold the letter up.

'So I hear.' He leans on his good shoulder against the door-frame. 'Why do you look annoyed? I thought you'd be pleased.'

'I am, but it's such a patronising letter that's as vague as always.

We don't even know how much by. We could buy something expensive, go to claim it back on expenses and be refused. There's no system for getting approval first so wishes have to be granted on the spot.'

'Maybe there'll be enough for anything you want.'

'Scrooge would never be that generous. He's probably allocated us an extra fiver each, which we'll only find out when we've spent a couple of hundred.'

'I'm with Nia.' Mrs Brissett taps her own letter. 'Either support us or don't. I've had enough of his ambiguous letters. And then to add that onto the end. He may as well be saying "keep up the good work" like he's in any way part of this. We're doing this to *fight* him. I don't want his patronising encouragement. Or his ever-changing budget, for that matter. If the papers phone him for a quote about all this, you can guarantee he'll take credit for it.'

'They'd be better men than me if they can get through,' Hubert says. 'I've been trying to phone him every day and it just rings and rings.'

'There were customers trying to get in when I arrived this morning,' James says. 'Shouldn't we concentrate on the positive things here? You've got what you wanted and we can carry on granting wishes. I've got another thousand nutcrackers in the back of my car and Nia's got more flags and bunting, right?' He looks at me questioningly and I nod. 'We'll bring boxes round today. We've got a week left until Christmas so let's make it the best week ever, rather than worrying about some guy behind his computer in an office.'

'Hear, hear!' Hubert says, always the first to support anybody.

As usual, James has got an eloquent and endearing way of saying things that's guaranteed to get people on board and make it feel like anything's possible. And he's got a point too. All we can do is try to make this week before Christmas the best week Nutcracker Lane has ever had and if that's the end of it, then at least it will have gone out on a high note.

Stacey goes inside to prepare for opening time, Mrs Brissett wafts away and Hubert wishes us a good day and goes inside his own shop, leaving me and James alone in the empty lane. He gives me a slow and deliberate wink 'See you at lunchtime? Maybe we'll manage to walk under a lamppost or two this time.' His smile widens as he nods towards the nearest bunch of dangling mistletoe, which is too far away for now.

It's enough to make me feel all flushed and overheated, but I can feel my lips twitching up in response to his smile and I force myself to turn away and go into Starlight Rainbows.

A very high note might be an understatement.

*

Stacey's on the till while I'm on my lunchbreak, but instead of wolfing down a sandwich and painting something out the back, I go to find James. His shop is shut but he isn't inside, although I keep seeing him walking up and down the lane with boxes of nutcrackers under his good arm, delivering them to shopkeepers who want more to hide around their local areas.

I head outside and meet him at his car where he's got the back seats down and he's leaning into the boot and attaching my laminated flags to the nutcrackers' hands. 'Do you know you're losing trade? Customers keep trying your door, even though your window is almost empty with the amount of stuff you've put out.'

'Don't care. I'd rather see people enjoying it than get a few quid for it.' He grins at me and lifts the box of nutcrackers. 'I'm taking these down to the snowglobe seller. Walk with me?'

For the first time this year, we're dodging customers. It's busier than I've seen it for a long while, and the school holidays haven't even started yet. People are clutching nutcrackers, and going into shops and coming out weighed down with bags, and instead of walking up and down the lane today, the carol singers are gathered in the recess outside the coffee shop and giving a concert. It's been

229

years since it was too crowded for them to walk up and down.

'There are definitely more,' James says in my ear and we stop for a moment and listen to their rendition of "O Holy Night".

'What?'

'Carol singers. Counting them seems to have become my new hobby. On that first day when you were in my shop and they walked past, there were only five. Now there's sixteen.'

I simultaneously half-laugh and realise he's right. The small group of carol singers has increased, and they sound so much better for it. Their harmonies filter from one end of the lane to the other, and someone's turned off the overhead music that feeds out through the speaker system so people can hear them properly.

'They stopped coming because no one listened,' I whisper to him. 'Angela has always said how disheartening it is to keep carrying on when there's no one to appreciate it, and now look.' I nod to the tip basket on the floor in front of her feet, full of coins. Divided by sixteen of them, it certainly won't put down a deposit on a yacht, but it must be nice to feel appreciated.

'Nia!' Angela beckons me over as they finish the song and shuffle their lyric sheets for the next one. 'Did you hear about the email?'

'What email?' I pull James with me as we go around the edge of the group of people gathered to listen.

'From Scrooge, saying he'd increased the budget for Nutcracker Lane and offering us a set wage to come every day until Christmas. Generous, too. Enough to get some stragglers back on board.' She nods towards the singers behind her, all dressed in their finest handmade Victorian outfits. 'I take it this is all your doing, you two.' She smiles at James as well.

'We had nothing to do with this,' I say because it's the first time I've heard about it. 'Scrooge is outdoing himself with the surprises today.'

'Well, it was jolly nice of him, no matter how unexpected.

230

Apparently we're "an important part of the Nutcracker Lane team and the sense of nostalgia wouldn't be the same without us". The man's a reformed character, I tell you!'

'He must've been abducted by aliens and replaced by a pod person overnight,' I mutter.

The rest of the carollers clearly want to get on with singing so we say goodbye and sidle out of the ever-increasing crowd, James being careful not to whack anyone with his box or broken arm.

'I never thought I'd see it like this again.' We stop and look back at the small crowd as the carollers start "O Tannenbaum".

'It's all your doing.'

'Mine? It's you, James. Without you …' I trail off as I think about what this season would've been like without him. 'It's every-body. The shopkeepers getting involved, you rallying everyone, not to mention providing thousands of nutcrackers …'

It's reassuring to see things busy as we head down the lane to the snowglobe shop on the corner before the wide expanse of the tree lot leads out into the car park. Even so late in the season, the tree seller has still got a few people wandering through her selec-tion. It's incredible. Last year, she'd closed up by mid-December because no one was here to buy any trees.

The snowglobe seller is so busy with customers that he barely has time to call out a thank you as James hands over the box of nutcrackers.

I check in with Stacey on the way back, but there's still ages left of my lunchbreak and she shoos me away again, and James takes my hand as we walk back up the lane. He doesn't say anything, just slots his fingers between mine like it's the most natural thing in the world, and I squeeze his hand back, because in a way, it is. I've never felt as comfortable with anyone as I do with him. It's never felt as normal to hold hands with someone. Maybe it's just because of his injuries – because holding hands has been "our thing" since that first night in the storeroom?

'Is that …'

'Oh my God, James, the chestnut seller is back!' My hand tightens around his so fast that it makes him flinch. 'It's been *years.*'

I point excitedly at the man with his Victorian-style cart setting up near the coffee shop. He roasts chestnuts on the spot and sells them in little paper bags, the most nostalgic taste of Christmas gone by. 'They were my granddad's favourite thing about coming here. My grandma didn't even like them but she used to buy a bag every time we came here after he died and we'd eat them on the way home.'

'He looks like he's ready for his first customers.' James tugs me in that direction, only letting go of my hand when we reach the chestnut seller and he digs his wallet out, cutting me off when I try to protest that I can get them.

'It's been some years,' I say to the man as he throws his nuts into the gas-powered oven hidden in the base of his cart.

'Yeah, Mr Neaser got in touch and explained about the drive to revitalise this place. I was only too happy to come back, even without the handsome incentive he offered. So many good memories here, but the place was fading into obscurity. Nice to see it looking like it did in the good ol' days again.'

'Mr Neaser ...' I mutter. Like that's his real name. I don't trust anything that horrible accountant does. He's got to be up to something. Increasing the budget, tempting back the carollers and now the chestnut seller, with only a week to go until Christmas.

'You're overthinking it,' James says in my ear, having clearly developed mind-reading abilities. 'Maybe he really did have a visit from three ghosts overnight. Maybe he can genuinely see that things are going well and he wants to help. Maybe he regrets what he's done and wants to make amends.'

I jokingly point a finger at him. 'I've told you before about sticking up for that awful man.'

He looks away, inhaling the gorgeous nutty smell as the chestnuts roast. Eventually the chestnut seller hands us a warm paper bag each and James digs in eagerly, pulling out a chestnut bursting from its crisp shell. 'I've never eaten one of these before ...'

'They're a key part of Christmas. Roasting on an open fire and all that.' I sing the first line of "The Christmas Song".

'Another thing ticked off my festive bucket list.' He shakes his head. 'And I can't believe I'm saying things like "festive bucket list". Before I met you, my festive bucket list was to make it 'til January without strangling anyone with tinsel or drowning myself in a vat of pine-needle-infused vodka. I think you found me just in the nick of time before I became a completely unfestiviable Grinch.'

As usual, I can't help giggling at his way of putting things as we head back up the lane, munching on hot chestnuts.

Carmen and Mrs Brissett are on wish-granting duty, but there's a lot more people than there have been in recent days, and it doesn't look like they're keeping on top of things. Rhonda from the hat shop is carrying a jumper and rushing about looking for someone she's obviously lost track of, and the florist has got a poinsettia under one arm and a snowglobe in the other and looks like he needs a map or a rescue by helicopter.

We're automatically heading towards the magical nutcracker anyway, but there's a young woman getting a nut out of the vending machine, and everyone else is already occupied by other wishes so no one's paying attention. James and I crouch down by the fence surrounding the nutcracker, at the back and out of the woman's sight, trying to make it look like we're mending a broken fencepost if we do get caught, although I don't know how because he's got an arm in plaster and we're both still eating chestnuts.

'I wish I could afford to give my family a proper Christmas.' The woman's voice breaks as she speaks to the nutcracker. 'Everything's been so hard since my husband left. I can't take as many shifts because I've got to look after the children, and they need things, and I can't afford a Christmas dinner, let alone any presents. Please help me give them the Christmas they deserve after such an awful year.'

James's eyes don't leave mine, and I watch his beautiful brown eyes get wider and sadder with every word she speaks.

'Heartbreaking,' he mouths, and I agree, trying to think of how we can help her.

'What about a hamper?' I watch over my shoulder as the woman throws her nutshell into the garden and starts walking away.

He nods enthusiastically and I shove both the bags of chestnuts at him and use his shoulder to push myself up before he has a chance because there's bound to be a bit of running involved. 'You stay, I'll go.'

'Nee?' When I turn around, he tosses his shop keys to me. 'There's a wooden crate behind my counter. Fill it with everything you can from everyone. I'll cover the costs.'

I don't have time to argue with him because the woman is getting away and he has to scramble after her. I wave to Stacey as I let myself into his shop, find the empty wooden crate and lock up behind me as I dash from shop to shop, filling it with chocolates from Carmen, sweets from Hubert, an armful of soaps and bath bombs, and a couple of scented candles from Mrs Thwaite. At the bakery, they give me a box filled with a selection of every cake in their display cases, the florist puts in an Amaryllis and a Christmas rose, and the coffee shop throws over a couple of bags of their flavoured coffee.

When I come out of my final shop, I grab a tree from the tree lot, and look desperately around for James.

'That way!' Rhonda points towards the car park. 'He went to get something so I've ended up watching him watching her in a vicious circle of stalking. You haven't seen a little girl who wants a pony, by any chance, have you?'

'No,' I shout back, hoping to all the reindeer gods that she hasn't got an actual pony hidden somewhere. Scrooge's budget might have increased but it would never go that far.

I finally see James at the edge of the car park, looking around

234

for me. There *has* to be a better system of doing this. The wish-granters of the past never seemed to run around like headless horseflies and lose half the recipients of the wishes they were meant to be granting.

'Excuse me?' James stops the woman just as she's about to get into a battered old car that looks like it's going to fall apart at any moment. She looks nervous at being stopped by a random man in the car park as I run up panting. You wouldn't think it was possible to sweat this much on a cold December day. If we come back next year, we're going to have to come up with a better wish-granting system.

'Hi, we work ...' Gasp. Wheeze. Choke. My new year's resolution needs to be to do some exercise. Again. One half-hearted jog last January clearly wasn't enough.

Thankfully James takes over, giving his usual sleek and endearing introduction while I try to get my breath back. 'We work for Nutcracker Lane. You're our hundredth visitor of the day and you've won a prize. We'd like to give you this hamper as a thank you for your custom.'

I hand her the wooden crate full of goodies, and she's clearly surprised by the weight of it when she takes it in her arms. I lean the tree against the door of her car, and James holds up an envelope and tucks it in down the side of the crate. 'Just a little something extra.'

It's a gift voucher for the out-of-town supermarket two roads away. I can't see how much it's for but I know James well enough to know that it'll be a large amount and that he paid for it himself and won't claim it back, and I feel my heart swell in my chest, and it's not *just* from being short of breath.

The woman bursts into tears. 'But I just said to the ...' Her finger points to the building and she stares at the entrance where the nutcracker stands before looking between us. I think she's worked out that we've somehow heard her wish and not that the nutcracker is actually magical, but she doesn't say it. 'I can't believe it,' she says instead, looking down at the array of goodies in the crate, which really would've been packed nicely and done up with some tissue paper and a ribbon if I'd had a few more minutes. 'Why would you do this?'

''Tis the season,' James says simply.

'You don't understand. My husband walked out, and I'm trying to raise two children, but I can't work as much as I was because I can't afford childcare, and they need clothes and school uniforms and school trip money, and all their friends have got the latest technology and it's Christmas next week and I don't have a penny extra …' She's trying to fight the tears but they spill over again. 'Thank you. Thank you, thank you. This is so wonderful.' She glances down at the tree leaning against her car. 'I couldn't even afford a tree and they keep asking when we're going to get one.'

I have to bite my lip to stop myself crying as she thanks us again and again and hugs us both, making James wince. He steps back as I help her get the tree into the back seat and we stand together and wave as she reverses out and drives away.

'You need to start wearing a sign that says: "My ribs are broken, don't hug me"'.

'Ah, it keeps me on my toes. Every day is a constant roulette of "will I get my lungs punctured today?"' He nudges his elbow into my arm. 'And there are some people I don't mind hugging me.'

I don't know if that was a hint or not, but I'm not missing an excuse to hug him. I lean up and settle my arms around his shoulders and pull him against me gently. 'You're lovely, you know that, don't you?'

'Oh, if only you knew.' He lets out a bitter laugh. 'And that was your idea.'

'I didn't run two streets and get her a gift voucher. This was never supposed to be about real money.'

'I know. I just saw a way I could help so I did. Believe me, Nee, I don't help many people in my normal life, and this is …' I feel him shake his head against mine.

236

I'm waiting for him to say something cynical about people coming here to see what they can get out of us, but he doesn't.

'We need to do more,' he says as he pulls away. 'People are struggling all over the country. So many other people must be in the same boat. It makes you realise how lucky you are if you can afford food every week. How lucky we are to work here with all these amazing people who are going out of their way to grant wishes. We could use this place to do something good.'

'They used to …'

'… but the budget was cut.'

'Exactly,' I answer, even though he doesn't phrase it as a question.

'You're right when you say everything feels nicer at this time of year. There's just a touch more kindness in the air, but people who need help need it more than ever. Helping people is the legacy I want Nutcracker Lane to leave.'

'I don't want it to go. I want it to *be* its own legacy for many more years than this. This place is amazing and no part of it deserves to be sold off for factory space.'

'Guess we're just going to have to answer some more wishes then …' He holds his hand out and I slip mine into it as we walk back across the car park, and I can't help thinking that one of mine has already been granted. Whatever it was that sent such a kind, sweet, and generous man into my life, there had to have been some magic involved somewhere, because for the first time ever, I think I've found a good one.

Chapter 15

I jump at the knock on my door on Monday night and glance at the clock as I get up to answer it – gone 8 p.m., cold, dark, and I wasn't expecting anyone, but I can't help the little flutter when I see James on the doorstep.

'I thought you were busy tonight.' I'm grinning because of how glad I am that he's not. It sounds ridiculous to say I was missing him, because I saw him as I left Nutcracker Lane two hours ago, but I *was* missing him. It's the 21st of December now and Christmas Day is on Friday. It's too late for online orders to be posted before Christmas, and all the gift orders have already been sent, so I'd just put the TV on and flopped on the sofa in front of a rerun of a Christmas edition of a game show, but the other half of my sofa feels empty without James here.

He hands me a bunch of festive flowers that he must've got from the florist – red and white roses interspersed with sprigs of blue spruce, pinecones, and stems of red berries and mistletoe. They're *so* beautiful and I inhale them gratefully while trying not to impale myself in the nose with the spruce needles.

'I am – hopefully with you. I had to check something first. And I have a question … Have you bought this year's nutcracker to add to your collection yet?'

I shake my head. 'I still haven't found the shop open. At least I have the one you gave me. And a box of about four hundred more in the spare room.'

'Good.' His grin is brighter than my porch light shining down on him. 'Do you fancy walking up to the lane with me?'

'Right now?' I ask and he nods. 'It's closed.'

'Ah.' He taps his nose, his cheeky grin saying he's not about to elaborate.

'Sure.' I shrug because I'd walk up to Orion with James if he asked.

He waits inside so he doesn't freeze while I get my coat, and once outside, he offers his arm and I slip mine through it, letting my fingers sink into the soft fabric of his mid-thigh-length black coat.

Christmas lights are shining from every window and twinkling in garden hedges and outdoor trees as we walk along my street and turn up at the corner where I meet Stacey every morning. I love their multicoloured brightness and how cheerful they make me feel. Some houses have got strings of chunky snowflake lights draped around their windows, some have got large silhouettes of Santa stuck to the glass, some have got inflatable snowmen in their gardens, and winter-dead trees have been given the illusion of life with green artificial holly-leaf lights. Some have left their curtains open and their Christmas trees twinkle inside, each one individual and unique, the living-room lights on, allowing us a glimpse into families' lives as they sit around watching TV or eating dinner.

My arm tightens where it's around James's and I snuggle a bit closer to him as he pulls my arm tighter against his side and holds it there.

He doesn't loosen his grip as we cross the icy shrub border and walk over the car park, and he only lets go to dig his keys out and let us in.

It's dark inside, illuminated only by the light of the moon

filtering in through the glass ceiling. James shoves his keys back into his pocket and holds his hand out, and I slip mine into it like I'm physically incapable of *not* holding his hand when there's even the slightest opportunity. Our footsteps echo through the empty lane, sounding loud in the complete silence that's the opposite of how noisy it is during daylight hours. Even with things as quiet as they've been in recent years, Nutcracker Lane is always full of noise – the hiss of steamers in the coffee shop, the jingling of bells and tinny music coming from battery-powered Christmas decorations, or the carollers or the hum of chatter from the few customers we do have.

'Where are we going?'

'You'll see when we get there.' He looks over at me and even in the darkness I can tell how wide his smile is.

'Are we supposed to be here? Are we going to get done for breaking and entering over this?'

He laughs. 'I assure you, we're good.'

We pass the darkened doors of the Starlight Rainbows and Twinkles and Trinkets until eventually we come almost to the end of the lane, and then he tugs us to the right, to the narrow corridor between us and the nutcracker factory.

The mechanical village we put there is still in darkness in its display case, as silent as everything else is tonight, and it's even darker in this part of the building without the see-through roof.

James stops in front of the door to the nutcracker outlet shop, pulls another set of keys out of his pocket and unlocks the door.

'What are you doing? How do you have the keys for that?'

He grins, but he clearly isn't going to let me in on his secrets, and the door swings shut behind him as he goes inside and floods the shop with light, bright enough to lighten up the whole corridor.

'This way, Madame …' He pulls the door from the inside and holds it open for me.

'I can't afford bail money, James.' I go through the glass door anyway and he closes it softly behind us.

'I promise I have permission. The shop's never open these days and you haven't got this year's addition to your nutcracker collection yet. I couldn't let Christmas pass without doing something about it. So there you go.' He gestures to the huge shop that used to be such an integral part of Nutcracker Lane. 'Take your pick. It's on me.'

'James …' I shake my head, struggling not to tear up at his thoughtfulness. Of all the things I thought he might be up to tonight, I was *not* expecting this. It's such a sweet, kind gesture, to go to all this trouble, to square whatever he had to square with the factory operators to let us in here after dark and get their keys, and how attentive he is to have given my nutcracker collection a second thought.

I feel like a kid in a sweetshop … well, like an adult in a sweetshop because I'm no *less* childlike when I go in a sweetshop even at the ripe old age of thirty-five.

The shop smells of freshly sanded wood and acrylic paint, the scent stronger than usual because the doors have been shut for so long. The carpet is a warm mulled wine colour under my feet, and every shelf is lined with silver tinsel and fairy lights in the exact same shade of purply red as the carpet. I look forward to stepping inside this shop every year, and I hadn't realised until this moment how much I'd missed it this year.

Nutcrackers line every shelf in any size you can dream of. There are thousands of them, standing like sentinels, holding swords and sceptres and drums. They range from tiny ones to hang on your tree to huge six-foot-tall display ones like the one I knocked over in James's shop all those weeks ago. Each shelf is crowded with them, from floor to ceiling at some points, rows and rows of their serious little moustached faces stare down at us, and while I can imagine that many of them might freak some people out, to me they've always been comforting. It's said they

241

bring good luck and guard a home by baring their teeth at evil spirits. I don't know about evil spirits in Wiltshire, but anything that wants to bring me luck is welcome.

This shop was always a huge part of the lane – the giftshop that children used to go in at the end of their school tours, a big draw for tourists, and the last place my grandma and I used to visit on our way home. It was the one thing that made Nutcracker Lane stand out from any other outskirts-of-town shopping centre at Christmastime. The whole lane developed from this one shop – from the factory needing a place to get rid of excess makes that couldn't be sold wholesale like the rest of their stock.

This is the only nutcracker manufacturing plant in the UK, and this little place gained a worldwide reputation. So many people came that they expanded the lane until it became its own self-contained little Christmas village. People flocked from all over to get their hands on these one-of-a-kind nutcrackers. And now look at them …

'Can I take some photos?' I say in a burst of inspiration.

James makes a "go ahead" gesture. 'Why?'

'I don't know … It's probably too late for this year, but this place is special, and I don't think it's been showcased online since the days of social media and viral news stories. Look at all these nutcrackers about to lose their home … As a story, it could have legs to it.'

'Lose their home?'

'Scrooge is shutting down this part of the lane. Selling it for factory space. This is the closest point to the factory – it's going to be the first to go. It can't be considered important because it hasn't opened its doors once this year, so it's certainly not going to have earned enough to stay.' I reach out and run my fingers over the furry hat of a sentry nutcracker. 'These chaps are going to be out on the street.'

'Nia, Scrooge isn't going to …' He trails off as I get my phone out.

'He'll probably sell them all for firewood.'

'You don't really think he's still going ahead with the competition, do you?'

'He hasn't told us otherwise. And Scrooge is the type of horrible person who refuses to go back on his word and admit he was wrong about anything out of sheer pig-headed superiority. Everything we've done could be for nothing because of that horrible man and his gigantic ego.'

He shakes his head as if trying to clear it. 'So what do you suggest? Run an adopt-a-nutcracker campaign? A series of posters emblazoned with "a nutcracker is for life, not just for Christmas"?'

'James, that's *brilliant*!'

'It is?' He sounds confused.

'I'm not even sure how yet, but it is. We could sell some of these off – really cheap, and use the profits for wish-granting. Christmas Day is on Friday – that gives us three days to find homes for some of these nutcrackers. And we could carry on after Christmas ... If Scrooge would let us. We could be rehoming nutcrackers for months rather than letting him destroy them. If he won't even let anyone open the shop this year, he can't think it's important.'

'Maybe he didn't think nutcrackers mattered anymore?'

I snap a picture of a shelf, pick up a nutcracker and hand it to him. 'Smile.' He does it automatically but he looks like he's miles away as I take a photo of him and the nutcracker. 'This is special. Where else in the UK can you see this many nutcrackers all together? People would love to see this. People would *come* to see this. And not just at Christmas. The factory operates year-round. The *only* one in the UK, James. There's historic significance here. We could use the lane as some sort of nutcracker museum throughout the year. You said yourself that one of the problems is that there's no interest outside of December. What if we could find some? We could showcase their history. We could run school trips. Oh!'

My voice goes so high with overexcitement that it makes him jump. 'We could run workshops and let people in to make their own! We could do story times for kids and read the original book *The Nutcracker and the Mouse King* and have painting sessions so they could paint their own. We could have nutcracker-themed afternoon teas. And the shops could stay. I mean, either we could do a Christmas-all-year-round theme, or they could be part of the museum complex. All museums have giftshops, and things like the chocolate shop or the sweetshop or the coffee shop don't have to be seasonal, and nutcrackers originate from Germany so maybe we could pull in some traditional German shops and make it like a year-round Christmas market. We could change things while still staying the same. Take the snowglobe seller – he could make summer globes, so he's still doing his craft but it's not out of season.'

James picks up a tiny nutcracker from a shelf and flips it over in his hand. 'What are summer globes?'

'I don't know, I think we just invented them.' I spin around and take another couple of pictures. 'Something like tropical scenes in the globes with sand, and shells, and glitter. Trees with tiny autumn-leaf confetti falling when you shake it up. For spring, he could have tulips and daffodils with falling cherry blossoms all around them. I don't know, I'm not a snowglobe maker – I just mean that we could change the seasonal aspect without changing the heart of Nutcracker Lane ... There's just one man standing in the way.'

'Maybe there's not. If you put your mind to something, I firmly believe you're capable of winning anyone over. And maybe you already have and he was rushing in the last letter and he forgot to say it.'

'Keeping us on our toes, more like. Keeping us guessing. Trying to keep the shopkeepers at each other's throats while he sits counting all the money *our* efforts are pulling in.' I sigh and take a photo of a row of six-foot nutcrackers lined up together except they're test pieces so they're all a couple of inches shorter or taller than their intended height. 'What do you think?'

'Why does it matter what I think?'

I stop in the middle of picking up a thirty-eight-centimetre ice-blue glittered nutcracker with a whisk in his hand and a cupcake for a hat and I stare at it for a few moments while I try to think of an answer. The air feels charged between us, like this is a key moment to say something important. 'Because I can't imagine doing this without you. Everything feels possible when you're here.'

He looks down. 'Nia, I …'

'I'm sorry, I wasn't thinking.' I backpedal as fast as I can. 'You've got your own problems with your father and your business to take over. I shouldn't have said anything.'

'Nee, it's not that. Believe me, it's *not* that. It's—'

'Sorry, I just wanted your opinion because you're good at figures and retail and stuff. I forgot you're not staying here after Friday and carrying on this fight. I'll call a staff meeting sometime this week and see if the other shopkeepers would be on board, and we can formulate some kind of business plan and get it ready to present to Scrooge.'

I try not to show the bitter disappointment that feels like it's bleeding out of my pores. The idea of doing this without him suddenly feels daunting rather than exciting. I force myself to push three bagpipe-playing nutcrackers together and take a photo of them. I knew he was only here for the month. I knew he was going back to his real life, his real job, and I'm one of the only people who knows about his father's illness and his trepidation about what he's facing. There's just something about being with him that makes the impossible feel like it's within touching distance.

I can feel the sense of sadness permeating from him as we carry on wandering the aisles, going in a different direction, drifting away from each other.

'There are old ones in storage.'

'What?' My head pings up.

'Not here. At the head office. They have old ones.'

'*How* do you know that?'

'The factory was founded in the 1930s. They have original ones from Germany, and some they bought from all over the world in an attempt to replicate what was already popular, and of course they have a copy of every one that's ever been made here to keep track of how they've evolved over the years. That could be an interesting exhibit.' He must notice my confused look because he adds, 'I saw them when I was collecting stock.'

'They have eighty-something years' worth of nutcrackers and they're not using them ...'

He scratches the back of his neck, his eyes intently focused on the nutcracker in his hand. 'Maybe they didn't realise they could be important.'

'And you said your parents might have newspaper clippings about the magical nutcracker. We could showcase his story ...'

'And wishes aren't just for Christmas, right? They could keep being granted all year through?'

I look over the top of the shelf at him in the next aisle. 'So you *do* think there's something in this ...'

He looks up and meets my eyes across a row of nutcrackers, and the look in his is intense and unwavering enough to make my breath catch. 'If you got that excited about going ballroom dancing with hungry sharks, I'd support it.'

'How would that work?' I furrow my eyebrows. 'Would the ballroom be in the water or would the sharks be in the ballroom? You might think the sharks wouldn't be too supportive of this idea. And quite heavy to do a waltz with, I would imagine ...'

'And how would they ever get their fins into dancing shoes?' His mouth twitches as he tries to stop himself laughing.

I force myself to turn away and pick up a purple nutcracker with a giant pinecone in his hand and a Christmas tree on his head and indicate around the shop with it. 'I can't believe you did this. You know how to surprise a girl.'

'I didn't know whether I'd be intruding. I know it was something you did with your grandmother and I didn't want to blunder in and encroach on that tradition in case you didn't want anyone else's involvement.'

Once again, I'm struck by how thoughtful and empathic he is. It's been a *heck* of a long time since I met a man like him. 'Things are different this year. You've shown me that even though a lot of Christmas is about nostalgia and remembering the years and people who came before, it can also be about making new memories and letting new people in when you never thought you would.'

I hear him swallow and clear his throat, and he has no idea how much I want to kiss him. 'We're going to be here all night at this rate. You choose this year's nutcracker for me. I don't mind what it looks like.'

'Me?' He sounds like I've asked him to pluck the stings from stinging nettles.

'Yeah. It's not about the nutcrackers so much as the memories of getting them, and believe me, I am *never* going to forget this one.'

He's trying to hide a proud smile as he wanders round, picking up nutcrackers, appraising them and returning them to their spaces on the shelves. 'This is not as easy as it looks. I'm trying to find the perfect one. I'd kind of like you to remember me fondly when you get it out next year. And have a nice big one to throw darts at when you hate me.'

Remember him fondly? Hate him? He talks like he's going away … Like I'm not going to see him after this. I know he's got a lot to face next year, and even though Nutcracker Lane will close in January and everything is up in the air at the moment, he's talking like he's going to disappear. I thought we had something here. Are we not friends … or whatever … who are going to stay in touch?

He only lives half an hour away. Even if my ideas for Nutcracker Lane turn out to be nothing more than a pipe dream and Scrooge bulldozes the whole place next year and I spend all my days in a panicked haze of jobhunting, I'm going to *make* time to see him. If he thinks he's going to get that cast off his arm in January without me holding his other hand, he's got another thing coming. And he's not dealing with his father's illness by himself either. But he talks like we're never going to see each other again after Nutcracker Lane closes.

Unless he *is* going to turn back into a wooden soldier on Christmas Day.

I'm pretty sure it's not the latter, but I can't find the words to say anything, so I concentrate on the nutcrackers instead. I don't realise I'm trying to find one for him too until I come across the perfect one. It's wearing all black apart from gold boots and an amber gem belt, but the Japanese art of kintsugi has been tried out on it, so it's covered in cracks but each one is patched up with fine lines of gold. It's got big brown eyes and black furry hair that's a bit longer than usual, and it's wearing a crown and holding an intricately carved wooden bell to ring in the season that dings when you push it. It's got a kind of regal look that's different to other nutcrackers. It's so *him* that it could have been made for him.

I'm so eager to give it to him that I'm glad when he yells 'got it' and thrusts a nutcracker in the air victoriously, and immediately regrets it when the movement pulls on still-healing ribs.

We meet at the checkout counter and he hands me the nutcracker he's chosen, one with green legs going down into furry white boots that I've never seen before, a red Christmas jumper with actual pom poms glued onto his wooden body, a tiny Christmas tree held in his hand and a Santa hat on the hair around his head that's almost the same shade of brown as mine.

'Oh, James.' I bite my lip to stop my eyes watering. 'He's amazing. *Exactly* the one I would've chosen myself. I even have a pair of boots like that. I never wear them because furry boots don't work so well with our English drizzle, but I get them out and admire them occasionally. And now I have a nutcracker wearing them …' I'm rambling to stop myself enveloping him in a bear hug. Out of the thousands of nutcrackers here, he's picked the exact one I would've grabbed if I'd seen it myself. 'Thank you.' I can barely get the words out as I take it from him. 'You know I'm getting one for you too, don't you?'

The smile that crosses his face is slow at first, gradually getting wider as I pull it out from behind my back and hold it out, waiting for his good hand to close around it.

He raises an eyebrow. 'It's broken.'

'No, it's not. The Japanese mend cracks with gold resin to illuminate each repair an object has undergone. They believe flaws should be celebrated and each break is a unique part of every item's history that only adds to its beauty.'

He swallows hard. 'Believe me, I celebrate these breaks every single day because I wouldn't have met you without them.'

'Aww.' I push my bottom lip out because I'm not sure if he's being sarcastic or not, even though the look in his eyes is soft and distant and he looks genuinely touched.

'I think that's the nicest thing anyone's ever said to me. I can honestly say no one's ever bought me a nutcracker before.' He takes the nutcracker out of my hand and runs the fingers of his broken arm across it. He seems to be considering saying something else but he eventually thinks better of it. 'We should pay. Can I …'

I know he's such a gent that he's going to offer to pay for his own nutcracker but I've already pulled my purse out, thankful I had the forethought to shove it into my pocket while he was waiting downstairs earlier. He goes behind the counter, opens the till to put the money in, grabs a notebook from underneath and writes a note saying "*Two nutcrackers gone, money in till. Thanks*

~ J" and I wonder two things simultaneously – is he really on such familiar terms with the factory owners, and how can even the way someone writes be sexy?

He must notice me watching him write because he says, 'What's the difference between the Christmas alphabet and the regular alphabet?'

It's got be another one of his bad jokes but I can't think of an answer to catch him out. 'I don't know.'

'The Christmas alphabet has no-el.'

I can't stop myself laughing, even though it's not because the joke is funny but because of how ridiculously proud he looks as he chucks an extra five pence into the till and takes a bag, carefully settling both our nutcrackers into it and handing it to me to carry.

After he turns the lights off and locks up behind us, he stops me at the edge of the alleyway before we turn into the main lane. 'One second.'

He pulls his phone out and opens an app on it, doing something until … suddenly the whole world lights up. Every pillar, every lamppost, every hanging garland, every extra tree that's been erected in the lane in the past couple of weeks, they all spring into fairy-light life. The nutcracker village starts up its mechanical movement behind us, and the first few bars of "Grown-Up Christmas List" by Kelly Clarkson filter through the overhead speaker.

'The decorations!' I look around in surprise. 'This is, like, all of them. Ever. Right?'

'I might've emptied the storeroom. And the shop. I wanted to make it like it was, Nia. I know there's only three days until Christmas and it's too little, too late, and I wish I'd met you earlier and we'd done all of this at the beginning of the season …'

I reach out and take his hand. 'I'm more concerned that you did this yourself with one arm.'

'I appreciate you thinking I'm Superman, but I couldn't have done this by myself even without the broken bones. I had help from some of the others. I wanted to make it special for you, just one last time, before …'

There's that "before" thing again. Like there's some kind of deadline coming up. Like by Christmas all this will be over. Does he know something about the lane that I don't? Has he overheard Scrooge's plans when he's been to collect stock and he knows that everything we're doing to save Nutcracker Lane will ultimately be for nothing? Or is he just naturally pessimistic? I decide that everything looks so beautiful and he's gone to so much effort that I don't want to think about it tonight.

I squeeze his hand. 'I can't believe you did this. It's perfect. You know this is one of my favourite Christmas songs, don't you?'

'I might've asked Stacey. I wanted it to be special.'

We're still in darkness, but the way is lit by fairy lights now, twinkling and sparkling in every direction. Every streetlamp is glowing orange and every post is wrapped with white lights. The rainbow-coloured candle bulbs stapled along the eaves of each shop are shining, and the green garlands draped above our heads are covered with white lights chasing each other in sequence. The giant baubles I remember from the olden days are suspended from each ceiling support by huge red satin ribbons, and curtains of white lights are cascading down like a waterfall, interspersed with blue snowflakes, while my favourite Christmas song plays quietly above us.

'I just wanted you to know someone's listening.'

'You. From that first night in the storeroom, you've listened to me. Even though you hated Christmas and I'm sure you weren't interested in Nutcracker Lane at all, you still listened to me. And now look at it. You've made it perfect again.' I let go of his hand long enough to spin around with my arms out, indicating all the lights around me. He laughs when I nearly clonk him round the head with the two nutcrackers in the bag as we wander back up the shimmering lane and I try to make myself behave like an adult.

'James …' I pick up his hand again, wondering when I ever became such a hand-holder. It's not something I've ever done before, but I feel like something's missing when my fingers *aren't* entwined with his. 'Thank you. This is amazing. I never thought I'd see it like this again. If this is the end of Nutcracker Lane, this is the best way it could've ended. Thank you for making this year so incredibly special.'

'It won't be.' He sounds a lot more confident than I feel. 'Thank you for showing me *how* special this place is.'

The song changes to the very fitting "Walking In A Winter Wonderland" and we're both wandering as slowly as possible. I don't want this to be over yet, and he's doing the same and hopefully that means he doesn't want it to either.

He stops when we get to the magical nutcracker and moves my hand so it's hooked through his elbow instead as he lays his arm on the picket fence and rests his chin on it.

'You okay?' I hang the bag containing the nutcrackers over one of the fence posts and use my free hand to reach out and stroke his hair just once, an excuse to touch him, twisting my arms like a pretzel because it's such an awkward position.

'Just thinking about magic,' he murmurs as his eyes drift shut, and even though I was only going to touch his hair once, he tilts his head towards me and it's not that easy.

'You? Thinking about magic? Have you been at the painkillers again? Are you about to start asking "how many iguanas are there in a mile?" or other nonsensical questions?'

He laughs. 'No. Being with you makes me feel like a kid at Christmas. I forget everything I've always hated, all the prac- ticality, all the cynicism. You make me believe in anything.' He sighs and shakes his head at himself. 'What would your Christmas wish be?'

'Nutcracker Lane,' I say without thinking about it. I turn around and look at the twinkling lane.

'What, all of it?' He turns around too, leaning back on his

252

elbows against the fence.

'No. I don't know. I just want it to survive. To thrive. To still be here next Christmas. Hopefully all year through, but I'm not holding my breath about convincing Scrooge to turn it into a nutcracker museum. I think that'd take more than a Christmas miracle.'

'Three weeks ago, you told me anything's possible at Christmastime. Make a wish.' He looks upwards. 'The stars are twinkling just right, and if I opened a door, I reckon the wind would ripple his beard ...'

Three weeks and one night ago, I made a wish and I think it might've come true. It feels like magic is dancing in the air tonight. There's an icy breeze foxtrotting down the lane, so real I can almost see the air glittering and hear the faint tinkling of jingle bells. When I look up through the glass ceiling, I can make out constellations in the winter sky. It's a night for making wishes.

I go inside the fence and take a walnut from the vending machine, keeping an eye on James in case this is some sort of wind-up and he's going to film it and put me on YouTube or something, but when I look back at him, his chin is resting on his arm across the fence again and he's watching me with a soft smile on his face.

He gives me an encouraging nod as I walk up to the nutcracker, place the nut into his mouth and reach around to pull the lever, something I've done many times before but somehow feels different tonight, enchanted somehow, like *this* wish is the important one.

I look up at the nutcracker's rosy-cheeked wooden face, the benevolent and homely face that you'd picture on a beloved grandpa, and I can't help smiling at him as I bring his lever down and the shell starts to split. 'I wish for Nutcracker Lane ... in whichever way it's going to survive and prosper for as many years as possible.'

I pick the walnut out of the shell and pop it in my mouth, and when I look back, James is still watching me with heavy eyes and a sleepy smile. I take a walnut from the vending machine on my way out and he makes a noise and scrunches the fingers of his hand so I grab another one and go back to stand next to him.

I deposit both nuts in his hand. 'Your turn.'

Instead of going to the nutcracker, he positions the seam of both nuts against each other in his good hand and presses them together, using just enough force to shatter the shells. He holds one out to me.

My eyes go wide. I had no idea that was possible. 'That's an impressive party trick.'

'Guess you could say I'm a real nutcracker.'

I choke on said nut. Why does he keep coming out with this stuff? As soon as I'm certain that he's really, really *real*, he says something like that. 'Aren't you going to make a wish?'

'I don't need to.' He swallows his walnut and looks me directly in the eyes. 'Mine already came true.'

I go hot all over and my traitorous knees threaten to give out at the idea that he means what I so desperately hope he means.

'Nee, that first night in the storeroom. I wished for someone to l—' He corrects himself quickly before he says the "l" word. 'To care about me, and you haven't stopped looking after me since.' He presses his lips together but they still twitch towards a smile, and I realise I've stopped breathing and have to gasp for air.

'Do you know how much I love that advent calendar? And it's not because of the chocolate – it's because every morning when I open a door, I think of you. The moment I met you, it was like something unclenched in my chest. I've never felt so instantly comfortable with someone. I've never been so instantly at home with someone. From that night in the storeroom, I'd have felt like I was cheating on you if I'd even looked at someone else, which would've been a complete impossibility because you've occupied my every thought since then.'

254

It's not just me. That's all I can think as he reaches out and entangles his fingers with mine again. I'm not sure there's been a fraction of a second that I haven't spent thinking about James in the past few weeks. He feels it too. My joy must reflect in my smile because I don't realise how tense his shoulders were until they drop with relief and he pulls me closer.

My brain has turned to mush and my hand has landed on his neck, making him shiver as my nails run over his skin, and I've ended up with my back against the fence, my other hand in his hair, his broken arm around me between the fence and my back, holding me tight to him, his good arm around one shoulder, holding the side of my face, his thumb brushing my jaw.

Our foreheads are pressed together, our noses alongside each other's, sharing each breath as he whispers, 'Can I ask you something?'

I nod minutely. I've never needed anything more than I need him to kiss me. My whole body is on fire with anticipation and I think I'm going to burst if he doesn't get on with it.

'Just so you know it's an option, but are you going to punch me in the ribs if I kiss you?'

I let out a marginally deranged burst of laughter. 'Oh my God, James, I'm going to punch you in the ribs if you *don't*—'

His lips are on mine before I can finish the sentence.

I tilt my head up to meet him, and even though I was more than expecting the kiss, I let out a whimper at how good it feels when our lips finally connect. I've spent a not-insignificant amount of time imagining what it would be like to kiss James, but nothing prepares me for the onslaught of feelings that flood through me.

It's ridiculously soft at first, so infuriatingly gentle, the sexually charged equivalent of that kiss at the side of my mouth the other day. His lips melt against mine, and it's such a relief after so long that it takes all my willpower to stay on my feet, constantly aware that he's bruised and hurt and I can't grab him with quite the force I want to. It's like he can tell I'm holding back and he

255

takes the lead, making the kiss more forceful, his thumb pressing carefully against my jaw, pulling me tighter when I'm trying to hold back for fear of hurting him.

From a distance, he looks clean-shaven, but up close, he's got the barest hint of five-o'clock shadow and it makes my skin tingle at every touch. My ears are ringing, every atom in my body is blazing towards my lips, and my hand is curled so tightly in his hair that it'll be a Christmas miracle if I don't come away with a few clumps.

I lose awareness of everything around me. There is nothing but his lips and the pressure at every point that his body touches mine, and as we hit the point where I don't think I can stop kissing him even though oxygen is becoming a severe issue, he pulls away, and our foreheads press together again as we both gasp for breath.

I've never ever felt this way after a kiss before. So unsteady that it's like I'm on a boat being tossed around by a stormy sea. I can't open my eyes because kisses like that don't actually happen in real life and if I open them, I'll wake up.

'Is the room spinning?' he murmurs.

'Everything's spinning.'

'Oh, thank God. It's not just me. Did we accidentally down six bottles of wine between the outlet shop and here?'

'We might have, but that was a lot more fun, and six bottles of wine would've made me start throwing up ages ago.' Talking about vomit in the middle of a kiss. Well done, Nia.

He lets out a howl of laughter and presses his lips quickly to mine again. 'Of all the times I've imagined doing that, that was *so* much better.'

'Oh, I don't know. I think we should do it again to make sure.'

'I like your way of thinking,' he says, each word peppered with a kiss.

I lose track of time as he kisses me properly again. Everything fades as my fingers curl into his body so tightly that he's going to have nail-shaped indents in the back of his neck, and it takes a long while for me to risk pulling away and opening first one eye and then the other, genuinely surprised that we're still on Nutcracker Lane because everything about that kiss felt like the world shifted underneath our feet and everything that hasn't been right for a long while is suddenly right again.

I look up at the giant nutcracker looming above us, and I'm sure his cheeks look redder than they did earlier. I doubt he's used to watching that kind of display. Eight-year-olds wishing for unicorns is more his usual scene.

'My wish came true too, you know.'

James raises one eyebrow and lowers the other in confusion.

'The night before I met you in the shop, I wished for Prince Charming.'

I thought it would make him laugh, but the smile he gives me is surprisingly tight and the look on his face is pained. 'I *wish* I was Prince Charming ... but I'm not, Nia. I'm so far from Prince Charming that I probably shouldn't have done that, but I didn't know how to go another second without kissing you, and—'

I cut him off by kissing him again, and he stumbles into the fence and groans in actual pain as it jars a bruise.

'Come on, let's go back to mine. If you think I'm letting you go home after that, forget it.'

He hesitates. 'Nee, I can't do, y'know, *that*. Not with these ribs. And trust me, you don't want to see me with my shirt off at the moment. I look like ... you know when you were a child and got your hands into some watercolour paints and mixed every colour together and it ended up an indistinct purple-tinged mess?'

It makes me giggle because I remember it well. 'We've got all the time in the world for, y'know, *that*. It was the last thing on *my* mind. And seeing under your shirt would make no difference to how gorgeous you are, but kissing you and staying upright at the same time isn't working out too well for me. And when you knocked, I was contemplating getting up to make a batch of mince

257

pies, so you can come and help with that, because it's December 21st and no un-Grinching would be complete without a mince pie hot from the oven and freshly whipped cream.'

He lets out a guttural groan of longing, and I gather up the bag containing the two nutcrackers.

'Just so you know, I think my un-Grinching is more than complete now. You've completely changed the way I see Christmas. You've changed the way I see everything.'

I can't help smiling as we walk hand-in-hand towards the entrance. He's certainly had a positive impact on my life too. I can't wait to see where this is going and where we'll be next Christmas, because for the first time, it feels like it might be even better than this one. It feels like there might be hope.

Chapter 16

My lips are actually swollen, to the point where Lily asks me if I'm wearing a new lipstick when she walks up to Nutcracker Lane with Stacey and me the next morning. School's out for Christmas and she's designated herself as our new sales assistant and muffin supervisor for the Nutcracker Lane bakery, and there's something really special about seeing her love Nutcracker Lane as much as I did when I was her age.

'Well, what d'ya know, looks like Flynn Rider's been to the same make-up counter.' Stacey raises an understanding eyebrow as we meet James getting out of his car.

His hair is still damp from where he's been home to shower and change, and for the first time, his jumper is not a Grinch one but a black and white Fair Isle patterned one with Jack Skellington's face in the middle of it. Typical James, nothing *too* Christmassy. If it wasn't for Lily and Stacey's curious eyes, I'd kiss him good morning as well as the many *many* times we kissed last night before he reluctantly went home, but he settles for dropping his good arm around my shoulder and squeezing me into his side.

Once opening time passes, Nutcracker Lane is busier than it's been in the past few years put together. With school holidays and most work breaks in full swing, there are families everywhere. The chestnut seller is doling out bags of chestnuts with such speed that his arms are a blur, like the scene in *Elf* when Buddy starts throwing snowballs in the park. The carollers have split up into three groups and are giving a synchronised concert near the magical nutcracker, the coffee shop, and the tree lot at the other end. Our line of little nutcrackers has been almost obliterated at the sides of the lane with people taking them, knocking them over, or trampling them, so now they only stand in proud lines through each shop window, an implied wooden middle finger to Scrooge.

With families off work, Carmen and Hubert have roped in cover for their counters and are getting in a few final chances to grant wishes. With only three days until Christmas, there might not be many more chances, and somewhere I have to find the time to formulate a real business plan to show them and find out who else would be on board with my ideas for the future of Nutcracker Lane before we have to get together and tackle presenting it to Scrooge. Safety in numbers and all that.

James seems to have given up entirely on his shop because it's shut and he's outside walking around, and I can't work out what he's doing because he just seems to be talking to people. The fingers of his broken arm can grip a notebook now and he's scribbling down comments, almost like some kind of customer satisfaction survey.

When I've watched him walk past for the sixth time, Lily puts her hands on my back and shoves me out the door. 'Me and Mum can manage here. Go and grant some wishes with your prince. He might turn back into a doll on Christmas Eve.'

'You weren't supposed to tell anyone *that*.' I raise an eyebrow at Stacey, making her giggle.

'It's not like it's actually going to happen, Nee.'

No, but I can't shake the feeling that something is. Even with all the kissing last night, and although we didn't actually define that we *are* seeing each other, it's pretty obvious we've been in some kind of relationship since the night in the storeroom, but he's still acting like everything is going to change after Christmas.

'What are you up to?' I ask as I catch up with him between the florist and the hat shop, dodging people walking around with poinsettias under their arms and novelty hats on their heads.

We're near enough to a lamppost that he can get away with the mistletoe excuse and he leans down to press a brief kiss to my cheek, which although lovely, is sorely lacking after all the kissing when we got home last night.

'Just seeing ...' He swallows, looking surprised that I've caught him. 'Asking what customers want. Finding out what they like and dislike and trying to pin down what we need to improve for next year.'

I like how strong his confidence is in that there will *be* a next year. 'Something we can put in the business plan to try and get Scrooge onside?'

'Er, yeah. Sure.' His dark hair has gone wavy on the ends where it didn't dry properly this morning and I resist the urge to tuck it back.

'What have you got so far?'

'Well, wishes are popular but what you said is right in that we need a better system and to employ dedicated wish-granters again ...' He stops as the sound of sirens reaches us from a distance and then carries on. 'Hubert has fallen off a ladder three times this morning from where he's pretending to fix a lamppost and Mrs Brissett has mopped the same imaginary spot on the floor so often that she's started to wear away the paving slab itself, and ...'

The sirens are louder now, and I feel the same sense of dread and discomfort everyone feels when they hear an ambulance.

'God, James, they sound really close.' I stand on tiptoes to see over the heads of shoppers between us and the door, fully expecting to see an ambulance speeding into the car park, but there's nothing.

A few shoppers have stopped and are looking for the source of the sirens too.

James points to the opposite side of the building where the factory car park is. 'It's coming from over—'

'Oh, thank God! I've been looking everywhere for you!' A middle-aged man wearing neon-yellow safety clothing rushes up to us, looking wide-eyed, sweaty, and out of breath. 'Sir, there's been an accident in the factory – you have to come now.'

James has frozen, looking between me and the man with his mouth half open.

'Please, Mr Ozborne.' The man is almost yelling in his panic. 'You're the acting manager – there's no one else to turn to. The paramedics are on site but they need someone for the official report. We need you *now*!'

Ozborne. The name sounds so familiar, even though this is the first time his surname has come up.

James still doesn't speak, so I do instead. 'He's not the acting manager of the factory.' I turn from the factory worker to him. 'Are you? How could you possibly be a manager of the factory? That doesn't make any sense.'

The factory worker is bouncing on the balls of his feet, clearly panicked to get back, but he's made a mistake here and the sooner he realises that, the sooner he can find whoever he's really looking for.

James swallows hard. 'I'm not the acting manager of the factory.'

There. I knew that. Something bad has obviously happened and this poor man has got confused in the chaos. I turn to him. 'Is everything okay? Can we help?'

'Nia, I'm the acting manager of the whole place.' James doesn't look up as he speaks, saying it to the rounded corner of one of the paving slabs, which he pokes at with the toe of his boot.

I laugh out loud even though this is very odd timing for jokes.

'You're not the acting manager of this place. Our acting manager is Scrooge.'

James doesn't respond. Hubert, Carmen, and Mrs Brissett are all gathered round, along with quite a few shoppers, unable to ignore the spectacle of the distressed man in yellow while sirens howl outside.

I let out a sound that's half-giggle half-gurgle. 'That would make *you* Scrooge. You're not seriously telling me that you're him, are you?'

Every nanosecond that passes without him speaking makes my heart plummet further into my stomach. It's not *possible*. It's more likely that he's genuinely a wooden nutcracker come to life than there being *any* possibility that he could be that awful, miserly accountant. Scrooge is the *furthest* thing from kind and generous James.

'I'm so sorry. I was going to tell you. I've tried to tell you …' he starts.

'Oh, come *on*!' I let out another snortle. 'You are *not* Scrooge. You can't be.'

'Mr Ozborne, I don't know what's going on here but this is an emergency and we need you right now. Please, sir.' The distraught man starts to run off in the direction of the factory, clearly expecting James to follow him.

He hesitates, looking me in the eyes. 'Nee, I …'

'Sir!' the factory man shouts, and James starts after him, still unable to run properly with the ribs.

'I'm sorry, Nia. This is not how you were meant to find out, but someone's hurt and I have to go. I swear to you, I'll explain later.' He shoves the notebook he's holding at me. I don't realise my hands are shaking until our fingers brush when I take it off him and I realise it's not just my hands. My whole body is shaking like I'm standing on one of those vibrating circulation booster things they sell on late-night shopping channels.

263

I stare at the empty space where he was stood for a long time. Shoppers move on around me, nuts are cracked and wishes are made, carols are sung, and there's the constant chatter of shoppers planning Christmas dinner and talking of plans for the next few days, but I ignore it all. If I just stand here without moving, he's going to come back and admit this is all a practical joke. If I stay right in this spot, it won't be real.

I don't move until Carmen wraps her arm around my shoulders. 'Must admit, I did *not* see that coming.'

She didn't? There is no way it can be true. James is the most trustworthy man I've met for years. James hates Scrooge. I've moaned about Scrooge endlessly *to* James. They *cannot* be the same person.

'You okay, Nia?' Hubert shakes his head as he comes over. 'No wonder he never answered his phone. You've gone pale. Do you want to sit down?' He digs around in his multiple pockets until he eventually produces a bag of sweets. 'Here, have a peppermint cream; that'll cheer you up.'

I take one of the soft round mints that are chocolate-dipped on one side, even though I think it'll take a bit more than a peppermint cream to sort this one out. I clutch the notebook to my chest, holding it against me like if I somehow squeeze it tight enough, he'll magically appear in front of me and offer a perfectly reasonable explanation about how someone's got their wires crossed and this is all a huge, gigantic, monumental misunderstanding. Any minute now …

Carmen is still smoothing my jumper down and Hubert is patting my shoulder and waving the peppermint creams in my face again, and I need space. I paste on my brightest smile and shrug them off in the politest way possible and head back to Starlight Rainbows. I can't make sense of my own brain. I've heard the words, but I don't understand them.

'What's all the commotion out there? Has something happened?' Stacey says as soon as I step in the door.

I half-snort and half-choke at the same time. '"Something" is an understatement.'

I must look as dazed as I feel because Stacey cocks her head to the side and appraises me for a moment, and without another word, opens the till and hands a tenner to Lily. 'Lil, run across to the bakery and get three hot chocolates and three cakes stuffed with the largest amount of cream, okay?'

This is one of the benefits of working with your best friend.

There are a few customers browsing and she serves a lady before turning back to me. 'What's wrong?'

'He's Scrooge.'

'Who? That guy in the yellow safety gear?'

'No. James.'

It's Stacey's turn to burst out laughing. 'No, he's not. Scrooge is old and decrepit and a grouchy, nasty, angry, bitter man who takes pleasure in making others miserable. James is adorable, funny, brings people coffee, and is so perfect for you that he could have been manufactured to your specifications. If he's anyone in disguise, it's Flynn Rider.'

'I'm not joking, Stace. He's Scrooge. He's been Scrooge all along.'

She shakes her head, still not taking me seriously. 'Well, what's he doing here then? If James hated Nutcracker Lane as much as Scrooge does, he wouldn't be here, would he?'

'I don't know.' I slap his notebook against the palm of my opposite hand. 'Come to gloat as he watches the lane he's taken such great pleasure in destroying glug its final glug and sink beneath the waves as Leo and Kate jump off it?'

'That was *Titanic*, Nee …'

'I'm serious though. What the hell is he doing here? Spectating? Getting himself a front-row seat to the final demise of Nutcracker Lane? Does he get some kind of sadistic pleasure from meeting the people he's personally putting out of a job? Has he sat there laughing while we've all run around like drunken giraffes trying to save this place *from* him?'

265

She finally falls in that I'm really not joking. 'This can't be right. There's got to be a misunderstanding somewhere.'

'There isn't, Stace. He made it *abundantly* clear just now. I've spent the past three weeks trying to Un-Scrooge Scrooge.'

She sucks in a breath. 'I think you've done a little bit more than that with him, don't you?'

'Oh, I wouldn't say that. I've only gone and fallen in love with the man I hate more than anyone else in the world ... You know, the same man who I was absolutely certain would never cheat on me like other boyfriends have, the one I let in and opened up to, the one I *knew* was a good, honest, trustworthy person? I'd rather he cheated on me than this. At least that would be a one-time thing. James has been weaving a carefully constructed lie since the moment I walked into his shop that first time.'

'He's got just as involved in trying to save the lane as everyone has. Nia, there *must* be something else going on here.'

'Humouring us. Having a laugh at our expense. Nutcracker Lane is a sport to him. Teasing us, giving us hope, dangling this place like a carrot, letting us think there was a chance while he gleefully slices our budget like Edward Scissorhands.' I'm still miming Johnny Depp's cutting motions from the film when Lily comes back in with a tray of three cups and a box of extremely creamy cream cakes.

Even they don't look appetising, but Stacey assures me fresh cream has medicinal properties and we both huddle behind the counter while Lily answers customer queries with more adeptness than I ever have.

'All the times his car's been in but he's been nowhere to be found,' I say with my mouth full. 'Where did I think he was? The North Pole?'

'Where was he?' she asks, struggling to keep up.

'I don't know. Over in the factory, I suppose. Being an acting manager. Poring over his expansion plans and which shops he can bulldoze first.' I take a sip of hot chocolate, which does nothing but remind me of James and the way he bought us one on the morning after he came home with me for the first time. 'Oh God, Stace, the keys. Last night, he had the keys to the outlet shop and I thought he must've gone to so much trouble to get them and do this incredibly special thing for me when they were his all along.'

She scoops cream out of her cake with her finger. 'I hate to be the voice of reason, but don't you think he's gone to a *lot* of trouble here? The decorations, the nutcrackers, talking the shopkeepers into getting involved in banding together against ... *himself*? Nia, it doesn't make any sense.'

'Nothing Scrooge has ever done makes sense. We knew he wasn't using his real name, but even in that, he was ... what, taking the mickey out of us? Laughing over his own Scrooge-like tendencies?' I lick my fingers as I finish my cake and sip my hot chocolate again even though it's still too hot.

His notebook is on the floor under my knee and I pick it up. 'I'm going to, I don't know, go and paint something. I should have been putting in more hours with my crafting, not spending every waking moment with him ...'

'You were trying to save Nutcracker Lane. That's a good thing.'

'The only thing I've been trying to do is *not* fall in love. And I failed.'

'Nee ...' she calls after me as I get up.

'It's okay. I should've known. From day one, I've said men like him don't exist in real life – turns out, they don't.'

I go through to the back room and put my hot chocolate cup and his notebook down on the workbench. I'm sure he only gave it to me because he had nowhere else to put it, but I can't resist the temptation to flick through. It doesn't say much, other than proving he was at least honest about what he was doing this morning because the first few pages really are full of customer comments, although why or what he intends to do with them is anyone's guess. Clues to the most popular shops he can bring back next year, I suppose. I shut the book in frustration. I don't know what I expected to find in there. An explanation that made sense, maybe?

I had a custom order for a snowman family with the names of each family member on yesterday that is being picked up tomorrow, so I sit down at the table and pull out my paint box. One of the things I've always loved most about making things is the escape and the ability to let your mind go and forget about everything other than the brushstrokes.

As I sit there dabbing white paint onto MDF snowmen, I can almost hear the gossip spreading down the lane like the leaves on trees leaning across to whisper to each other on a windy day, and it isn't long before Carmen, Mrs Brissett, and Hubert bustle into the back room to find me.

Hubert puts a bag of peppermint bark down on the desk in front of me and I thank him and put a huge piece of the jagged chocolate into my mouth so I can avoid answering their questions for a while.

'We had no idea, pet,' Mrs Brissett says.

'What a shock,' Hubert says.

'And he seemed so nice,' Carmen adds.

The shop's obviously quiet because Stacey pokes her head round the door and gives me a wink of solidarity.

'But what about the good things he's done? It was James's idea to put the decorations back, and he's done so much of it himself, even with the arm,' Carmen says.

'And I've lost track of how many jumpers he's bought now,' Mrs Brissett says. 'That first day when we met him, I thought he was way too uptight to wear a Christmas jumper, but you had such a positive influence on him.'

'All those wishes he's granted. Why would he do that if he was going to shut us down?' Hubert holds up a finger to halt us. 'And look at how happy it's made *him*. He's been genuinely touched by some of the people he's helped.'

'He practically ran to that supermarket the other day to

get that voucher even though he was obviously in agony,' Mrs Brissett adds.

I think about standing in the car park with him as we watched that woman drive away. He *was* genuinely touched. He talked about Nutcracker Lane's legacy … because that's all it will ever be to him – history.

'The rivalry between shopkeepers,' I say, because I can't combine the James I've got to know with the Scrooge who's been sending us condescending letters for months. 'That was *his* idea. Every budget cut. Every little thing that's gradually been siphoned from the lane. That was all him.'

'What about all he's done this year?'

'All I can think is that he wanted to get hands-on with his factory expansion plans. As well as the sales figures for each shop, he wanted to *see* for himself which ones are performing best. We all said straightaway that it would be impossible to judge from figures alone because of item value, and he obviously knew that too and inserted himself smack bang into the middle of Nutcracker Lane where he could carefully monitor comings and goings and do customer satisfaction surveys.'

'But he increased our budget this year.'

'Yeah. I don't get that bit,' I admit. 'One final joke to pep us up before he pulls the rug right out from underneath us, maybe?'

'The chestnut seller said he personally asked him to come back, and the carol singers have been rewarded handsomely. I don't understand, Nia,' Carmen says with imploring eyes, like I somehow *do*.

'But he's such a nice man,' Hubert says. 'Maybe we've got it wrong. Maybe Scrooge is on holiday and he's the acting manager for the acting manager. The *acting* acting manager.'

The words "clutching" and "straws" spring to mind.

I end up sitting there nodding along with them while working my way mindlessly through the bag of peppermint bark until they leave.

I feel like I've been hit in the face with something heavy and I'm probably suffering from some sort of concussion because I can't connect what happened this morning with any sort of reality and I feel like I'm floating above the shop and watching it like I'm not really here.

As evidenced when I paint a snowman pink because I'm not concentrating.

I'm hyperaware of what James said about explaining later and I'm a nervous wreck for the rest of the day as the clock creeps towards closing time and it gets more likely that he's going to come in.

I must admit that I'm … kind of worrying … about him too. We have no idea what happened at the factory this morning, only that the ambulance raced off at full speed not long after James left and the factory hasn't been operational since then. Hubert tried to go over but was refused both entry *and* information by a security guard. Stacey's even changed the Christmas songs for the local radio station in the shop in case any news makes it there before it makes it to us. I tried to man the till, but I kept making mistakes because I was so obsessed with watching for him – ready to dive into the back room at the first sign because I do *not* want to see him at the moment.

Simon collected Lily an hour ago and confirmed his car wasn't in the car park. The skies are dark outside, and it's a few minutes to our later pre-Christmas closing time of 6 p.m. when I'm finally brave enough to venture from the back room and help Stacey tidy the shop.

'Nia.'

I squeal at the sound of his voice and dive up the step into the back room so fast that I stumble and hit the wall, shaking the entire cabin and knocking several display pieces loose.

He goes to follow me but Stacey plants herself squarely in his path, hands on her hips, feet wide apart. 'She doesn't want to see you.'

270

I hide on the other side of the open doorway. He's mere feet away, but there's a wall between us so I can't see his face, but I'm pretty sure he could get round Stacey easily.

'I see that, but there's an explanation for this.' He sounds exhausted. How can I know him so well after such a short amount of time that I can tell every nuance of his voice? And at the same time, I clearly know *nothing* about him.

'I'm sure there is.' I can hear from her tone that she's folded her arms and is probably tapping a foot expectantly.

'I'm not going to shout it across the shop. I need to see her. Please, Stacey.' I can envision him pushing a hand through his hair and sighing when it falls forward again straightaway. 'I'm sorry it's so late, but I had to go home and change because I was covered in someone else's blood. I've been at the hospital all afternoon. I got back as soon as I could.'

Even after all this, I *still* want to go and hug him. He sounds like he needs a hug. Just as I'm thinking that maybe I should go out there and hear what he has to say, I remember he's Scrooge and force my feet to stay rooted to the floor.

I know Stacey when she's in protective mode – last seen when Lily was being bullied at school – and I hear her shuffle forwards and imagine her barging him towards the counter so he doesn't get a chance to follow me while she gets his notebook out from where we'd put it ready to give back. I hear her shove it at his chest. 'I don't think now's the time.'

'Nia?' he calls. 'I know you haven't gone far, please let me explain.'

He knows me too well too. I can barely hear over the blood rushing in my ears. I close my eyes and lean my pounding forehead against the cool wall. I *want* there to be an explanation – I just don't think there *is*, and I'm not in the mood for hearing James try to talk himself out of it and tangle himself in more lies.

I take a deep breath. 'Answer me one question.' I'm surprised the words are audible because even I wasn't certain they were going to come out. 'Are you, or are you not, the Scrooge who's been merrily cutting the budget every year and gloating and preening over how much more damage you can do?'

Please be *not*. Please let this all be a misunderstanding.

'Yes.' He takes a few steps closer to the door into the back room and I automatically back up. 'But it's not what you think.'

'You would say that!' I don't realise I'm going to shout until the words come out deafening in the quietness.

'Nia, please—'

'Go away, James.'

I can almost hear him glance between Stacey and the open doorway and I hear her footsteps as she moves to stand in front of the step, blocking his path again.

After a few long moments, he speaks again. 'Fine, I'll go for now, but I'm not giving up on this. I'm not giving up on *us* because you made me believe in Christmas magic. You made me believe that no matter how impossible something seems, anything is possible at this time of year.'

And in the process, I've made absolutely damn sure that I do *not*. Christmas has suddenly lost all its magic for me.

I hear Stacey lock the door behind him, and within seconds, her head pops round the back room door. 'You okay?'

I can't manage anything more involved than a shrug.

'If it helps, he looked distraught.'

I *know* he did. I could hear it in his voice even without seeing him. 'Good,' I say, although I can't hide the wobble in my voice and Stacey hears it too.

She comes over and gives me a hug. 'Come on, let's finish tidying and then you're coming home with me. Simon's taking Lily ice skating tonight so you and me are going to put on a Christmas movie and eat three times our bodyweight in ice cream.'

I appreciate her efforts, but I think it's going to take more than festive romantic comedies and ice cream to fix this. I don't remember being this upset after Brad cheated on me and I'd been dating him for years. I've known James for three weeks and my heart feels more broken than it ever has before, and I don't know if it's because of him, or because I'm absolutely certain that whoever he is and whatever he's playing at, this will be my last year on Nutcracker Lane.

There is no more hope of saving it. Both the man I was falling for and the Christmas village I've loved since childhood are gone.

Chapter 17

Yesterday, I was shocked and numb, but today I've barely stopped crying. It's December 23rd, the penultimate shopping day before Christmas, and Nutcracker Lane is bustling with festive cheer. These few days before Christmas when most things are done – cards are posted and presents have been delivered to people you aren't spending the day with, visitors have visited and office Christmas parties are hazy memories – these are my favourite days. There's a certain satisfaction once last posting dates have passed and you're officially too late to buy any more gifts or add any more food to your Christmas grocery delivery. A sense of "that's it, if it's missing now, we'll just have to go without it", absolving yourself of your festive to-do list and looking forward to a few days of eating too much and not getting up from the sofa unless it's absolutely necessary.

Everything Christmassy has lost its appeal now. I forced myself into a Christmas jumper and holly-leaf headband this morning solely because I knew Stacey would march me across the lane to the jumper shop to buy another one if I turned up in ordinary clothes. She's already held me down and inserted a pair of flashing Christmas bulb earrings into my ears. I couldn't risk anything that would make me leave the safety of the back room.

Going across the lane is out of the question because James could pop out at any moment. His car wasn't there when Stacey and I got in this morning – early, to avoid any risk of running into him – but Hubert has reliably informed us that it's now in its regular space, although his shop is shut so he must be over in the factory.

Lily's dressed up as Rapunzel from *Tangled* and is dancing around the shop, belting out "I See The Light" like some sort of summoning ritual, but she's too adorable for me to ask her to stop.

'Auntie Nia, why won't you let an actual Disney prince into your shop?' she asks me for the eleventh time this morning.

'Because Disney princes only exist in Disney films. They never, ever step into real life. I should've known that.'

Despite her love of Flynn Rider, she promises to hit James with her fairy wand if she spots him lurking nearby. Stacey has taught her well.

I spend most of the morning in the back room. Well, *all* of the morning because Stacey shooed me away when I did go onto the shop floor and was so obsessed with watching for James that I knocked over an earring stand and sent forty pairs of bauble earrings flailing across the floor. I spend most of the morning painting sets of gingerbread man bunting sprinkled with iridescent glitter, even though it's a bit late for Christmas decorations now, and if I was thinking clearly, I'd have made good use of the time and started on Valentine's Day stock instead.

The afternoon brings with it a slew of last-minute custom orders that customers buy for collection tomorrow, and to give the paint and varnish ample drying time, they need to be done as quickly as possible.

Usually I get annoyed at last-minute orders, but it's like Nutcracker Lane knew I needed the distraction today, and I appreciate the ability to lose myself in the work and not think about anything else.

Except for every voice in the shop and every hint of a footstep near the open doorway to the back room. Except every 0.02 of a second when my mind drifts to him and where he is and if he's going to come in and try to talk to me again.

When I finish the last custom order for a set of standing reindeer pulling a 3D sleigh and screw the cap back on my red acrylic paint bottle after doing Rudolph's nose, the last of the cup of tea Stacey made me before she and Lily left for the day has gone cold and the clock shows it's past seven. Stacey asked me to go home with them, but I didn't want to impose again, and now I'm going to have to run the gauntlet of avoiding James alone.

He'll have gone by now, I tell myself.

I had a desk lamp on my work, but the main light in the back room is off because it was still daylight when I last looked up. I get up and stretch my back out and flip the main light on, blinking in the sudden brightness.

I sidle to the edge of the doorway and peer out, expecting to see James's shop in complete darkness like the rest of the lane at this time of night.

It's not. It's just as bright as it is in daytime.

The windows are empty compared to how they were at first because almost his entire stock has been repurposed to decorate the lane itself, but he's definitely still there.

Bollocks.

I pace around the back room. There's loads of work I could do. I could stay here all night if need be. I've got a kettle and plenty of teabags, and Carmen has been over to cheer me up with some ridiculously expensive-looking Christmas chocolates in a matte black box with gold ribbons and gold paper inside, and it's full of a selection of her handmade festive-flavoured delights like peppermint, gingerbread, hazelnut cinnamon, stollen, and mince pie truffles dusted with sugar, so I'll be set for a while, just until he leaves and I can walk home without worrying about running into him.

I never thought I'd say this, but I can't wait for Christmas to be over. No more Nutcracker Lane and having to dance the dance of avoiding James on a daily basis. It's only been a day and I'm already exhausted.

Just as I'm thinking how weird it is to be opposite him on the lane, knowing he's there and he must've seen my light come on so he'll know I'm here too, there's a knock on the door.

I freeze.

'Nia, it's me.' His voice is muffled through the door, distant with the space of the shop between us.

Of course it is. Who *else* is it going to be at this time of night?

I don't know what I should do. Should I tell him to go away? He did when I told him to last night. Maybe I should stay silent and pretend the light is on an automatic timer to deter burglars. That's reasonable, right? There doesn't have to be anyone here. Maybe if I stay still, I can get away with turning it off in ten minutes and pretending it's an automated security measure.

'I can see your light, Nee; I know you're in there.'

I don't respond. Staying silent is the best option. He'll have no choice but to go away eventually.

'You know how difficult it is for me to get up off the floor so I'm going to sit down out here just so you know it's worth the pain for a chance to talk to you.' He doesn't hide the groan as he obviously lowers himself down on the other side of the door, and there are a few clunks and bangs as he gets comfortable. 'I suspect you're hiding in the back, too scared to move in case I see you through the window, so now you know my back is turned and you can move freely. And I really hope you come to the door because I need to talk to you, Nia.'

I step down from the back room onto the shop floor. Perceptive as always. Scrooge has no right to be that perceptive.

'And if you really have gone home and left the light on by mistake, I hope someone's CCTV has captured this so you can see what an absolute plonker I look talking to myself through a door.'

277

The giggle bursts out unexpectedly and I clamp my hand over my mouth, horrified at myself. That wasn't supposed to happen – not laughing at him *or* giving away my position.

He's quiet for a few moments, but he's obviously heard it because his tone is lighter when he speaks again. There was a hint of doubt in it before, but now he clearly knows I'm listening.

'I can pinpoint the moment I fell in love with you.'

I fall over my own feet and stumble into the wall, knocking a huge holly-leaf plaque loose, and I grab it before it hits the floor. As I stand back upright, pleased at my unusual display of agility, I accidentally elbow a basket of hanging wooden Christmas pudding baubles and send them clattering to the floor loudly enough for Good King Wenceslas to hear, never mind James sitting right outside.

He can't mean that. He's just saying it to get a reaction. I set the holly-leaf wall plaque safely on the floor and look over the scattered baubles. He certainly got one. I ignore the mess and creep a bit nearer. I still don't have to let him know I'm in here. He has enough trouble with getting up from the floor that I'll have ample warning when he moves and there'll be plenty of time to dive out of sight, and as for all the noise ... Well, how does he know we've not been invaded by giant festive pigeons and it could be them in here breaking up the stock?

'That night in the storeroom. When you made me sit down and reached up to push my hair back. It was the kindest, most gentle, thoughtful touch, and by the time I opened my eyes and touched your wrist, I was smitten.'

My breathing is shallow and my lungs feel too small for the amount of oxygen they suddenly need. I move closer to the front of the shop on autopilot.

'And since then, I've fallen head-over-jingle-bells for you, Nia,' he continues. 'Please don't let it end like this, because I think we've got something worth fighting for and I'm not giving up, just like you haven't given up on Nutcracker Lane.'

The mention of the lane brings me back to my senses. Hearing that someone you're in love with is also in love with you is enough to knock anyone a little off their skis, but remembering the lane is enough to remind me what this is all about and I yank my hand back from the door I was about to pull open.

I flex my fingers in surprise. I have no intention of letting him in. I shouldn't be anywhere near this door, and yet I'm so close to it and my legs are so wobbly that I'm likely to fall into it at any second.

He's quiet for a long while, so long that I almost lean into the window and press my nose against the glass to make sure he's still there, but I also realise that he knows I need a moment to process what he's just told me, and he's giving me that, and the fact he knows me so well is enough to make me feel even more unsteady on my feet.

I grip the doorframe and lower myself down too, knowing he can hear me and now even the giant pigeon excuse will sound unfeasible. The door thuds as my back hits it and I wriggle around to get comfortable. Well, as comfortable as possible while sitting on the floor with a wooden door as a backrest.

It's weird to be sitting here so close and yet so far. The thick wooden door could be three miles wide for the amount of distance I feel between us.

'Please say something.' He speaks in barely more than a whisper, obviously in no doubt I'm sitting right behind him.

There are so many "somethings" I could say. *I'm in love with you too – I can't pinpoint the exact moment, but it started in the storeroom and the process was pretty much complete by the time you kissed me on the side of the lips while we were making the gingerbread house. I thought we had something special too. I thought you were the first man in a very long time who wouldn't lie to me. You crashed through my defences and I let you in from day one because you were so trustworthy.*

I thought we were trying to save Nutcracker Lane together. For

*a couple of weeks now, I've thought we were going to. I've thought
about spending nights curled up on the sofa with you, waking up
next to you and walking to work on Nutcracker Lane with you every
morning for the rest of my life. I'm not someone who rushes into
things, but I've made new memories with you, and until yesterday
morning, I was excited about making more.*

I don't realise I'm crying until I go to speak and all that comes
out is a snot-filled gurgle.

I pinch the bridge of my nose and take deep breaths. This door
isn't thick enough for him *not* to have heard that.

'How can you be him, James?' I say eventually. The tell-tale
wobble is still in my voice. 'You're a *good* guy. You're kind and
funny and a good listener. You care about people. You go out of
your way to help people. It was *you* who granted the first wish
and started bringing the magic back to Nutcracker Lane. I don't
understand.'

He goes to speak but I cut him off. 'And what about us, for
that matter? What were you going to do? Spend Christmas with
me and *then* tell me? How much further was this going to go if
that man hadn't come looking for you yesterday?'

'I don't *know*, Nia. I didn't plan this. Nothing like this was ever
meant to happen and then I met you and everything I thought
I knew disintegrated. I never intended to deceive you, and as for
Christmas, I wanted to spend it with you so desperately that I
couldn't say no even though I knew it could never happen.'

Doesn't he realise that makes it worse? When was he going to
tell me? When he didn't turn up for Christmas lunch? After we'd
spent a few glorious days together on my sofa, neck-deep in old
movies and fancy cheeseboards?

'I was going to tell you.' He thunks his head back against the
door. 'I've been *trying* to tell you and every time I start to say
it, I think about you never speaking to me again and I chicken
out because I don't know how to cope with you never speaking
to me again.'

'Congratulations, that went well.' My sarcasm is somewhat mitigated by the fact I am, indeed, speaking to him.

His sigh is so deep that it reverberates through the door. 'You changed me, Nia. Everything I thought was true changed at that exact moment you pushed my hair back. I'd been alone and bitter and closed off from the world for a really long while. I thought people were always out for themselves and only wanted what they could get out of you. I thought I had to play them at their own game to survive. That touch, how kind you were, how you didn't want anything in return – you just … cared about me. Being near you made me happy. Talking to you made me happy. Listening to you made me happy. You dragging me headfirst into Christmas made me happy. Hearing what you thought about this place and how much you loved it was inspiring. You made me see it in a different light.'

'Oh, come *on*, James,' I mutter. 'You've been lying from the very first moment I met you. The "Help Wanted" sign for a start.' I think back to that first morning when I knocked over the nutcracker in his shop.

At least he has the decency to hesitate before replying. 'All right, there was that. But that was a little white lie because I couldn't tell you who I really was. None of the shopkeepers would've spoken honestly to me. You would've held back and treated me as an enemy.'

'I can't imagine why, can you?' I snap.

'Of course I can. I deserve it, I know that. But what I said to you before is true – Scrooge's ideas sounded right on paper but seeing the actual human impact of them changes things. And, believe it or not, I *did* come here to find a way to save Nutcracker Lane.'

I scoff so hard that I choke myself and he has to ask me if I'm okay before he carries on.

'What I told you is true. I came here to find some Christmas spirit, and you gave it to me in spades. I know it's too little, too late for this year, but I've been trying to make amends with the budget increase and asking the people I'd forced out to come back.'

'Oh God, James.' I groan out loud at the memory of standing in the lane with our letters last week and telling *him* how Scrooge had increased our budget. He must've had such a good laugh at my expense. At all our expenses.

Trying to fight *him* with an army of nutcrackers. He must've thought I was such an idiot. It even explains why he was talking like there was some sort of deadline. Not because he was going to turn back into a wooden soldier on Christmas Day, but because he knew I'd find out sooner or later.

'I came here because I wanted to understand what this place means to people. I've always hated it here, resented it with every fibre of my being. You're right, it's always been my first option when looking for ways to cut spending. It had reached a tipping point this year – do or die, and I knew there were a heck of a lot of people who wouldn't want to see this place close down. I told you I didn't "get" Christmas or why people loved it so much, and without understanding that, I couldn't see what the point in Nutcracker Lane was.'

'So you invented a pseudonym for yourself and infiltrated our ranks, pretending to be someone you're not?'

'What? No.'

'So why E.B. Neaser then?'

'Just a joke. My stupid sense of humour. I knew what the shopkeepers were calling me and decided to play up to it. If you'd gone back to the accounts from when I first joined the company, you'd have seen that everything was signed J. Ozborne. It was never intentionally done to mislead you, but I've been signing all informal correspondence to Nutcracker Lane with E.B. Neaser for years now as a joke, a way of playing up to the Scrooge nickname.'

I wasn't here then. I've never seen any official paperwork from that long ago, but he's probably telling the truth on that one.

I've never thought the name was anything more than a joke, but finding out something like this makes you question everything.

'Coming here has changed me, Nia. I really am like Scrooge now. I've seen the error of my ways. You've single-handedly been my ghosts of Christmas Past, Present, and Future. I didn't expect to find the community spirit, the way the other shopkeepers have welcomed me with open arms, the amount of love there still is for this place. I didn't expect to discover how much I missed the creative side of this business, or to feel like a child again, or to remember how much I used to love nutcrackers and how much Christmas used to mean to me too, and how much I wanted it to be like you make it.'

I picture that lonely little boy sitting in front of a Christmas tree again. Maybe it's understandable, in a way, why he would grow up hating Christmas.

'I know you hate me, and I'm sorry, Nia. I can't say that enough. I couldn't tell you because the whole point was to experience Christmas on Nutcracker Lane as the people who love it do – to see it through their eyes – and then things developed between us and I knew I needed to tell you, and I couldn't pluck up the courage because I knew you'd never forgive me for lying, and now it's all spiralled out of control and it seems so much worse than it was ever intended to be. All I wanted to do was keep to myself, sell a bit of excess stock, and see if spending the season in the middle of a Christmas village could give me a burst of inspiration for what to do about this place. I never meant to fall in love.'

Tears are streaming down my face as I listen. The way he speaks makes it sound reasonable and understandable, and even after all this, the only thing I want to do is open the door and wrap him in my arms.

But it isn't that easy. Nothing changes the fact he's been lying to me – to everyone – since the moment I met him. Yet *another* man who can't be honest and upfront.

I lean my head back against the door and try to get my breathing under control without sniffling too much.

'Are you okay after yesterday?' I shouldn't care. I shouldn't even be listening to this, I should walk away and forget all about him, but all I can think about is how absolutely drained he sounded last night.

'Me?' I know he didn't expect the question because I can almost hear the raised eyebrow. 'I'm not the one who had the accident.'

'Well, that makes a welcome change.' I sigh. 'Seriously, James. It sounded like a bad day for everyone. Was the guy badly hurt?'

'There was an incident with one of the machines. A guy thought the woodcutter was switched off and put his hand in to unblock it. Without getting too graphic, you can probably imagine what happened. But the paramedics and hospital staff were great and they were able to save everything and think he should make a full recovery. The factory was closing for Christmas today anyway, but we'll have a full health and safety review in January before reopening.'

'Good. Any more accidents like that and the factory will be in so much trouble that bulldozing the lane will be pointless.'

'Bulldozing it …' He sounds confused. 'After everything that's happened in the last few weeks, you think my plans haven't changed?'

'I don't know, James,' I say honestly. 'You're not who I thought you were. I don't know what's real and what isn't.'

'Nutcracker Lane isn't going anywhere, Nia. *You've* saved it. We're coming back next year stronger than ever. That notebook you read yesterday was a blueprint of what this place needs straight from customers' mouths. I wanted to know what people like and dislike, what's been working and what hasn't. Like I said, we'll hire some proper wish-granters again and start doing charity drives and … everything. Everything like it used to be. Everything you've told me about since that night in the storeroom.'

'And you're going to give us the budget for all that, are you?'

'Of course I am. One thing I've learnt from being here is that you get back what you put in. The more things are cut, the less people come. Look at this place in the past couple of weeks. People are talking about us all over social media because of what *we* did. If we put that kind of effort in all the time, more people would come.'

I'm crying again and I don't know why. It sounds too good to be true, and if there's one thing I've learnt recently, it's that things that seem too good to be true *always* are. Even if you think they're different this time. 'How the hell can I ever trust you again, James?'

He doesn't answer for a long while, so long that I think he might've managed to sneak away without me noticing. 'I don't know.'

And that's all there is to say. The only thing I wanted from James was for him to be an honest, decent guy, and while I *do* think there's some truth in everything he's just said and he's definitely decent, he's very far from honest.

He's quiet, but I hear the movement as he pushes himself up from the floor and hesitates, like he wants to say something else, but he doesn't. His footsteps echo down the lane as he walks away. In the silence of the night, I hear the engine rumble of a car starting up and pulling out of the car park.

I don't know how long I sit there for, but it takes me a while to wipe away the tears and get back to my feet.

I get up and collect my things, and walk home in the crisp, cold night air, every breath billowing in front of my face as pavement salt crunches under my shoes. I stop to look at the array of Christmas lights I pass. It's two days until Christmas and I've never felt less festive.

Chapter 18

I'm woken up the next morning by a sharp hammering on the door. I bolt upright and stumble over the duvet cover that's tangled around my legs. It was a restless night's sleep and I feel like I've woken up every twenty minutes thinking about James, which on the positive side, has meant I've not spent the night panicking about the Christmas dinner I've got to cook tomorrow and instead how he *won't* be here for it.

The hammering comes again and I scrub my hand over my face and rush down the stairs.

It's half past seven. Who the hell ...

My eyes are stinging in the brightness as I snap the hallway light on and drop the keys twice before I fumble one into the lock and throw the door open. I only realise I haven't looked in the mirror when the courier takes a step back in alarm and then starts giggling to himself. 'Woke you up, love. Sorry.'

I suspect he feels more sorry for himself at being faced with the sight of me first thing in the morning. At least it's still dark out. A full daylight view would've probably turned him to stone, the poor man. At least the festive pyjamas are sure to have brightened his morning. It's not every day a woman answers the door wearing much-loved, bobbled and faded flannel red-and-green check pyjamas with two giant candy canes on the front forming a heart shape. I'm probably one of those stories he'll go back to the office and tell his colleagues about.

He hands me his machine and I scribble something that doesn't even vaguely resemble my signature, and then he holds out a cardboard document envelope, takes his machine back, and wishes me a merry Christmas on his way down the path to his van.

I close the door behind him and accidentally catch a glimpse of myself in the hallway mirror. Wild Animal Control will probably be along any minute. I smooth my fringe down and shake my hair back so it only goes in four directions as opposed to the seventeen it's currently sticking out in as I tear the strip off the document envelope, wondering who on earth is sending me documents on Christmas Eve.

And why they look so official.

My eyes scan over the sheet of paper I pull out, although it may as well be written in gobbledegook and I have to put it down and go to the kitchen to splash water on my face in an attempt to make my stinging eyes work again and to double-check I'm not dreaming.

I pick up the letter again and blink a few times because underneath the embossed official header and addresses, it can't possibly say what I think it says.

Dear Miss Maddison,

We act for Nutcracker Enterprises Incorporated, trading as Nutcracker Lane. We are writing to inform you that you have been named as a co-proprietor of Nutcracker Lane Christmas Village. Please make contact with our office when we reopen on January 4th and arrange a meeting to officially sign over a third of Nutcracker Lane into your name.

Please ensure you bring proof of identification with you.

If you have any enquiries, we will be happy to assist.

Yours sincerely,
B.G.D. Solicitors

Well, that's one way to wake up. The equivalent of a bucket of ice water to the face. I read the letter again and again, but it still doesn't make sense.

I scan the document for any mention of James's name, because surely this *has* to be something to do with him – his final idea of a joke, but it doesn't look like a joke. I know you can mock up official letters online, but this is printed on ridiculously high quality watermarked paper with embossed gold logos and proper-looking headers and footers.

My phone is still upstairs on the bedside table and I go back up to get it. My fingers have automatically scrolled to the photo of James with the nutcracker in the outlet shop and dialled his number before I've considered what I'm doing.

He doesn't answer. Which is fair enough considering it's not even daylight yet on Christmas Eve. And probably for the best considering we didn't exactly part on good terms. Or on any terms at all, really.

I dial the solicitor's number from the contact details at the top of the letter, but unsurprisingly on the day before Christmas, they don't answer either, so I dial my most-dialled number instead.

'Nia?' Stacey sounds bleary. 'It's not even 8 a.m. on Christmas Eve. Even Lily's not up yet and *nothing* keeps her in bed when there's advent calendar chocolate to be had. This had better be good.'

'I think I own Nutcracker Lane,' I blurt out.

'Very funny. You haven't started on the mulled wine already, have you? We still have to work today.'

'Not all of it. Part of it.'

'The mulled wine?' She sounds confused and I hear her mouthing my name to Simon, who I've undoubtedly also woken up on one of his very few days off.

'No. Nutcracker Lane. A courier just came with a letter from a solicitor saying I've been made co-proprietor and I need to make an appointment with his office when they reopen in the new year to sign the paperwork.'

'Sounds like a scam. Like those phone calls you get saying your internet's about to be cut off or you've been charged a membership to something you've never heard of and they'll reverse it if you phone back and give them all your bank details.'

I run my fingers over the indented logo. 'It's very elaborate for a scam. And a scam would've come in the normal post. This was same-day courier …'

She grumbles something unintelligible.

'I'm going to walk up there …'

'The courier?'

I think I scared the courier more than enough for one morning without adding stalking to the mix. 'No, to the lane. Just to see if there's anyone around who can explain this.'

She sighs and I hear the throw of a duvet cover and the groan as she gets out of bed. 'I'm coming with you.'

I know everyone thinks their best friend is wonderful but mine is more wonderful than most.

I pull on sweatpants and a Christmas jumper, brush my teeth and hair, and yank on a coat as I go out the door, papers in hand to show Stacey.

When I get to the corner where we usually meet, she's trudging up the hill towards me, a coat on over her nightwear, as baggy blue pyjama bottoms with arctic foxes all over them flap in the breeze.

'The solicitor exists,' I say before she's reached me. 'I googled him. It genuinely looks legit.' I can't hide the flutter in my voice as I think about the possibility of this being real.

She gives me a pre-coffee grunt and takes the envelope out of my hands, scanning over the pages while we walk up the rest of the hill towards Nutcracker Lane as the sky turns from charcoal to light grey in the space of a few minutes. It's too early for most people's Christmas lights to be on, so the houses are dull and the pavement is damp with early morning mist.

'His car's in.' After weeks in the habit of looking for his car, it's the first thing I notice when we reach the top.

Stacey doesn't even need to look up to know who I'm talking about.

My heart feels like it's in my throat and simultaneously like it's pounding out of my chest. And I *still* feel the familiar flutter of butterflies in my stomach at the prospect of seeing him.

Stacey slots her arm through mine in solidarity and hands the envelope back to me.

'It looks legit, right?' My voice is hoarse and shakes on the last word, because I don't understand it but I can't ignore the shot of excitement about what I don't understand.

Apart from James's car, the car park is completely deserted, and Stace and I go in by the tree lot, which is now bare except for a few spindly stragglers and decorated trees in pots, which probably haven't got much hope of finding a home on Christmas Eve. We're nearer our shop from this end, but the lane is dark and silent as we walk up towards Starlight Rainbows.

As we approach the wood cabins, I wonder what I expected to find, because this part of the lane is no less dark and silent than the rest of it.

'There's no one here,' Stacey whispers, tugging my arm a bit closer.

Except there is. I come to such a sharp halt as we approach the two shops opposite each other that I nearly trip over my own feet and Stacey bangs into my side.

'What the ...' She follows my gaze to the window of Twinkles and Trinkets.

The shop is now completely empty except for one thing – standing alone in the darkened window of James's shop is the six-foot-tall nutcracker I knocked over on day one. The handsome one with flushed red cheeks matching the blush on his wedge-shaped nose, wearing his green-trimmed red outfit, with his black boots and gold crown. His broken arm is mended and instead of the jagged line joining the wood together, the break is wrapped with a string of tinsel, and the flashing candle bulb necklace James bought from our shop is around its neck.

'Is that the …' Stacey asks.

I nod.

'He mended it then …'

I look around the lane. It's so eerily silent that there can't possibly be anyone else here. 'He mended it. *Or …*'

'Turned back into it?' she offers.

'Well, it's not beyond the realm of possibility, is it?' I extract my arm from hers and go up to the window for a closer look. I stare up at the life-size nutcracker who is grinning woodenly down at me from his plinth in the otherwise empty display. 'What if James really was …'

'A magical nutcracker come to life?' she finishes for me.

I don't reply. The nutcracker has got wood-brown eyes that are darker than James's, and hair that's the exact same shade of such a dark brown that it looks black in most lights. It *could* be him. I mean, obviously it *couldn't* because this is reality and nutcrackers don't come to life outside of nineteenth-century children's books and Tchaikovsky ballets, and definitely not in little Christmas villages in Wiltshire.

'You don't really think …' Stacey trails off. Neither of us seems able to finish a sentence this morning.

I reach up and touch the window where one of the nutcracker's wooden ball hands touches the glass from the inside, like if I can get close enough, he'll blink or give me some hint … 'Don't you think it's weird that this has been missing the whole time, and now James has disappeared, it's returned?'

'He was probably mending it and it's taken him this long because he's been so busy trying to save Nutcracker Lane. And he's only got one functional arm – that must slow things down.'

'You think he was really trying to save it?'

'I think everything he said to you last night is true,' Stacey

291

says because I texted her the basics when I got home. 'I think that when you knocked that nutcracker over, you *metaphorically* knocked him off his feet. I know a man in love when I see one, and I certainly know you well enough to know you're snowballs-over-mittens for him too.'

'And what if he's ...' I gesture to the nutcracker in the window '... that.'

She doesn't answer, and it hits me how devastated I'm going to be if he is *that*. If he somehow doesn't exist ... if he somehow wasn't real. What the hell am I going to do without him in my life? I already miss him like a Christmas tree with half its branches cut off and it's only been two days. The thought of this being *it* ... of never seeing him again ...

My eyes fill up with tears as the thought passes through my head. Never seeing him again is unthinkable. No matter what has happened between us, he can't just be gone. If he's turned into a wooden doll, I'm going to be even angrier with him.

I sniff hard, swipe my hands over my eyes, and square my shoulders. There is *no way* he wasn't real. Wooden men don't make you feel alive like he did. 'Okay, sensible, *non*-magic-believing head on. He cannot be that nutcracker. It's not possible. And what about this?' I slap at the envelope in my hand. 'What the hell is this?'

'I don't know. What exactly did he say to you last night?'

I repeat the shortened version of everything I told her in the message I sent when I got home.

'So, what, you think he's trying to prove you can trust him by giving you a third of the lane?' Her face screws up in confusion. 'But it's not his to give away. He's just the accountant, isn't he?'

'I don't know. I don't flipping *know*, Stace. I don't know what he is. He told me he worked for a Christmas cracker company.'

'Okay, let's work backwards, retrace your steps. What happened before yesterday? When did you last see him?'

'Before the accident in the factory. The night before. I told you about the outlet shop and the decorations and then there was kissing and we made a wish on the magical nutcracker.'

'What did you wish for?'

'Nutcracker Lane.'

'What?'

I look up the lane towards the magical nutcracker, obscured from view by the curve in the street. 'I wished for Nutcracker Lane ...'

We share a glance and both turn towards the upper end of the lane. My hand is frozen in mid-gesture towards its general direction.

'Well, they say wishes come true here ...' Stacey says slowly.

'Yeah, but it's a wooden statue. It's a lovely story, but it doesn't actually grant wishes. James was the only person who heard—' I cut the sentence off as realisation finally hits and all the pieces I haven't understood slot instantly together. 'James was the only person who heard. Stace, that's *it*! That's what this has been about this whole time.'

'You've lost me.' She's shaking her head.

'He's not just the accountant. He's the new owner. *This* is the family business he has to take over in January. He doesn't work for a Christmas cracker company at all. That was something he made up because he couldn't tell us where he really worked. This is what he's so scared of destroying. *This* is why he's here. He wanted to find the festive spirit he needs to save his parents' Christmas business, and *this* is it. It's Nutcracker Lane.'

She tries and fails to stifle a yawn, clearly not following my epiphany.

'He said he resented Nutcracker Lane. Why would you resent something you've only visited a couple of times as a kid? He *resented* the business that took his parents away at Christmas. He told me that. He specifically said his parents sold the illusion of a perfect Christmas.'

I throw my arms out to the sides and spin around to indicate

293

the lane surrounding us. 'But their own Christmases were all about work and material-value toys. This is why he was talking like there was a deadline to our relationship – because if I'd got as far as meeting his parents for Christmas dinner tomorrow, I'd have realised they were the darling couple who used to run Nutcracker Lane. Mr and Mrs Ozborne. The ones who haven't been around much in the past couple of years – the same time his father got ill. They loved this place *so* much – it would break their hearts to see it go under. What he said yesterday was true – he came here to find a way of saving Nutcracker Lane. It's his father's dying wish.'

I think back over all the things James has said to me. He's always been cagey about his job, but every so often, things have slipped out that, if I'm honest with myself, made it blatantly obvious he wasn't talking about Christmas crackers. 'And to be fair, if we'd have known he was Scrooge, we *would* have avoided him—'

'I was hoping you'd find your way up here.'

We both scream at the unexpected voice in the quiet lane and turn to see James walking out of a fake-snow-covered gap between the shops, one hand shoved into his pocket, and the fingers of his broken arm clutching a few envelopes.

He's wearing jeans and a red shirt with a white reindeer pattern all over it, and my first instinct is to run at him and jump into his arms, which is not advisable for his injuries. What I actually do is burst into tears because he's real and not a giant nutcracker come to life.

'What are you doing here so early?' I stutter out eventually.

'Putting letters through everyone's door informing them that they now collectively own a third of Nutcracker Lane. I own a third, you own a third, and now they own a third between them.' He closes one eye and tilts his head to think about it. 'Could be *interesting* if there are disagreements.'

The sight of his smile makes the tears fall harder. 'Why would you do this?' I hold up the envelope in my hand so it hides my face as I try to get my emotions under control.

'Because you once said to me that if I can't take over this business, I need to find someone who can. And I found someone who can, and more importantly, I found someone who makes me believe that *I* can. And I *can't* do this without you, Nia. I can't imagine going to work every day without you next to me. And if we're going to open as some kind of nutcracker museum year-round, we need permanent staff.' He glances at Stacey, and he's even enough of a gentleman not to mention the pyjama bottoms. 'With plenty of time off for craft fairs, of course.'

'Well, now you've found your nutcracker prince, Nee, I'm going to go home because Lily's probably bouncing on the bed by now and I need to shower and change before work. See you both at nine!' Stacey backs away with a wave, looking like she can't get out of here fast enough.

I turn back to him and waggle the envelope around. 'What are you playing at, James? What is this? Trying to buy me off? Typical Scrooge. As always, everything's about money with him. And you.' I realise I *still* can't reconcile that they're the same person, and that nothing I've said so far makes sense. It's hard to hang on to my anger when I look at him, chewing his lip, his thumb fiddling with the corner of one of the envelopes in his hand, but if this is some attempt to throw money at a problem and hope it goes away in typical Scrooge style ... I'm not willing to let my guard down yet.

'It's nothing like that. I don't want or expect anything from you. I *know* this can't undo how much I've hurt you, but I wanted to prove that I want what's best for Nutcracker Lane, and *you* are what's best for it. Even if you hate me. Even if you never want to talk to me again, Nutcracker Lane needs you at the helm. And the other shopkeepers – *they* are what makes Nutcracker Lane so special. They're the heart and soul of this place. All of you are the ones who've kept the festive spirit up here despite the circumstances. I don't want to be their employer, a boss they've got to answer to; I want us all to have an equal say in what goes on here. For the first time in my life, I feel like I'm part of something here – a real little community – and everyone deserves an input into a community.'

It would be so easy to drift closer and my fingers twitch with the urge to touch him, to run them over his reindeer shirt, but I force myself to stay rooted to the spot. Trying to remind myself that this is Scrooge I'm dealing with – there has to be a catch somewhere. 'You really think the museum thing is a good idea?'

'I think it's a fantastic idea. Adopting nutcrackers, make-your-own workshops, guided tours and school trips, wish-granting, giftshops, themed afternoon teas – everything you said. I talked to my folks last night and my dad cried with happiness. They want to meet you. I know things are weird and I know it's going to take more than this to prove you can trust me, but Mum's putting on a Christmas Eve tea tonight and she wants you to come. They remember you and your grandma, and they trust you with Nutcracker Lane a heck of a lot more than they trust me.'

I want to snap something about it serving him right, but he looks so genuine, and no matter what has happened, I find it hard to distrust him. On this. On everything else, I don't trust him as far as I could throw him using a teaspoon as a catapult.

'Please, Nia. You've shown me that every moment counts and I'll never get this time with my family back. It's the last Christmas Eve I'm ever going to spend with my father and I want you to be part of it.'

His voice wobbles and that does it for me. My eyes fill up with tears again and I blink furiously, attempting to hold them back. I give him a single nod, trying not to let him see how much of an emotional wreck I am this morning.

'Can I pick you up at half past seven tonight?'
Another nod.
'Are you going to thump me in the ribs if I try to hug you right now?'

I nod again, but this time a giggle bursts out too.

It makes him grin and he holds both hands up like he's surrendering, and his lips twitch into a smile. 'Okay. Point taken. But I'm not giving up on us. Someone once told me that magic can happen at Christmas. Even the impossible.'

He salutes and turns to walk away, and it takes every ounce of my willpower not to run after him, throw my arms around him, and kiss him like there's no tomorrow.

In that instant of thinking he might really have turned into a nutcracker, the thought of never seeing him again made me feel like I'd been punched in the chest … hard enough to wonder if learning to trust him again wouldn't be so impossible after all. Stranger things have happened on Nutcracker Lane.

Chapter 19

Why am I so nervous? Why am I holding James's hand on his parents' doorstep? Why did I ever agree to this? It's 8 p.m. on Christmas Eve and I have at least a thousand things that need doing to prep for the Christmas lunch tomorrow, but instead I'm looking up at a three-bedroom detached house in a pretty area, with a garden that doesn't look as well kempt as it clearly once was.

His hand squeezes mine, and in my head I'm telling myself to extract my fingers and step away. Nothing changes the fact that he lied from the moment I met him, and that is not something that can be undone by even his grand gesture this morning. That's the sensible corner of my brain. What I actually do is squeeze his hand back and look up to catch his eyes, and he gives me a muted smile as Mrs Claus opens the door.

She's not actually Mrs Claus, of course, but that's how I remember her from Nutcracker Lane, back in the Nineties when she and her husband used to be there every day. He'd walk from one end of the lane to the other, dressed as Santa, jingling a Christmas bell and "ho-ho-ho-ing", and she'd hand out freshly baked cookies and stop to chat and take photos with children.

'Nia!' Instead of stepping back and letting us inside, she comes out onto the step and envelops me in a bear hug. 'You have no idea how wonderful it is to finally meet you. Again. I know we've met before in years gone by, but lately, we've heard *so* much about you.'

It makes my heart swell as I hug her back. James has been talking about me. Maybe they're as fed up of hearing about me as Stace is of hearing about James.

'Come in, come in.' When she releases me from the hug, she keeps hold of my hand and tugs me inside, calling into the house. 'They're here!'

It's certainly the warmest welcome I've had in a while. She lets us into a burgundy red hallway with wooden floors and a festive rug running the length of it, and waits while we take our coats off and hang them on hooks by the door and leave our shoes underneath. She gives James a hug too, and takes both our hands and pulls us through the hallway, around a tight corner, and into a wide, spacious living room.

James's dad is sitting at the dining table, his laptop in front of him and a pile of papers to one side. A mountainous stack of open files on his other side have slipped and scattered across the table.

'I'm Judy, this is Raymond.' She pauses. 'Sorry, you already knew that, didn't you?'

I did, but it's been years since I saw them, so it's nice to be reminded.

Judy's got blonde-grey hair, smooth and straight to her shoulders, and she's wearing a tinsel headband with a pair of Christmas trees sticking out like cat ears, and I'm glad I went for my understated silver headband with a small pair of elegant, sparkly reindeer antlers. I wasn't sure what to expect, if this would be formal or posh, or if they'd be happy to see me or annoyed at me for blundering into their family Christmas Eve.

Raymond is wearing a Santa hat, which hides his head, bald from treatment, and they're wearing matching his and hers Christmas jumpers depicting the bodies of Santa and Mrs Claus, so their own heads emerge from the neckline. It's adorable in a way I hadn't expected.

'We're so pleased you could come. Thank you for making time for us on Christmas Eve – you must have a lot to do.' Raymond reaches out to shake my hand, and then quickly closes his open laptop and starts shuffling away paperwork.

Working. Even at this time on Christmas Eve night. Like James said he would be.

Judy disappears into the kitchen and refuses any help when I offer, and Raymond leans across to push a chair out for me, and I can't help looking around as I sit down.

It's a spacious living room, at least three times the size of mine, but there's a cold and clinical feel to it. There's a hearth but the real fire has been taken out and replaced by a screen that has digital flames waving on it, and in a corner by the floor-length curtains, stands a three-foot-tall plastic tree with bent branches, like someone's just got it out of a box. There are no haphazard piles of presents stacked under it. The only lights are fibre-optic strands sticking out of the crushed branches, and the decorations are worn-looking plastic things fused to the tree itself.

James's words about Christmas being a box-ticking exercise float through my head.

There are hardly any decorations. A few touches here and there, like a candle on the mantelpiece and a pair of robin cushions on the sofa, but nowhere is really decorated for Christmas. It looks sleek and minimalistic – more like a magazine photoshoot than a family Christmas. When I was growing up, chaos would have descended by this time of night – everyone would be wearing their new Christmas pyjamas, the TV would be on, the cooking would've started, and everyone would be playing with the one present they'd been allowed to open on Christmas Eve.

From everything James has said, I expected his parents to be quiet and reserved, and I still can't quite reconcile the fact they're the owners of Nutcracker Lane who I used to see there all the time, who were on first-name terms with my grandma and always used to stop for a chat. When I was little, I remember being convinced they were the real Santa and Mrs Claus, and I imagined them living in a warm and homely castle in the North Pole. This house is the opposite of what I expected.

James has taken the seat next to me, although the table is so huge that it feels like there's at least a mile between us, physically and metaphorically. He smiles a gentle half-smile when I catch his eyes, and then jumps up to help his mum when she reappears with a tray full of bowls, but she shoos him away in case he drops something with his one hand.

Judy sets out bowls of buffet food, more suited to a summer salad bar than Christmas Eve dinner. It's all neatly arranged lettuce leaves and summer veggies like tomatoes and cucumber, and finger sandwiches, breadsticks and dips, and a cheese and cracker selection. It's nice but it's not exactly festive. Maybe it's easier. She knew I was coming for dinner and didn't have a clue what I might like, so it makes sense that there's a selection.

'You've been busy,' I say as I thank her and help myself to a mini sausage roll.

'Oh gosh, no. Fresh from the caterer. I would *never* have the patience to do all that.' She looks thoughtful as she sits down. 'Sorry, it's probably not the kind of family Christmas you're used to. We do Christmas all year round. By the time it's December, we don't have the headspace left for a real Christmas.'

Well, she's got a lot on her plate. I know they're worried about the business and Raymond's illness and how she's going to cope when the worst happens. If I was dealing with what this family are, I wouldn't have time to potch about with Christmas dinner either.

Raymond has taken some food but isn't eating, and I can't help noticing his hollow cheeks and pale skin, a world away from the jolly Santa he used to be.

'Nia, I must apologise for rejecting your application every year. If we'd known …' he starts.

'It's okay. I think everything happens for a reason, and it turns out that this was the perfect year to finally get accepted.' I look

301

over and catch James's eyes again, and he smiles, but I quickly avert my eyes when I catch Judy watching us.

Things aren't right between us – I know that. He was almost silent on the way over in the car. He put a Christmas radio station on quietly for me, and I got the impression that he didn't want to push me or pressure me in any way. The gift of a share in the lane was one thing, and I think he's terrified of making it seem like he's trying to buy me off or expecting anything in return.

'I love your ideas for the lane,' Raymond says, still not touching his food. 'When James told us, we both smacked our heads and wondered why we'd never thought of something like it ourselves.'

'Our past few years have been so caught up with budgeting and profit margins that you forget what it's really about. I haven't even been able to steel myself to go down there because I knew it would upset me too much, and with Ray ...' She trails off.

I fight the urge to get up and give her a hug.

'And him and his arm right before opening day.' Raymond picks up the conversation, indicating towards James and I follow his line of sight.

His arm. James's cheeks are red and there's a plea in his eyes when he looks at me. They have absolutely no idea that his injuries extend further than a broken arm.

'It's all been too much this year,' his father continues. 'I've got so caught up in searching for ways to cut costs and hunting for prospective investors, and other potential sources of income to save the lane, we didn't even consider the possibility that the lane could save itself.' He grins a toothy grin at me. 'With the right people on board, that is.'

It makes me go warm all over and I can't help the little thrill that goes through me at the thought of being part of Nutcracker Lane permanently.

'We haven't been the right people for a while now ...' Judy says.

'All of these.' Raymond waves a thin hand towards an armchair where the files are now dumped. 'Potential investors who wanted

302

Nutcracker Lane to become something else. We couldn't bear to sell it and see it destroyed, but my energy has gone into … other things.'

The unspoken words hang in the air. Judy swallows hard.

'James taking over the accounts was a godsend, although we'd started to think it had gone too far downhill to be saved. Of course, we didn't know *quite* how bad things were …' A look flies between him and James.

It makes me understand something I didn't really understand before now.

Just like they clearly don't know how badly he's hurt, James tried to save them from the worry of Nutcracker Lane's finances. When he took over a few years ago, he must've been trying to fix it himself, before they realised how bad things had got. His solutions like budget cuts and rent increases and reduced opening hours *were* "perfect on paper". Maybe they would've worked for any other retail establishment. Maybe he really was just doing the best he could as someone who hates Christmas and didn't see the importance of Nutcracker Lane … until he saw it for himself.

'This year is the first time things have started looking up.' Raymond taps the closed lid of the laptop still on the table beside him.

'For all of us,' James says.

I look over and meet his eyes again and he gives me a small smile. There's an awkwardness between us and he's been quiet until now, and I think he's still being careful not to make this about anything other than business.

'James said you have old nutcrackers from years gone by …' I say before they sense the awkwardness too. I have no idea how much they know about what's happened between me and him, but it's probably as little as possible.

'A garage full of them!' Raymond's eyes light up. 'Even more at our head office. We have nutcrackers dating back years, a copy of every nutcracker ever made by the factory. And I've always been in touch with German museums from the Erzgebirge region where nutcrackers are said to have originated. I'm sure they'd be happy to let us borrow some pieces, and there's bound to be some cross-advertising opportunities for us and them …' He hesitates and then corrects himself. '*You* and them. Not us. It's long past time for us to hand over the reins.'

'And you don't …' I swallow and try again, unable to think of the best way to word it. 'You don't mind James giving me, and the other shopkeepers, such a huge share of *your* company, something you built up from scratch? I know how much it means to you,' I say, because it's obvious. Their eyes light up when they talk about it. It's not that they stopped caring, like the rumours circling the lane have suggested, it's that there's so much else going on in their lives – an unthinkable, life-changing illness that's obviously had a heartbreaking effect on them all.

'Nutcracker Lane would be nothing without the shopkeepers. Those loyal people have stuck with us through thick and thin. And I know you as a customer. I know you've been coming to the lane for as long as any of us can remember. James has made no secret of how much you love it, and if you hadn't come along this year … well, I dread to think what would've happened to it under *his* control. And now look at him.' He smiles at his son. 'Wearing a Christmas jumper. Getting excited about nutcrackers and granting wishes and something called summer globes, whatever they are, but I'm sure they fit in somewhere.'

James starts telling them about our idea for helping Nutcracker Lane fit in with the seasons, and by the time we've finished giving them a run-down of everything he and I have already discussed, he's pulled his chair over and has got his right elbow on the table, leaning around me to gesticulate with his broken arm, his fingers brushing my shoulder occasionally, and the sparkle is back in his Disney prince brown eyes. I feel myself fizzing with excitement as their enthusiasm and ideas spark off more from both of us. Judy pulls her chair closer to Raymond until they're holding hands on the table, lost in memories of Nutcracker Lane when they first took over the factory and expanded around it.

'Your enthusiasm reminds me of us when we were your age,' Judy says wistfully. 'And this one ...' She points at James. 'Whatever you did to him, feel free to keep doing it. He's like a different person since he met you. If you can make him love Christmas, you're capable of anything.'

'I think "love" is going a bit far,' James mumbles, although the smile twitching at his mouth says otherwise.

When I go to the bathroom, I catch sight of a door ajar to a hospital-like room downstairs, presumably because his dad isn't strong enough to climb the stairs, and it makes my breath catch. Before my grandpa died, we all knew that he wouldn't be with us the following Christmas, and it made everything so bitter-sweet. My mum and grandma tried hard to make it a Christmas to remember, but I caught my grandma crying in the kitchen because it was a time that would be impossible to forget for all the wrong reasons.

When I come back, Judy has cleared the table and instead of the multiple buffet bowls, there's now a neatly stacked tray of perfect Christmas cookies, and I slide my hand across James's shoulder as I sit down, glad he hasn't moved his chair back to its original position.

I can feel his eyes on me and I pick out a blue-iced snowflake cookie. 'Did you make these?' I ask Judy, remembering her cookies from years ago.

'Oh, heaven's me, no. Who has time for that? I ordered them from the caterer too.'

I glance at James, who's picking the icing off his cookie silently.

The illusion of a perfect Christmas. Christmases are messy and rushed and chaotic. Cookies are made with love and flour fights, and iced with unsteady hands. Rudolph always looks like he's had a few too many sherries and snowmen look like they've been on the business end of a rugby scrum. There are mismatched decorations everywhere, a tree dropping needles and slurping water at a fast enough pace to ensure a daily panic about dehydration. But everything in their house is picture-perfect, and everywhere I look, I can imagine James at Christmas, the lonely little boy who grew up wanting more than material things and resenting the festive season itself for always bringing disappointment.

Judy must clock the look on my face because she says, 'I hope you will always find time to bake with your children.'

The idea of children makes me choke on the cookie. Either that or I've eaten so many mince pies lately that I look like I'm expecting triplets.

'Well, now you're stepping down from the business, maybe you'll have time to,' Raymond says.

'I could get on board with that,' James adds. 'It's never too late, and I'm beyond a lost cause in the kitchen.'

'You could run classes at the lane,' I say. 'Kids love baking and decorating cookies. Parents could leave them and go off shopping for half an hour while you run a cookie decorating class. The more options we can offer, the better.'

Raymond smiles at me. 'James said you were good, but wow. You've got a head for this stuff.'

I blush. 'We could make them nutcracker-themed. Decorate your own nutcracker cookie.'

'I love it,' Judy says. 'I'd like to do that. Even though I'm stepping down, I'd like to still be involved in some way. And I'll need something to occupy my time.'

'The other shopkeepers talk about you two with such fondness. They'd be overjoyed to see you there again,' I say. 'Cookie decorating classes could be just the beginning. You could give talks or take people on tours of the factory. I mean, who knows more about the history of Nutcracker Lane than one of the people who founded it?'

The unspoken certainty that Raymond won't be here for long hangs in the air between us. It feels terrible and wrong to be making plans that won't involve him, and yet, I can see the tension in his shoulders easing as we speak.

He must catch me watching because he meets my eyes and gives me a small nod. Maybe knowing that Judy won't be alone and will have something to keep going for is all he needs at the moment. 'All we've ever wanted for Nutcracker Lane is someone who will love it as much as us, and will do everything in their power to ensure it's still standing in another forty years' time.'

'And I think that's you two,' Judy adds. 'I don't know how James managed to find you, Nia, but if I didn't believe in the magic of Nutcracker Lane before, I do now.'

'You will come for Christmas dinner tomorrow, won't you?' The words are out of my mouth before I realise I'm going to say them.

I feel James stiffen beside me.

'Is the invite still on?' His mum looks between him and me. Maybe he has told her something after all.

I nod. 'I'd be honoured to have you. I've always thought Nutcracker Lane was like a little family, and Christmas is always better with family.'

*

'I didn't think you'd still want us to come,' James says. I can hear the sigh of relief at finally getting the words out.

We're outside in his parents' garage, looking through boxes of nutcrackers, and he's clearly been itching to say something since the moment we were alone. Raymond and Judy are still indoors, and the flickering light in the garage is illuminating aged pallet-wood boxes, containing nutcracker treasures from years gone by.

I think about it for a long minute. 'I meant what I said. You've helped me with so much Christmas stuff, it wouldn't be right to *not* spend Christmas with you.'

'Even though you hate my guts and would like to feed me to some cannibalistic reindeer?'

I burst out laughing.

'I'm sorry, Nia. I know they're just words, and I know you can't trust me—'

'It's okay.' I cut him off, my fingers running over a handwritten "1975" on the front of a box. 'Meeting them, seeing where you grew up, how you spent Christmases ... I get it. I understand why you hate Christmas. And why you resented Nutcracker Lane, and how much your family is going through, and I do realise you came there to try to set things right this year.'

I slide the lid off the box and pull out an old-fashioned nutcracker wearing a red coat and yellow trousers with the year stamped on its base. 'They don't know the extent of your injuries, do they?'

'I didn't want to worry them. They've got enough to deal with. Believe me, if I could've hidden the broken arm too, I would have.'

There's something about him hiding his injuries and dealing with so much on his own that makes me want to hug him, but it's also made things start to make sense. 'You've been hiding the extent of the finance problems and trying to deal with it yourself and save them the worry too, right?' I think back on the things he's said over the weeks. 'Burying your head in the sand, slashing the budget, hoping that one day you'd slash it enough to make a dent in the deficit? Not turning to anyone for help, thinking you can't trust people and can only rely on yourself ...'

His teeth chew on his lip as he ducks his head. 'That changed when I met you, Nee. Within a day, I'd been more open with you than I had with anyone else in my life. Apart from this one stupid lie ...'

I suddenly don't care who he is, or was, or who he said he was or wasn't. There are some things that no one can lie about, like that softness in his eyes, his gentle smile, and the surprise on his face whenever he said too much and let me in more than he meant to. There was nothing dishonest about that. Those heavy-lidded eyes and slow, sleepy smile. He wasn't hiding anything in those moments. I think for the first time in a long while, he was letting someone see the *real* him.

He's changed me too. Until him, I thought I was doing well on my own. I convinced myself I was a strong, independent woman and I was happy being alone, and that I was smart to always keep men at a safe distance and never let anyone in or share any part of myself with someone.

Without even trying, he changed that. Somewhere in the middle of trying to make him believe in Christmas, he made me believe in love again. He made me *want* love again. He made me let my guard down and trust someone again, and it felt better than I expected. I always thought I'd feel weak and vulnerable if I let someone in again, but with James, I felt empowered. Being with him made me feel like anything was possible.

And even though he wasn't exactly honest, he made me trust someone again, and somehow I *still* trust him, and the thought of this ending because I'm too stubborn to forgive him makes my heart race and my palms sweat, and suddenly nothing matters but the way I feel when I'm with him.

'I'm sorry for lying to you,' he says before I have a chance to say anything else. 'You have to realise it was never meant to go as far as it did.'

'It's okay.' I jump in before he can continue. 'I know why you couldn't tell us. I also know you've been more honest with me than you probably intended to be, and I get it. I think you started the job there thinking that the only way to keep Nutcracker Lane going was to reduce the budget for it, but actually seeing it was the best thing you could've done because now you get it.'

'You think I'm officially un-Grinched?'

I nod, my smile so wide that my jaw is starting to protest.

We reach out at the same time, and the moment our hands touch, a flood of emotions releases inside of me and I let out a breath as relief crashes through my body, and I can't hold back anymore. The spell of slow awkwardness is broken and I throw my arms around him as carefully as I can, given how desperately I need to touch him. My arms go round his shoulders, tangling in his hair and pulling him down, making him laugh as I hold his head and smother his face in kisses.

I don't even realise I'm crying until he pulls me in against him, almost certainly tight enough to be uncomfortable, his good hand curling into my hair and holding me close, his mouth against my ear. I lose track of time as we stand there for endless minutes. I feel his shoulders relax as unseen tension drains from them and I manage to stop myself from crying for long enough to get my breathing back to normal, because everything feels right with the world again. Like it has since the moment I met him.

He pulls back and slides a hand down my face, tilting my head until he can touch his lips to mine in the softest, gentlest, most loving kiss I've ever felt. I pull him impossibly tighter and get lost in kissing him, letting it sweep away everything but this moment.

Nothing matters but the two of us, right here and now. I can even ignore the eyes of the multiple nutcrackers watching us from the shelves of his parents' garage, given the way his fingers curl into my hip and how his hair feels in my hands, the feel of his skin against mine and the freedom of knowing that it's all out there now. There are no secrets between us, warring with the excitement of knowing this is the start of something special. Everything about kissing him feels different than it has before.

Hands move and arms tighten and it's all I can do to stay on my feet. I've never known a kiss that's so desperate with desire and so careful and loving too. I run my fingers down from his shoulder to the top of the cast and back up again. He doesn't hide the shiver and I push myself up on tiptoes and kiss his stubbled jaw.

'Did you really think I was the nutcracker come to life?'

'No.' I huff and my cheeks burn. I'm *so* glad he overheard that conversation with Stacey this morning; I was hoping he hadn't. 'Maybe. For, like, *one* moment.'

He laughs and I pull away but his arm tightens around my back, holding me close. I duck my head against his shoulder and hide my burning red face in his chest. 'It was gone and you were on the floor where it fell. It's the same arm, James! All you said at first was about getting "knocked over"! I'd made a wish for a nutcracker prince! You know the story of the broken nutcracker turning into a prince as well as I do! The coincidences added up.'

He moves his shoulder to get me to lift my head, and I look up into his wide brown eyes.

'Do you know something? I never want to live my life *without* someone whose obvious train of thought is not something normal like I'd picked up the nutcracker and got down to collect up the debris but that he'd come to life and turned into me. Never change, Nia.' He kisses me. 'You make me believe in magic.'

He makes me believe in a lot of things I didn't think I believed in too as his lips touch mine again and the kiss sweeps everything else away.

'You have no idea how tightly I want to hold you, how much I want to pick you up and spin you around, and I can't because of the injuries, but—'

I shut him up by planting another kiss on his mouth. 'There'll be plenty of time for that. Plenty of time for everything.'

'Plenty of time for making wishes come true?'

'Exactly. There's something magical about Nutcracker Lane. Now it's up to us to share it.' My heart swells so much that I feel like the moment in *The Nutcracker* ballet when the tree begins to grow. It feels like the start of something that's going to change Christmas forever.

Epilogue

'You owe me four hundred pounds!'

'You're the dog, I'm the iron ... aren't I?'

'Oh no, don't tell me that's a hotel?'

'Do not pass Go! Don't you *dare* take that two hundred pounds!'

Somehow, with our combined total of three arms, James and I managed to make dinner, so far no one's noticeably gone down with food poisoning, and now the whole lot of us are sitting on my living-room floor. My mum, two cousins, my brother and his girlfriend, James and his mum and dad, surrounded by piles of presents, tubs of chocolates, crackers and paper hats.

It's the biggest family Christmas I've had for years. It's been chaotic and fun and so lovely to catch up with cousins I haven't seen for years, meet my brother's girlfriend, and see Mum relax for a change. Even Stacey, Simon, and Lily turned up this afternoon with presents and *more* chocolates.

I wanted James's present to be something special and was thrilled when I managed to track down a vintage game of Monopoly from the Eighties with the red and white striped box, exactly as he described when he mentioned his favourite child-hood gift, and it was worth everything for the look on his face when he opened it this morning.

There are still balled-up shreds of wrapping paper strewn throughout the room, a minty candle melting in the candle warmer, and tree lights twinkling while the fire crackles. There's only eight tokens so James and I are squashed together like some sort of hybrid three-armed player. I've got my arm wrapped through his and my head on his shoulder, and every time he looks at me, his eyes are shining with happiness and he's got that cheeky smile that makes my heart flutter and he squeezes minutely closer, and the fact we're in polite company only serves to build the anticipation of kissing him later.

He's wearing Grinch lounge pants and green-and-blue striped fluffy socks and his first *really* Christmassy Christmas jumper with "Noel" written in a wreath of silver stars, along with the perfect shade of navy party hat from a Christmas cracker. My hat is green and I've got it on over the top of a Santa hat because it doesn't matter how daft you look at Christmas, and I'm wearing my baby-blue kissing penguins jumper and three pairs of fluffy socks – all the ones I've unwrapped this morning.

We've all got mugs of hot chocolate each, despite the fact everyone is still uncomfortably full from the Christmas dinner, and everyone keeps delving into the Quality Street tin despite protesting that they couldn't eat another thing – exactly what Christmas is all about, and I can't think of any better way to spend it, or any people I'd rather spend it with.

*

The cousins left early, Mum and my brother and his girlfriend have walked back to Mum's house, and James has run his parents home while I clean up and make a start on the pile of washing up that's so huge, I expect mountaineers and explorers to be along any minute and stick a flag in the top of it.

I get halfway through it before I hear his car pull up outside, and a couple of minutes later he comes in and kisses me so passionately that I nearly drop the plate in my hand. 'You have *no* idea how badly I've needed to do that all day.'

'Oh, I do.' It's my turn to kiss him. 'I *really* do.'

The washing up is forgotten as I lose myself in him until he takes the plate away from me and starts drying up, always the perfect gentleman.

In the living room, Christmas music is still playing quietly as I pull a bin bag around and fill it with discarded wrapping paper and polystyrene packing from presents. "Little Drummer Boy", the song that always reminds me of nutcrackers, comes on and James goes over to turn the light off. He comes back, takes my hand and pulls me against him, holding on tight as he starts gently dancing us around the room.

'We seem to have done this before.'

'We can stop if you want,' he murmurs against my hair, sounding like Santa popping down the chimney to say he's misplaced a reindeer is more likely. My hands curl into his shoulders hard enough to leave him in no doubt that I'm not on board with that idea.

It's a perfect Christmas evening. The room smells of peppermint and woodsmoke from the fire, and now everyone's gone home, there's something about it just being the two of us and an evening of relaxing and eating sandwiches made of leftovers for supper later. The lights on the tree twinkle and flash, and the six-foot nutcracker with the mended arm that he gave me for Christmas stands silently in the corner, watching over us.

'I wanted to say thank you.' James moves his head until he can whisper in my ear. 'Thank you for making me "get" Christmas. Today was incredible. I already know that's one of the best memories I'm ever going to have of my dad.'

'He looked well.'

'He looked happy. For the first time in years, he and my mum know that their beloved business is going to be okay because of you.'

314

'Because of both of us. *All* of us. Everyone who's got involved in restoring Nutcracker Lane to its former glory. Because none of it would've happened without you.'

'I guess we make a perfect team.' He leans down and presses his lips against my cheek. 'I just wanted you know this was my best Christmas ever.'

'Good. Just so long as you know that neither of us are getting up off that sofa for the next few days unless there's a national emergency.'

'I am absolutely okay with that.' He wraps both arms around me and I reach up and cover the fingers of his broken one and let myself relax in his embrace.

I know there will be challenges ahead. We both know it's not going to be an easy year, but some people are like magic personified and make you feel like you can face anything with them beside you. And who knows, when the wind whispers just right and the stars twinkle on a Christmas night, maybe wishes can come true after all.

*

**Swept away by Nia's romance in *The Little Christmas
Shop on Nutcracker Lane*? Don't miss *The Little Bookshop
of Love Stories*, another heart-warming love story
from Jaimie Admans. Available now!**

Acknowledgements

Mum, thank you for putting up with the giant 6ft nutcracker in your living room for the past year! Unfortunately he didn't turn into a handsome prince on Christmas Eve! Thank you for always being there for me, for the constant patience, support, encouragement, and for always believing in me. I don't know what I'd do without you. Love you lots!

Thank you to an amazing author and one of my very best friends, Marie Landry, for making me feel not-alone in this strange year and for being a highlight of every single day. I'm so grateful for having you in my life! Caru chi!

Thank you so much to Lor Bingham at Calico Bespoke Gifts (https://www.etsy.com/uk/shop/CalicoBespokeGifts) for her endless patience and kindness in answering my questions about her gorgeous crafts and decorations to make sure Nia knew what she was talking about!

Bill, Toby, Cathie – thank you for always being supportive and enthusiastic!

An extra special thank you to Bev for always taking the time to write to me, and for always being so encouraging and supportive and kind!

Thank you, Charlotte McFall, for always being a tireless cheerleader and brilliant friend.

Thank you, Jayne Lloyd, for being such a good friend through hard times. Fingers crossed that 2021 will be a better year!

The lovely and talented fellow HQ authors – I don't know what I'd do without all of you!

All the lovely authors and bloggers I know online. You've all been so supportive since the very first book, and I want to mention you all by name, but I know I'll forget someone and I don't want to leave anyone out, so to everyone I chat to on Twitter or Facebook – thank you.

The little writing group that doesn't have a name – Sharon Sant, Sharon Atkinson, Dan Thompson, Jack Croxall, Holly Martin, Jane Yates. I can always turn to you guys!

Thank you to all the team at HQ and especially my fabulous editor, Belinda Toor – thank you for not laughing when I pitched an idea about magical nutcrackers!

And finally, a massive thank you to *you* for reading!

Keep reading for an excerpt from *Snowflakes at the Little Christmas Tree Farm* …

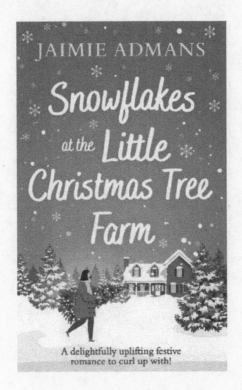

Keep reading for an excerpt from *Snowflakes at the Little Christmas Tree Farm*.

Chapter 1

I am never drinking again.

Please tell me that pounding, throbbing sound is not coming from inside my own head. I peel one eye open and severely consider not bothering to open the other one.

I'm slumped on the living-room floor and propped upright by the coffee table, with my face smooshed against the keyboard of my open laptop. My movement jogs the mouse and the dark screen comes back to life, and my eyes hurt at the sudden brightness. I wince and push myself away, instantly regretting it when my stomach rolls at the movement.

When I can bring myself to peer blearily at the screen, there are loads of new emails in my inbox – and most of the subject lines say 'congratulations'. More spam, no doubt. 'Congratulations, you're the sole benefactor of a millionaire Nigerian prince. Give us your bank details and we'll pop a million dollars straight into your account. Totally legit, honest.'

There are three empty bottles of Prosecco beside me, and my phone is worryingly nearby. Why do I remember squealing 'thank you, luffly robot voice, we're moving to Scotland!' into the phone at some unmentionable hour of the night? While sitting on the

321

living-room floor? With my computer? And my phone? I glance at the empty bottles again.

Oh God, Steve. On the desk in his office. With Lucia from accounting. That's why I'd broken out the emergency Prosecco. And then the *emergency* emergency Prosecco. That bare bum thrusting in among the spreadsheets was enough to drive anyone to drink. I'd never seen it from that angle before. There in all its spotty, hairy glory. And all that grunting. Did he ever grunt like that with me? I'd always thought it was sexy, but when you walk into your boss's office and find him humping your colleague on the desk, it sounds more along the lines of 'stuck pig'. Which, conveniently, is exactly the way I described Steve yesterday, with a few choice swearwords thrown in for good measure, as I clambered onto a filing cabinet and announced to the whole office what had been going on, quit my job, and stormed out with a satisfying door slam. I'd then sat in the fire escape stairwell and let the tears fall, hurt and annoyed at myself for trusting him. I hadn't, at first. I knew he flirted with everyone and didn't really believe he liked me, but he was so charming, so believable, and I'd let myself be taken in. Why did I ever think it would be a good idea to get into a relationship with my boss? Why did I ignore the rumours that circulated the office about him? Why did I drink three bottles of Prosecco last night? Why ... wait, why does that email say 'receipt for your payment'? I must've gone on eBay and bought another pair of shoes that look pretty but, in retrospect, were obviously designed for women much younger than me and with much slimmer feet and more attractive legs than mine, who also possess some ability to walk in heels, which I do not.

I squint and move closer to the screen. That email's from an estate agent. Scottish Pine Properties. I recognise the name because I've been daydreaming about their listing for a Christmas tree farm all week ...

I sit bolt upright, ignoring the spinning room and thumping head as I click on the email.

I didn't ... did I?

Dear Miss Griffiths,

I'm pleased to congratulate you on your purchase of Peppermint Branches Christmas Tree Farm. Thank you for your fast payment. I look forward to meeting with you to show you around your new property and hand over the keys. Please give my office a ring at your earliest convenience to arrange a meeting.

I *did*, didn't I?

It suddenly comes back in a flood. Oh God, what have I done? Why did I think looking at the online auction for a Christmas tree farm that I've been fantasising about since the first moment I saw it was a good idea after so much Prosecco?

Why do I remember shouting 'Hah! Up yours R-five-hyphens-81, it's mine!' at some ungodly hour of the morning, probably scaring a passing cat?

R-five-hyphens-81. The other bidder in the online property auction – privacy maintained by the website only allowing you to see the first and last letters of your opponent's name. The buzz of the auction last night. Watching with bated breath as they put in a bid with ten minutes to go on the countdown timer. So I put in a bid. Then they put in another. And I added another. We went round in circles until there were four seconds left on the clock. I hit the button one last time. And I won it.

Now there's a multitude of emails in my inbox that say things like 'Congratulations on your purchase' and 'receipt for your payment.' The automated phone call from the bank, the robot voice asking me to confirm that it wasn't a fraudulent transaction, that it was really me requesting to transfer the small sum of fifty grand to Scottish Pine Properties in Aberdeen.

I've actually done it. I've spent almost all of Mum and Dad's money on a Christmas tree farm. In Scotland. What was I thinking?

I glance at the empty bottles again. That Prosecco has got a lot to answer for.

Note to self: change security questions. Must be something unable to answer when drunk. The origins of pi or long division or something. Unfortunately I still remember my mother's maiden name and my first school even after three bottles of fizzy wine.

You know how you get overexcited at eBay auctions and you only want that skirt if it doesn't go above £1.50 and you're there right at the end and people are bidding and suddenly you've won the thing for £29.77 and you're absolutely exhilarated until the invoice email comes through, and you realise you do actually have to pay £29.77 plus postage for someone's manky old skirt that's probably got moth-eaten holes in it and stitching coming out, and when you get it, it smells of stale cigarette smoke and clearly has never met a washing machine before? This is like that, but I've bought a Christmas tree farm. This is so far removed from anything I'd ever normally even consider doing. But somehow, it doesn't feel like a mistake. That money has been sitting in a savings account, waiting for something to happen to it. I wanted to make something of it, to use the money from the sale of Mum and Dad's house to honour their memory or make them proud or something. I've never known what. That's why I haven't touched it since it came through.

Dad grew up in Scotland and always talked about selling their house and buying a farm there in their retirement. He always wanted to return to his Scottish roots. He never got a chance to live that dream. And as I stared at my laptop last night, that auction suddenly seemed like the answer. It wasn't *just* because I was slightly worse for wear. It was because, without that Prosecco, I'd have talked myself out of it and convinced myself to do the sensible thing and *not* buy a Christmas tree farm in Scotland.

I should be terrified. I should be getting onto the estate agents and begging for a refund on the grounds of diminished capacity. Obviously, this is a mistake. Of course I don't actually want a Christmas tree farm in Scotland. I live in the tiniest flat known to mankind in the centre of London. What am I supposed to do with Peppermint Branches Christmas Tree Farm in the little village of Elffield in the northernmost corner of Aberdeenshire?

That's what I expect myself to be doing. But the very small part of me that doesn't feel completely sick from the hangover is fluttering with excitement. I *don't* want a refund. I don't want to back out. I saw that auction over a week ago and have daydreamed about it ever since. How amazing would it be to own a Christmas tree farm? I've spent hours picturing wide-open fields, rows of lush green trees, snowy ground, sleigh rides, and the scent of pine needles hanging in the air. Subconsciously, I knew exactly what time that auction ended. I didn't inadvertently stumble across it just as it was ending, and accidentally enter a bidding war with the other anonymous bidder, driving the price up by a grand each time, until my final bid went in at £52,104. With estate agent fees and whatever other expenses will be added on, that leaves me with under £2,000 left in my savings account for whatever investment the tree farm needs. The price was so close to the amount I got from the sale of Mum and Dad's house that it's almost like fate.

It wasn't a drunken mistake. I wanted it, and in the cold light of day, I still do.

And coffee. I definitely want coffee.

Dear reader,

Thank you so much for reading *The Little Christmas Shop on Nutcracker Lane*. I hope you enjoyed Nia and James's story, and getting wrapped up in the festive magic of Nutcracker Lane!

I've always loved nutcrackers and have been collecting them for years, as well as loving the Christmas ballet, and I've wanted to somehow incorporate both of these into a book for years, and it's never worked out … until now! Various versions of this story have been in mind for years, and when this idea popped into my head in December 2018, I *knew* it was 'the one', and I spent most of last year waiting to start writing it at Christmastime!

I really enjoyed writing about a traditional British Christmas and getting to relive so many of my own festive childhood memories – Argos catalogues, Monopoly, tins of Quality Street, and of course, Nineties foil decorations! Does anyone else really miss them?

If you enjoyed this story, please consider leaving a review on Amazon. It only has to be a line or two, and it makes such a difference to helping other readers decide whether to pick up the book or not, and it would mean so much to me to know what you think! Did it make you smile, laugh, or cry? What would you wish for on a magical nutcracker? What shop would you most like to visit on Nutcracker Lane? It's Carmen's chocolate shop for me!

Thank you again for reading. If you want to get in touch, you can find me on Twitter – usually when I should be writing – @ be_the_spark. I would love to hear from you!

Hope to see you again soon in a future book!

Lots of love,

Jaimie

Dear Reader,

We hope you enjoyed reading this book. If you did, we'd be so appreciative if you left a review. It really helps us and the author to bring more books like this to you.

Here at HQ Digital we are dedicated to publishing fiction that will keep you turning the pages into the early hours. Don't want to miss a thing? To find out more about our books, promotions, discover exclusive content and enter competitions you can keep in touch in the following ways:

JOIN OUR COMMUNITY:

Sign up to our new email newsletter: hyperurl.co/hqnewsletter

Read our new blog www.hqstories.co.uk

https://twitter.com/HQDigitalUK

www.facebook.com/HQStories

BUDDING WRITER?

We're also looking for authors to join the HQ Digital family!
Find out more here:

https://www.hqstories.co.uk/want-to-write-for-us/

Thanks for reading, from the HQ Digital team

ONE PLACE. MANY STORIES

If you enjoyed *The Little Christmas Shop on Nutcracker Lane*, then why not try another delightfully uplifting romance from HQ Digital?